The Tiergarten Tales

Paolo G. Grossi

The Tiergarten Tales

Published by The Conrad Press in the United Kingdom 2021

Tel: +44(0)1227 472 874
www.theconradpress.com
info@theconradpress.com

ISBN 978-1-913567-75-0

Typesetting and Cover Design by: Charlotte Mouncey, www.bookstyle.co.uk Cover design inspired by Gebhard Fugel self portrait 1890 and paintings of the Tiergarten by Lesser Ury between 1900s and 1910s.

The Conrad Press logo was designed by Maria Priestley.

Printed and bound in Great Britain by Clays Ltd, Elcograf S.p.A.

The Tiergarten Tales

Berlin. Its boys. Their stories

Paolo G. Grossi

Unlike the puerile loyalty to a conviction, loyalty to a friend is a virtue - perhaps the only virtue, the last remaining one.

Milan Kundera

Contents

The lodger

Grey sky. It has been so for the last few days, or weeks, months perhaps. It had been his decision to move here so there is no one else to blame. That irks him no end, no one to blame, no one to shout at.

Up here on the sixth floor one can barely hear the traffic below and there is never much of it anyway; it's early morning and he lives on a quiet and leafy street, upmarket, expensive, unaffordable for most people.

The air is warm and all he wears is pyjama bottoms; he prefers to walk around the apartment barefoot though he misses a soft thick carpet. But more often than not homes come with beautiful wooden parquet here: beautiful but uncomfortable for his feet which have lost some of the supple elasticity they used to have. Age, always age; he wishes he could log out from thinking about ageing.

Coffee time. He walks back inside through the French doors and inserts a capsule in the machine, the mechanical noise reassuring, another morning with the same routine.

Frau Greta is on her way and he needs to get out. It's his rule number one or, rather, hers: get out of the cleaning lady's way, you're just a hindrance and when she took on the job she dropped a few stern hints which allowed no debate. Very German, he smiles.

No breakfast at home; he'll walk to the Bismarck Bistro for mid-morning brunch. The temperature is warm enough to sit outside with just a light jacket and watch the world go by.

Except that it never does. The bistro is quaint and the fare of good quality but it never seems to be that busy, though the lack of a crowd has lately developed into a pleasure rather than a shortcoming.

Either way the bistro is close, reasonably priced, and on the edge of that vast and wild forest in the centre of the city peculiarly described as a 'garten'.

He's ready now and he feels pleasantly casual: slacks, a polo and a light blue jacket. A scarf around his neck protects him from the light breeze.

And sunglasses. He has spent a good chunk of his previous life in a part of the world where everyone wore sunglasses, outdoor and indoor. You could never see anyone's eyes. Beautiful eyes, old eyes, blue, green, black, it didn't matter; they were all behind dark lenses. All the fucking time.

But he has kept the habit; perhaps one day he'll lose it. Habits come and go.

He strolls along the oak-lined paths before turning towards the bistro. Empty roads. Is that Sunday? Perhaps not, but the roads are always empty here anyway. Which he loves. Or not. He's not yet sure.

When he reaches the bistro, he lazily scans the area: a few tables outside, almost empty as usual, one middle-aged guy tapping away at his laptop in the far corner.

He takes a seat and then remembers the free newspapers

inside so he gets up again and strolls in to pick up a copy of the Morgenpost.

Ella is at the till. The owner greets him in a low voice and with a smile. She must do that with all the regular customers, he thinks, but he likes it as it makes him feel special even if he is dead sure he isn't.

After three years his German has improved dramatically. He has subjected himself to a gruelling and eye-wateringly expensive blitz of private tuitions. He can now finish reading long-winded and often completely irrelevant opinion pieces. Nothing much ever seems to happen here anyway. He prefers books to news but he forgot to bring one along.

'Good morning sir, what can I get you today?'

Not Ella's voice. It sounds soft and warm, young, almost female though clearly not.

As he turns, a young man of perhaps less than twenty stands there with a smile and detectable eagerness. The eagerness of the new employee, the excitement of a new job, the freshness of a new chapter.

The boy gently shifts the wheat blond fringe along his forehead; a pair of black framed spectacles sits on his angular nose, the thick prescription lenses magnifying his light blue eyes.

'Good morning, let's see: a cappuccino for a start, I haven't decided on the food, may I have a minute?'

'Sure, sir, I'll get the drink ready for you, take your time.'

The manners are calm and polite. Unassuming, he ponders.

After a few minutes the young man returns with the cappuccino and briefly stands there, clearly waiting for the order but with no impatient insistence.

'Oh, thanks, how embarrassing, I still haven't decided. Sorry.'

'There is no worry, sir, give us a shout when you've chosen. I'm Karl, I'll be inside.'

'Very kind, thank you. I'm William. I'm quite a regular here, you must have just started today.'

'Yes, first day. Part-time. Or, more precisely, when I have the time available I call them and come to work.'

'Student?'

'Yeah.'

'Nice to meet you Karl, I'll take a look at the menu, I almost know it by heart anyway.'

A little laugh of approval, not the most original humour but still something, he thinks.

He's back at the Bismarck after a couple of days and Ella comes to take the order. He chooses not to enquire about Karl though from time to time over the last few days he has sprung unannounced into his mind; fleetingly, pleasantly and most conspicuously never sexually. He has felt no enthusiasm for picturing him naked or walking around in his underwear, or any other vaguely lewd fantasy. Most of the times it does happen. He has mostly recalled his voice and his few words, the not yet deep tone of his voice: neither a boy nor yet a man.

Then business calls and he has to fly back to his former workplace. He has virtually retired but his expertise is prized and they never discuss the fees of his consultancy; sometimes he receives his first class return ticket before

Jack, his former boss, even calls him. They are busy men.

Karl freely floats in and out of his mind but in his mind only. He remains rather puzzled at the thought of a geeky young man failing to arouse his low instincts. The voice and the smile stay lodged, though he can hardly remember his body. Did he actually look at it?

After a few weeks he's back and finally taking full advantage of the much improved weather. He can now idle outside in a polo shirt holding the Morgenpost wide open in front of him.

'Good morning, Herr William.'

He lets the paper fold in half and looks at Karl unsurprised as he did say he was to work whenever he was free from university. He knew that one day or the next he would have seen him again. That never worried him.

'Good morning, young man.'

'How are you, sir? We haven't seen you for a while.'

'No, indeed. I had to go abroad for a week.'

'Where to? Anywhere nice?'

'California. But on a business trip.'

'Thought you had a start of a tan. Had a few breaks between work then?'

'Yes, thank you. I managed to have a couple of days at the beach.'

'Lucky you, sir. Would love to see California. Love swimming. Is that where you are from?'

'Boston actually, only worked there.'

'Your German is cool.'

'Still a strong accent though, and my cases are rather

deplorable, I'm afraid. Sorry.'

'It's not that.'

'Thank you, what is it?'

Karl throws an engaging laugh, friendlier than ever before.

'It's the "thank you" and "sorry", you put one of those every three words.' William reddens a bit. 'It sounds funny. We don't really apologise or thank so much.'

'Oh, I'm sorry.'

Karl opens his arms and his eyebrows lift: 'That's what I mean.'

'I'll try.'

'Oh no, don't. It's funny but cool. Cappuccino?'

'That would be awesome.'

He thinks he should stop interjecting Americanisms in his German; he has been living in Berlin for three years and, except for business phone calls , his conversations are mostly in German, though everyone here speaks perfect English anyway. Karl seems to rather like the term 'awesome' though, as he repeats it with a thumb up. And a smile. That smile.

He has come to realise what is so attractive about that smile: it lacks malice. It seems bereft of a second motive and it is neither forced nor flirting.

The following day Karl comes to the table with a cappuccino on his tray. He loves the fact that he no longer needs to order and he makes him feel like part of a family. Patently absurd yet harmless.

'I haven't asked you what you are studying.'

'Chemistry, uber-nerd.'

'I am, well, was, in IT, that's the Silicon Valley bit. Kind of retired but still offering my services from time to time.'

'You're dead young to be retired, perhaps I'm studying the wrong subject.'

'Not that young.' And he worries about Karl asking his age: just shy of forty-five though fit and healthy and with all his greying hair; Karl remains oblivious to it anyway.

'Do you live with your parents?'

'Student hall and a nightmare if you ask. Loud, not that clean, drinking and shouting, had enough already.'

'How come you don't join in? I did.'

'I said I'm a nerd?' They both laugh, first time together, almost in unison. 'That is why I got this job, would like to move out but not that easy.'

'Rents are cheap here.'

'Still not that cheap for me though. I'm in the humiliating process of begging my parents at the moment, not going super well.'

'You might make some good friends in the student home.'

'I have, don't get me wrong, they are all good guys, no troubles. Maybe I'm a hopeless loner.'

A young couple has just arrived and taken a table. Ella has to slightly shout to shake Karl from whatever dream he seems to be trapped in. He nods and leaves but he clearly shows displeasure at having to stop this chat.

He takes the order, serves the customers and swiftly returns to William's table, the place as usual very quiet. William folds back the Morgenpost again and sits up with his hands in a fist under his chin.

'I had an idea, Karl.'

'Yes?'

'What do you think about renting a room at my place?'

'Sounds interesting.'

'It's a smallish room at the end of the corridor but all furnished and with a single bed. Oh, and it has a desk, for your studying.'

'Where do you live?'

'Not far from Viktoria-Luise-Platz.' The location sets off a whistle from Karl.

'Nice area. More than nice.'

'Your own bathroom too. I can't give you one of the guest rooms as my older brother and sister do come to visit sometimes, without mentioning nephews and nieces. An uncle in Berlin seems to be cooler than the previous one in California these days.'

Karl frowns.

'How many rooms do you have?'

His tone is mildly reproachful of suspected wealth yet only in jest as he's neither capable nor willing to be reproachful. He's not in the least interested in the answer anyway, the question was rhetorical and William just shrugs it away.

'Sounds amazing but also unaffordable, how much would the rent be?'

'How much do you pay at Uni?'

'Around three-hundred, subsidised. No bills.'

'Good enough for me.' He sees a hint of suspicion in Karl's face and with reason, he thinks.

'I know what you are thinking: where's the catch? There isn't one. It's not charity. I don't need a tenant but I'm away a fair bit and could do with a presence of some kind in the apartment when I'm not there. It's very safe, of course, but also very big. I'd like someone else living in it.'

Karl has listened attentively; he always listens before replying and he never interrupts.

'Why me though?'

'I wouldn't advertise and I'm slightly weary of strange characters or total loonies turning up anyway. Only thought about it when you said you wanted to move out of your quarters.' There is a trace of excitement in Karl's expression while William hears his conscience tapping his shoulder and whispering in his ear that he's a reprehensible liar.

'And you're not a serial killer or an axe murderer, are you?'

'I'll leave the machete at my parents' then.'

They laugh. Together. Again.

'You know how many landlords it has slaughtered in its career? My most treasured possession.'

'Can you spare the life of the next one?'

'I'll see what I can do.'

A touch of barbaric humour, William thinks, but it has nevertheless broken the ice.

'No pressure anyway, come around and see the place.'

'I think I will, sir.'

They agree the day and the time and Karl is making his way back into the bistro though he briefly turns around.

'Very kind of you to think of me, sir.'

He turns up on time and rings the entry phone of an old sandstone mansion block with an imposing oak double door as its main entrance. He feels overwhelmed by the elegance and the cleanliness and for a moment he considers that perhaps this isn't suited for him. A voice comes through when the video camera flashes white.

'Top floor, come up.'

He walks tentatively through the grand lobby and he's pleased by the absence of a concierge because he now feels even more inadequate for the place.

William opens the door. Slacks and red Lacoste, colourful socks.

'Better take my shoes off.'

'You just guessed the first rule of the house. Don't worry, there aren't many others.'

He nods and comes in, leaving his battered Converses on the side. He whistles in appreciation: the small hallway leads to a vast sitting room split in two sections by large and fluffy sofas; two tall French windows are casually ajar onto a square terrace where some wooden furniture is sheltered by a white and yellow awning. The taste of the interior design is impeccable; modern minimalist, but with occasional period pieces of furniture. The walls randomly host exquisite - and authentic - works of art. Though he's only eighteen, Karl can recognise refined taste.

'Come through. Here is the kitchen.'

Another state-of-the-art little gem. He follows William onto the terrace.

'Wow, what a view. You can see the Siegessäule sticking out of the Tiergarten.'

'I understand we're not that far from your college. By the way, there is storage for your bike in the underground garage.'

Karl puts his thumb up. He's starting to feel the excitement about a possible move and he's afraid that he's struggling to conceal it.

'Follow me.'

They are back to the small hallway and stroll into a long corridor flanked by several doors.

'This is my room and bathroom, then the two guest bedrooms with the guest bathrooms, and here we are. It's the last at the end but it means it's quiet and private. I imagine you as a diligent student?'

A self-deprecating smile appears on Karl's closed lips.

'I try.'

The room is much bigger than Karl had imagined and elegantly furnished with a single bed made up with a fresh and fluffy white duvet, a wardrobe, a chest of drawers and a desk. The window is large and a warm, golden light filters through the off-white curtains.

'Your bathroom is right in front of your door. And that's just you using it.'

Karl is silent. He sees himself living here, he really does.

'Well, I've just realised how rude I have been. Would you like some tea or coffee or even a beer, it's already late afternoon.'

'What?... Ah, yes.' He was dreaming of himself here, his imagination flying.

They walk to the sitting room.

'A beer sounds a good idea, why not?'

'Great, go and sit on the terrace, I'll be along in a sec.'

Karl slumps into a comfortable armchair and he turns it in the direction of the Tiergarten, awed.

William comes back with two bottles and no glasses. The informality relaxes and pleases Karl: one thing he's a bit worried about is how to behave in this plush apartment as he has never lived in one of these in his still young life. The beer bottles without glasses have eased his worries. He was mildly concerned that William was expecting him to behave like a young aristocrat.

'So, what do you think?'

'Well, wow. It's an amazing place you have here. Just wow.' Both have a sip.

'Life here is not as pretentious as the apartment, Karl. Don't feel intimidated. You can walk around as you please. I do. Slack on the sofa, watch rubbish TV, lazy Sunday mornings and all that. Fridge-wise it's, well, help yourself really, just add whatever you feel eating that I might not order online at Edeka. I haven't kept up with teenagers' culinary tastes. I do like to cook, welcome to join me for dinner anytime.'

Karl struggles to explain to himself why he never feels any discomfort in William's company, why he's always at ease and feels he can say whatever he likes without thinking it out first. Not that he ever does. He always thinks before speaking.

'Further rules: Frau Greta, the cleaning lady, comes Tuesday and Thursday from eight to three. I strongly suggest to get out of her way. Actually, I don't suggest it, I'm telling you for your own benefit as she made it clear when she started that no one is to be in the apartment when she cleans. On those evenings we can have dinner on the floor as it'll be cleaner than an operating table.' Karl nods and takes another sip. 'She will blitz your room and laundry, I warn you.'

'I can't possibly ask that.'

'You won't be able to stop her, trust me. Last but not least. Guests. I'm uber-liberal, so whoever comes along, no problem: Grindr, bars, whatever. As long as you check out they are not coming along with that machete of yours.'

As soon as he finishes the sentence it dawns on him that he has just assumed something which he never actually asked. He freezes and a panic sets in. He has made a big mistake and he might have offended him. He has so far assumed but he now remembers that he was never hundred per cent sure and Karl might not be what Bill thinks he is; not all straight boys are brutes or football fanatics, some are sweet and sensitive. Polite. Respectful. Sensible.

Fuck, he thinks, how stupid he has been.

Karl stares ahead at the Siegessäule, bottle in his hand. He doesn't turn to William.

'Is it that obvious?'

Relief in William's heart.

'No, not really. I fear I have offended you.'

'Nah. I'm not easily offended, sir. I don't hide it, I'm out at uni and with the old folks, just thought that perhaps you hadn't guessed.' He waits and then grins. 'Or perhaps I just wanted to keep you guessing.'

'No hidden motives either by the way. I mean, I'm a gentleman.'

Karl turns.

'I know you are.'

'Most importantly, whether you move in or not, I would

really prefer if you stop this "Herr William" and "Sir" stuff; back in the US they call me Bill.'

'Bill?'

'Yes.'

'I like that. Yeah. Bill.'

He moves in the day after as there is really no notice to give to the hall, they have a waiting list for new students.

Bill is around when he appears with a big rucksack, an even bigger holdall and the nowadays indispensable IT paraphernalia.

'I can help with the rest of your stuff, though I don't own a car.'

Karl chuckles.

'There is no other stuff. I haven't lived long enough to hoard other stuff.'

He starts to settle in at a pleasant, slow speed. Every day a small piece of Bill's routine fits in with Karl's which is not especially demanding as routines go. They learn each other's coffee tastes so they can always put two cups under the machine when they fancy a flat white.

He's introduced to Frau Greta who shows no sign of suspicion or disapproval. If anything, a hint of thirst for the challenge presented by a much younger thus vastly more untidy person veils her gaze. She holds a bottle of bleach in her right hand, a mop in her left and she's not afraid to use them.

'Herr Brackman, I'll sort out socks and underwear between you two, I have two boys and a husband at home, I have a system.' And Frau Greta has a system for anything, the household relies on her one hundred per cent as Bill is not that good at housekeeping.

'Karl doesn't want to be a burden, he's happy to do his own laundry.'

She frowns in mild but unmistakable disapproval; her apron, her slender figure and spectacles exude authority in the housekeeping field, an authority Bill knows best not to challenge.

'Ah, Herr Brackman, that is not a good idea. As I said, I have two young ones at home and their idea of laundry is below any remotely acceptable standard.'

Bill looks at Karl with the 'I told you so' expression which begs to accept Greta's services. He offers an extra two hours for the extra work and she thanks him while declaring that one will suffice.

Karl feels that he's receiving too much in the deal and volunteers an extra small contribution without being sure if he can actually afford it. But Bill declines, explaining that he prefers Frau Greta to be in charge of everything: 'You'll see what I mean'.

And he does.

He returns from college and notices the Teutonic trail of order and cleanliness Frau Greta has left in her wake but nothing prepares him for what his room has transformed into.

Over the previous few days he had already managed to mildly 'teenage' his room: not a cataclysmic event of plastic bottles and crumpled duvets, or a tornado of scattered clothing; rather a gentle forgetfulness to re-stow any items back where they belong.

He opens the door and his jaw drops: the bed is made up - *did she use a ruler?* She must have - the linen changed, the parquet polished and everything is stowed away. His laundry is arranged in equidistant piles of items on the duvet. He checks: there are no socks or underwear belonging to Bill, they are all his.

How did she do it? He laughs to himself, thinking that perhaps, while he shops in C&A, Bill wouldn't be seen dead in there. His socks are probably all from Gant.

The desk has not been tidied up but there is a note on it:

Herr Karl, you might have left the papers on your desk in some studying order as my sons do, so I thought better not to re-arrange them. Let me know if you would like that next time. Greta.

He looks outside, even his small room window has a very pleasant view of the city. He's happy.

The settling in continues. Unhurried, gradual, unintrusive, and Bill is true to his word: he is a gentleman. Karl leaves the door of his room open at night and walks around in his pyjama bottoms in the morning, sometimes all day. He was afraid this slobbish habit would annoy Bill but it appears not to. At times he flirts in jest. Bill remains the gentleman he said he was.

He's a quiet boy with sporadic periods of deep introversion, outgoing yet reserved. Sometimes they bump into each other in the kitchen, sitting room or on the terrace, exchange a few words or jokes, ask how is everything and that is all.

On some evenings Bill cooks dinner. They discover that they are both fridge-grazers so it seldom happens and Karl cannot cook to save his own young life.

When Bill feels in culinary mood he always invites the young man to join him and Karl loves these rare occasions, though he feels rather guilty as he's unable to contribute much to the grocery shopping. When he does, Aldi's labels start to appear between small cans of caviar and pots of Belgian pate'.

Before dinner he pointed that out to Bill while sheepishly implying that he would struggle to add further to the shopping. Bill gently dismissed him.

'I'm not expecting a student to fill the fridge with Reblochon and bottles of Crozes-Hermitage.'

Karl doesn't have the foggiest of what on earth these two items might be but the names sound prohibitively expensive.

During the conversation he had been standing by Bill who, while pouring the wine, had ruffled his fluffy blond hair before taking the glasses to the terrace where the starters laid ready. He had never done it before and it stirs a sudden hurricane inside Karl. He struggles to define what it is but he keeps feeling it over a chatty dinner. It has a strange, unsettling power.

'So, time to ask you after a few weeks. How do you find it? I mean, living here?'

Karl takes a sip of the wine. A blazing pink sunset marks the sky behind the Siegessäule and a warm breeze sweeps the table at irregular intervals carrying the soft noise of the sparse traffic below. The weather has improved over the past few weeks and they are both barefoot, in shorts and t-shirts; super casual as Bill had promised. Everything that Bill had promised has actually happened.

'It's alright, I suppose. Still getting used to it.'

As he says that, he sees Bill's mildly disappointed expression as he grabs his glass and nervously downs a sizeable quantity of the content.

'Ah. Well. Ok.'

Karl puts down the glass and bursts in a spitting laugh while kicking him under the table.

'Ah ah, I got you there. Who am I kidding? I'm so fucking happy. To be here, I mean.' Bill's face lightens up, the disappointment gone. 'God, you fell for that one. I guess I must be the lodger from heaven?'

The carefree chatting, the banter, the wine, the complete lack of fear of saying something wrong. He feels at home. He really does.

Bill has yet to form an opinion on whether Karl is the lodger from heaven. All he knows is that his arrival has injected a fresh and animated climate in the former single household. A sprightly fountain of youth. Hard to define as there is nothing special Karl does or says to cause that. A few times they have watched television together, though the young man has Netflix on his MacBook and, like most teenagers, is partial to bingeing on series which invariably involve vampires and zombies or a combination of the two joyously massacring each other.

It's his presence, or just the mere thought that he's in the house while he's away. Although he's not away as much as he pretended when he mentioned it to Karl while trying to convince him to rent the room. It was a lie, of course it was.

He rarely travels back to California nor takes regulars breaks or holidays. He's not even out in the evening that much. He thinks his lodger has forgotten about it but he hasn't. He has been here nearly three weeks now and Bill hasn't left Berlin once. Karl smiles when he remembers him saying it.

He has cleared the table and has brought out two espressos. One thing they definitely have in common is coffee overconsumption, not yet a problem on Karl's young constitution, not so on Bill's more time-worn one.

'Tell me to piss off if I'm a nosy troll. You haven't told me much about your time in California.'

'Didn't think you'd be interested.'

'Why not?'

'Older gay man's baggage.'

'Your calling yourself old is annoying, you know that, don't you?'

'Wallowing in self-indulgence is a certified human right, young man. Are you trying to stop me from feeling sorry for myself?'

'I am, fire away then.'

'It isn't that exciting, I warn you.'

'That's for me to decide.' And he takes a sip of the espresso.

'I was there for about twenty years, give and take a few breaks. For the best part of them I shared my life with Mark, my partner. An odd life if you ask me.'

'I do.'

'Mark was born in Nevada but he became a very successful Hollywood producer and talent-scout when he moved to L.A. We met in a bar in San Francisco, you know, those places where you picked up guys before the internet swept them all away.'

Light laugh from Karl.

'Some have survived.'

'True. Anyway, we sort of moved in together though I couldn't leave the valley and Paramount held him in diamond-encrusted chains in Beverly Hills.'

'The valley?'

'The one made of silicon.'

Karl nods.

'So we kind of commuted between the two, a pain in a way but we fell in love; we were just a bit older than you at the time though I was five years younger than him. Both professions paid well, allowing us to afford an amazing lifestyle, though at times it got a bit out of control. It always does in America.'

'In what way?'

'After a while we quietly abandoned monogamy and went a bit wild, but we never went for the drugs stuff. You have no idea how stoned out of their wits some of the film stars you see on your Netflix thing actually are.'

'You've met some then?' Karl's childish excitement amuses him.

'Some. Mostly when they were boys, before their big break. You see, Karl, what happens with the starlets happens with the boys too. Exactly the same. It doesn't come out that much because most of the boys forget about it and move on, depending on how nasty or pleasant their experience was. Mark became a big shot at Paramount and a stream of aspiring, willing young men started to flow.

Overflow, rather.'

He notices Karl listening in full awe.

'I couldn't blame him, really. You should have seen the sheer desperation to get a part, even the smallest one. A line. I don't know, serving a drink to Brad Pitt in his next production, taking Nicole Kidman's luggage at the hotel lobby, you name it.'

He realises that he is a bit tipsy and in need to take it to the next level.

'I have an idea, what about a brandy?'

Thumb up from Karl. He doesn't get drunk very often but he likes it when he does and he loves the company. Cognac remains mysterious to him but it has alcohol in it and that can't be bad.

Bill returns with two large glasses, too large for comfort but tonight Karl feels comfortable. More comfortable than he has ever felt. They both take a good sip.

'It didn't bother me and I still loved Mark. I know he didn't care about the boys, most of them were just beautiful things who couldn't carry a tune or blurt out a line to save their lives. We used to joke that they needed a teleprompter in bed too.'

They laugh out loud.

'Did you play along?' Even in the fog of rapidly progressing intoxication, Bill detects a worried pang in Karl's question.

'Not a lot. It got a bit boring, my work was pretty demand-ing anyway and with entirely different people.'

'Such as?'

'Geeks. Some of them barely your age and already on three figure salaries. Most of them spotty, ripped jeans and hoodies. Patently unwashed. The hood was almost always down on their forehead even as they scoffed Big Macs and Coke, which was all they consumed. Pretty sure they didn't even know what they were earning but the brains under the hoodies were truly frightening: they could hack the CIA just for the fun of it.'

More brandy.

'I don't know how you can feel sorry for someone on that kind of money but I did actually. Some were clearly sociopaths in need of help.'

'Did you? I mean, help?'

'One thing they didn't have is social skills. Once I was working on a project with this kid and in the middle of work, he turns and asks: "Would you have sex with me?"'

'What?'

'No shit. I couldn't tell his age and I was so taken aback that I struggled for words. He looked about twelve. I told him that if he wanted to experiment, maybe a young guy of roughly his age would have been a better idea. He told me he was twenty-seven and never had proper sex before. Still not sure what he meant for 'proper'. Fuck me, talking of arrested development.'

Karl finishes the brandy but Bill has brought the bottle to the table. There is a heavy gold medallion on it, something eye-wateringly expensive.

'And did you…?'

'He said I was the first man he met who didn't scare him to death. He told me he felt I wouldn't tease him for being ugly.'

'Was he? Ugly, I mean.'

'He only thought he was.'

'He was probably bullied at school. Geeks and nerds are the most obvious target.'

A pause of silence. Karl's agitation for the hair-ruffling has returned.

'Mark wasn't a predator. First, he was a very handsome guy. Fit, tanned, impeccable manners. I've got the feeling most boys didn't mind it, considering what they might have had to put up with when falling prey of lecherous fat directors and brutish studio bosses. And he was good to them. He always found them a way into the studios. Sometimes risking his reputation too. I overheard a few famous directors raging at him on the phone that if he really insisted in sending his catamites to them, could he stick to fucking the talented ones.'

'I thought you said that it wasn't exciting? Try growing up in Spandau.'

More laughter.

Bill has left the table to look over the railings. It's dark now, the light of the table lamps is filtering out from the sitting room.

He stares pensively at the French doors while Karl is still sat at the table hazily observing his profile. His sharply cut grey hair shines against the glow, his blue eyes glitter from the alcohol, one hand is in his pocket, the other one holds the brandy glass. He looks into it and then ahead. Karl would like to get up too but his legs feel a little jelly. They are both pickled.

'Why did you split up? Sorry, I assume you did if you are here.'

'We didn't. Just as we were starting to tire of sinful Babylon and were tentatively planning a secluded existence on Malibu beach, Mark got cancer and passed away. About four years ago. It was swift so there wasn't an awful lot of suffering. We both hated all the schmaltz that comes with illness.'

'Oh man, I'm sorry to hear that.'

'No worries.' He comes back to the table. 'I tried to carry on living in California but with all my good intentions, I couldn't. I couldn't stand the people anymore. Mark left me everything in an unassailable will. There wasn't much of a family to contest it anyway. He only had an older gay brother who had stayed behind in Nevada and was comfortably settled with his partner. A real old-fashioned queen. I offered to share the legacy but he was happy for me to look after it, as he put it. He and his partner were what we were about to become. Didn't look that bad to be honest, except for the Nevada bit. A year later I moved to Berlin. I still don't know why but I don't regret it. I think.'

One in the morning and there is no Karl's tale. Suburban childhood, Grundschule, Gymnasium and the Abitur exams to get into university. There's a lot of schooling at that age. Long and grey. No seedy Beverly Hills underworld to brave and conquer.

They head for the corridor, both rather unstable on their feet. They are at Bill's door. He opens it and turns to Karl.

'Thank you for the evening.'

'Thank you Bill, was awesome.'

When he reaches his door he hears his name: 'Karl!' He sees Bill leaning on the frame of the door. 'It's…it's great to have you here.'

He nods and enters his room. He undresses and lies on the bed staring at the ceiling, not feeling too well: the toxic mix of champagne, Crozes-Hermitage and brandy rumbling noisily in his belly. And then the hair-ruffling returns, spinning into his hazy head. He crosses his hands on his smooth, ivory chest; most nights they travel south, along his naked body, seeking a Sisyphean relief from desire.

Not tonight. One of them travels north and ruffles his hair instead.

He's studying hard for an upcoming exam. Bill and Frau Greta seem pleased with his diligent efforts, making him feel like he has been adopted rather than lodging.

She has allowed him to stay in his room while she blitzes the apartment and both come in regularly with various types of coffee to keep him awake.

When Bill comes in, he leaves the mug on the desk and ruffles his hair, leaving him vaguely upset when he forgets to do it. He feels entitled to it now.

On some evenings Bill finds him slumped on the desk, completely out. He carries him to the bed with nervous care, takes his jeans off and covers him with the duvet. Then he picks up the cup and the plate on the desk, turns the light off and leaves as silently as he can.

On one of these nights he impulsively kisses him on the forehead before leaving.

Karl was not that out and he felt that. He turns and buries himself in the pillow, a nuclear reaction of sudden euphoria exploding inside his chest.

When he passes the exam with flying colours he returns home with the news and gets his first hug from Bill.

He lingers in his arms, lulling in the rush of warmth hitting him, mildly resisting Bill's discreet attempts to end it.

Although a quiet and reserved lad, Karl is far from being an asocial loner. He has straight and gay friends, some remnants of school days, some acquired at the faculty of chemistry.

He met his best friend Lukas when they joined. They went back to his room and, without much ado, proceeded to sleep together on the very first evening. A wild night of passion which fizzled out a bit on the second one. On the third it was all over in the proverbial flash though they agreed to stay best friends and so they did. Boys would never allow bedroom fun to get in the way of a good friendship.

Exams passed, they chill on the sun-drenched patio of the Bismarck, staff-discounted Lattes on the table, Karl noisily slurping the last drop of his.

'Do you think I'm ugly?'

Lukas raises his crystal grey eyes to the clear Berlin sky and pushes his matt black hair back in theatrical exasperation. He's an extraordinarily patient boy and with Karl he has to be.

'I thought I said, no-more-Bill. I am Billed-out, can we change subject?'

'I was talking about me.'

'No, you weren't. You were asking because you believe that Bill finds you ugly and that is why he hasn't burst into your room at night with the intention of raping you.'

'That's crude. And he would never do that to anyone, he's a gentleman.'

'So why do you want him to behave like a brute?'

'I don't.'

Lukas noisily drops and bangs his forehead on the table. He loves Karl, he's his best mate, even when he drives him to despair. Like. Right now.

Karl gets up.

'Another coffee?'

'Cappuccino Crush for me.'

Annoyed grin from Karl.

'Haha, very funny.'

He comes back with Ella holding the lattes and gives the five euro note back to Lukas with a smile.

'I got one free. Ella loves me.'

Lukas glances at her with a hand gesture seeking an ally in desperation.

'Who doesn't?'

Ella nods in agreement.

'We all do.' And she kisses him on the head.

After a brief silence he crosses the red insecurity zone again.

'I don't think I'm that attractive, you know. I mean, the fact that we're young doesn't make everyone attracted to us.'

'Thanks, so now I'm ugly too?'

'If you were I wouldn't have slept with you?'

'We all have different tastes.'

'I think he finds me ugly. And plain. My spectacles are so thick and without them I can't see shit. These bloody spots never clear. And all that time in Hollywood, surrounded by beautiful boys, if you think about it. I must look so uninteresting. So boring.'

'I think I'll go mad. Listen mate, by the far too vast information I have from you about him, it frankly looks to me that he fucking adores you. I don't remember my landlord kissing me goodnight in bed or giving me a long hug after I passed my exam.'

'Your grades were shit and your landlord is old and fat.'

'Immaterial. Perhaps Bill just doesn't sleep around or he had enough of sex or fuck knows. Maybe, maybe he has a boyfriend or a lover you don't know of.'

Lukas could kill himself for saying that. You don't say that to Karl right now. He sees a dejected, worried thunder on his face and he needs a quick fix.

'Sure he cares the hell about you though.' He's desperate to change the subject and he has an idea now. 'Are we still on for the beach tomorrow?'

'Yeah.'

'Tell you what. Why don't you invite him?'

He looks suspicious but not uninterested. Lukas drops his shoulders.

'I have no intention of stealing your Bill.'

'He's not "my" Bill.'

'Whatever, ask him?'

'Ok.'

He accepts the invitation. That makes Karl happy and worried at the same time that Bill might not like his friend or Lukas might say something stupid.

But the day sets off in good spirits. They are all fit cyclists and they cover the distance to the Wannsee Beach in good time. The sun is blazing hot, Lukas and Bill have exchanged a few words about various nonsense and Karl relaxes as he sees them getting along well.

Changed into their swimming trunks they head for a secluded and quiet spot. They arrived fairly early and there is ample choice of locations but Bill has forgotten his water bottle in the changing booth and returns to reception to retrieve it. Lukas promptly bashes out his first impression.

'He's dead fit, I grant you that. And you were right, he's a gentleman.'

The conversation flows, Bill asking the boys about uni and their plans for life in general. Being here with them makes him feel young which is, of course, nonsense; all the same a comforting one.

'Did you say you brought a ball along?'

Lukas nods. Bill slaps his shoulder.

'Game on then.'

They run to the lake. The water is cold for the boys and freezing for Bill as his stoic resistance to glacial temperatures has inexorably lowered with the years going by.

They play a few games, splashing around, shouting, arguing stupidly about their freshly invented rules. They let the ball drift away and the boys take turn to climb on Bill's shoulders to jump in the water with back-breaking somersaults.

After all sorts of aquatic games Lukas heads for the shore, leaving them to play at wrestling and drowning each other as boys do or, more precisely, as Bill did when, as a young man himself, used to spend the best part of his summer holidays at the family home in Nantucket.

He's now keeping Karl's head under water and the young man is furiously paddling with his hands while trying to free himself. When he succeeds he accidentally resurfaces between Bill's arms with his back to him.

A moment, only a moment.

His arms gently close in around Karl's bony chest, his nose breathing on his neck, their bodies close. He grabs Bill's forearm from below with both hands. His body shakes. Bill figures out the imminent burst and frees one of his hands to seal Karl's mouth seconds before a long, muted moan is discharged.

He's breathing heavily and he just wants to die. There. Now.

But Bill turns him around by grabbing his upper arms with his strong hands. Karl looks down, unable to meet his eyes; he's so embarrassed he would like to be drown for real.

Bill squeezes Karl's skinny upper limbs repeatedly, in a tender, reassuring way.

'Hey!'

Then he lifts his chin with his thumb and fingers but the young man is too ashamed for words. Almost in tears.

'I'll go ahead, see you on the beach.'

He leaves him to clean himself up without mentioning it. As a gentleman would.

Lukas has gone for a toilet break and Bill is lying on his stomach facing the woods while Karl sits still, silent, staring at the water. The shore is now busier and noisier.

He knows the young man is mustering all the courage he can find.

'That was gross. I'm so sorry. I couldn't stop it.'

Bill fails to move, without looking at him he'll be able to let it all out and get over it.

'And you shouldn't have tried. It's nature.'

'Nature?'

'Did you know that a man's sexual power is at its peak at exactly your age?'

'Fuck me, I do now.'

A small laugh from Bill reassures him. A thoughtful pause.

'How angry are you with me?'

Bill gets up.

'What? Why should I be angry? I'm most certainly not.'

'You sure?'

'Positive.'

'Thanks for...you know...'

'I couldn't possibly know how noisy you might be.'

'I'm a fairly noisy bastard.'

They burst into a loud laugh as Lukas approaches. He wants to treat them to a Flammkuchen and a beer at the Wannsee Brasserie so they set off in earnest.

The day gets better and better, the beers on the table multiply by magic but they are sweated off on the long bike ride home.

Once there Karl has finally convinced himself that Bill is not angry with him and Bill has exhausted all his Freudian knowledge in trying to reassure him that he's not a sexually incontinent animal. He reckons he has succeeded, but with Karl one never knows.

His parents still live in Spandau. On a sunny day he cycles all the way there for the weekly dinner.

When he's back he has to re-adjust to the unglamorous lower middle class abode of his folks. His father is an electrician and his mother works part-time in a doctor's surgery. They have looked after their only son well and he has repaid his debt by growing into a fine young man. Sensitive, studious and polite.

When he goes to his old bedroom to look for some old books, he realises he misses its unpretentious simplicity. Living with Bill has never made him envious of what he has or who he is. He's not and never will be ashamed of his parents.

He forces himself not to talk too much about his glamorous landlord, following Lukas' advice to skip the detail that he's only five years younger than his dad; although Bill looks like a man in his thirties while his father has slumped into a premature sixty-something decline.

There are men and there are gay men.

Karl has left now and his father is on washing-up duty since they have never bothered with the purchase of a dishwasher. Between rinsing and drying he stares out of the window in silence while his wife clears up the table. She speaks while piling up plates by his side.

'Karl seems to be very fond of this Bill.'

He's a Prussian of few words and none forthcoming at this very moment. She tries again.

'He sounds very wealthy, he didn't say how old he was though.'

No reply, yet the thinking is louder than words. The

self-questioning. The nagging feeling that perhaps a gap is being subconsciously filled and by someone he cannot compete with. All nonsense, he repeats to himself to no avail: nonsense is what keeps us awake and he will get no sleep tonight.

He's sorting out some documents. He has a working lunch at the Adlon with Jack, who sometimes tires of pretending to be such a busy man and has flown in from Palo Alto. It's a hot, sunny day and he wears a white Ralph Lauren shirt over a pair of blue slacks; as he puts on a light tweed jacket with a pink pocket square, the entry phone rings. He tries to recall if he's expecting some delivery but he's convinced he isn't.

'Hallo?'

'Herr Brackman?'

'Yes, it's me.'

'Hallo, my name is Jonas Schaefer, I'm Karl's father. I hope I'm not disturbing you.'

He is startled for a second. What for, he's not quite sure. He's Karl's landlord and he has not behaved inappropriately in any way he could think of.

'No, not at all, please come up. Top floor.'

He WhatsApps Jack immediately, delaying lunch by about thirty minutes.

While Herr Schaefer waits for the lift he surveys the grand and spotless lobby. He has worked in such apartments and knows the value of these places.

Bill opens the door and invites Herr Schaefer in, shaking his hand.

'Pleased to meet you Herr Schaefer.'

'Pleased to meet you Herr Brackman.'

'Would you like a coffee or anything else? I believe Karl is at the faculty for a lecture right now.'

'Oh, I know that. No, I don't want to impose, thank you. I just wanted to check his new arrangements are safe and sound; you see, for my wife and me Karl is still our little boy.'

'Rightly so. Well, here we are, all open to inspection.'

He has tried to look at Bill while unobserved and he can tell he's not much younger than himself. Herr Schaefer's clothes are simple but of decent quality, modest and practical. On the other hand Bill's understated, Anglo elegance is on an entirely different scale and an unreachable one for Herr Schaefer. The patrician nonchalance of his manners is mesmerisingly intimidating.

'You must be very proud of your son, he's doing well with his studies.'

'We are, thank you, Herr Brackman, we are.'

Karl vaguely resembles his father and Bill notices the fine features that have given life to his angelic, angular face. The look in his eyes is also as vulnerable.

'Karl tells me he's very happy here. He was very, how can I say, informative about this place. And about you, of course.'

'I'm glad to hear that, Herr Schaefer, he's a very good lodger; quiet, respectful, a delight to have around.'

'Yes.'

There's not much else to say: words don't come easy to Herr Schaefer and he's uncomfortably staring at Bill from time to time.

'Well, I better be going, I think my son is in safe hands.'

'You haven't seen Karl's room.'

'I'm sure it's really good, no need.'

'I think you should see it.'

He nods while Bill leads the way. Frau Greta has been there the day before so Karl hasn't had enough time to un-blitz his room and it's still in a reasonable state.

'His bedroom was never that tidy.'

'Frau Greta, the cleaning lady.'

'I see.'

'And this is his desk.'

He points at the desk. There is an insistence in Bill's manners which Herr Schaefer only comprehends when he notices the picture frame on it. No need to pick it up. He can clearly see himself and his wife with a younger Karl in his shorts and sandals. It's a holiday shot, they are all smiling, probably Majorca or some other bucket and spade destination.

'Thank you, Herr Brackman. By the way, boys of his age don't take well to parents checking up on them.' Bill guarantees his discretion with a restrained nod.

Herr Schaefer leaves and strolls in a haze toward the nearest U-Bahn stop.

It took a long time to accept what Karl told them only a few years before. His wife got there faster but, as much as he tried, the pain would not shift and he struggled to hide it from his son. He still does. He so wanted Karl to believe everything was fine when it really wasn't. It never is, we just delude ourselves that it is.

He was still dreaming of girlfriends and wives, grandchildren and a safe life, or what he believed to be a safe life.

Then he sat them down to relieve a burden he had achingly carried for the best part of his sixteen years.

That night young Karl had been shaking with fear but not for himself. He had worked out all the possible ways to avoid hurting his parents, all too alert to being their only creation, their only purpose, a purpose which he was about to shatter.

Herr Schaefer had stayed silent before reading the terror in his son's eyes, the wrenching pain at seeing his mother crying. He had tried to reassure him as best as his broken heart was allowing him to utter any word of comfort: this was still his home and he was still their boy.

And perhaps he so miserably failed in his deception, Karl sensing that despite the reassurances, his own father was drifting away, silently withdrawing what little affection a born and bred Prussian man could afford to display.

Abandonment seeps in people's lives by stealth, between casual phrases linked together by distracted, perfunctory conversation; words that mean no harm yet betray indifference. Small talks are really that small.

He feels a stir and, having walked by several U-Bahn stops, sits on a bench at one of the entrances of the Tiergarten. He stares ahead and thinks of Bill. And it hurts.

Bill is on the balcony, hands in his pockets, his Ray Bans shielding glistening eyes. He has watched him walk away, slightly hunched, his dejection all too clear.

He knows all things and more: Karl poured it all out over another evening fuelled by a couple of good bottles of Beaujolais, needless to say, fastidiously chilled to perfection.

The pair of them slouched on the sofa, Bill digging deeper and deeper at his Palo Alto analyst's experience in a vain effort to stem Karl's torment. He had tried his best to relieve the agony fuelled by the inner guilt of having let his parents down by virtue of being something he had never asked to be.

Yet he had also confessed how much he had always loved them though Bill could never reveal such truth to Herr Schaefer while he was at the apartment. It would have been graceless and uncalled for. Ungentlemanly.

But he had previously noticed the photo on Karl's desk. That was all he had in his armoury and he gave it his best shot.

* * *

- staying at my folks tonight, going straight to uni in the morning x -

- no probs, catch you later x -

The WhatsApp exchange is brief and to the point. They both hate to linger: teenage hurry against businessman's busy habits. Liberating brevity.

He finds his auntie joining them for dinner and taking possession of his room for the night, so he cycles back home. It's late but the night is warm, the breeze caressing his hair while he speeds back home through the deserted streets of the city.

But like every other night, the ruffling of his hair, the kisses on the forehead and the hugs on the sofa resurface stronger than ever.

And like many other nights, he stops by Bill's bedroom.

He must be fast asleep. He keeps doing it: he lifts his hand up in a fist barely an inch from the door, ready to knock, while whispering to himself any possible line, any credible excuse:

I feel lonely.

Just wanted to check if you were alright.

Would you mind if I snuggle up?

Perhaps one night he'll find the courage, tonight maybe.

He awakes at about eight and heads for the kitchen in his boxer shorts and socks, rubbing his eyes, his hand through his hair a few times to shock himself into the day ahead. He hears the sound of the coffee machine and instinctively calls out before going through the double doors.

'Morning, Bill!'

A naked young man is at the machine, ineptly playing with it, Nespresso capsules falling and rolling all over the floor with a ticking noise.

He freezes at the door.

The boy turns without any discernible embarrassment and he's worse than naked, he's semi-erect, tumescent.

The sudden pain running through his bones is like an earthquake, he has to hold onto one of the chairs for fear of fainting. The boy smiles.

'You must be Karl. Hi, I'm Klaus.'

He can only stammer out a reply.

'Who...who are you?'

He's holding onto the crazy idea that he might be one of Bill's nephews; and it's crazy because his name is Klaus and he has just addressed him in unaccented German. Besides,

46

a nephew would hardly walk around naked and in a semi excited state: those straws are just too thin to be clutched at.

'I did say it. Klaus?'

'Yes, I heard that, I mean...'

'Oh yes. Well. A friend of Bill?'

'A friend.'

'Well, I mean. You know what I mean.'

'No. I don't fucking know what you mean. Tell me.'

He feels the anger rising to uncontrollable levels. Klaus has a worried expression. He's not sure why Bill's lodger now has this tense, disfiguring rage appearing on his face.

They vaguely look alike, possibly the same age, maybe a little older. In a brief and parallel universe the resemblance somehow reassures him but it's indeed brief. He's burning inside.

Klaus grabs the improbably ready coffees and makes a move taking the furthest possible route away from Karl.

'I better be back.' And his last hope is shattered by seeing him leaving with one mug in each hand. That's what he has spent nights after nights dreaming he would do. One day. And now never. And it's killing him.

Klaus walks into the bedroom and closes the door behind him. He leaves one of the catastrophically made coffees on the table by Bill's side. He's sleeping on his stomach and Klaus gently jumps on him, kissing his neck, aroused, wanting more of him in the morning dew, dripping with hazy desire.

While chewing away at his ear he whispers in it.

'I've just met your lodger.'

Bill's eyes open in sudden, sheer horror.

'What? Karl?'

'Yep.'

'That's impossible. He's at his parents'.'

'Well, he's in the kitchen.'

He leaps out of the bed.

'Fuck! Oh my fucking God. Oh fuck! Oh Jesus!'

He finds his briefs but once worn they show his morning erection, something he has no intention to walk into the kitchen with. He keeps swearing obscenities while searching for his baggy pyjama pants hoping to lose his excitement which is instead fed by his blood boiling in panic. He punches the wardrobe with a savage grunt; Klaus is terrified and, above all, he struggles to understand what's happening, why it's happening and if perhaps it's all his fault. He hides under the duvet in fear.

'I don't understand. What's going on? I've just met your lodger.' But Bill, now besides himself, shouts at him in a rage.

'Just shut up! Just shut the fuck up!'

He has found the pants and the size of his manhood is returning to visually acceptable levels. He violently opens the door which slams against its hinges and runs to the kitchen shouting.

'Karl! Karl!'

He's not in the kitchen. He makes his way to the balcony via the double door and walks around the corner which leads to the sitting room entrance. He leans over the edge, scouring the street below, the tarmac, unconsciously listening out for screams. He has always been painfully aware of how brittle Karl's confidence is.

'I haven't thrown myself off the balcony if that is what you are checking out.'

He jumps, startled. Karl is sitting cross-legged on the sofa, still in his boxers and socks, his hands holding his ankles, a flood of tears the size of an Atlantic high tide scars his red, bony cheeks.

Bill covers his face with one hand.

'Oh God. I am so sorry, Karl. I don't know what to say.'

'Why sorry? I'm only your lodger.'

He shakes his head and sits up in the armchair, only a couple of feet from Karl.

'No. You are not. You know that.'

'Do I?'

Klaus comes in, tentative, walking on egg shells. At least he has finally put some pants on. He sees the state Karl is in and he hazily understands or not. It looks complicated to him.

'Hey. Are you guys ok? I'm a bit freaked out here.'

Karl gets up and points at Klaus in anger and sadness. He has no idea what he's about to blurt out, he's in a distraught, unhinged place. His voice trembles.

'A hustler? A fucking hustler? Why do you need to hire a hustler? I was...'

But he stops. Does it matter that he was? Bill gets up in a defensive pose.

'Wow, wow, slow down. Klaus is not a hustler. He's a student exactly like yourself who has in the past overspent a bit so I'm slowly sorting out his debts.'

'Well, technically that makes me a hustler.'

'Klaus! Shut the fuck up.'

'I like spending the night here though. So maybe not. Oh, I don't know.'

Bill likes Klaus; he's a much simpler soul than his lodger but he's at the end of his forbearance and darts an unmistakable look in his direction.

'Klaus! Do you mind? I'm trying not to make it worse here!'

'I'd better go, I think. Catch you later guys.'

Neither acknowledge him leaving, the wreck is between them and them only.

The silence they both love so much falls across the room: heavy and punctuated by Karl's light sobbing. Bill knows all too well the cataclysmic angst raging inside his young friend but this time he's a gentleman without answers and without solutions; he has to think hard at what to say as he has presently increased his insecurity by a thousand pegs. He exhales.

'Please, don't hate him, he's a harmless kid.'

Karl, who has returned to his previous position on the sofa, nods: hate doesn't come to him, not for Klaus, not even for Bill.

'I'll apologise,' he stammers. 'I've made an absolute idiot of myself. Sorry about that.'

'No, you haven't. Perhaps, well, perhaps I'm not such a gentleman after all.'

Karl stares at the floor, worried about what he's about to say.

'Do you want me to move out?'

The question is tentative: even after this, it hurts him to imagine life without Bill.

'What? No, I don't.'

'It will be embarrassing though: I've got it all wrong. I feel so fucking stupid.'

Bill gets up, hands in his pants' pockets. He stares at the Siegessäule commanding the beginning of a new day.

'You haven't.'

'You must have had a good laugh at my clumsy attempts at seduction. Those Calvins cost me a fortune I didn't have.'

'The socks though? I didn't get that one?'

'That wasn't seduction. The tiles of the kitchen floor are fucking freezing.'

A small laugh, he's getting through.

'You also forgot there is an anti-burglary camera covering the corridor.'

'Oh. Fuck.'

'Some nights I was behind that door. I could almost hear your whispering.'

He pauses to weigh his words.

'You cannot even commence to imagine how much I care for you.'

Karl feels a shiver.

'You have a funny way of showing it.'

Bill is desperate. And no longer capable of holding anything back.

'If a car were about to hit you, I would run in front of it.'

Karl's eyes are out on stalks now.

'I've seen how sex sometime ruins everything. I was afraid of it actually happening. Then what? Maybe jealousy, fights, all sorts of emotional blackmail. And losing you. The shenanigans of Mark and myself you know too well. In the end it made us arid, lifeless. Which is why we were all too ready to drop it: lust has no longevity. You being here is all I care for.'

He jumps up, runs to him and falls into his arms. He feels his hand clutching his neck, the shivers a stabbing pleasure; the tightest, longest embrace he has ever had and one he'd like to last forever.

Neither of them can let go. Bill grabs his still trembling arms and looks outside, then at Karl's face, ravaged by the incessant crying.

'Glorious weather. I was wondering?'

Karl's smile appears and it's huge, the biggest Bill has ever seen on this tortured soul's lips.

'Wannsee Beach.'

'What about the lecture?'

'Must skip this one. Special day.'

'Ready in thirty minutes, young man.'

'Make it twenty, old man.' And he punches Bill's stomach in a boxing move.

He walks towards his room but bounces back out like a troll on a spring while Bill is still standing at the terrace door.

'Bring your helmet, I'll race you this time.'

'You're on.'

'You have no chance.'

He's in the shower, the water rinsing away the tears. He turns the tap off and leans with his hands against the wall tiles, staring at himself in the mirror, drops falling from his wet hair on his wet body.

If a car were about to hit you, I would run in front of it.

While drying himself he sits on the edge of the tub and covers his face with the wet towel, immersed in thoughts full of hope.

He now knows it will happen; he has no way of knowing when but he knows it will.

But this is Bill, and it will be truly sensational. He'll wait for an evening carefully choreographed by a blazing sunset; there will be champagne, a candle on the terrace table, a soothing jazz tune playing in the background, some insanely expensive bottles of red wine with unpronounceable names and food Karl has never heard of.

And then he'll bring the espressos and the brandy bottle with the gold medallion. And they will sip them while standing on the edge of the balcony, the city telling them it's past their bedtime. That it is time.

Infatuations rarely survive the mundanity of a humdrum existence; one without vintage Claret and elegant terraces. With its invisible cruelty, time robs us of the thrilling dynamics of insecure yearnings. Those very yearnings erupt in obsession and abate in routine, finally descending into indifference and often resentful hostility.

And perhaps they know it. Yet their lips are meeting, their bodies bare, their limbs trembling with bristling shivers.

A solution

Breakfast is a formal event in the Kimmich household. Walther, their butler, has prepared the buffet, now displayed on the oak-panelled credenza, to his customary exacting standards: cold meats and cheese, warm pastries delivered daily by the household-appointed Konditorei, fresh fruit and juices. Coffee is served at the table by himself and Maria, the maid of Polish or vaguely Slavic origins, no one has ever been sure of her exact provenance.

Master Felix prefers tea, the most anglophile of his habits and decidedly un-Prussian; while Walther's coffee's freshly roasted aroma swaddles the room with an uplifting and refreshing whiff, his tea-making abilities are unmistakably Prussian, thus of the most unpleasant variety.

He never verbalises his distaste as he has by now endured Walther's barbarity for years on end: the young man had entered service as a stable boy first with Herr Kimmich the elder when barely nine years of age and had then developed into a competent butler. Upon their marriage, Felix and Charlotte had purchased a large and elegant villa of uncertain gothic architecture in the most sought-after location of Kaiser-Friedrich Platz and renamed it Villa Augusta in honour of his mother.

Frau Kimmich, upon surveying the size of the mansion,

had fallen into a still unabated state of excitement in calculating how many grandchildren those numerous rooms could comfortably accommodate. After a year though, Charlotte is not yet with child.

Walther is only a few months younger than his master. That was, among several other reasons, why he had jumped with childish joy when Felix had asked him to leave his father's service and join his young family at their new abode in the heart of the city.

Perhaps because of his still tender age and his unassuming sweet nature, Felix is the most gracious and agreeable of gentlemen: polite, collected, undemanding and generous. Walther, Maria, the cook and Jurgen, the carriage driver, are well paid and treated with considerate respect. Four servants and some part-time gardeners are at this time barely adequate; the advent of posterity will unquestionably warrant more.

Felix and Walther had courageously endured the windswept steppes of Brandenburg as the playground of their childhood, effortlessly bestriding their deep class divide. Gerhardt Kimmich, Felix's landowning father, had never felt any objection to the two lads being partners in the well-known crimes young men invariably get involved in.

When in trouble for the customary youthful mischiefs, they were referred to - and shouted at - as the 'Kimmich' boys and were both punished by the whip of Felix's father, an endeavour which gave them a proud feel of equality.

Herr Kimmich had actively fostered their adolescent bond. He was a very wealthy landowner but not one of aristocratic stock. He had always made a point of being contemptuous of the otherwise prized 'Von' prefix and not against a healthy mingling with the lower classes. Walther would give Felix, a sensitive, delicate and daydreaming lad, a badly needed taste of street life: games which end when knees can't possibly bleed any further and fist fights which are settled with the reward of new and loyal friends.

He had secretly instructed Walther's widowed mother not to address his son as 'master' when the boys stopped over for their afternoon snack at her modest cottage on his farming estate. No special food either, and he had been unequivocal to Frau Klara:

'If it's good enough for Walther, it's good enough for Felix.'

Prussia meets Sparta.

Herr Kimmich's plan had worked to perfection: his son had grown into a fine and charming young man who, after a five years stint at military school, had returned home to take over the administration of the family's estate with outstanding results. He had proved a conscientious and capable administrator: every morning he would lock himself in his study and no invoice or bill ever went unpaid. Documentation, permits and financial transactions were diligently dealt with and inspections frequently carried out to survey farmers and harvests. Herr Kimmich the elder had safely relinquished most of the administration in the knowledge that the family estate was now in safe and capable hands.

Felix had pleaded with his father for an improvement in the treatment of the land tenants, arguing that it would have contributed to better returns. Herr Kimmich had reluctantly agreed though beamed with pride once informed of the results.

Unbeknown to Felix, Herr Kimmich had summoned his butler into the study shortly after his move to the new household had been agreed. He had invited an astounded Walther to take a seat in one of the leather armchairs in front of his oversized mahogany desk and pushed an envelope forward in his direction.

'This is for you, Walther. For your services to the family.'

'Sir, I can't possibly...'

'Nonsense. Frau Augusta is in a state of utter despair at the idea of losing your services.'

'Very kind of you, sir.'

He had stood up to leave, feeling uncomfortable in the armchair. Important personages had sat there; no place for humble peasants.

'Just another thing, Walther.'

'At your service, sir.'

'Watch over Master Felix.'

'We have received a letter from Weimar. Your parents. I took the liberty of opening it.'

Charlotte is buttering her bread.

'Same old same?'

He nods. She puts the knife back on the plate and listlessly looks at her husband.

'We didn't think about this when we decided to proceed with our plan.'

Felix has a sip of the tea, his face cringes in disgust.

'Would you consider being a mother?'

She stares at the tall French windows, peering between the heavy drapes.

'We have the first snow.'

'They won't relent, neither my mother nor yours.'

'That much I know. Would you consider being a father?'

'Do you think I would be a total failure as a father?'

'No, on the contrary, but that's not the issue.'

'Charlotte, I honestly don't know what to do. I'll do what you want.'

'Could we find a medical excuse?'

'Possibly. Bear in mind, your mother is the most important patron of the Weimar orphanage. I'm convinced she would get on the case as soon as we inform her of the sad news.'

'At least they would come ready-made.'

He nearly chokes on his croissant.

'Charlotte…'

She knows her husband as the sensitive soul he is and regrets her coarse comment.

'Let's think it over. Don't forget we have afternoon tea at the Kaiserhof. The Von Mutthes.'

'That oaf, thank you for reminding me.'

'The Baroness is a charming lady though.'

'Married to an oaf. Do we have to?'

'That oaf, as you are fond of calling him, is a long-standing member of the Prussian Cavalry Club; your father is keen on you being well regarded in there.'

'I've only been there once.'

'Yes, your father has remarked that to me with a certain dose of regret.'

'He knows I'm not fond of the members.'

'Well, we don't have all morning to list all of the things which fall short of our fondness in the current society.'

Felix's complaint is boyish and mostly out of boredom; his father's wish has always been imperative to him and he would never displease Charlotte. She dries her thin lips with the tip of her embroidered napkin.

'Carriage at three.'

The Kaiserhof tea room is the place to be found, admired or criticised, most often both. The afternoon is the busiest time of the day, drawing ladies with the best couture in Berlin enviously eyeing other ladies with better ones still.

It has snowed all morning, dispersing spellbinding winter magic over the boulevards leading up to the Wilhelm Platz. The main thoroughfares have been promptly cleared with Teutonic efficiency and Jurgen has negotiated his way to the hotel without much difficulty.

The Von Mutthe's name has commanded one of the best tables in the house; Felix can't help remarking to Charlotte that only the Kaiser could have secured a better one. They are at the centre of the orbital sphere of Berlin's high society and their fellow guests at the Kaiserhof bow and pay homage to such status when fortuitously or intentionally ambling by their table.

All out of deference and good manners of course. Felix's opinion of Baron Von Mutthe is widely shared across the city's circuit; everyone thinks that he is an insufferable oaf, including his long-suffering wife.

Everyone also briefly stalls their strolling to linger and admire the elegant and beautiful young couple at their table; virtually unknown yet resplendent against the sight of the overweight Baron.

And Felix is indeed a handsome young gentleman: the deep blue veins marking his silky hands gracefully disappear through the cuffs of his tailored jacket; the physique is slender and wiry, the deportment deer-like, the golden moustaches soft and fluffy, the pupils two precious emeralds, the complexion levigated alabaster. He still wears his light brown hair parted on the side, in a stripling's fashion, blithely unaware that it bestows upon him an adolescent poise: a feature widely derided by the likes of the Baron or other equally boorish brutes at the Cavalry Club.

Charlotte is in a white dress dotted with pink roses, sporting a daring décolleté which reveals her smooth, rosy complexion. Once her hat was removed in the ladies' powder room, her golden locks, masterly coiffured in a graceful bun, had raised gasps of admiration.

The Baron leans gracelessly onto Felix's armchair.

'Bah, this tea business is an English nonsense. Ladies have tea! I'd rather be at the Club with a good beer and some brave Prussian officers!'

Charlotte and Baroness Von Mutthe have been sidelined in the conversation by the Baron. He hardly bothers to conceal his embarrassment at being forced to take part in such a womanly event. Felix gathers all his diplomacy.

'Baron, it is well known that our English cousins allow time for tea with the ladies before repairing to their clubs.'

'Cousins? What cousins? Nonsense! Our Kaiser has nothing to do with this rabble of effeminate, posey aristocrats.'

'The Kaiser is Her Majesty Queen Victoria's grandson.'

'Ach...So?'

'I would consider that quite a relation, wouldn't you?'

A boorish grunt.

'And you are a Baron, sir, you'd rather find that your title classifies as aristocracy.'

The Baron shakes his fist.

'Victoria or not, we are Prussia! Or Germany, as they call us now; we have a young and strong Emperor, we don't take orders from anyone!'

'I don't recall Her Majesty imparting any.'

His inability to match Felix's debate skills riles the Baron no end. He bursts into a rage at the arrival of a bottle of champagne at the table.

'What's this French nonsense?' And he snaps his fingers at the waiter while repeatedly banging his stick on the floor; adjacent guests turn.

'Bring me a beer, dear chap.'

Baroness Von Mutthe darts a disapproving stare at her husband, Charlotte looks on at her in silent commiseration.

To his relief the ladies rejoin the conversation and skilfully sideline the Baron. The Baroness lays her hand on Charlotte's forearm.

'I am still in awe of your grand wedding. A lavish reception. Impeccable taste. The elegance! Charlotte, you looked magnificent and, of course, Herr Kimmich, you were so handsome and charming. If you don't mind, when my children marry I will ask for your advice and implement it without any alteration at all.'

'You are very kind, Baroness. I of course chose the dress but I left most of the organisation to Felix, his skills in that field are second to none.'

She lifts the champagne to initiate a toast.

'Then I will need the advice of both!'

The carriage is tardily negotiating the wide and slushy boulevards; the Baroness, immersed in her thoughts, peers through the narrow window at the silver branches of the trees as the cab slices through the Tiergarten, now a dazzling canvass powdered by the early snowfall.

'Charming couple, I am determined to see more of Frau Charlotte.'

The Baron stares ahead, hands over his stick, motionless.

'I am determined not to come across that insolent brat ever again.'

She shuts her eyes. A life of stoical endurance. He grumbles while looking away.

'Men are not supposed to be "handsome and charming".'

'And pray tell, why not? Herr Kimmich's attire is also exquisite, akin to a real English gentleman.'

'I wouldn't become too close to them.'

'Why shouldn't I?'

He pauses, shakes his head a few times, then finally darts a disdainful, affronted look at his wife.

'I don't remember organising our wedding. Men don't organise weddings.'

They have an early night after the vexing afternoon and reconvene at breakfast amid a much improved atmosphere.

Charlotte has some uplifting news.

'I have invited Edda for dinner tomorrow.'

'Ah! What a splendid idea. An evening with Fräulein Kahler is what I need to recover from that adipose bore.'

'I knew it would cheer you up.'

'Count me in.'

'She's very fond of you too, but you already know that.'

'Well, of all your charming acquaintances, she is the most ebullient company I can think of. Fräulein Kahler restores my faith in humanity.'

'Are you dining at home tonight?'

'I think I'll go out. I have a lot of work to do over the day.'

Charlotte pauses. Her eyes lift towards Felix. A teasing smile.

'Chez Franz?'

'Chez Franz.'

Jurgen is at the door, snowing has restarted and he questions himself on the wisdom of travelling all the way to the Reinickendorf district in such weather. The two black horses attached to the carriage however seem to relish a good gallop in the thick snow.

Walther opens one side of the hefty double entrance door and Felix emerges from the end of the long hallway wearing a long black cape with a heavy fur collar over his evening suit, his top hat low over his eyebrows, his stick in his hand.

There is no talk. He glides down the steps and hurries into the carriage, Jurgen promptly closing the door behind him. The driver then turns to Walther who nods to him. He nods back in agreed conspiracy.

Jurgen whips the horses and they ride at speed along the perimeter of the Tiergarten, noisily trundling along the deserted avenues of Charlottenburg towards a lesser area of the city, one inhabited by lesser tribes.

Jurgen knows the drill. He stops the carriage very close to the entrance door; it's standing no more than twenty inches from it and he can barely squeeze in between to open the cab's door. In silence and at speed Felix transfers from the cab to the grand lobby.

Once inside, the butler takes his cape and hat with a bow and leaves promptly as Felix is in no need of directions: he's a regular. Not a frequent regular but a regular still.

'Herr Hagelstein, honoured by your presence!'

Franz is standing at the entrance of the main salon: a grand affair of plush armchairs and *chaises longues*, almost all upholstered in a florid, rather lurid red satin. The heavy velvet drapes are drawn close, no light or noise seem to be allowed to escape to the outer world. Oversized candles flicker away in every available corner and a bar counter runs along one of the walls. The temperature is positively roasting.

'I have no words for thanking you for your latest contribution. It was immensely generous of you, Herr Hagelstein!'

He discreetly waves his hand.

'No need, my dear Franz, no need.'

The host is a short man with thin, macabre moustaches and far too much pomade in his hair; he wears a white tie evening suit though this is no Konigliches Opernhaus. He snaps his fingers at the barman.

'Hans! Champagne for Herr Hagelstein, fast!'

Felix approaches the bar and sits on one of the stools to sip the champagne which has landed in front of him at lightning speed.

Some of the boys he knows. With some he has acquainted himself closer than others; a few are aimlessly loitering and a small number of them sit on the knees of distinguished older gentlemen: judges, doctors, lawyers, landowners, servants of the empire, noblemen, Feldmarschalls. Emperors even.

Everyone is finely attired, including the boys; this is a sophisticated concern: upstairs, and upstairs only, nature is allowed to unleash its irresistible temptations.

Franz approaches the bar and he's not alone.

'Herr Hagelstein, with your kind permission, I would like to introduce Florian to you. He has been with us for the best part of two weeks. While your business engagements were keeping you away, I have taken the liberty of relaying to the boy what a fine gentleman you are.'

A reply is of no interest to him. He bows and glides away like a retreating tide. Felix finds Franz oily yet harmless and kind.

Florian is possibly on the wrong side of twenty. Or the right one, depending from what angle you look at the boy. And it's undoubtedly hard to avoid looking at this fresh acquisition.

He wears a white shirt with the sleeves rolled up, a tweed gilet and a beige cravat. He is also blessed with a shy and unsettling beauty. The small blue eyes, the platinum blond short hair, the sculpted small limbs; Felix wonders whether Buonarroti himself has secretly painted an angel in front of him. Here. At the bar.

'Delighted to meet you, sir.'

'Delighted to meet you, Florian.'

Another glass of champagne lands on the bar. This is not a cash-friendly establishment. There are no bills to settle.

Not Franz, not the barman and, most importantly, not the boys. You volunteer 'contributions' to the running of the house. It maintains a surreal aura of authenticity and a precarious shield from illegality. The members are wealthy and demand discretion.

Florian stares at him with those tiny blue gems forged by the masterful hands of Poseidon. He's thrilled yet unsure: Felix is handsome but also young. Too young for this venue.

'Your moustaches, sir.'

'Yes?'

'They look so soft. Can I touch them?'

He nods. Florian feels the softness under his lithe white fingers. They both shiver, almost at the same time.

'May I ask you something?'

He's already breaking the golden rule of the house: you don't interrogate the distinguished members. Ever.

'Of course.'

'Looks like you and I are of the same age?'

'Would that be a problem?'

'Of course not but, well, unusual?'

'I can assure you, young man, that I must be older than you, if that helps.'

Florian throws a cocky wink.

'I wasn't needing any help.'

'Twenty-seven.'

'You look younger, and that's with the moustaches and the gentleman's outfit.'

The boy looks away.

'Nineteen, me.'

* * *

Not all the members are mature or unattractive. The year is 1890, however old or young you might happen to be, the possibilities are scarce and the venues even scarcer. Young gentlemen of means occasionally join this small community at the edge of the city. It's safer than other conduits. But not always.

A few months earlier the most peculiar misunderstanding had happened to Felix while sitting at the bar. An older gentleman with a jungly beard and a monocle had approached and complimented him on how strikingly handsome he was. Over the conversation his hand had landed on Felix's thigh.

He had found himself amused and ready to play the part with relish, had it not been for Franz rushing over in a panic to frantically explain to the old gentleman who Felix was and, above all, what he wasn't.

The flustered host had been about to escort the apologetic man away but Felix had stopped him with a gentle yet firm wave of his hand. He had then ordered another glass of champagne while asking Franz to be left alone with the old folk.

His conversation had turned out to be of the most pleasurable variety. In the midst of it he had grabbed the gentleman's hand and repositioned it back on his thigh, holding it. When they had been about to part, he had taken the man's wrinkly old hands in his and kissed him on the cheek, brushing his skin with his soft, irresistible moustaches, the man's eyes watery with emotion.

* * *

They are upstairs now, where nature is allowed a safe haven to satisfy its earthy creatures in the best bedroom of the house, heated and lit by the glowing embers in the fireplace.

Once close, Felix lifts his right hand to caress Florian's cheek. The boy abruptly jolts back, startled and afraid.

He thinks intensely for a moment before speaking.

'They...they don't beat you here? Do they? Because if they do...'

'No. They don't.'

He grabs Felix's hand and brings it back up to his cheek. Youth erupts: their garments fly off onto the floor while they head to the four-poster bed, devouring with animal hunger each other's svelte, hairless frames. All of them. To the last dab of flesh. To the last finger. To the last toe. Until the lips are singed by the savage kisses which they find impossible to bring to an end. Until the ears are chewed bloody by the brutal bites. Until there is no resistance left to the virile thrusts. Until the last drop of nectar has been relinquished by the glowing, expended bodies.

It's nearly midnight and he can't bring himself to look at Florian; he's ready to entangle himself with him anew and spend another few hours of his life in the upper circles of heaven. Florian turns to kiss him again and with a mischievous grin they eye each other's manhoods, ablaze and unbeaten by the cataclysmic pleasure already inflicted on them.

Florian lifts two fingers in the victory sign.

'Bathroom break, excuse me.'

As he gets up, Felix can finally see his scrawny back against the light of the fire. He had detected something not quite right while caressing it but the thundering avalanche of pleasure had brokered no time for enquires.

When he returns he stalls him once back on the bed and tries to turn him around; he puts up some resistance but Felix wins, ending up holding him in a lock while looking at his back. He gulps.

'Who did this to you?'

The scars are healed but they are deep and cover all of his back. He's now caressing them.

'Please sir, don't.'

'How?'

He frees himself and lies down on his back; the scars evidently embarrass him and he prefers Felix stroking his chest, his tummy, his rapidly saddening face.

'Caught in the act. Feldmarschall Von Luthenberg. Father. I thought I was going to die and I think he genuinely wanted to kill me. I lost consciousness after I saw the blood spreading on the floor. Until then I was screaming like a pig but he had locked the door, neither Mother nor the servants could help me. He left me for dead, in a pool of blood, his whip on my back.

He confined me to my room until I was well again. Then a servant appeared at the door carrying a case packed with a few clothes. He escorted me to the entrance of the estate and gave me a letter.'

Felix holds his hand.

'He doesn't want me to set foot in the house ever again and has forbidden Mother and my brothers to contact me. He asked me to no longer consider myself his son. The valet who was with me was beaten too and sacked on the spot.'

He spreads his arms wide. In defeat.

'And here I am, sir.'

The kiss is without ending, comforting and tearful as the renewed passion briefly sends the ghosts away.

He's putting his clothes back on, it's almost one in the morning and Jurgen has been waiting. Florian is sitting up on the bed.

'Do you have to go?'

'I do.'

He pulls the rope by the curtains, the butler appears almost immediately.

'Tell Franz I will keep the room for the night and Florian can stay here until tomorrow. Tell him I don't want the boy to be disturbed before midday. Call my carriage.' He hands over a couple of coins, the butler bows out.

He rummages through the pocket of his coat, plucks a few hundred Marks notes out of it and leaves them on the table.

'Hide them before anyone comes in tomorrow.'

Once fully dressed, Felix opens his arms and Florian runs into them: still bare, still impossibly beautiful. Upon releasing from the embrace he notices the sum on the table.

'You are a kind and generous gentleman, sir.'

A silent nod.

He rushes out and transfers onto his carriage in haste. In such a haste and so absently that he can't possibly notice a man in a black coat and top hat, standing in the snow at the far corner of the street, calmly writing on a small notebook in his hands.

But Franz does. He parts the drapes an inch or two with his gloved fingers and sees him folding his notebook and boarding a black carriage which has just appeared from nowhere. His Walhalla is often circled by malevolent ravens.

He has no means to warn Herr Hagelstein. Not his real name, of course; no one here would be so careless as to use their real names. And he has no idea where he lives either or which remote part of the empire he might come from.

Franz's house is a haven for gentlemen of standing; yet for every gentleman of standing there might be one standing outside.

Fräulein Kahler and Felix enjoy an animated conversation by the glowing fireplace. Edda is ethereal and slender; elegant, but not by costly means. She's also a committed socialist though not a fanatic one and Felix drinks her political theories over workers and women's rights with relish. He has no real political opinion of his own: as the wealthy son of a wealthy landowner his leanings should be clear but they are not. He feels sympathetic to Edda's causes and Charlotte, while playing a few sonatas at the grand piano with lithesome concentration, glows at how her husband and her dearest friend fire the house up with their connection.

Dinner is a roaring success, Walther happy to see the Kimmichs enjoying the company of their guest. There aren't many occasions such as this one at Villa Augusta and he had been excited all day long. His *mise en place* was nothing short of sensational. The three diners lavish heartfelt compliments on his competence and attention to details and after a brandy round in the drawing room they are ready to retire.

Baron Von Mutthe would explode in a fit at the mere

thought of a man sharing a brandy with the ladies after dinner; Felix can almost hear him in his head: *Bah! A brandy with the ladies? What has Prussia come into? Cigars and whisky at the Cavalry Club! That's the right place for a Prussian soldier!'*

'I'll check a few papers in my study before retiring; you will stay for breakfast, Edda, will you? You are unaware of my sadistic streak, so I insist in subjecting you to Walther's tea.'

'Is that bad?'

'Torture.'

An earthy laugh by the trio.

'Goodnight ladies.'

He kisses both on the cheek and leaves. The two women slowly walk upstairs and turn right towards Charlotte's boudoir: a large drawing room with annexed bedroom.

His private quarters are smaller and more modest: when it came to choose, he insisted in his wife settling in the best wing of the villa: 'It's more suited for a lady and her friends,' he said, 'I am in no need of additional comforts.'

Two days later Jurgen knocks at the study's door and is admitted by Felix who notices his discomfort.

'Is there anything wrong, Jurgen?'

'Sir, a valet from the Cavalry club came to the house about half an hour ago.'

'Yes?'

'He said…he said he had been instructed to remove the Club seal from the carriage, the one allowing me to wait for you in the reserved holding area.'

'I wonder if there has been some sort of misunderstanding.'

'That's what I thought, sir. I protested that it was all nonsense but he wouldn't leave. He took the seal and left a letter.' He hands the letter over to Felix. 'I hope everything is in order, sir.'

While absently turning the envelope in his hands, he notices the Prussian Cavalry Club seal on it.

'What?…Yes, yes, or course, everything is perfectly fine, thank you, Jurgen, thank you for promptly informing me.'

Jurgen bows and leaves. He's stopped by Walther in the hallway, they exchange sombre looks. The butler whispers.

'Did you see anyone around the house?'

'No. I waited away from it and did regular checks. Master Felix was very late, one o'clock perhaps. I didn't spot anyone. It was snowy and foggy, I might have missed.'

The next day, with dusk gradually plunging the study into darkness, Felix is still diligently immersed in paperwork, Charlotte out on the Kurfürstendamm for shopping and chores. Walther knocks.

'Yes, come in!'

'Sir, your father is here.'

'Oh, please, let him through.'

Herr Kimmich has already relinquished coat and hat to Walther but has retained his stick with the carved ivory head. He seldom separates himself from it.

He is a slender country squire of perhaps fifty-five, elegantly attired, yet without the frills of a city gentleman. His manners are brusque but sincere, polite and unthreatening. His grey beard and moustaches are finely trimmed and at close inspection one can detect the angular features inherited by his younger son.

'Father.'

'Son.'

Neither an embrace nor a handshaking.

'I apologise for the unannounced visit.'

'You have no need to announce yourself. Sadly, Charlotte is out shopping.'

'I have come to see you.'

'Very pleased, let me get Walther to fetch some coffee, you know very well about the tea.'

'What about some beer?'

'Father, you know very well that Mother…'

'Yes, yes, but she's not here.'

He darts a mildly reproachful look at his father as Walther walks in. Herr Kimmich pats the butler's shoulder.

'Walther! Bring at once two large carafes of the best Brandenburg beer. I hope you maintain a good stock in the house!'

Felix flashes a worried look at Walther who nonetheless bows in agreement.

'We do, Herr Kimmich.'

But they don't. Young Kimmich detests beer, though he never had the courage to reveal that to his father.

After closing the study door behind him, Walther jolts out of the entrance door without putting his coat on and runs to the household-appointed liquor store, thankfully located only a few blocks away. He's back at flashing speed, carrying a heavy casket of the most expensive beer he could find, panting and darting straight to the kitchen.

'Would you prefer to move to the drawing room, Father? Or would you like to inspect the accounts?'

'I prefer your study. It's a good study, though I have no need to inspect the estate's accounts. They are in safe hands, I trust.'

Felix bows. Herr Kimmich frowns in wonder.

'Anyway, where are those damn beers?'

The large carafes are now on the desk, a delight for the father, a torture for the son. Herr Kimmich grabs his carafe by the handle to toast but when Felix gets hold of his by wrapping his delicate hand around it, he coughs and thumps the floor twice with his stick. He stares at his son who, without reply, swiftly switches his fingers in a firm grasp of the handle. The firmest he can muster.

'Prost!'

'Prost!'

His father guzzles half of the huge carafe and so does Felix, his eyes bulging in displeasure, sipping not allowed: this isn't some French bubbling nonsense.

* * *

Felix had skilfully managed to fool his father up to his fourteenth birthday, when the luck that helps the brave ceased to shield the reckless.

One warm and sunny day of spring, Frau Augusta had travelled to Lubeck with Felix's older brother and younger sister for a planned three days visit to her family, leaving her husband to look forward to enjoying a solitary ride with Attila, his favourite horse.

But when he walked through the stables and reached the

hay stack to get hold of some forage, he heard some heavy breathing and the most unusual of groans. His heart then briefly stopped upon the disintegration of his world.

He stood frozen while, like two frightened rabbits caught in a hansom's beam, Felix and Walther frantically scuttled to retrieve their clothes while trying to cover their bareness. In the end they gave up and stood still, hiding their rebellious manhoods with their shirts.

Shaking in fear and shame, they felt unable to meet Herr Kimmich's eyes, but they had seen the whip in his hand and accepted that they were about to die and that they thoroughly deserved it.

No tears, as they thought better: it would have only enraged Felix's father further, or so they thought.

But Herr Kimmich was no Feldmarschall Von Luthenberg: he was a man of strong temperament yet contemptuous of bad temper.

He turned around, walked back to the house and didn't resurface from his study until the return of Frau Augusta some three days later.

The boys dressed in silence while exchanging worried glances. Without a single word they beat a hasty retreat to their respective homes, Walther not sure if glad to be alive and in horror at what was about to befall on him and his mother.

Felix climbed the stairs to his room in distressed haste and developed a running fever, prompting the servants and his loving governess to attend to him in frenzied worry.

He would have preferred to have been whipped to a pulp, the shame for his father having to witness such unspeakable sin gnashing at his stomach, the worry for what was to happen to his loyal companion filling him with remorse. In the privacy of his room, the tears finally breached the dam and flooded out until there were no more.

Herr Kimmich sat motionless at his desk from dawn to dusk, sleeping a few hours in the morning on the *chaise longue*, the servants at a loss at what could have possibly happened.

Stephan, Felix's older brother, meant nothing to him: a layabout of embarrassingly limited intellect for whom Herr Kimmich nurtured next to no hope; his younger sister Renate was in the meantime developing into a frivolous and cantankerous princess who riled him no end.

His cards were on Felix. And now this. It was breaking him into little pieces. The pain, the shame, the regret and the guilt brought on by the conviction that in the end it was all his fault: he would have never turned out like this without some horrible mistake on his part.

At first he tried hard to convince himself that perhaps it was boys' play: innocent adolescent games. He remembered fooling around at military school himself, no girls at hand to assuage a torrent of hovering, uncontrollable hormones. There had been a few raunchy games here and there to release their inexhaustible energy, yet when reveries of young ladies had started to creep into their tender minds, it had all been swept away. Dispersed in the Brandenburg fog. No one would mention anything because there was nothing to mention: time for girls.

But it was a forlorn hope. Whilst wholly uninterested in Stephan and Renate, Herr Kimmich had kept a close watch on his favourite and a few of his singularities started to fall into place in the torturing jigsaw forming in his mind: these were no boys' games.

As a country landowner in the endless eastern steppes, yet a reasonably learned man of the world, Herr Kimmich knew all too well the dangerous and unhappy milieu his son was destined to join if sent into a shaming exile. After two wretched and sleepless nights in his study, he had resolved on his course of action.

He called for a bath and clean clothing and resurfaced a refreshed man in time for the return of his wife. In the official version devised for Frau Augusta, Felix had merely developed a fever and he was now getting better.

The fourth day after the incident, one of the footmen opened Felix's door and announced in no uncertain terms that Herr Kimmich was ordering his presence at dinner.

Everything was ready: a bath and clean clothes. The footman wasn't anticipating any resistance and none was to be forthcoming; Felix had no truck with disobedience.

He entered the dining room in respectful silence, his frame about an inch smaller after days of voluntary starvation. Blue and red marks showed under his eyes, where his skin was at the most transparent, dotted by minuscule freckles.

He had been told nothing. He had no idea who knew, who didn't, or if anyone had been informed at all. He felt surprisingly calm yet unable to look at his father in the eyes.

'I am satisfied that your health is considerably better, son.'

'Yes, Father.'

'Very well, your mother has been feeling very apprehensive since her return.'

'I am very sorry, Mother.'

She grabbed his hand, the soft feel and the realisation that his father had said nothing to anyone lifted him from the dead. When a footman appeared at Felix's side with a jug of lemonade, Herr Kimmich knocked loudly on the table. The footman turned to wait for fresh orders.

'I think it's time for Master Felix to have some wine. Half a glass would do.'

The footman bowed and returned with the wine.

'Gerhardt, are you entirely sure? He is not yet fourteen.'

'Oh, he's quite a man, Augusta.'

Felix's face flushed into a deep shade of crimson; the insinuation in his father's statement twisting through his heart.

'Son?'

He lifted the glass for a short sip. He had secretly tasted wine before, of course, but with his father's permission it was somehow tasting better.

'Your holiday has been far too idle, young man. Tomorrow you will join the farmers in the fields until the day you are due to return to school. Walther is coming to collect you at four. You two are in need of some hard toil. Be ready or I will personally make sure you receive a good thrashing at the hands of the head farmer.'

Frau Augusta stirred but a stern glance from her husband shot down in flames any attempt at protest.

Then he met his father's severe gaze: no smile but no anger either. Of only one thing he was now sure: the incident was closed.

It was never revealed to Felix that his partner in crime had found some reckless bravery in his young heart and had requested to be admitted by Herr Kimmich, rightly believing that he had nothing to lose: if he so wished he could thrash him all the way to Berlin and back.

Trembling down to his last bone, he had entered the study cap in hands and stood respectfully at a distance, blaming it all on himself: he had volunteered to take extra whipping on behalf of Felix with the promise to leave as soon as possible. His discretion would bring no shame on the family.

Walther's courage and loyalty had moved Herr Kimmich: except for their stubborn carnal proclivity, neither boys were natural transgressors. On the hay stack they had been genuinely prepared to subject themselves to a rightful raging carnage, far more distressed by the shame they had brought on themselves and the family name.

Furthermore, Herr Kimmich had always nurtured a soft spot for his stable lad: good-natured, hard-working, respectful and with no ideas above his status; the most suitable of childhood companions for a still wispy Felix.

Besides, he had always felt that protecting everyone on the estate, from his dear wife down to the last peasant, was his duty and he took pride in such endeavour.

So he had thumped the floor with his stick, raising his voice and causing Walther to jolt in terror.

'Nonsense! Felix will be better tomorrow and he will join you in the fields until the end of his holiday. Come and collect him at four. If you two are late the head farmer will give you a good thrashing on my behalf.'

Walther had felt unable able to move, his eyes wide open.

'Now…don't you have some stables to attend to, young man? What is this estate coming into? Off you go. Now!'

* * *

The carafes lie empty on the table, Felix's tummy already rumbling: large quantities of beer don't agree with his delicate digestion.

Herr Kimmich takes a folded paper out of his inner pocket and puts it on the table.

'Your brother is in trouble again; that womanising, gambling scoundrel!'

'Don't be so hard on him, Father.'

He waves a finger at his son.

'For the life of me, I have never understood why you have always defended that good-for-nothing. And he has been constantly ungentlemanly and mean to you.'

Felix shrugs.

'He's my brother.'

He wishes some hardening of the heart in his son's personality but that's some hope. Secretly, though, he feels proud of his unflinching sweet nature.

'That is the list of the creditors, one of them is one of those houses. May I ask you to take care of it?'

'Will do.'

The finger is wagging again.

'No money directly to him, understand? Do not send him money!'

Yet he knows that Felix helps his brother with his reckless finances and out of his own income.

Herr Kimmich stands up and walks to the window, his hands holding his stick behind his back. A long silence follows but long silences have never embarrassed their bond, they give space and time to weigh their words as they both prefer to.

'I presume you have by now heard from the Club.'

'Father...'

But he gently turns and raises the palm of his hand.

'I will talk.'

Felix obediently retreats with his hands behind his back.

'I had lunch with the other members of the Club's committee: Von Mutthe, Count Von Stolberg and the General Secretary whose name I'd be damned if I could ever remember. The matter will remain between us four gentlemen, I am the chairman and you are a Kimmich after all, discretion is in everyone's interest.'

Felix nods. He's not quite sure why as his father hasn't turned from the window.

'The suspension is for six months: "minor infraction to the code of conduct". It's not an expulsion. At least not yet.'

Then he bangs his stick on the wooden parquet with a mighty thump, his voice raised.

'Damn hypocrites! For the life of me, I wouldn't trust half of those swines in a cadets' dormitory! You should have heard Von Stolberg. That oily oaf. Claiming he was only doing this for my honour. My honour? As if my son's reputation doesn't count!'

Felix lowers his gaze, a pang in his heart at the thought of the ordeal his father had to go through. For him. For his sins.

'And Von Mutthe, you know Von Mutthe? That pig. Do

you know what he said to me thereafter at the bar? "You should advise more discretion to your son". The swine! Do you want to know what I told him? "And so should you to yours. My spies might better than yours."'

But they both know it to be a hollow threat. Von Mutthe's son is rumoured to be a regular patron at Mireille's, but young gentlemen's visits to such joints are not frowned upon. Most young offspring of Prussian aristocracy bois-terously relay their exploits when back at the Club: tales of willing young ladies interposing between a cigar and a whisky.

Herr Kimmich calms down and a restful silence returns; daylight is starting to fade, a few thin snowflakes are hitting the window pane. He turns, his son still there, hands behind his back, head bowed.

'I am most thankful, Father, I trust Mother doesn't...'

A prompt, negative nod. Throughout his married life he has successfully sheltered his wife from her children's misdemeanours, financial or otherwise; in any case, Frau Augusta hauls from one of the most respectable merchant families of Lubeck. She wouldn't be remotely aware of what Felix's disposition might be: for her and for many others such men cannot possibly exist.

He sits back in the armchair, hands on top of his stick, his gaze lowered.

'Son. Is it really necessary to visit such places? Is Walther still a loyal brother-in-arms?'

That is what Walther became in Herr Kimmich's mind since that faithful day at the stables. He came up with the clever term to make it acceptable for himself and it worked.

Almost.

'He is...I...I...'

But words fail him. Herr Kimmich is a man of the world but Felix has no way of explanation and deep down he's convinced his father does indeed understand why he visits such places, he just fears for him.

'Von Mutthe detests you and your kind: that much is clear; he called you an insolent brat. In my presence! If I didn't find duels so distasteful...'

Felix trembles. He wouldn't allow it. He would first kill Von Mutthe himself and face the consequences.

'They have no quarrel with me, they are the ones who appointed me to the chairmanship. I strongly suspect that he just wanted to teach you a lesson, to show you your place. I don't anticipate this happening again but there are other dangers: the law. Blackmail.'

Felix can only nod. If he could defeat his recurring, pulsating urges, he would have done it by now. They both know that there is no chance of that happening. At least not in the prime of his time.

Herr Kimmich stands up, Felix makes for the bell to summon Walther but he stops him.

'Your mother is most disappointed at not having seen you and Charlotte for some time for either dinner or Sunday lunch. She misses you terribly.'

And so does he, but those are words which will never leave his lips.

'We will rehabilitate ourselves very soon.'

'I'm counting on it, she is driving me utterly insane with this talk about grandchildren, I sure hope Stephan doesn't sire any rabble. What about you and Charlotte? Have you considered it?'

He is not merely aware of the solution. He arranged it. Felix and Charlotte had known each other since childhood and their respective families had always been close. He had discovered her inclinations in a vastly less traumatic way than the scene at the stables. When they had reached a certain age and everyone down to the last cousin was demanding marriage, he had successfully talked them into it, throwing in the purchase of Villa Augusta while leisurely pointing out that the first floor had enough space for comfortable and separate apartments. Herr Kimmich. A resourceful man of the world.

'Do you think I would make a suitable father?'

He knows it's a serious dilemma his son nurtures, not a quip. He shrugs and waves his stick.

'I've seen worse.'

He heads for the door. He turns before leaving but there are no more words, only a devotion which refuses to waver.

Walther appears in the lobby with his hat and coat; once dressed, Jurgen comes in and exchanges glances with him. His hands wave apologetically.

'I hid the carriage and did regular checks, Herr Kimmich, I must have missed.'

He pats Jurgen on his muscular arms.

'These vermin are becoming smarter, dear Jurgen, I wouldn't fret.'

Jurgen propels his big fist forward and shakes it in a menacing pose. In his spare time he's a skilful boxer at his working men's club. He could floor an ox.

'If they hurt Master Felix I'll have them eating dust, Herr Kimmich, I promise you...'

He grabs Jurgen's shoulders.

'Hopefully that won't be necessary. I keep my trust in you gentlemen.'

Felix loves his mother dearly and seems to be biologically unable to disobey his father, so the young couple travels to the family seat for a whole three nights over a frosty January weekend.

Cocooned by the idyllic grand estate under a blanket of heavy snow, his parents ecstatic at their presence, they spend four blissful and restful days. Felix had left his child-hood home in great sadness and his excitement at being back rapidly infects the household with fresh merriment, his old governess fussing over him like he had never gone past the age of ten. The second day Charlotte catches him in his old nursery, staring at the fields outside the large arched window, some of his old toy soldiers in his hand. Unnoticed, she tiptoes away.

Frau Augusta monopolises Charlotte to gently pressure her on the subject of grandchildren whilst Herr Kimmich makes sure he and his son are left alone in the drawing room after dinner. Slouched in the leather armchairs in front of the fire, they down whisky and brandy, smoke cigars, and interpose a few careful words between long, thoughtful silences.

They also have long drives around the estate, the farmers always pleased to see master Felix, some still remembering him trotting around the estate in short trousers. On a stop at the cottage of Walther's mother, Felix reassures her that he will be scolding her son for his far too scarce home visits.

Frau Augusta is only allowed a few moments alone with her dearest boy and in one of them she softly strokes Felix's finely parted chestnut hair in deep satisfaction.

'Your father is a changed man when you are here.'

And never tiring of gazing into Felix's shining emeralds while caressing his smooth cheek, she dreams of how beautiful and sweet-natured her grandchildren will be if her beloved son would only be so kind to produce any.

On one of their drives, Felix dares to enquire why Stephan has not been invited and why Renate has been sent packing to some cousins of hers.

'I made sure they were not to be around, of course!'

He smiles in disapproval at his father's brazen favouritism.

'With your permission, Father, I would like to appoint Walther as my private secretary. I need one: the amount of paperwork is increasing and I'm not sure I can maintain reasonable standards all on my own. He has educated himself while in service, I've checked. He has completed a typing course and with some extra training he'll shine on the job.'

Herr Kimmich nods in assent.

'A lad of grit and integrity. He has my trust. He'll look after you well.'

Felix turns with a benign grin of endearment.

'They all do. His Majesty couldn't claim a better Imperial Guard.'

His father's stick hits Felix's arm twice in jest.

'Don't mock loyalty, son, hard to find these days! Make

sure the new butler is of the same stock.'

'I think I'll let Charlotte choose, what's your opinion on this?

'My full confidence in Charlotte's judgement is well known.'

Another long silence to digest their conversation. Felix leans against his side of the carriage and after carefully weighing his words he tries to speak.

'Father, I wish I...'

But Herr Kimmich has already raised the palm of his hand to intimate silence.

'I know you do.'

On the way back home they have no choice but to return to the subject, the only part of the solution so far not functioning to specifications. Charlotte sighs in mild exasperation.

'We'll have to decide what to do.'

'Have you asked Edda's opinion?'

'We are still only dear friends.'

He's mildly disappointed as he adores Fräulein Kahler and she makes his wife happy which matters to him a great deal.

'I would like to see both our parents happy, Charlotte, I admit. You know very well that I'm prepared to make it very, how can I put it, sterile? Sorry, dreadful wording. Professional?'

Charlotte contemplates his humble, reticent bearing: he's still the boy who can't harm a fly. She's in a mood for a little and innocuous taunting though.

'Men don't disgust me, you know? I hope you don't think

you do. Even Edda finds you terribly good-looking.'

He turns a shade of pink. Not an inch of vanity runs through his diminutive bones. He belongs to the inconspicuous pantheon of those few human beings whose beauty is neither common nor absolute though enchantingly subtle.

'I don't think that.'

'Would it be your first ever?'

He's now positively crimson.

'Yes. You?

'Yes.'

They pause, perhaps realising the surreality of their dialogue.

'The physical aspect doesn't worry me, Felix. But when our children are older there might be issues.'

'Lovers?' Charlotte nods. 'That worries me too.'

'Felix, I genuinely believe you would make a wonderful father.'

'That is kind of you, but we might fall prey to rumours, blackmail, the law. My predicament carries a far bigger amount of risk than yours. What if...' He lowers his head, Charlotte now afraid of hurting him.

'Perhaps the solution wasn't as perfect as we thought it might be.' She says.

'We knew that from the start. Still, could you think of anything better? How is Edda faring?'

It's her turn to lower her gaze, fiddling with her gloves.

'Her family is driving her insane. Ghastly suitors nearly every day, questions, suspicions.'

'My point.'

'I do worry when you are at Franz's, perhaps a stable and

reliable fellow gentleman?'

Felix sighs. He knows who she means.

'Regardless of our inclinations, Charlotte, we're still men. It's not the same as man and wife.'

She grabs his hand and kisses it. Their love might be unconventional, yet it's deep and considerate. When his father had proposed the solution, he had reassured her at the end of their conversation: 'Save for one thing, my son will be a better husband than any of the ghastly brutes out there.'

They're deeply asleep, swathed in the winter light starting to filter through the semi-closed drapes. Felix is behind him, his right arm wrapped around his chest.

It's nearly eight; Walther awakes, brushes his face with his hand then turns. His master's eyes are still closed, something resembling a smile under his moustaches. He sweeps his thumb under them, stirring his lips.

'Sir. Sir.'

Felix stretches out, his lanky and hairless body gleaming in the blue hue of a winter dawn.

'I won't be able to set for breakfast. Too late.'

A huge yawn from Felix as he dissolves into a fluffy pillow, laziness always his morning ploy. His words are muffled.

'I'm sure Maria will attend to Charlotte perfectly well.'

It doesn't happen very often now but when it does it's still as magical as when they were barely fourteen of age. Two or three times a month perhaps, sometime a few more. Walther brings a hot drink up to his master's apartment and politely enquires if anything else will be required of him.

Felix, routinely already in his night gown, takes his hand and kisses him, their mutual passion flaring up.

They also delight in sleeping entangled as nature made them, while on their celibate days they respectfully remain in their pyjamas. They are not quite sure why, but eccentric habits can occasionally take hold in enduring affections.

From time to time they also share the bath tub. It had started at a very young age and they had never found a plausible rationale to give up a quirk both thoroughly enjoy.

Only once it had led to an unserious and vigorous adolescent game whose ending had generated a glutinous and grungy quagmire which had caused the pair of them to succumb to hysterical laughter. Nowadays he mostly holds Walther in his arms, kissing his wet hair, at times listlessly drifting into a light sleep.

He sits on his side of the bed while Felix still lies on it: arm at an angle under his cheek holding his head up; ruffled, dishevelled hair tumbling over his forehead.

'I have news for you.'

Walther has started to dress.

'Yes, sir?

'We're hiring a new butler.'

He turns with a worried expression. What has he done? Felix hits him with a pillow and a laugh.

'Easy, Brother, you're my new private secretary from, well, now. Or at least from when we find a new butler.'

'Seriously?'

'Now we need a pact: when you spend the night up here, I'm Felix.'

'I don't know.'

He rises on his knees and, still bare and fired up, hugs him tightly from behind.

'I'm not prepared to accept a refusal.' He's kissing his neck now, he has no intention of leaving his boudoir early this morning.

'Are you entirely confident in my clerical abilities, sir? I mean…Felix.'

'I most certainly am. And you have the full seal of approval of His Imperial Majesty.'

Walther turns with a confused frown.

'Father.'

He's about to thank him but he's caressing his athletic chest, his hands like feathers on Walther's silky skin. Their lips are one again.

* * *

Charlotte had always nurtured the secret hope that Walther would one day become the stable young gentleman in her husband's life. She had soon acknowledged that Herr Kimmich's mischievously hatched up term of 'brothers-in-arms' more pertinently fitted the nature of their union. Consulted for an opinion, Edda, clever Edda, had summed it up:

'Friendship is everything for boys. But they are incapable of giving up their freedom.'

Walther had always been given generous time off. While he had never been the cut of gentleman for Franz's, either because of scarce financial means or by virtue of being as young as his master, he had nevertheless never failed to set out for a few adventures of his own, whether at the Charlottenburg Baths or at any new joint which could suddenly appear on the clandestine circuit of despicable pleasures. These escapades had never amounted to a big deal in first place.

Presently, his needs, while hardly ever overpowering in first place, are already in slow decline. On the other hand he fears Felix's urges are at times dangerously off scale. The occasional nights spent with his master are starting to give him enough satisfaction to live with. More often than not he now takes to his bed in the early hours of the evening in the company of some decent literature. On the other hand, Felix's night raids at Franz's are increasing in quantity and, unbeknown to Walther, in intensity.

* * *

With the boys still ascending the lower circles of heaven, it is left to Charlotte to answer the bell to find a young lad of no more of ten years of age standing on the steps, holding his cap and a letter.

'Good morning, Frau Kimmich, this is from Baroness Von Mutthe.'

'Thank you young man, I'll fetch a shilling.'

'The Baroness has asked me to wait for the reply, Frau Kimmich.'

Charlotte is taken by surprise but shrugs unperturbed.

'Very well. We can't leave you out here waiting in the cold though. You can wait in the kitchen; I'm sure Maria will have a cake ready for you and you'll still receive a shilling for your services.'

'Most generous, Frau Kimmich, thank you.'

My dear Charlotte,

First and foremost, I would like to take the opportunity to thank you for the delightful company at the Kaiserhof, despite my husband's regrettably unkind disposition towards Herr Kimmich.

As previously mentioned, I would love more than anything else in the world to invite you over at our residence for tea; however this is sadly forbidden by the Baron.

Therefore I would be grateful if you could forgive my effrontery in asking to be received at your residence at your convenience. It would sadden me greatly if my consort's unfortunate disposition prevented us from developing our acquaintance further.

Young Matthias is my private maid's son and he is trusted. Please forward your reply through him and him only. Please do not send any of your servants, they might be recognised by the Baron.

I trust you have an entrance for deliveries. If you could include directions for my carriage driver, it would be most useful.

I am deeply sorry for the necessity of these precautions which I am confident have your full understanding.

In kindness.

B.V.M.

Charlotte has had both tea and coffee brought over to the drawing room; once Baroness Von Mutthe takes the first sip of the tea and the expression of her face mutates in a polite cringe, Frau Kimmich casually remarks that perhaps coffee would be a better choice in winter time. The Baroness nods in agreement.

She is a truly grand dame in a stately white dress crowned by a sumptuous hat. A lady of not yet sixty of noble, commanding yet serene and unpretentious deportment. She is frequently received at court.

Amid tentative small talks she insists on switching to first names as terms of address. Due to the noblewoman's higher rank, Charlotte somehow struggles with the friendlier approach. In the end she finds herself unable to drop the *Sie* pronoun.

Over the second cup of coffee the Baroness takes hold of Frau Kimmich's hand, their chairs only a foot apart.

'Charlotte, it's time for me to unreservedly apologise for my husband's behaviour towards Herr Kimmich.'

'There is no need, Sophie, we still enjoyed the afternoon at the Kaiserhof.'

'That is not what I was referring to.'

She feels a squeeze of her hand. The Baroness humbly lowers her gaze in a short but thoughtful pose.

'The Baron is responsible for your husband's suspension from the Club. It pains me immensely to reveal this to you but I find my consort's actions so despicable, I felt I had to make you part of such malign intentions. It was his spy who reported Herr Felix back to the Club.'

Charlotte's turn to squeeze her hand.

'My dear Sophie, we suspected as much. But we never doubted that you couldn't possibly be involved in this.'

'That is most kind of you. At least he thought better than reporting it to the authorities. I would apologise to Herr Kimmich in person but I fear it would cause embarrassment. He comes across as such a sensitive soul.'

'You are right; in any case Felix doesn't harbour any bad feelings towards you or even towards your husband, you have my word on that.'

'I am so relieved, Charlotte. I must say now, and do not misinterpret my words: I find Herr Felix most charming and of the most delightful disposition, however I cannot help wondering how you deal with his inclinations.'

Charlotte needs to think quickly what to answer. She would love to make the Baroness fully aware of their arrangement but she fears her revelation might foster a renewed defensiveness in a lady who, as far as she knows, is not of similar predisposition.

The Baroness is close to sixty but Charlotte is well aware that some people feel under threat upon discovering that their gender could be the object of desire by someone formerly believed to be a harmless acquaintance.

'Dear Sophie, Felix and I are happily married under an arrangement. A solution.'

The Baroness frowns in wonder.

'My husband and I are of the same persuasion.'

She is in no need to explain it further; Baroness Von Mutthe is a lady of intellect and wit who had to bow to family conventions and marry into fellow aristocracy with an extraordinary amount of misfortune.

'My dear Charlotte, I am most relieved.'

'Relieved?'

'Of course, my dear. Weren't for a reciprocal arrangement, it would have meant a great deal of suffering for both of you.'

'I don't expect you to approve, Sophie.'

'And pray tell, who am I to stand in judgement? And with a husband like mine?'

The ice smashed into smithereens, they relax and laugh.

'I safely assume that you might have never encountered the likes of us?'

'You forget I am frequently received at court, my dear. Baron Von Mutthe is far too blinkered to see that the very people he so vehemently despises are standing right next to him at the palace.'

Another laugh.

The Von Klausen's status is far higher than the Baron's, her brother a Margrave of the Empire. The frequent invitations to court land on her doorstep solely because the Kaiser and her family are well acquainted and he greatly enjoys her company rather than the Baron's, whom, like almost everyone else in Berlin, he thoroughly despises.

Many a night her husband is left fuming in a corner of the ballroom. While His Majesty and his close courtiers joyfully entertain a positively ebullient Sophie Von Mutthe, he has no choice but to ruminate patriotic and militaristic manure with Chancellor Bismarck, quite an oaf himself.

'I hope for the sake of that wonderful young man that he keeps safe and sound. You would be astounded by the intrigues at court. I am myself acquainted with some impossibly charming young officers at the palace who notoriously stray to the most unsavoury districts of Berlin.'

'I trust they receive some stern motherly warnings from you, Sophie.'

'Well, I couldn't stop them even if I locked them up. That is men, my dear.'

Walther serves more coffee and pastries.

'Now, Charlotte, I won't be able to stay much longer but I have a question.'

'Please.'

'A charming young lady like yourself must have a circle of lady friends. Do you meet up regularly? Is there a special lady in your life?'

Charlotte blushes; Baroness Von Mutthe's unexpected, disarming frankness elates her.

'Yes and... yes.'

'And they are all of your inclination or of a more mixed milieu?'

'Fairly mixed.'

'Well then, I wonder if they would be pleased to make my acquaintance.'

Charlotte's eyes widen.

'I am sure they would be delighted. A word of warning though: some of their political leanings might not agree with your position in society.'

'Socialists? Women's rights? Is that what you mean?'

'More or less.'

'We will have to make sure the Baron remains safely unaware of our encounters then. Nothing would give me more pleasure than him finding me plotting with socialists but I have a position to maintain, though I am in no way certain how much good this position is to me.' She lowers her gaze on her diamond ring, elegantly adjusting it with her lithe fingers. 'Well, our world might have run its course anyway.'

Wenzel is punctual to the second on his arrival at Villa Augusta: clean, well dressed, carrying a small leather case and a letter of introduction by Herr Kimmich the elder in his hand. In the end he had chosen for them and Wenzel is a young man just shy of thirty, son of one of the estate's farmers: 'A hard-working lad whom I have reasons to trust for his loyalty and discretion', the letter reads.

And he is as such, though not quite the butler. Walther has to remain in his position for a few more days to see to some training but the young man proves to be a fast learner. He swiftly gains the approval of the household: respectful, well-mannered and not of the meddlesome type. He's tall and gangly, with angular features, deep dark eyes and matt black hair.

Herr Kimmich's choice wasn't a random one. Wenzel's older brother, still a farmer on the estate, is rumoured to prefer the company of gentlemen and Herr Kimmich had discreetly investigated his feelings about his sibling. No much progress had been made though, as Wenzel was of the reticent type (which he preferred), but Felix's father had arrived at the conclusion (and the hope) that perhaps he was rather oblivious to it.

In any case the solution is nowhere near as water-tight as the brains behind its inception would like to believe.

Suspicions and rumours do not exactly abound yet they are hard to dispel when they creep up. Fortunately, they noticeably fail to hurt them due to their casual aversion to society outings. Perhaps even some members of their respective families might be aware of something. Perhaps Felix's matchless charm is enough for such details to be glossed over. They have no way of knowing. It's a recurring chance they are taking and Wenzel is just one more.

Nonetheless he is settling into his position and Walther is first sent to the family's tailor to be fitted with some decent suits, ties and cravats for his new role.

When he comes back wearing his first outfit, Felix's eyes glow with pride, prompting a night of bedchamber games in celebration. Walther is nervous though: he has attended typewriting and bookkeeping courses, yet he's afraid of disappointing his master. An unnecessary apprehension as both young men are diligent and conscientious when it comes to work; a smaller desk is moved into the study, a typewriter placed on it and some files, bills and invoices assigned to Walther to deal with. Moreover, a telephone is finally installed at Villa Augusta.

Throughout the whole day they both work in stony silence, Walther in a state of nervous, brain-melting concentration. After a few days Felix performs some checks on his work and he's ecstatic at the progress.

After a week, in the middle of a working afternoon, Wenzel comes in with two large carafes of beer and leaves them on Felix's desk. A bewildered Walther raises his head and looks on in puzzlement whilst his friend grabs one of the carafes and almost slams it on his new desk. He does have at times some endearing 'master-of-all-he-surveys' moments.

'I have decided on some changes and we deserve a toast for our hard work. We will toast at every change I am announcing.'

Walther nods.

'First: this "Sir" and "Master Felix" nonsense is terminating today, as from now. Bedroom or non-bedroom. And be warned, Charlotte demands to be addressed by her first name too. Prost!'

He tentatively grabs the carafe, vaguely afraid that Felix has taken leave of his senses. He's well aware that he detests beer and the rumbling tummy that goes with it.

'Prost!'

They take a big swig.

'Second: Wenzel has arranged one of the guest rooms for you to take over. We never have any guests anyway. You are not to sleep downstairs from tonight. Prost!'

He's speechless.

'Prost!'

'Third: Fräulein Kahler is coming over tonight and you are joining us for dinner. Not an invite but an order.' He knows too well Walther would try to decline an invite.

'Prost!'

'Prost!'

The carafes are almost empty. Felix lays a hand on his rumbling tummy. Never mind.

'Fourth: stand up!'

And he meets his lips.

He's walking back from the waste depository at the far end of the garden, where he has diligently stowed the remains of the day. He takes a slight detour towards the study as he hasn't been able to clear the high pile of snow obstructing the kitchen's entrance. All his life young Wenzel has been told to walk upright, looking straight ahead in pride and dignity.

And that is what he does. And that is how he sees them: embraced, their mouths to one, their hands in each other's hair.

On that very moment Felix's eyes break from the dreamy pleasure to meet Wenzel's. They clock wide open, neither scared nor shocked. His life. Their lives. To be found out or existing in fear of being found out: over and over. No rest, no respite. Ever.

He gently releases himself from his friend's embrace while Walther senses something is wrong and turns towards the window. He's still there, his head and shoulders covered in snow and in a state they struggle to ascertain: fear, anger or disgust. It's usually one of them or all three, most often all three. What they are almost sure of is that until now he had been an unsuspecting soul; his death-like, startled expression betrays a shattered innocence.

He squeezes Walther's hand as Wenzel breaks out of his stunned state and quietly leaves.

They stare at each other. They have been there before. Together. And there was a father and a whip. How many more times will it happen? How many more lives do they have left?

'I must talk to him before dinner.'

Walther nods and sits back at the desk, seriously doubting

he will be able to finish any work today.

He's not in the basement's kitchen; Felix walks straight to his room at the end of the corridor in the servants' quarters and finds the door open. He finds him sitting on the bed, his arms around his knees.

'May I come in?'

He nods. Felix stands with one hand in his pocket while he wipes his face and eyes a couple of times with the other to give himself some time to think what to say.

'My apologies that you had to see that. We've been trying to be very discreet; lapse of judgement! I'm sorry, Wenzel.'

'Sir.'

'I...we...this household is...'

He struggles to find the right words. Are there any right words? He can only summon the wrong ones.

'If you feel you cannot continue your service here, I fully understand.'

Wenzel is torn. His parents were highly pleased when Herr Kimmich offered the position at Villa Augusta to him. They had heard of the good rate of pay, the fair treatment, the comfortable lodgings, and they knew first hand of master Felix's gentlemanly disposition. After all, several of the most brutish landowners of the Brandenburg estates were still whipping their farmers to this day.

And he's undoubtedly happy at Villa Augusta; he was starting to settle in. He holds no inimical feelings towards them for the genuine reason that he has never witnessed such act. He is simply conflicted on what to do.

'I appreciate some people, very likely most people, might recoil at the very idea of associating themselves with us, therefore I fully understand if you want to leave.'

'They say Klaus is like you and master Walther, sir.'

Felix frowns.

'Who's Klaus?'

'One of my brothers.'

'Yes, we are not the only ones in the world, Wenzel.'

'I'm confused though: are you both masters of the house or it's you and your wife?'

'Walther is my private secretary now. Frau Charlotte and I are the rightful heads of the house. If it makes sense. Which probably doesn't.'

Wenzel nods.

'I think I better leave you to think it over; if you can't serve dinner tonight, let Walther know, he will take care of it.'

He rightly feels he should not linger any further in conversation and promptly leaves.

Upon Edda's arrival the ladies are informed of the event and the four of them convene in the drawing room for evening cocktails. In the absence of any service they will know their new butler has left.

The double door opens and Wenzel and Maria emerge with trays and glasses. They then transfer to the dining room where the table is neatly set up for dinner.

Once the ladies have retired, Walther takes another glass of brandy from the tray and addresses the young man for the first time.

'Wenzel.'

'Sir?'

'My heartfelt apologies for today.'

'I don't recall anything of exceptional relevance to apologise for, sir.'

In every household tempestuous spells regularly alternate with serene lulls. Villa Augusta is no different and the onset of spring ushers in a period of deserved tranquillity. Wenzel proves himself a good butler and Walther a skilled secretary.

When visiting his parents, Felix and Charlotte find them glowing with delight at reports of a happy family though of course still despondent at the lack of news on the grandchildren front.

Herr Kimmich sees first hand Walther's competent handling of more and more of the estate affairs and he is now regularly invited along, his mother brimming with pride. Felix's father is still unsure on what to wish for though. He secretly hopes that a stronger and lasting bond between the two young men would finish off his son's hazardous gallivanting for good; equally, he wishes that he would at least visit Charlotte's quarters to fill the nurseries.

Master Felix has now more time at his disposal to treat Charlotte as a proper consort and proceeds in earnest to lavishing presents and dinners on her and Fräulein Kahler; the harbinger of spring also allows them languid afternoon strolls along the Tiergarten's paths.

Still at heart a country lad, he tentatively braves a night at the Koningliches Opernhaus and for the occasion Charlotte is presented with a diamond necklace, the result of a secretive blitz with Edda to the family's jeweller.

The crowd in the Opernhaus' foyer parts like the waters of the Red Sea when they grace its marble floors, ladies and gentlemen alike awestruck by their youth, beauty and Charlotte's magnificent couture, the diamonds around her sinuous neck dazzling under the bright light of the chandeliers. Most whisper in each other's ears, demanding to know who they are, wondering about their provenance and status.

Once they reach their box on the second tier, they are surprised to find it empty as they were told they would have been sharing it with Lieutenant Werner and fiancée.

Charlotte takes her seat on the chair at the front while Felix stands behind her. Etiquette demands that he'll have to endure that position for the whole performance, still he has resigned himself to his ordeal with stoic devotion.

They catch sight of Baroness Von Mutthe in the Imperial box, her husband not at her side: some French nonsense is performed tonight. Their box is close to the royal one, though they humbly wait to be acknowledged, in full awareness that it might not happen. Diamonds have no title.

But the Baroness turns and sees them. She verifies her find with her opera glasses and discreetly nods, meeting a prudent smile and a restrained bow.

Charlotte stands up at the Kaiser's entrance. He kisses the bowing Baroness' gloved hand and takes his seat. The box is strangely still empty. In silence and darkness Iphigénie en Aulide commences.

Holding a glass of French nonsense, they stroll along the corridors during the interval, among further bows and whispers; when they reach the door of their box, a young couple is standing by it.

The young gentleman is in high uniform; lanky, light blond hair, short moustaches and glacial blue eyes. The young lady has a suave countenance, perhaps slightly absent or naive.

They formally greet each other and proceed to introduce themselves. The officer clicks his heels while bowing his head.

'Lieutenant Werner and fiancée. At your service, sir.'

'Felix Alexander Kimmich, sir, and this is my wife Charlotte. Delighted.'

'Sadly, we were late. Some trouble with the carriage's wheel. We missed the first act.'

'Glad you arrived in time for the second.' He points at the door. 'After you.'

The gaze was an instant longer than expected. Direct and deep. Martial yet inquisitive. Eager.

The ladies take their seats and the lights dim for Clytemnestre to plead with Achilles to save the life of her daughter Iphigénie from the cruel intentions of her father Agamemnon. Werner's right hand is on his fiancée's shoulder.

Par un père cruel a la mort condamnée,

Side by side. Staring at the stage.

Et par les Dieux abandonnée,

Sleeves brush against each other.

Elle n'a que vous seul,

Fingertips touch for a moment.

Vous êtes dans ces lieux,

Then for more.

Son père, son époux, son asile, et ses Dieux,

Nothing in between.

Vous remplirez mon espérance,

A shiver and a palpitation.

Vous défendrez des jours si précieux,

Through their spines and their hearts.

Le courroux éclatant,

The hands search.

Qui parait dans vos yeux,

And find.

M'en donne l'assurance,

The heads turn.

Sans vous, sans vous secours,

Unyielding pupils.

Nous la perdrons tous deux,

Seeking endorsement.

C'en est fait de ses jours.

Unearthing collusion.

Von Mutthe's opera glasses have missed nothing.

The Kaiser stands up and, amid the loud applause, bends down and whispers inquisitively in his most trusted confidante's ear. She flicks her fan open to cover her mouth, her watery eyes betraying excitement. When her arm is up for the Emperor's hand, the surrounding Feldmarschalls click their heels.

'Emeralds and sapphires, your Majesty. The most dazzling in the house. Irresistible. Full of desire.'

The two couples are in their coats and hats, the foyer has started to empty.

'Perhaps, with the consent of the ladies, Herr Kimmich would care to join me at my Club for a brandy and a cigar?'

Felix shudders.

'Which Club are you member of, Lieutenant?'

'The Imperial Officers, sir.' While clicking his heels again, he fails to notice the relief on Felix's face.

'It will be an honour.'

They are alone in the drawing room of the Club, it's late and most of the officers and their guests have retired. Lieutenant Werner's fine features are shadowed by the flickering flames of the fire, their brandy glasses warm in their hands, the room heavy with the smell of their cigars.

'I was at military school myself. Five years.'

'I thought as much.'

'You did?'

'Cadets' posture. Was it your decision to leave?'

Felix smiles at the insinuation, not entirely sure if there is one.

'I wasn't asked to leave if that is what you meant. I was never caught.'

'I wasn't insinuating...'

'No offence taken. One has to be careful. That's a warning for you, Lieutenant. Rather daring of you by the way. At the opera, I mean.'

Lieutenant Werner stares at the fire.

'And a disgrace. With my fiancée there. My hand on her shoulder.' He leans forward, throws the almost finished cigar in the fire and holds the glass in both hands, staring in it.

'I feel I can be frank with you, Felix.'

'I'm honoured, what makes you feel that way?'

'Your look is determined and strong. But kind.' He takes another sip and waves at the cadet behind the bar for a refill. He stares at the fire.

'I'm scared.'

'Of?'

'This.'

'We all are.'

'Why didn't I pull my hand away?'

'Because you can't. There is an inevitability to it.'

'Your eyes. The green in them. They turned me into stone. I'm incapable of seeing such beauty in my fiancée.'

The green of his eyes is now golden. Unblinking. A fiendish, irresistible handsomeness. Hushed yet piercing.

'I've ordered a suite.'

'As a member, I have permanent lodgings here.'

'I assumed that to be the case. You'll learn in time to be always a step ahead, Lieutenant. Our kind lives in scrutiny.'

'Wise.' He stands up and clicks his heels. 'The last door on the right at the end of the corridor. First floor.'

A reassuring nod.

The morning light beams on the small knots of his spine, as smooth and white as unbaked bread buns. Felix is getting dressed, a cigarette between satisfied lips while ogling the godly creature lying between rumpled sheets. Ivory. Blue. Tamed. His shimmering yet vulnerable sapphires hidden by the almost transparent eyelids. His flaxen short locks listlessly gracing his eyebrows. Herr Kimmich the younger is a man of no illusions about his world: not one for remorseful souls.

Sophie Von Mutthe is now fully involved with Charlotte's ladies' circle and spends her time at court receptions relishing her next rendezvous with 'that posse of crazy women and mad revolutionaries'.

But what delights most Herr Kimmich the elder is Jurgen's off the cuff invitation to Wenzel to join him at his boxing evenings at the working men's club, swiftly followed by Walther and belatedly by Felix too.

'Finally, some manly action!' He shouts at dinner, causing Frau Augusta to fret to distraction at the idea of 'her dear little boy in the hands of sweaty brutes'. At that sentence Walther is unable to contain a giggle and promptly receives a good kick from Felix under the table while Herr Kimmich proudly slaps his son's shoulder.

'Nonsense! A few bruises and a black eye have never hurt anyone!'

And on the first evening Wenzel does indeed return with a bruise on his cheek; on the second one he sports a black eye. This is fun.

Walther, always the Dickensian street lad, joins next and one evening his black eye proves irresistible to Felix, winning him a round of vigorous wrestling on the bedroom floor: 'You are a boxer now, Brother,' he says as he pins him down in that thrilling instant between the end of virile tussle and the onset of gratification.

Walther suggests to him to join up though Felix dismisses the proposition in mocking self-deprecation:

'Have you gentlemen seen the size of me? There is no way I will be returning in one piece.'

Walther has none of that.

'They pair weights, they won't have you boxing Jurgen. Besides, we are still in training, no matches. Though you do get punched about.' He points his finger at his now purple eye socket.

Jurgen nods though he is slightly concerned. Their ultimate duty is still to protect their master, not to take him to a boxing club to be reduced to a pulp.

His fears prove unfounded: Felix is of small but not frail constitution and wasn't raised a dainty little snob either. Besides, he has a well-known side taste for the less fortunate districts of the city, the boxing club being located in one of the roughest.

Jurgen's main worry is the class difference. Neither boys are in the least of the effeminate type but Felix's German is of the highly educated variety though somehow deprived of charmless hauteur. Furthermore, after training, substantial quantities of beer are downed in the smoke-filled filthy canteen of the club which, to Jurgen's astonishment, seems to greatly appeal to his master.

On the first evening his instructor pairs him with a boy almost half his age as he's the only one they could find who they hope won't floor him as soon as he steps onto the ring.

But his supple little muscles, wiry body and deer-like agility prove a surprising asset and, this being Felix, he diligently listens to the instructor who knows by experience when a young man is in need of tough love. He never argues or complains when his sparring partner floors him with a good left-hander: he just gets himself up (sometimes with great struggle) and apologises with his hand up for having been downed. At the end of the training and without a single protest, he subjects himself to a tough schedule of hits to his stomach 'to shape up' his abdominal muscles. He focuses and follows his trainer's instructions to the letter while Walther and Wenzel act a bit too silly and are repeatedly reprimanded by Jurgen and their instructors. One day he's caught shirtless by Walther in the study, punching the armchair with his gloves on. Unfazed by his secretary's mocking grin, he softly punches his nose with the right glove:

'Training tonight, Brother.'

One evening, ready to head for the showers and a beer in the canteen, they are told Felix will stay behind. They leave shrugging and come back finding him on the floor doing sit ups, panting and sweating while his trainer stands by with his arms folded. Their jaws drop. The instructor, a burly no-nonsense chap, turns to them.

'Sloppy tonight, no good.'

Felix drops on the floor near expiration.

'Did I tell you to stop? Another ten of the best, young man.'

Felix, eyes bulging, his bare chest dripping with sweat, drops of it trickling from his moustaches, barely lifts himself up.

'Yes, sir! Sorry, sir!'

In the carriage his companions have taken to a giggle but he's quiet and serious though he never really minds to be made fun of. He looks at his bruised hand.

'You two should be more respectful of your trainers.'

But the giggles continue.

'Yes sir…sorry sir…!'

It is, of course, no use: friends make fun of you.

He jumps in Felix's bed still in his pyjamas. He's in his, sitting up with an arm behind his head. Felix warns him straight away.

'Don't take that off. I don't have a single muscle left working.'

'Not even the one?'

'Don't be vulgar.'

Walther takes his now almost purple hand and kisses it.

'I've come to say sorry.' A grunt. Walther squeezes his biceps. 'This is making you very fit.'

'If they don't break me in a thousand pieces first.'

'I'll collect them all one by one with a spoon.'

'Make sure it's silver.'

'Still angry?'

'Very.'

'No, you are not.'

'Then I'm not.'

Walther kisses him and turns, Felix hugs him lashing out some moans of pain.

They have grown fond of Wenzel. He seems to be now completely oblivious to their liaison and, most importantly, he makes sensational tea, whose quality Felix childishly never fails to remark in Walther's presence.

Their thrice weekly Boxing Club escapades are more fun than they ever expected and Jurgen reports back to Herr Kimmich that the three young men are having the time of their lives, though he will continue to keep a close watch on them.

Outside the Boxing Club nights their relationship remains the most professional and respectful one and even during those evenings Wenzel continues to address them with 'sir' or 'master'. They wouldn't dream of embarrassing him by asking to move onto more familiar terms of address. The boundaries don't seem to prevent Wenzel joining in to make fun of each other anyway, especially after a few beers which still make Felix's tummy rumble; at least in the boxing club canteen the noise is so loud no one can hear it.

The pair spend their day in the study, diligently immersed in their work; Walther is often dispatched on errands to the estate to deal with farmers, rents and other affairs. His competence is growing along with his salary and the family's wealth.

As he has progressed much faster than his friends, Felix's instructor arranges his first match.

His focused agility and his now more athletic, nimble little frame are no match for his adversary and, after having taken a few nasty hits, his newly acquired skills floor his opponent.

He punches the air with a roar. His nose is bleeding, there is a cut on his eyebrow and one on his lower lip; he cannot quite feel his ribs yet he's pretty sure they are still there, only of a more bluish variety.

The working club's hall erupts. Little Felix has won the day. He's snatched from the ring by the drunken, chanting crowd, lifted on some man's shoulders the size of a wardrobe and paraded around, sweaty and bloody, everyone patting his legs, arms and tummy. All of which ache atrociously.

His sight is slightly hazed by the blows and the hall's dense and smoky atmosphere. When he's lowered down to be presented with a grotesquely oversized carafe of beer in celebration, he struggles at first to recognise the gentleman standing in front of him, Jurgen towering behind.

He wipes the sweat from his brows emitting a grunt of pain and freezes wide-eyed.

'Father?'

He's not given the time to witness Herr Kimmich shouting at the burly sailor standing next to him:

'That's my son! My son has just won the match! That's him!'

Rivers of beer. Much later the three young ones return home in a state of disgraceful inebriation and juvenile euphoria: singing off-tune, hugging a sober Jurgen and slurring some declarations of love for each other. The loyal driver patiently puts them to bed one by one, buckets at the side.

The following Sunday, Felix, Charlotte and Walther visit the family home for lunch. When they alight the footman immediately congratulates Felix on his victory. It can only mean one thing: his father has spent the last few days relaying the tale of his triumph to everyone. Charlotte and Walther smile; Felix only wishes he could as his lower lip has a nasty cut, the bruises on the eyebrows hurt every time he changes expression and his nose has a plaster on it, producing a muffled sound in his voice. He also has the middle finger of his right hand in a stick and a bandage so he keeps that hand in his pocket when they enter the drawing room.

At the sight of the condition of her dearest son, Frau Augusta almost faints. She tries to hug and kiss him but he has to politely push her away with an apology.

'I'm very sorry, Mother, everything is rather brittle right now.'

Frau Kimmich is incandescent with her husband.

'Gerhardt! What is the meaning of this? Are you trying to murder my poor Felix? This crazy enterprise must stop at once! I won't have my dear boy reduced to this by these brutes. Charlotte, this is impossible. Say something!'

Charlotte looks at Walther for support but he has a fair dose of wounds and bandages himself as training at the working men's boxing club involves a good deal of punches. They say it toughens boys up.

'Have you all gentlemen taken leave of your senses? Charlotte, you don't approve of this? Do you?'

Charlotte really has no opinion in the matter so she merely volunteers what she feels.

'They seem to be enjoying the nights at the club.'

'Oh, for the love of God! Everyone has gone mad. My Felix!'

She forgets about her son's pleading and she grabs his arms which, covered by the jacket's sleeves, are not showing the bruises. He cries out in pain.

'Mother!'

She takes her handkerchief to her eyes.

'Mother, it's quite alright. I'm not dead; well, not yet. It will take a few weeks and I'll be like new. I won the match though!' And he raises his fist in victory, triggering another cry of pain.

'Nonsense, Augusta. You should have seen him: left hand, right hand, eyes fixed on the opponent. Focus. Athletic jumping. Good tactic, son, good tactic. Masterful, simply masterful; that chap didn't have a chance with Felix, I am telling you...'

'That is quite enough, Gerhardt, lunch now, my boy needs to eat. The madness!'

When the soup lands in front of Felix, he forgets and takes his hand out of his pocket. His bandaged finger positively shows over the mahogany table. Walther makes a warning gesture but too late. Frau Augusta shrieks.

'Oh dear God! Gerhardt, Felix must remain here for a few weeks to recover from what these murderers have done to him.'

'Mother...'

'I will hear no objections. You have all lost your mind.'

Conspiratorial glances are exchanged between Herr Kimmich and the two young men: this is a match they aren't going to win.

After lunch, as custom, he invites the boys in the drawing room for brandy and cigars but Walther leaves after downing his glass. Herr Kimmich deserves some glowing time with his son.

'Well, that instructor you have. Good man, good man. And the Club, you know, strong, hard-working folks. With a spine!'

'Father, half of them are criminals, the other half probably murderers. I genuinely doubt anyone does any "working".'

'Now, now. Men of that stock get into all sort of trouble.'

'Father, we had the best of time at the club. I agree, they are decent folks after all. But you know very well that Mother will never talk to you again if I continue to be battered like this. Besides, I'm not so sure I want to continue to be battered like this. It hurts.'

'Fair enough. But you had your victory. It's important to win something. Did they have some sort of trophy?'

'Yes, it's in the carriage. I thought that perhaps I'll leave it here if you don't mind. My present.'

On the following visit the trophy, a cheap affair of granite, metal and ribbons, is on the drawing room's mantelpiece, Felix's name engraved in the base. He turns with a frown to Walther while holding the trophy in his hands.

'I don't remember it being engraved, do you?'

Walther nods in a warning to avoid pointing that out to his father and he quietly puts it back on the mantelpiece.

To pacify Frau Augusta they all agree that Felix will stay and recover at the family seat in full peace and serenity. Without much ado his mother dispatches the servants to prepare his old room. The thought of having two or three weeks fussing over her dear boy sends her in a frenzy and Walther is now more than capable of running the estate on his own for a few weeks, fully trusted by Herr Kimmich the elder.

He proposes a stroll at dusk, pleading with his friend that he's about to face weeks of Mother's dawn-to-dusk resolute attention. They have a minute or two before Jurgen drives in to collect Walther and Charlotte so they use them to amble down to the family chapel and rest on the low wall by the lake.

'Never seen your father so proud.'

Felix's face darkens while he stares in silence at the grass.

'He believes this makes me a man.'

'You are a man.'

'A real one.'

Walther shrugs.

'When he caught us he didn't kill us. He could have done. The feeling of degradation must have been unbearable.'

Felix sputters a devilish tiny laugh.

'You were the one being degraded.'

For that he receives a good shove which rolls him onto the grass in cries of pain.

'That hurt!'

'Serves you right.'

A smile, then a giggle, and a laugh. He grabs Walther's hand and lifts himself up, Jurgen is walking down the hill.

His instructor is sad to see him leave but he understands.

'My mother will have a heart attack if I continue to turn up in pieces. And the heavy drinking is killing me.'

He laughs and shakes his hand with a big pat on his back. The motley crew of murderers and rascals are also sad to see him leave. They proceed in earnest to give him a good old send off by arranging the heaviest of drinking sessions for the three young men until Jurgen finds them semi-unconscious on the filthy floor of the club's canteen.

Walther leaves the club too, seeing no reason to continue. Wenzel carries on for a little while and then a sweetheart appears from nowhere and that promptly marks the end of his fledgling boxing career. In the meantime Felix has hired an under-butler and a private maid for Charlotte while promoting Wenzel to head butler, giving him an excuse to increase his wages.

'He has a sweetheart now, he might want to treat her to the funfair, the dance hall, you know what they are like, the ladies.'

Walther smiles in amusement while updating Wenzel's salary in his register: no, he does not, how would he?

The boxing fun brought about some beneficial side results to which the two young men remained genuinely oblivious: it stopped their less respectable activities in their tracks.

Felix wasn't seen at Franz's for weeks and Walther, exhausted by work and training, made for his bed earlier and earlier as the days went by. When in bed together they had felt no need to go beyond mutual warmth.

On one of the training evenings, an unsuspecting and handsome young lad had joined them in the filthy showers of the club with the sole disappointing intention of, well, showering. Unseen by their fellow boxer, Walther had winked in jest. In the changing rooms, Felix had taken his towel off, whacked Walther's backside and sternly pointed a finger at his face.

'We are here to train.'

Among the frenzied camaraderie of the club, Wenzel had unwittingly forgotten what he had witnessed through the study's window and had stopped thinking about the peculiarity of his new mates' relationship. When unleashed, fun, friendship and youth steamroll fears and prejudices away from our minds.

La Bête humaine

Fräulein Kahler is now a regular guest at Villa Augusta. Sadly, her family fails to share her enthusiasm for 'that household' and insists in subjecting her to a never-ending parade of moronic upper-class suitors who rile her all the way to the end of the North Sea.

Charlotte is frequently upset at her friend's predicament, something which hasn't escaped her husband's attentive eye for people's recurring states of unhappiness. All the same, he has no solutions to the problem and all he can offer is the full hospitality of Villa Augusta.

'Edda is welcome here, as guest or otherwise. You know that.'

Walther is no longer 'invited' for meals. His chair and *mise-en-place* are now permanently set up in their rightful place. Two copies of the Berliner Zeitung are now delivered to the villa. Wenzel places them on Felix and Walther's desks on weekdays and on the tables by their armchairs in the drawing room on Saturdays and Sundays.

Unlike most gentlemen of the day, Felix has banned newspapers from the breakfast table.

'The ladies,' he points out to Walther, 'basic good manners. How would you feel having breakfast with the events of the day?'

Felix repositions his cup on the saucer.

'Wenzel, this tea is magnificent!'

Walther, who has by now heard the jibe endless times, ignores it outright.

'Perhaps it's about time you stop poking fun at our Walther.'

Charlotte has taken to call him 'our Walther' and he still blushes when she says it. She lifts a paper from the table.

'I have received a letter from Weimar.'

'How is family?'

'All well, thank you. We have been invited to Baden-Baden for the season.'

'For the whole season? Surely not at their residence?'

'They have taken an extensive property, you know Father.'

'I'm in agreement on Baden but allow me to insist that we take our own property. I hope this will not offend your parents?'

'It will.'

'And after a profuse apology?'

'They'll revert to adoring you.'

She grins. She never minds her family being fond of her husband yet the letter in her hands had caused her eyes to raise to the dining room ceiling in exasperation: 'Your brothers are looking forward to rides and games of tennis with Felix'. 'You know very well how your younger sisters already fret at the mere idea of having Felix here with us'. 'Your father has already organised a shooting expedition in Felix's honour'. When she had finished reading it she had dropped it on the floor; her name barely featured in it.

'I intend to take Jurgen and Wenzel with us. A long stay

requires your own servants, perhaps all of them. Besides, with Walther and, I fervently hope, Edda, joining us, it would be an unacceptable imposition on our behalf, don't you agree?'

Walther jolts and turns to him.

'Me?'

'Well, where do you propose to while away the season?'

'Why, here. Working. I'm your secretary.'

Charlotte is by now highly skilled in spotting and defusing any tension between the two young men.

'Perhaps we should let Walther decide?'

'I can't see what all this fuss is about. You were with us last season.'

'As a butler.'

'Are you seriously proposing to be away from me, I mean, from us, for the best part of four months? Charlotte won't have that, would you my dear?'

She throws a comforting smile at Walther, whose face exhibits a shade of crimson.

'Walther, you know how greatly it will please me if you could join us.'

'Thank you, Charlotte, very kind. But what about the estate business?'

Felix shrugs.

'Father can still run it while we are away, he isn't a demented old fool yet.'

But Walther is now staring at his plate.

'They all know I was your butler.'

'And now you are the family's administrator, that is a title and that is how we'll introduce you.'

'Have I been promoted again?'

'I must have forgotten to inform you.'

His head hasn't moved. The paralysing power of humble roots.

'I'm the son of peasants.'

'Nonsense! You have always possessed some fine manners.'

'You sound like your father.'

Felix shrugs again, unsure whether to treat that as a compliment. In the meantime his long-suffering friend runs through a mental list of items and events which will hopelessly embarrass him in Baden's grand society circuit.

'I can't shoot.'

'You can ride. We've been riding since we were eight. And the boxing is gone, I'll book some tennis lessons.'

'I'm not jumping into a mud bath!'

'I'll throw you in. Anyway, why are we discussing this? Your attendance is requested at Baden.'

Walther is now confused.

'By whom?'

Felix's look is astounded, in his unique mocking way.

'By me, who else?'

He's still perusing some documents at his desk, an additional piece of furniture he requested for his new bedroom in order to be able to review the last small accounting details before bedtime. A knock on the door.

He's in his pyjamas and gown and so is Felix who leans on the door frame, hands in his pockets.

'Up for a game?'

They have taken up chess. They both find it rather lame after the adrenaline-fuelled boxing days but at least their noses are not bleeding anymore and Frau Augusta was positively ecstatic at the news.

'I'm reviewing the banks' letters of credit.'

'I have the brandy ready.'

Walther throws the papers on the desk with a sigh.

'I never win.'

'You need to focus.'

'You taught me the game. I think you cheat.'

'Of course I do.'

He follows Felix into his bedroom. What's the use?

'Checkmate!'

Walther expires on the armchair. Felix raises his hand apologetically.

'I didn't cheat, I promise.'

A big yawn. Walther gets up.

'That's me for tonight.'

'Stay.'

'It's late, and I'm due to the estate tomorrow, Jurgen has the carriage ready at seven.'

'Hug, kiss, lights out.' Felix lifts his right hand's fingers in the pledge way. 'Promise.'

'Sounds like your dormitory at military school.'

'Without the kiss.'

'Seriously?'

Felix winks.

'Of course not.'

The heavy velvet curtains pulled open, Walther's round brown eyes are locked on the birches furiously battered by the first winds of spring. They have hugged and kissed and Felix is holding him. His hand rests inside the collar of his jacket, his thumb gently caressing the base of his neck. The duvet is up to their noses, holding in the sweet smell of intimacy.

'We can wrestle in a mud bath.'

He turns with a sharp movement.

'Really?'

Felix sputters.

'You idiot.'

He's back staring at the trees.

'I have offended you today.'

'Nonsense. But it hurt.'

'What hurt?'

'We've never been apart for four months. It's an eternity. Are you trying to kill me?' He feels Felix's fingers interlocking with his, almost crushing his hand. His moustaches are now tickling his neck. 'I wish you would now count yourself as part of the family. I've always considered you as such anyway.'

'Well. I was your father's stable boy. Then the family butler. Then your butler. Then you wanted to use first names and now I'm your secretary, or "administrator", as you called it.'

'You forgot "lady-in-waiting".'

A quick, sharp hit of Walther's elbow in Felix's ribs.

'Ouch!'

'I need time.'

'I know. But it's important to me.' Walther feels a swift peck on his neck. 'Lights out, Brother.'

Villa Augusta is the largest in size amid the handsome mansions gracing the lime tree-lined Kaiser-Friedrich Platz. Ever since the Kimmichs' arrival, its gardens have been taken care of by occasional contractors. Felix is now determined to preside over a more and more splendid abode and, upon his father's recommendation, he hires Tobias, a worker at the estate. The new gardener takes along his young son as Herr Kimmich points out that he might come of help as a messenger for small errands.

He isn't a landscaping gardener as such but Felix is adamant that he'll learn on the job. When Tobias realises how well-treated the servants are, he strenuously applies himself to the task in fear of losing such a position.

With a fast-expanding number of servants, Felix and Walther's competent team work in the running of the estate and spring on its way, the atmosphere in the household is ebullient and serene. The servants are, however, of the same opinion of Frau Augusta: children would make it just perfect.

But Charlotte and Felix have temporarily abandoned the subject and there is a sad wedge in between this bliss: Fräulein Kahler's parents are increasingly insistent that their daughter should no longer frequent 'those people'.

It hurts him. He would love to see Charlotte happy with her companion at her side and he cares for Edda a great deal himself. Sometimes, after heated political debates, Walther and Charlotte rile Felix with pointy remarks: 'She's turning you into a socialist!', they declare with a giggle.

He also believes that it would be much better to have Edda around the house if children were to be sired. He's doubtful of his paternal instincts and, despite his liberal approach to life in general, he has a grain of old-fashioned Prussian conviction that ladies will be far better than himself or Walther in raising children. He has made this clear to him a few times: 'They don't get into as much trouble as we do.'

He has also gone back to Franz's, though not on a shopping spree, rather to regularly visit Florian. The young man is charming, discreet and, of course, too impossibly beautiful for Felix to resist, and he's notoriously incapable of resisting anything.

As it always does, the passion subsides after the first few weeks, though this enhances their relationship instead of damaging it. He has organised a small room at Franz's for Florian to occupy on permanent basis and they now meet in the afternoon as well as at night-time. At times he leaves without indulging in carnal entertainment.

After private lodgings are secured, he can no longer countenance the thought of Florian having to be in the company of other gentlemen and demands exclusivity. Franz names his price and gets it.

Everyone in the household cannot avoid noticing how happy master Felix is, though not yet aware of any special person in his life.

He takes Florian to a modestly-priced tailor in Reinickendorf who fits out the boy with a full wardrobe for the price of one of Felix's suits at the family's tailor on the Unter den Linden.

Their afternoons are carefree and playful. His present occupation is the result of cruelty and he's no street kid: he doesn't swear or use slang and he listens before answering questions. If he's not consulted he doesn't volunteer an opinion.

When Felix proposes to linger for an hour or so at a concert in the nearby park, he fears Florian will be bored to distraction; instead, the boy remains in his seat without fidgeting and later comments on how beautiful the music was.

Sometimes Felix sits reading in the only armchair of the room and when Florian is asked if he'd like to read something too, he gets a nod of approval. He brings along some easy novels and the young man proves an avid reader.

The evenings are still fired by authentic youthful passion and Florian doesn't seem to regard it as a 'service'. Felix never stays over at night-time: waking up at Franz's doesn't exactly appeal to him; as a consequence they never had a morning waking up embraced, hazy and excited.

He would prefer to wrest Florian from Franz's clutches as he's not entirely sure that they don't force the boy into other services when he is not there and, after all, a boy house is a boy house.

Walther is the first to learn of his plans over a pillow talk; they would never discuss such subjects in the study: they remain very professional when at their desks.

'The lad is from a good family: the Von Luthenbergs.'

Walther nods.

'There is always a place in the household, what did you have in mind? Would he lodge in your quarters?'

Walther's head lies on his bare chest, Felix stroking his hair.

'What? No. Men don't do that. We don't do that.'

Walther laughs.

'You'll have to draw up a schedule for us, or put one of our names outside the door.'

He pinches his ear hard.

'That is in bad taste.'

But he's in giggling mood now.

'Well, what about if we cross each other in here by mistake?'

A mischievous silence. Perhaps a plan. Walther springs up in mock outrage.

'And that is not in bad taste?'

Felix winks at him and grabs his head back onto his chest.

'Maybe.'

'But you're thinking about it, aren't you?'

'Well, no more of that.'

His cheek feels the heat rising from Felix's body; welcoming, reassuring. The delayed gratification of sporadic couplings.

'Just lodging or with some occupation?'

'I was thinking, perhaps some education. He's rather bright. You'll like him.'

'Does he know about us?'

'Yes, I haven't revealed our address though, not while he's at Franz's.'

'Wise. Well, it's late. You know that what you decide is law for me, you're the master.'

He feels a gentle slap on his cheek.

'We are brothers. Lights out.'

He's ecstatic at having Walther's approval. His secretary is still dutiful and devoted; for him Felix is still his master and he prefers it that way. He finds it comforting.

Felix, on the other hand, no longer takes any important decision without consulting his brother-in-arms, though he had to act brutally to lure him to Baden, well aware that Walther is already sick with worry at having to brave the season's grand society outings.

He dithers though. One evening he arrives at Franz's and sits at the bar waiting for Florian. He has agreed to treat him for dinner at a local bistro.

Hans greets him and places the silver mat on the bar for the glass of champagne which usually follows. When he withdraws his hand, a small envelope lies by it.

He stares at the barman but he meets no expression. Hans is an attractive man of perhaps thirty, formerly employed in the house's more lucrative pursuits. Unable to move on, he had opted to stay in a less demanding position. It gives him an invaluable insight into the various going-ons of the house, of which there is never a shortage.

Dear Herr Hagelstein,

I have to be brief. You have been the kindest gentleman I have ever come across and I am deeply grateful to you for taking care of me so well.

I do accept that you have a family and other commitments which prevent you from taking me away from this place.

I understand, but I cannot stay here any longer. The other boys now hate me because I have a steady gentleman who pays for a private room. While I am here it is impossible to look for a position, not that I am trained in anything though.

Another gentleman has kindly offered to take me away for the season; perhaps while I am away I might find something more respectable to earn my keep.

I hope I am not offending you too much by accepting but I am rather desperate to leave Franz's.

I do consider the days I spent with you the best of my short life so far and I will treasure them forever.

Please, do not be angry with me.

Yours, Florian

Hans is impassive. He knows all too well what has just happened, he has seen it happening countless times. He has seen them departing. There is really nothing new for Hans under the Berlin sun.

Felix hides the letter and the envelope away in the inside pocket of his jacket and sticks a cigarette between his lips, Hans prompt with a match.

He likes Herr Hagelstein: polite and refined, a breath of fresh air among the brutish ogres loitering about the place. Before Florian came along, he used to discreetly warn him of boys of unsuitable temperament while recommending the ones who in his opinion were more befitting for such a trusting and considerate gentleman.

Felix rummages in his trouser pocket and leaves a fifty Reichsmarks note on the bar.

'I don't suppose you're acquainted with the gentleman?'

Hans sweeps up the note.

'Maybe.' Another note but this time Hans returns it. 'That's generous enough, Herr Hagelstein.'

'I have no intention of going after them. I'd like to know if Florian is in good hands.'

Hans must lie.

'A gentleman, good manners, generous. Very taken with the boy.'

There is no mawkish sorrow between them. There has never been. Men they are. Boys maybe. Ladies, never.

'How do you know Hans is lying?'

'I do.'

Felix is standing at his bedroom's door. Walther is holding Florian's note in his hand.

'I'm worried he might be in trouble.'

'We can hire people. I can track them down.'

'No use.'

Walther is prepared to rotate Prussia onto its axis to find them yet certain endeavours are sometime best not attempted. Felix grabs his hand.

'Stay with me tonight.'

He's not the type for endlessly dwelling on misfortunes. He finds it 'womanly'. Florian is a boy and boys move on. As he does. He continues to oversee a blooming household: wealthier and happier.

In the meantime Walther has diligently subjected himself to an artillery barrage of tennis lessons: he's determined to take Baden by storm or be swept to the high seas by it. After a few days of angst over Florian's destiny, Felix returns to form and challenges him to a match.

'I have a fantastic excuse to buy him some exceedingly elegant "whites",' he remarks to his bemused wife.

He has arranged the rental of Villa Hildegard in the Kaiseralle of Baden-Baden, a monumental compound only a walking distance from the residence to be taken over by the Dessauers: 'The whole household can transfer with us,' he announces to Walther in deep satisfaction.

A shimmering afternoon sun, carafes of iced lemonade on the tables. The Schöneberg Tennis Club grounds are dotted with white jumpers knotted around the shoulders of privileged, flaxen-haired people; the boys are warming up and about to play.

Six-zero, six-zero, six-zero.

He's at his wits' end. He sits panting in a pool of sweat at the edge of the court, his head almost between his legs. Felix is sipping from a glass of lemonade, his moustaches now golden; his hair, which turns curly when wet, flutters in the light breeze. The instructor sits mortified in one of the corners of the court.

'You are not to allow anyone to challenge me, I'm an embarrassment.'

'Nonsense! You've just taken it up. By the time we are there, you'll smash them.'

'Who's them?'

'The toffs.'

'I have bad feelings about this.'

'I'll be there. Incidentally, those "whites" make you unbearably attractive, you must know that.'

'You don't look too bad yourself in them.'

'Flattery will take you nowhere. Let's try another set.'

The season is still some time away, Berlin is in bloom and Walther is turning out a formidable administrator. Herr Kimmich the elder has started to dispatch him to bank managers and stockbrokers, receiving glowing reports in return: 'That young chap you sent. Very smart, Herr Kimmich, very smart.'

After a dinner at the estate, he stands up and, laying a hand on Walther's shoulder, he calls out:

'Well, ladies, if you don't mind, I'll take my boys to the study for some urgent business we have coming up next week.'

He fears Felix might take offence at his parents' now well-established inclusion but he seems pleased instead, proud. When faced with some important decisions he now solemnly turns to Walther: 'I think Father would be glad to hear your opinion on this.'

Walther's competence is now giving Felix some extra spare time: he uses it wisely and sometimes not so wisely.

He has all but stopped his escapades to Franz's as a period of reflection has been ushered in by Florian's flight. Walther almost chokes on his coffee when he catches him shirtless in the garden with a shovel in his hands, helping Tobias dig a flower bed.

Felix and Walther have drained their brains to fumes in

trying to find a way to help Edda to fight or altogether flee her family but they have no power; in the end Felix cannot help but to be a little shameless to lighten up the gloom: 'Perhaps we should hire a hitman from the working men's club to murder them all.'

For a while he had suspended his visits to the Charlottenburg Baths but he now looks forward to a relaxing day out. He loves the Baths, not merely for the obvious reasons which would no doubt spring to the minds of the most cynical readers, but also for the exercise, the peace of the reading loggia and the decor: a plush blend of Greco-Roman columns and balustrades surrounded by some garish baroque and gothic features. He's never been sure how such architectural schizophrenia can possibly work, but it does: there is something of the unashamed about it.

Like himself.

Two days a week are reserved for the ladies, all the other days are gentlemen only. Swimming and Turkish Baths are to be attended as nature created you, fluffy white bath-robes are provided for all the other areas. A charitable rule indeed: unlike Felix, the vast majority of the visiting gentlemen hardly springs from the loins of Apollo.

There are also private cabins for massages. Felix has his personal one which he reserves well in advance at considerable expense. It resembles a small studio in which a gentleman can shave, smoke and relax on a comfortable armchair.

Kadir is his masseur. A strapping forty-year-old man hauling from one of the many lands of the Ottoman Empire: swarthy, sinuous muscles, oversized and luscious moustaches, far too much pomade in his hair.

Felix is no orientalist when it comes to matters of the flesh. When he had booked Kadir for the first time, he hadn't entertained any diversionary intentions.

Like many gentlemen of middle-eastern origin, Kadir, though not necessarily of Hellenistic persuasion, could rarely remain indifferent to the sculpted silhouettes of athletic bodies. When Felix had lain undressed on the massage bed face down, his supple, sinuous body all exposed, Kadir had rightly guessed that such celestial work of art deserved the most divine of treatments. Felix's calves are wiry and muscular, his vertebrae stand out like a masterful bas-relief and, except for where it should be growing, hair is not to be found on any other part of his body.

Kadir's hands had journeyed to previously undiscovered paths and had caused Felix to jolt: neither in fear nor in anger and positively not in rejection. He had let his masseur fly him away from earthly fears, his eyes shut over a journey culminating with Kadir laying his hands flat on Felix's tummy, his body spent, his eyes unable to re-open. Afterwards, he had covered him with a clean sheet and, after washing his hands, he had joined them in front of his mouth in a pose of eastern respect, bowing out in silence.

Kadir is off duty on Thursdays. Thursday is the mysteriously and unofficially allocated day for the pursuit of events of illegal nature: discretion essential, possibilities endless.

Mature gentlemen might freely remark how a handsome squire would represent a suitable husband for their daughters. Others who would rather have the handsome squire for themselves, wisely keep their counsel. Felix often finds himself the target of such remarks.

He goes for a good swim. It's eleven in the morning and the pool is empty as Thursdays become busier much later in the afternoon. As they would.

He swims for a good hour, then slips into his gown and walks to the loggia where he lies on the lounger with a copy of La Bête humaine, Zola's new bestseller. Like many educated Prussians of the time, he's fluent in the author's language and didn't have to wait for a decent translation to appear at his regular Charlottenburg bookseller.

He reads for an hour or so before returning to his private room. He leaves the book and heads for the Turkish Baths, a spacious room with marble walls and silver bowls for the sadistic purpose of throwing cold water on steaming bodies.

He leaves his gown on a hook outside and enters. A cloud of white vapour escapes from the glass door.

He has to adjust to the dimmed lighting and the steam which prevent him seeing where he's heading, though he knows the layout anyway: the marble benches are all around the wall, intercalated by fountains of cold water with the bowls positioned under the running taps.

It seems deserted though there is no way to see to the other end of the room. It pleases him: when the room is empty he can stretch out on a bench and close his eyes, the steam enveloping his whole body. Yet he sits for the time being with his eyes shut.

After a short time he hears the hinges of the glass door creaking and feels the presence of somebody walking around. Then this somebody sits by him. Close.

After an instant or two of tense silence, the sound of a voice jolts him out of his dreaming.

'Herr Kimmich!'

He freezes. Not in fear, as he is known here and no improper conduct has so far been entertained.

'Yes?'

He turns but he's unable to distinguish the features of the gentleman at his side. When the steam's spout allows a short respite, he can eventually discern a much older man, about three times the size of him, with a very hairy body and what appears to be a scruffy set of beard and moustaches. He's also radiating a gut-wrenching whiff of tobacco and whisky; poor dental hygiene's effluvia emanate from his mouth. As he has addressed him by his name though, he's clearly not in pursuit of Thursday's special activities.

'I'm ever so sorry, sir, but the steam prevents me from recognising you.'

'Yes, of course. Count Von Stolberg.'

His heart jumps.

'Ah, yes, of course. Pleased to see you, Count.'

Felix doesn't move away, believing that in the absence of second motives, it would be discourteous, though the Count has not necessarily been the best of friends lately.

'Do you come here often, Herr Kimmich?'

'Only two or three times a month if at all.'

He doesn't enquire how often the Count comes here. He's not interested. He would rather leave.

'I see.'

The Count breaths in with his nose and exhales, Felix's face turns the other way in disgust.

'Sorry business, the Club's suspension.'

He's puzzled by the goading. Why is he doing it anyway? He has already won.

'Well, I understand I'm suspended for another four months or so.'

'That's what I understand. It could go either way though.'

His heart jumps a little more.

'What do you mean by that, sir?'

'The suspension could be lifted or turned into an expulsion.' Felix closes his eyes. 'I'm the president. I take the ultimate decision.'

'Then, Count, I place my trust in your magnanimity.'

'Very wise to do so, Herr Kimmich, very wise.' As he proffers those words, his sweaty big hand lands with a loud slap on Felix's thigh. The upper part of it. It stays there.

Felix freezes in horror, his back glued to the marble wall, unable to move, his eyes now wide open.

'Count?'

'You see, Herr Kimmich, I think we both agree that an early reinstatement, the charges dropped, and a return with full honours would please your dear father no end.'

While he says that, his hand moves up; it now rests between his thigh and his private parts. He feels the Count's huge fingers rustling the fluffy area. Felix has started to shake.

'On the other hand, a final expulsion with ignominy would break his heart, don't you think?' The Count's hand is now grabbing his private parts, squeezing them, toying with the more delicate ones. Felix is winching and breathing heavily.

144

'Count, please. Someone might come in.'

'You are right, young fellow. Perhaps we need a more private venue for such a transaction.'

He withdraws his hand. Felix has to think fast but the shock is preventing him from doing so. All he knows is that his father would be deeply hurt by his expulsion. He exhales and sighs in resignation. He has to ask though he fears the answer.

'Would it be a single transaction or...instalments?'

'Here. Now. Today. And no more.'

'Here? But...'

'I have a private room. As you have. Number three. I'll be waiting.'

He knows about his private room. Has he been stalking him? Does it matter now?

He pats Felix's tummy twice and leaves.

He's not sure whether drops of steam or tears cover his face. He feels numb but he has no time to think it over: the Count might conclude that he has decided to decline the offer and leave with his expulsion in his pocket. He can't let his father down, he has already done it so many times.

He has had liaisons with much older men before, Felix's taste for adventure always thirsty for new emotions; but they were handsome and charming. And clean. The Count is beyond the realm of the repulsive. He lets his face drop in his hands. He tries to think what the Count's intentions could be and recoils in horror. Will he just want to savour his body or expect some active action on his repugnant one? Will he expect to kiss? He feels sick but he has no choice. There is no escape.

He leaves the room, dons his gown and walks slowly in the direction of room number three. The corridors are dimly lit. He consoles himself with the single nature of the transaction: *I'll get through this as fast as he allows me to and it'll be over.*

He opens the door of the room. It's dark, only a tiny table lamp on. Von Stolberg is standing in the middle, arms folded; he hasn't showered but then neither has Felix, the smell of the steam might shield him from the other rotten odours.

No instructions are forthcoming so Felix leans against one of the walls and waits for his fate. The Count approaches and with sharp movements snatches his robe and throws it in a corner, Felix is trembling.

His fears of having to run a kissing gauntlet were unfounded. For the Count this is a Prussian soldiers' covenant. A men's game. An acceptable form of camaraderie. All this nonsensical insanity articulated in his mind over years of guilt-ridden and quasi-suicidal angst. This has to remain virile to be justifiable in his tortured soul.

But the relief is brief, the mercy even briefer.

He bites his neck hard. Felix is about to scream but the Count slaps the palm of his hand on his mouth with a stern intimation: 'Quiet, boy!'

Felix's breath is noisy, his eyes wide in terror. The Count stoops and tries to bite Felix's nipples. They are pale and transparent, tiny, flushed. Walther and Florian had always and only kissed them gently, stroked them with tenderness.

His hands close in fists of pain as the Count's hands are now everywhere: squeezing his buttocks, grabbing his genitals with ferocity.

He tries to plead.

'Count, please.'

It enrages Von Stolberg. This is not a man and woman affair. This requires violence.

The backhand hitting his cheek is of such strength it almost knocks him unconscious. He hits his head on the wooden wall and falls on the floor. Von Stolberg approaches and from his standing position, grabs Felix's hair with his right hand. Once he has nailed his head to the wall, he forces himself through. All the way. Savage, furious blows. Felix tries to push the Count's hairy thighs back as he believes he's going to be sick any minute now. But it's no use: the grunts are porcine, the sound almost subhuman. He's fearful the Count will spend himself. It lasts an eternity or at least what he thinks is an eternity.

He withdraws, Felix coughs violently and about to beg for mercy once more but there is no letup. Grabbed by his skinny arms, he's thrown onto the massage bed, his face violently smacking the leather mattress. Von Stolberg grabs a pillow and positions it under his face which is then smashed into it with renewed force.

Felix is now besides himself with fear. He begs again.

'I've never...'

And no, he has never. With Walther, Florian, Werner, Franz's boys and even with older gentlemen, Felix is the man.

But not today.

The plea is a fatal mistake. Purity and virginity, either of the female or male variety, hold the diabolical power to bring men like Von Stolberg to unhinged levels of arousal.

The Count's eyes are bloodshot, his nose snorting like a raging Minotaur, his manhood ready.

But not yet. Cruelty is the game.

The slaps are of herculean fury and he's almost thrown off the bed by them. Von Stolberg grabs a branch of birchwood, more commonly used by the Russian masseurs to gently stimulate the circulation of their clients, and whacks it on his buttocks with a loud snap.

Felix buries his face into the pillow. He can't scream, people will come. He knows he's bleeding, his inner thighs feel wet. His tears are wetting the pillow, his face red, disfigured by pain. A brief letup ensues, but only for his legs to be hit by Von Stolberg's feet kicking the insides of his ankles to pull them apart. He feels the drops of the massage oil dripping into the crevice. His face lifts off the pillow for a split second:

'No...'

The Count's hand pushes his head back down. The first thrust quarters him with such savage vehemence, the bed knocks the wall in front of it with a loud thump. All he can do is to punch the wall to fight the unendurable pain; he releases a stream of white foam from the corners of his mouth.

He's about to faint and he would prefer to. An avenging spirit is keeping him conscious during his ravishing.

After an interminable few minutes the Count withdraws, moves beside Felix's face, sharply turns it with his hands and forces himself in again.

Then he repositions himself behind him for a final assault which no longer meets futile resistance, Felix's body now no more than a disjointed, discarded puppet. When he is indeed close to either fainting or expiring, a subhuman grunt flies above his head: the sound of a speared boar. The Count's teeth stab the tender flesh of his neck. Von Stolberg is inside him forever.

He withdraws and looks at Felix's lifeless body in contempt as he no longer feels any urge to touch him, he actually disgusts him now.

He wipes himself with a white towel and throws it in the paper basket at the head of the bed. Felix is conscious enough to see the blood marks.

Von Stolberg hurriedly dresses himself while Felix lies frozen on the bed, his arms and legs dangling, red streaks running along them.

'Shower here. There is a cubicle. Don't go to the communal ones.'

Before turning he kicks Felix's calf with his boot and spits on his ravaged body.

A few minutes go by before he can barely stir. With nervous caution he tries to lift himself from the table but his battered legs are unable to support him and he disorderly tumbles on the floor, crouching down in a foetal position in the corner: he can't feel the lower part of his body. Sobs pour out, uncontrolled, his head buried in his arms.

Another few minutes and he tries to wipe some of the mess off his face: tears, blood, saliva, foam.

He only has one thought and not for himself: no-one must ever know, Jurgen would murder Von Stolberg with his bare hands.

He must find the strength to reach the shower cubicle

but his legs give way again so he crawls along and almost throws himself in it. By gathering all his strength he manages to stand up and open the tap. The water is cold and he fumbles with the lever to adjust it. He senses the dirt draining away from his body but when he looks down he's horrified by the pool of red water streaming into the hole: it doesn't seem to stop.

He will not leave until the water turns clear and he's afraid of touching the wounds so he can only hope the bleeding will cease.

Eventually the water turns clear and after a tentative soap up and a rinse he leaves the cubicle. He dries himself; his sight is hazed by the pain but he is able to witness the aftermaths of the carnage on the floor and feels sick again.

Once he's more or less sure that he's somehow presentable, he dons his bathrobe and carefully opens the door, cautiously peering in the corridor. It's still empty and he reaches his room without awkward encounters.

He's not sure whether to shower again or not but he wants to leave this place as soon as he can. He dresses and positions his hat low on his brow; with his hands bandaged by two flannels and covered by his gloves, he walks through the reception area with his head down.

It'll be difficult to avoid Jurgen noticing anything but he tries: he hides his face by pretending to hold onto his hat with his hand, then he just whispers to him while climbing into the carriage.

'Just drive.'

Jurgen becomes immediately suspicious and takes a detour through the Tiergarten, knowing something is wrong.

Felix leans against the side of the carriage as tears run down his cheeks; besides the indescribable pain, he struggles to comprehend the wanton savagery, the frenzied violence. He accepted his blackmail; he went of his own volition to the room and was prepared to subject himself to his lust. Then why? He's at a loss but a more urgent issue is arising: he's not feeling as well as he thought he was.

The lower side of his body is still numb and he's hot in the face; he's afraid of fainting and worried that once home he might not be able to climb the stairs and lock himself in his apartments.

He knocks with his stick on the carriage's roof. Jurgen stops and lowers his head by the side. Felix leans out, trying to cover his face with his hand.

'Doctor Falckenberg.'

Jurgen drives to Doctor Falckenberg's surgery as fast as he can, now more than convinced that something has happened.

The young receptionist knows him well and immediately understands that something is very wrong.

She storms into the consulting room and she's quickly back, holding an elderly lady by her arm while explaining that there is an emergency and she'll be seen as soon as it's resolved. She then takes Felix inside and leaves.

'Felix!'

'Doctor Falckenberg...'

* * *

Doctor Falckenberg is a thin and tall man of sixty with gold-rimmed spectacles and grey hair parted on one side.

He has been the Kimmich family's doctor since his graduation, actually delivering Felix. That was inevitably followed by a regular and constant attention to bloodied knees, cuts and bruises, childhood ailments and the recent boxing craze.

After the fateful discovery in the stables, Herr Kimmich had consulted him in strict privacy about what he considered a disability, albeit one he was somehow prepared to accept for his son's sake. Doctor Falckenberg had responded calmly to the news.

'Herr Kimmich, as a matter of fact, there is a new school of thought in Vienna which has come up with some interesting new theories about Felix's condition. They don't seem to accept that as an illness. I have studied their findings with the utmost interest and I say I am minded to agree.'

'My son is not ill?'

'They are still researching the matter and I'm confident they will soon reach some new and even more interesting conclusions. But I tend to concur with the idea that your son might not be responsible for his preferences. By that I mean that he is unable to fight them.'

'Felix is not a pervert?'

'I live in hope that physicians will no longer utter that word one day, Herr Kimmich.'

Doctor Falckenberg was no psychoanalyst but had referred young Felix to a colleague of his who also happened to be a staunch Freudian. He had helped him to come to terms with at least some of the aspects of his sexuality and he remained deeply grateful to Doctor Falckenberg who, needless to say, was a wall of discretion.

When he had started to realise that Felix was expanding

his horizons beyond his loyal brother-in-arms, he had demanded his attendance to his surgery every month for a full check-up, on each occasion taking the opportunity to warn the young man about potential medical consequences of excessive sexual activity.

* * *

He opens his eyes. The last thing he remembers is Doctor Falckenberg's worried face and the world going dark. He's lying on the consulting bed, covered with a clean white sheet, a small pillow under his head; he understands that he has no clothes on. The lights of the consulting room have been switched off though there is a ray of afternoon sun slashing the wall beside his bed.

He hears the water running. Doctor Falckeberg now stands at his side, drying his hands with a white towel.

'Felix.'

He stares at his doctor in shame, but he's met by a comforting, non-judgemental half-smile.

'Doctor Falckenberg.'

'How do you feel, young man?'

A pause, he's not quite sure.

'I don't know.'

'Understandable; I have sub-ministered you a mild seda-tive. If you're wondering what happened, you collapsed in my arms upon entering the room. You've been out for almost an hour now.'

'One hour?'

'Calm down, Hilde has brought some coffee to Jurgen and we have explained that you have contracted a rather nasty infection which has had a severe and immediate effect on your body.'

'You have.'

'Yes, I've spoken to him personally. I'm confident you have no intention for the true version of events to be made public?'

Felix closes his eyes, a small tear appears in one of them.

'Good. Now, young man, I need to perform a couple of tests on your legs to check that you are able to walk.'

Doctor Falckenberg lifts the sheet and grabs Felix's calves and feet, moving them up and forward in gentle motion. His hands are soft and smooth and produce a soothing sensation on his fragile nerves.

'Any pain?' A negative nod. 'Good. Now, Felix, I have medicated all your wounds. Some are serious but thankfully they don't need hospitalisation as that would require an explanation and I'd rather avoid that endeavour. I do need to ask you this though: was this a non-consensual accident or a new development in your psyche which you have decided to act on? You know you can be honest with me, I'm your doctor.'

'An accident.'

'I'm relieved. I hope I'll not see you here in these conditions again.' Another negative nod. 'Felix, the person who did this to you. Is he known to you? I mean, personally.'

'Yes.'

'And are you likely to have to meet him again?'

'Hopefully not.'

'This is a painful question but I need to know. His...fluid?'

The tears are streaming now; Doctor Falckenberg takes

off his spectacles and lowers his head with a sigh, pinching the bridge of his nose in resignation.

'I see. I'll have to keep checking for symptoms of potential infections ten days from now and then at regular intervals.' Felix nods. 'I'll leave you to rest for a while, then you'll get dressed and I'll take you home. I'll make sure that Frau Charlotte and Walther don't see any of the wounds and I'll return tomorrow to check up on you. Hilde has gone out to buy some new undergarments for you. You will wear my gloves.'

'Thank you, Doctor Falckenberg.'

'Felix, you ought to be aware that while your body will heal in a reasonable time, your mind will take longer and perhaps never will. Your dreams will change. Starting tonight.'

He nods but he is drifting off.

Doctor Falckenberg is held in high regard by the Kimmichs and his plan works. Over the following week he visits Felix every day and he's pleased with the improvements. Charlotte, Walther and the whole household follow his cleverly crafted instructions to the letter, the cleverest of them all being that Felix's infection might still be contagious. Jurgen is not entirely convinced but he fully trusts Doctor Falckenberg too.

As he predicted though, from the very first night the dreams have darkened and have turned surreal, frightening, convulsive.

He reports that he wakes up screaming in a pool of sweat and when he relays to him some of the contents of the nightmares, Doctor Falckenberg becomes concerned. He notices that while Felix's body heals, a dark shade circles his eyes, his stare is hollow and sometimes worryingly absent. He has studied the consequences of such actions and he's not too hopeful that they will disappear soon.

After a week or so, Edda, who is becoming increasingly more assertive with her family, volunteers to clear up the dinner of soup and bread which has been served to Felix in his room. Whilst politely listening to Wenzel's attempts to decline the offer, she quietly insists that it will be her pleasure to see him and that Doctor Falckenberg has now relaxed some of the restrictions. Walther and Charlotte agree: it will be good for Felix to briefly see Edda whom he loves and esteems a great deal.

Although a young lady of only twenty-five, Fräulein Kahler is in possession of a more mature and serious deportment than everyone else at Villa Augusta: Charlotte's stronger side.

She carefully opens the door and tiptoes to his bed. He has fallen asleep on his back and she quietly moves the dinner trolley table to one side. She approaches him and gently unbuttons the jacket of his pyjamas; he doesn't stir. She notices his eyes surrounded by the dark shades and the pillow drenched in sweat. Taking care to avoid touching him, she leans over his neck and moves her silent gaze down on his chest and ribs. She buttons his jacket up again and sits on the chair at the side of the bed absently reading a book previously dropped by Felix on the floor.

About fifteen minutes later he wakes up and sees her by his side.

'Edda, what a pleasure.'

'My dear Felix, how have you been feeling today?'

'Slightly better. Doctor Falckenberg sees it as a long recovery.'

'Doctor Falckenberg is arguably the best physician in Berlin, if not in the whole of Brandenburg. Some water?'

She takes a glass of water to his lips and while he drinks, she notices a small patch on the left-hand side of his head where hair is missing. She also observes his hands whose healing is not yet completed. He tries to hide them under the sheets.

He drinks avidly, like a child after a strenuous street game. A restful silence follows after he slumps back with an exhausted sigh.

'This infection has really flattened me. How is everyone holding up?'

'Naturally we are all worried for you, but Walther is on top of everything. He can't wait to see you up and running again. He misses you terribly; although, you know, he'd never admit to that.'

'Walther...'

She discerns the sudden veil of gloom over his eyes; she pauses then lowers her head, staring at the now closed book.

'Felix, I know what has happened to you.'

His eyes are fixed on her now. He has no intention of deceiving her.

'You have nothing to worry about. I understand why you don't want to divulge such a thing. It is the most terrible thing. No one will know.'

He knows that he can trust her. She leaves the chair, sits on the side of the bed and takes his lifeless hand in hers.

'When I was sixteen my family took all of us children to visit our auntie and uncle in Kiel. A carefree and playful few days: big lunches in the garden, sailing, visits to the funfair.'

She briefly gazes at the window.

'On the third day the whole of the family went into town for some shopping but I wasn't feeling too well so I remained at home. My uncle claimed to find shopping too frivolous and he stayed behind to look after me as they didn't have any servants. They weren't rich people.'

She looks intensely in his eyes, they are welling up. She gently squeezes his hand. 'I fear the violence of your ordeal to be much worse than mine, but my tender age and the mere fact that he was a relative made it unbearable. I was more or less in your same condition for days and notably I disguised it in similar fashion: an infection.

Like you, I didn't want anyone to know. To what end anyway? The scandal would have been horrific. Would they have even believed me? He was a respected member of the community after all and I was just a girl. Girls have fantasies.

I spent days in agony. I know you wake up at night screaming, I know you meet him in your dreams at night. I know because so did I.'

She lowers her head, staring at the floor.

'I spent weeks in fear, waiting to know if I was with child, thinking of what I would say or do. I was comforted by the knowledge that they were childless therefore he might have not been fertile. I had a lucky escape. If you can call it that.'

His head is turned on the side now staring aimlessly ahead.

'There are no words which can comfort you, that much I know. But you have a family downstairs, your parents. And Walther. They desperately need you.'

'And you.'

She smiles.

'I believe that your generosity is greater than any pain that this man has inflicted on you. Mine was. You can't cry in their arms. Do it in mine.'

Fräulein Kahler is right. The household has plunged into a slow-motion despondency, missing his infectious energy and shameless banter. Tobias and his young son miss the days when he would join them in tending the garden and sit down for a chat and a coffee over their break.

They are all greatly worried for his health and Edda also suspects that, secretly, everyone nurtures some vague suspicions on the nature of the illness though they are mercifully never close to the true source of it.

She cleverly uses the trust they place in her to interpose bogus knowledge about infectious diseases when in conversation with Charlotte, Walther and the servants, taking advantage of their total incomprehension of medical matters. In the end all they want is their master to heal and recover.

In the meantime Jurgen is summoned by the clerk of the Prussian Cavalry Club; upon being presented with the seal for his carriage, he snatches it from the terrified valet's hands and walks away in quiet fury. He somehow perceives the existence of a connection between his master's illness and his reinstatement at the Club but cannot arrive at a meaningful conclusion.

Count Von Stolberg is a sadistic rapist but one of his word: Herr Kimmich the younger is indeed reinstated with full honours after a short investigation which finds the charges bogus.

Von Mutthe is incandescent with rage but unable to override Von Stolberg and resigns himself to the possibility of having to acknowledge 'that insolent brat' in the corridors of the club; something which, unbeknown to him, will never happen as Felix has no intention of ever gracing its steps as long as he lives.

At least his father is beside himself with joy while Doctor Falckenberg reassures him on his son's recovery.

Wenzel quietly opens the door and wheels the trolley inside; for his convalescence they have been instructed not to knock as he might be resting. He catches him at the window, in his night gown, motionless, taking in the dusk.

He turns around. He hasn't shaved for days but his skin is still of the youthful type and there is hardly any shade; his moustaches though have been trimmed in perfect shape by the very same Wenzel. He approaches the trolley with his hands behind his back.

'Wenzel, I know all too well Doctor Falckenberg's instructions but I think I have by now tasted every possible variety of vegetables harvested on the fields of Brandenburg.' The butler's eyes widen in hopeful expectation. 'What are you serving downstairs?'

A plucky happy smile appears on Wenzel's lips.

'Sauerbraten with Kartoffelsalat, sir. And…Pinot?'

He inserts his finger between the buttons of Wenzel's waistcoat, pulls him closer and whispers in his ear.

'I don't suppose you can sneak some of that up, can you? No need to tell Doctor Falckenberg, of course.'

He bursts into the kitchen in a frenzy, unable to contain his happiness.

'He's up! He's up! He wants some proper dinner! Master Felix is well again! Quick! Quick!'

A rush of excitement sweeps the hall. The cook sets aside the best veal and Kartoffelsalat, Maria sits at the table with her hands together, thanking the Lord in Polish or whatever dialect she might speak (no one is quite sure still); Wenzel intimates secrecy whilst pouring the Pinot in a small carafe: no one ought to say anything to Charlotte, Walther or Edda yet.

When the three of them enter the dining room for breakfast, the first thing they notice is four places set up at the table and Jonas, the under-butler, standing by it with a happy grin over his young face.

They only have the time to briefly look at each other as Wenzel bursts the double door open and Felix, bathed, shaved and resplendent in his best morning suit, walks in.

'Well, good morning everyone. Why are you standing there like stones? I am positively ravenous. Now, Walther, we have a long day ahead: I must catch up with all the affairs of the estate. Charlotte, Edda, you look radiant this morning.'

One by one they take his hands in theirs and relay their

joy at having him back; Walther's eyes glisten with relief. When it's Edda's turn they hold their hands together a moment longer, their gaze fixed on each other until he leans by her ear.

'Thank you.'

Baroness Von Mutthe is increasingly exasperated at having to alight from her carriage at the servants' entrance of Villa Augusta for her afternoon teas which now occasionally involve Felix and Walther.

After all, Herr Kimmich has now been reinstated at the Cavalry Club which also counts her brother among its members: Wilhelm Von Klausen, the Margrave of Brandenburg.

Von Klausen happens to be a highly respected Feldmarschall and firmly in the Emperor's inner circle of loyal aides. When his father had consulted him for an opinion on pairing young and fragrant Sophie with the Baron, he had made his distaste crystal clear: 'I'd rather Sophie married a stable boy.'

Von Mutthe is about to leave the club. He has been handed his hat and coat but when he turns around he almost bumps into the chest of a much taller gentleman also in coat and hat.

'Von Mutthe!'

'Margrave.'

He's aghast; Von Klausen not only never addresses him at the club but he makes a point of walking by without even a tiny nod to greet him.

'Perhaps you would like to join me for a quick brandy?'

The Baron nods. Once at the bar the Margrave orders for him. The barman, a cadet on club duties, places the glasses on the bar and bows. When the Baron's hand moves to grab one of them, it is smacked down and glued to the wooden surface with a sharp blow by Von Klausen's stick, its ivory head almost knocking one of the glasses off. The young cadet is in state of shock, Von Mutthe frozen.

'Baron. I would like you to appreciate that I do take exception to gentlemen behaving beastly with the ladies, more so if they happen to be their consorts. Or, worse, my sisters.'

Von Klausen is a man of power: the Baron knows it, the cadet knows it. He's not anticipating a reply, Von Mutthe knows better than volunteering one. The Margrave's eyes narrow as he leans across; he's a strong man, the stick is holding down the Baron's hand with determined force.

'His Majesty would be most displeased to learn of such behaviour, you can rest assured of that.'

The Baron is seething, Von Klausen hasn't let the cadet go and the young man can only leave when dismissed. He's being ruthlessly humiliated in front of a hapless private.

'I trust I will have no more cause to endure your company again?'

He nods in fuming resignation and the stick lifts, leaving a red mark across his wrinkly hand.

'Enjoy the brandy.' And he finally turns to the stunned cadet before leaving. 'Dismissed.'

Master Felix recovers well. When he's almost sure that his nights are not besieged by nightmares and sudden screams, he gently leads Walther back to his room with the excuse of a game of chess.

He has stopped his escapades to Franz's, preferring the companionship of his private secretary, whose care and affection have been considerably heightened by the unexpected vulnerability of his brother-in-arms, displacing the sexual side of their relationship in the process.

This hasn't displeased Felix who sorely needs a period of reflection away from carnal activity; when they are back at it, Walther notices a hesitation when he touches him for the first time. He's taken aback by what it seems to be a worried fear, an emotion which he'd never thought would have emerged in his characteristically audacious companion.

On some nights he wakes up sweating and screaming and Walther has to hold his head on his chest to calm him down. He apologises and reassures him, though he remains tense and agitated until morning.

Time is healing him though: there are moments of sad stillness in which he stands by the window or sits for a few minutes on a bench in the garden; but the bashful banter is gradually returning with the effect of re-energising life at Villa Augusta.

One should know better than to enrage Margrave Von Klausen: the Baroness' carriage now solemnly comes to a halt in front of the imposing steps of the villa. Some of their neighbours have now seen her a few times joining the Kimmichs for tea and for the first time she is invited for lunch.

Wenzel and the rest of the servants enter a phase of panic

overdrive: the Kimmichs are indeed wealthy but bereft of any title; they are members of a landed gentry not exactly renowned for a sophisticated lifestyle. More often than not the city's nobility passingly describes their milieu as 'trade' or, worse, 'wealthy peasantry'.

Felix is no different: perhaps because of his nature, his wardrobe, lifestyle and manners are a sizeable notch above his peers but he remains a country lad at heart. At times he misses the military school years where the banter and play were rough but honourable. Or the boxing sessions at the working men's club. He's fond of remarking to Walther that he was 'bloody good' at it.

The day before Baroness Von Mutthe is due for lunch, he is at his wits' end with Wenzel and the rest of the staff; he descends the staircase to the kitchen hall at lunch time after a small snack hurriedly consumed in the study. They all rise when he enters.

'Well, dear fellows, I demand this senseless panic to cease at once. Wenzel, the crockery, silverware and glassware are absolutely fine. No, we don't need new ones.' He turns to the cook. 'The Baroness is a light eater, a small herring salad perhaps, very little meat. We all like your cooking, why shouldn't she?'

The cook comes forward while drying his hands in his apron.

'But, sir, she dines at court.'

'This is not the court, I'm not the Kaiser and she will eat what you prepare.' The cook bows. 'I think it will be a sunny day. We will have lunch in the garden. Tobias, some nice flowers on the table, please. Elegant but informal. All of you, stop worrying, she's a socialist anyway!'

Among the dropped jaws, Jonas, a lad of almost sixteen, turns wide-eyed in shock to Wenzel at his side.

'The Baroness is a socialist?'

For that he receives a good clip to his ear and is told to go back to his lunch while Felix walks up the stairs with a satisfied grin on his lips.

Jonas has been sort of adopted by the family. When Felix mentioned to his father that he wanted to recruit an under-butler, Herr Kimmich replied that he had just the man. An orphan, hard-working and respectful, though not the sharpest tool in Tobias' garden shed. Once he had settled down, Felix had remarked to Walther that 'perhaps it will be highly beneficial for young Jonas to be sheltered here rather than to face the world on his own.'

And he's happy at Villa Augusta, though not that happy when Felix, now back to form for an entertaining prank, mendaciously informs him that the Baroness has specifically requested his services at the table, ushering in a sleepless night for the hapless lad.

Tobias's display is rather successful; he has by now mastered some remarkable gardening skills and, beyond his wildest expectations, he receives a brief compliment from the Baroness for his 'delightful flowerbeds'.

A sunny day of spring, the sky terse, the breeze warm. Felix sits at the head of the table, the Baroness at his side.

Jonas' hand shakes so much while pouring the wine for the noblewoman that a fairly good quantity spills on the glass table, mercifully bereft of a white cloth; she turns to Felix with an amused smile while Jonas retreats, nervously drying his forehead with a crumpled handkerchief.

To everyone's relief she greatly enjoys the food and, above all, the company. Before rising for coffee in the drawing room, she addresses Felix and Charlotte.

'Kaiser-Friedrich Platz is very charming. Are you well acquainted with the neighbouring households?'

They exchange a perplexed glance. Edda and Walther lower their heads. Charlotte receives a nod of assent from her husband.

'Only on superficial terms, Sophie, many families would rather not have any dealings with us.'

'You mean you do not receive invitations?'

'We don't resent it.'

'I see. Felix, my dear boy, I believe your family to be of long-standing and solid Lutheran faith?' Felix nods. 'And I trust you and the servants attend service on Sundays?'

'We do. Except for Maria, of course. She's a Catholic. I think.'

'And where, if I may enquire?'

'St. Clemens, not far from here.'

'I am familiar with Pastor Brestrich: his sermons are often noticeably critical of the unfortunate predilection for war currently sweeping the nation. I never fail to make a point of reporting them to His Majesty as it riles him no end. Of course His Majesty takes immense pleasure in being riled by me. Very well, time for coffee, I believe.'

On her way to the drawing room the Baroness briefly pauses by Jonas, standing in military attention, his face crimson. She gently taps his shoulder with her fan.

'Thank you, young man. Most excellent service.'

He receives a gentle kick in the ankle by Wenzel as the mere fact of being addressed has made him forget to bow. When he finally manages a clumsy one, she lightly nods in approval; a little pride will lodge with him for a long time.

The following Sunday most of the congregation is assembled on the small opening in front of St. Clemens, thirty to forty minutes before the start of the service; another fresh, luminous day of the Brandenburg spring.

Two carriages arrive in convoy and come to a brusque halt at the end of the path which leads to the church's steps. As one of the main activities of the faithful flock is chiefly to ascertain who does and, most importantly, who does not attend church, necks and eyes turn in earnest.

Jurgen opens the door of the first carriage and bows when Charlotte and Walther alight, causing a few wondering glances. Instead of walking up the path, they stand in dignified pose, waiting for the appearance of the occupants of the second carriage.

In one of his most elegant morning suits, Felix alights first and offers his hand to the Baroness, clad in one of her most exquisite couture. The white silk of her dress, her feathered hat and the three lines of pearls around her neck dazzle in the morning sunshine. Charlotte and Walther bow and follow behind on a slow stroll to the entrance, leaving a few jaws stuck open along the way.

At the end of the service Pastor Brestrich is the first to approach the Baroness.

'Your Excellency, I am most honoured.'

'I was very impressed by your sermon, Father. I will relay the most interesting passages to His Majesty at the earliest opportunity.' A veil of worry appears on the Pastor's face. 'You are in no need to concern yourself: His Majesty's opinions on the future of the empire tend to fluctuate one day to the next. I will make sure I choose the right one.'

Quite a few members of the congregation are fellow residents of the Kaiser-Friedrich Platz area and the Baroness' closeness to the Kaiser is well known; the news spread like a deadly disease.

The high court judge who resides with his family in the same neighbourhood and had, until now, repeatedly advised his wife to 'keep a salutary distance from the Kimmichs' slams his stick on the hallway's table upon reaching home, startling the terrified servants.

'Baroness Von Mutthe in church with the Kimmichs! These scurrilous rumours about Herr Felix must be false! Of course they are! Why did you listen to them? It's obvious: all slander! Why have you never sent an invitation? Are we to ignore a young couple who as far as we know might have already been received at court? We cannot possibly be so discourteous. Woman, send a servant at once!'

His wife can barely proffer a word.

'But you always said...'

'No matter what I said! At once!'

A few weeks have gone by. They decide to stroll back in the late evening warmth, after the umpteenth invitation to dinner has been honoured. They are both silent, arm in arm.

'Talk about results exceeding expectations.'

She smiles at his complaint.

'I suspect you'd rather go back to being an outcast.'

His eyes sadden.

'We can't bring Walther and Edda along.'

'No, we cannot do that.'

He stops to pick a gardenia, turns and offers it to Charlotte.

'These people are no fun.'

She nods. The season is upon them.

The woods of Baden

The journey has been comfortable enough but they are now exhausted by its length. Felix had booked the best part of a first-class carriage as he had in the end decided to bring everyone along, with the exception of Tobias and his assistant as Villa Hildegard comes with gardeners and stable boys included. Most residences for the season are offered with the services of local staff, but Felix's motives were of more generous nature, as he pointed out to Walther: 'At least they'll have one day a week to enjoy Baden: parks, swimming, funfairs.'

The journey from Berlin to Karlsruhe took the whole night, followed by an early afternoon departure. The changing of trains was indeed cumbersome due to the vast amount of trunks and hat boxes, but Jonas, Wenzel and Jurgen were of great help to the porters.

Fräulein Kahler hasn't been able to join them. The epic war of attrition with her family rages on and this obviously saddens everyone a great deal.

Villa Hildegard and Villa Augusta are approximately of the same size, making the task of allocating rooms and boudoirs rather uncomplicated, upstairs and downstairs. There are some fine horses in the stables and the owners proudly parade them to Felix and Walther while enquiring on their riding skills.

They decide to reconvene for tea as they all need a good early afternoon rest; the weather is superb and they are now perched on some fine cushions complementing an elegant set of white iron garden furniture. A vine-entangled pergola, white afternoon outfits and straw hats shelter them from the blazing rays.

Without being announced, a young man of more or less the same age of Felix bursts into the garden: tall and with a wavy set of blond hair, though quite brusque and not immediately handsome. He's still wearing a morning suit with the cravat untied as the heat has started to rise.

'Felix! Charlotte!'

They all greet each other and then Felix introduces Walther who hopes the young visitor will not remember him as the former butler.

'Walther, Reinhardt, my brother-in-law.'

'My pleasure.'

Plans for the season are now in full flow: tennis games, horse rides, swimming at the Kurpark, balls and soirées at the best summer residences with the cream of the Empire. Walther fidgets nervously at every proposed arrangement.

'Father wanted you over tonight but Mother has forbidden it. She sends her love and she's in such a fret to see you and Charlotte, but she has insisted you rest after the journey; we were exhausted when we arrived last week. Tomorrow night though is white tie and high uniform for us, sir.'

When his time at military school had come to an end, Felix had left with a great deal of regret: he had risen in rank and had quickly become one of the most promising officers, on his way to the rank of Feldmarschall. Once a year he is recalled for a month of training: something he always looks forward to. As a consequence he is entitled to keep the high uniform and encouraged to wear it at formal events.

'Game of tennis tomorrow morning though, you can make that for sure?'

Felix nods. Reinhardt's gregariousness is of the thundering variety, one which doesn't broker an easy refusal. He appears not to have recognised Walther or if he has, he discreetly keeps it for himself. He slaps his shoulder.

'Walther! Do you play?'

'Me?...I...'

'Of course he does. Not a bad shot either!'

Felix is highly amused at Walther's murderous look.

'Perfect. Julius is up for it so it's a double.'

The four young men are strolling toward the court, racquets in their hands, white jumpers on their shoulders. The breeze is cool and ideal for a good game, though beads of sweat are already running along Walther's forehead. When they reach the court, Julius, Reinhardt's younger brother, casually turns to Felix.

'You gentlemen want to stay a team?'

'Let's make it more interesting,' prompts Felix, 'Reinhardt, would you like to team up with Walther?'

Walther's lips tighten in a thunderous grin.

'If Walther wishes me as partner.'

'What?...Yes...of course.'

But Reinhardt is a good player and, to Walther's astonishment, they win: he has given it all and he's elated when Reinhardt shakes his hand in congratulation.

They are almost ready for dinner at the Dessauers'. He's in his room, the double row of gold buttons on his deep blue jacket shining under the chandelier's light, the white trousers with a red stripe on the side perfectly ironed, his neck hidden by a flaming red mandarin collar. He's standing at the window, a cigarette in his hands, reflecting on a placid, silent dusk. He has treated himself to a long and restful visit to the barber: his hair is parted with fastidious precision, his moustaches golden and fluffy.

After a quick knock Walther comes in; although he has seen his brother-in-arms in high uniform before, he feels a knot in his throat when Felix turns away from his moment of contemplation.

'And there I was, thinking you couldn't get any more handsome.'

'You should be ashamed of your sycophantic flattery.'

He's fiddling with his white tie.

'Can't get the tie straight.'

'Come here.'

He stubs his cigarette out in the ashtray on the mantelpiece and grabs Walther's arm, gently leading him in front of the mirror. He's standing in front of it now, in tails and white tie, his brown hair parted in the middle, his round brown eyes nervously seeking refuge in his companion's glistening emeralds. And he's behind, his arms encircling his shoulders while trying to straighten the tie, his moustaches tickling his neck.

Their pupils meet on the mirror's surface, unblinking and covetous. Felix winks.

'You're spending the night here, Brother.'

The terrace at the villa is lit by the long shade of the chandeliers' brightness filtering through the French doors. The Dessauers are a wealthy merchant family partial to largesse when it comes to entertaining their guests: their soirées are sumptuous and protracted affairs.

Walther's worries quickly disappear once introduced to Herr Dessauer: whether or not he has recognised him as the former butler, the old man snatches him away with a hand under his arm at cocktail time.

'Felix, I'm going to steal your administrator for a good talk if it doesn't offend you. Now, young man, old Kimmich is reporting to me than some of your innovations in his estate's administration...' While concentrating on the incoming fire of business questions, he catches a conspiratorial wink in Felix's eye.

As predicted, Charlotte's barely teenage sisters incessantly fuss over her compliant husband, subjecting him to a barrage of invitations for youthful pursuits. And so do her mother and brother, who is greatly excited at introducing his fiancée to his military school comrade.

At around eleven they escape back to the terrace, in dire need of fresh air and a cigarette. The white tie has been choking Walther all night but he receives a stern warning when he's about to dismantle the intricate knot.

'Don't! We'll have to go back inside.'

They stare ahead. They can still discern the contour of the oaks at the end of the extensive lawn. From the moment they arrived there has been something Walther has been wanting to ask.

'Do you think they know?'

Felix exhales a long puff of smoke.

'Reinhardt. But he's a gentleman and a man of honour. Everyone else..., maybe. They are no fools.' He shrugs. 'We have been inseparable ever since we were toddlers. People notice those kinds of things. Well, if they do, they maintain their discretion in the most admirable way. After all, Charlotte is happy.'

Walther throws his cigarette away and exhales the last puff of white smoke.

'Thank you for this morning.'

'I have no idea what you are talking about.'

'There is no way I could have won. Even with Reinhardt as partner.'

'That is the most ludicrous accusation ever thrown at me!'

Walther smiles and shakes his head. Felix throws away his cigarette and positions himself no more than two inches from his face, his moustaches almost touching his lips, their breath mixing.

'Let me get this into your head once and for all: I will never allow anyone or anything to do you harm. Is that clear?'

A nod, their eyes transfixed on each other.

'Now. My afternoon has been completely and utterly seized by Charlotte's sisters. If I don't attend their Badminton games and various picnics, they'll positively murder me. But I have to come up fast with some outlandish excuse to free myself tomorrow morning: I have secured two of the best horses in Baden. Much better than the ones in the stable. We're going for a ride, the two of us.'

'What? But I had planned to do some work tomorrow, your father...'

Felix turns. That mocking grin.

'How do you plan to escape from my room tomorrow morning?'

He shakes his head while trotting behind him. What's the use?

* * *

Reinhardt had been a contemporary of Felix at military school. Their families already well acquainted, they had quickly become comrades-in-arms and were soon known as the inseparable Dessauer and Kimmich pair.

Both excelled in all fields: fencing, artillery manoeuvres and leadership skills. Above all, they were highly regarded by both their fellow cadets and the training officers and it was encouraged to have a close companion: it fostered loyalty and comradeship.

Reinhardt was above any suspicions but, as usual, rumours never lived far away from Felix.

One day a group of six to seven fellow cadets had gathered around a table in the refectory during a break from exercises and manoeuvres. Reinhardt had arrived unnoticed, though in time to hear one of the cadets relaying some lurid reports he had been passed on: Felix had enthusiastically accepted the protection of senior officers. A whole group of senior officers.

In less than a split second the table had flown over the boy, nailing him to the wall, Reinhardt's sword firmly pointed at his neck, the tip of it snipping at his skin.

'You will withdraw your scurrilous accusations now or defend them at dawn.'

His fellow cadets terrified, blood dripping on his white vest, the hapless lad had apologised at once and without reservation; Reinhardt was the best fencer of the school and a duel to defend the honour of a comrade would have probably been permitted, albeit with senior officers - perhaps a whole group of them - at the ready to declare satisfaction before a deadly outcome.

Sword withdrawn, he had offered his hand in friendship, his standing among his fellow cadets now at a new high: men of integrity never humiliate their adversaries.

'Gentlemen. I trust that the matter is closed and will not be sent forth beyond these four walls.'

Bows of agreement but, of course, it spread like wildfire.

Felix learnt of the event from Johannes, a fellow cadet two years his junior. Ashen-faced, the boy had listened to the reporting of the friendly kermesse in worried silence, waiting for his name to come up next. It hadn't, but he knew that it was just a matter of time before it would.

The storage room in the Armoury was far away from the barracks; the ground of the academy was vast and strategically dotted with secluded and seemingly safe little havens. Over agreed rendezvous, Felix willingly entertained officers and cadets alike with his manly vigour while ethe-real Johannes repeatedly subjected himself to theirs.

The two of them were still retrieving their scattered uniforms. The senior officers had left first, one by one, discreetly.

He was already partial to shameless banter. Recklessly lighting up a cigarette while polishing his boot on a box of ammunition, he blurted out a tasteless insult.

'You ought to go easy, comrade, you might be with child by now.'

But Johannes wasn't laughing. He had stopped getting dressed and was sitting on a box, staring at the filthy floor, fighting back flashbacks of the officers' bodies around him. Taking turns. The pungent scent of their loins.

His nose had started to bleed. Relatively new to these gatherings, thus unaware of their unspoken rules, Johannes had tenderly met the lips of a handsome Lieutenant. An indignant backhand had restored the officer's wounded pride. Oddly enough, the very same officer had hardly objected to being repeatedly dishonoured by Felix's angry thrusts.

Young Kimmich immediately regretted his jibe and stooped down to attend to the boy's nose with his crumpled handkerchief, holding the back of his head with his hand.

'My apology, that was uncalled for. There is no shame in it. That is what you like, that's all. Don't try that kissing business again. It offends them.'

Felix sighed at the appearance of a tentative tear on Johannes' cheek.

'Give it a rest. That offends them even more. And you are

safe anyway, you are Von Richter's boy.'

Feldmarschall Von Richter's infatuation had, however, a dangerous side: letters.

Words expire the moment they are uttered. They can be retracted or denied in injured outrage. More often than not, they are forgotten at the end of every conversation. Letters are smoking guns.

It was Felix who found him. A week later. The ceiling pipe of the storage room would have probably collapsed under a grown man's weight, but Johannes was fifteen, lithe, and, save for a few lusting officers, invisible to everyone. His uniform was neatly folded on a box of ammunition, almost as if he had wanted it to explode with them.

Felix stood frozen for a few seconds before noticing a small notebook and a letter on the floor, signed by Von Richter. He picked it up and started to read it: previous correspondence had already fallen in the wrong hands.

Silly old fool, he thought.

He crumpled up the paper and threw it away in angry contempt. He then grabbed one of Johannes' dangling feet with one hand and kissed it. He managed with a great deal of effort to untangle the rope by climbing onto a big box, carefully sliding Johannes' body first on the floor, then in his arms. He held him for a while before alerting anyone, kissing his flaxen short hair, whispering in his ear, perhaps regretting his mocking.

'You're safe now, little one. You're safe.'

Von Richter vanished in the drizzly mist of the Brandenburg autumn, blown away by its falling leaves of propriety. Transferred perhaps. Possibly discharged. Retired. Jailed. Executed. No one knew.

No bulletin was ever pinned to any wall, no service ever held. Once Felix had returned to his dormitory, he had found Johannes' belongings gone, his name plate removed, his bed stripped and ready for a new recruit.

On a grey day of November he spotted a black carriage through the window of the dormitory. It was parked at the far corner of the esplanade; a wooden cart attached to a single horse stood behind it, the silhouette of a small coffin barely discernible in the morning fog.

Then he noticed a man and a woman in black clothing leaving the entrance of the officers' quarters and walking at a slow pace towards the carriage. Still in his vest and trousers, he donned his boots in haste and ran to meet them.

They turned and saw him standing there. The lady gracefully folded her black veil above her hat, her eyes watery, her gaze perplexed.

He lifted his arm, the notebook in his hand.

'Johannes left a diary, sir.'

The expression of revulsion stabbed him through the heart. The lady lowered her veil and hastily climbed into the carriage. Her husband followed her without acknowledging him.

Shaking in anger, he raised his voice.

'Your son left a diary. Sir!'

The gentleman's stick hit the frame of the carriage with a sharp knock and the small convoy started to move. He wiped his eyes and threw the diary against the back of the coach, shouting.

'Johannes left a diary...Sir!'

His voice then broke in knots, speaking only to himself, the carriage and the cart already through the gates.

'He left...a diary...sir.'

He heard the sound of steps on the gravel and saw Reinhardt walking by, on his way to calmly collect the diary. Then he felt his arm around his shoulders, gently turning him and leading him back to their dormitory.

An adolescent, perhaps remorseful audience followed their retreat, hidden behind the high arched windows of the barracks, the now lifting mist cruelly exposing his humiliation.

The following week Felix and Reinhardt attended Sunday's service at the academy's church: a humongous white and yellow building, matching the ever-present baroque features of the school.

At seventeen, they were now in the countertenors section of the choir, facing the older officers lined up in the bass-baritone side.

Felix spotted the Lieutenant who had hit Johannes, possibly shattering the boy's illusion that love and affection could remotely feature in the raw and frenzied couplings down at the storage room.

They exchanged cold and resentful glances during the sermon. Afterwards, Reinhardt noticed Felix's hands holding the score of *Ein deutsches Requiem* with reddening fists. His voice was in tune, yet louder than their fellow cadets and coloured by an incandescent rage at the top of the thundering crescendo of *Denn Fleisch, es ist wie Gras*.

He noticed the officer on the bench opposite. Staring at Felix. He then placed his hand on his friend's now trembling fist and he calmed down, the Lieutenant still taunting him.

Sunday afternoons were free. While strolling back to the barracks in the suffused light of a winter sun, Reinhardt proposed a trip into town. On these outings, a small crowd of flirting young ladies would quickly assemble around the two young men in high uniform, Reinhardt shame-lessly taking advantage of his friend's irresistible charm and beauty. Felix willingly lent himself to the ploy, the endgame never amounting to more than a furtive kissing session behind a wall in the park. Once the most beautiful of the young ladies (often already in love and enraptured by marriage fantasies) had disappeared with his friend, Reinhardt would have the rest of the field for himself. The pair would then amble back along the riverbank path in hysterical giggles.

'Kimmich!'

They froze. Reinhardt looked at his friend's face and saw his eyes shutting in anger. He turned around and stood to attention, clicking his heels.

'Not you, Dessauer. Kimmich?'

Felix was standing still. Reinhardt kicked his ankle and whispered between closed lips.

'Turn, you stubborn fool.'

He turned, his eyes stabbing through the officer's severe gaze.

'That took some time, Kimmich. One hour detention.'

'Yes, sir.'

'To be taken today, at three o'clock. In the Armoury.

Alone.'

'Yes, sir.'

'Dismissed.'

They started walking, Reinhardt shaking his head.

'Don't go.'

'You don't understand. He wants...he wants to be...he wants to expiate.'

'What for? What have you done to him? Why does he hate you?'

'He doesn't. He feels responsible. He can't admit it to himself, but he does.'

'Johannes?'

Felix nodded. Reinhardt sighed in exasperation.

'On my heart, at times I do find it impossible to understand your lot.'

'Don't try.'

When the officer pushed the squeaky door of the storage room, Felix was already there, perched on a box of ammunition, underpants and a vest his only garments, his bare right leg dangling. The Lieutenant undressed and knelt down, kissing Felix's foot, working his way up to the calf, any self-control swept away by a lacerating obsession. The sole of the foot hit his face and pushed him flat on the floor. Felix jumped off the box and pinned him down, their mouths now barely an inch from each other. The officer started to kiss him, unable to fight his infatuation. Felix let him savour the lips of Apollo before detaching himself.

'And what now? Another backhand? I see. No audience, no shame.'

He stood up, lit a cigarette and started to collect his

uniform and boots.

'Don't flatter yourself. He didn't do it because of your slap. He only wanted to kiss you. Big deal. Find another cadet to mount you like a bull on heat. I've had you.'

He opened the door and turned around, the officer now crouched on the floor, his head in his hands.

'With your permission, I'll finish my detention outside. Sir.'

For a while Reinhardt hardly left Felix's side and discreetly started to hide ropes, knives and pistols away. He also kept finding excuses to join him on the occasional solitary saunter.

One day, exasperated, young Kimmich snapped at him.

'You should not concern yourself. I will never give them the satisfaction.'

When Felix and Charlotte's engagement was announced, Reinhardt, as the eldest son and anointed heir, had been summoned by a concerned father.

'Young Kimmich was your companion at military school for five years.'

'I am still humbled by such honour, Father.'

'As the first born and heir, I demand and value your judgement.'

He had turned to avoid his son's gaze. His hands together behind his back.

'There are rumours.'

Reinhardt had stood silent. Martial. Loyal.

'It will be my honour to have Herr Kimmich as

brother-in-law. Charlotte will be happy, Father.'

* * *

'My tailor says he takes immense pleasure in dressing you. You fit everything with extraordinary grace.'

And he does. Walther has picked a dark green fabric for his riding outfit since his riding partner's is of the more traditional flaming red variety.

Felix has selected a strong and lively white thoroughbred for himself and a slender brown one for his friend.

They are still tired. The previous night was one of intense social interaction and rivers of wine, followed by hours of youthful Olympian passion. At the onset of an early summer dawn they had just laid down their weapons and were contemplating the baroque motifs of the ceiling; motionless, their hands clasped together, their energy finally extinguished, their eyelids flickering until shut.

They intend to head for the woods south of Baden.

'If you thought you were going to have an easy day, you were mistaken. I intend to race you.'

Walther is testing the horse's docility, trotting a little around the stables ground. He throws a resigned look.

'With the intention of winning, no doubt.'

'Naturally.'

They are both outstanding riders; once out in the woods, they launch themselves into a furious race, recklessly jumping tall and dangerous bushes, splashing into a few streams, occasionally spying each other when they find themselves side by side.

When they finally come to a halt under an imposing oak,

they dismount and pat their charges, sweat dripping from under their black caps, their white riding pants splattered in mud.

Felix grabs him from behind and they wrestle for a good while, laughing, shouting obscenities at each other in childish jest. They end up flat on the grass, panting, their jackets unbuttoned, the heat rising, the tranquility of the surrounding countryside interrupted only by the sound of the cicadas and the blowing of their horses.

Walther perches himself on his elbow and watches him resting, soaking up the sun, his moustaches wet with sweat. Felix opens his eyes with a sharp blink.

'What?'

'Will you ever grow up?'

Walther smiles and reclines back, arms behind his head, eyes shut in the warmth of the midday rays.

'Do I have to? That is such a sad thing to do.' While saying that, he sits up and takes in the landscape. 'I loved military school. And yet I was constantly counting the days to my next leave. To be with you. It felt like being without food and water. I feared that growing up would put distance between us. I still do. As children, each other was all we had.'

They fall away, led into short dreams, hand in hand.

Not a long nap. They have to be back for Charlotte's adoring sisters before the start of the afternoon. Back on their saddles they trot at leisure to prepare for another fast dash back to Villa Hildegard.

A long silence, broken by a pensive Felix.

'We are inseparable.'

Then he turns. A long stare and a wink: 'Try and catch me.'

Taking advantage of his sisters' monopolisation of Felix's afternoons, Reinhardt lures Walther to a game of tennis. Fired up with renewed confidence, he accepts and they have a good one; Reinhardt only wins by a few points.

He is ready to walk home but Reinhardt heads for the showers, making him slightly uncomfortable. He knows that he knows.

Yet he seems oblivious to it. He laughs earthily as they exchange banter and small talk next to each other, under the steamy flow. Once wrapped in their towels and perched on the benches facing each other, Reinhardt speaks out.

'You ought to know that I am aware that the nature of your loyalty to Felix differs from mine.' He dries himself a bit more with a spare towel. 'All the same, I believe them to be equal in worth. You ought to know that too.'

Walther looks up.

'Few men would be this brave to think as such. And say it.'

'Not as brave as you gentlemen. I appreciate the challenge of your ways.' A thankful nod. 'My sword once defended his honour. I was prepared to kill or be killed for it. For him.' The stare is now inquisitive. Searching. 'Would you? Die for him?'

'Yes. I care not for myself. Only for him.'

Reinhardt stands up, his spare towel in his left hand.

'No hesitation. That was all I needed to know.' He forwards his hand. 'My friendship.'

Walther rises too.

'And mine.'

The shake is strong and powerful. Felt.

They stroll back in silence to the villas. Reinhardt had needed a men's situation to say what he had to say. The changing rooms, where most men would have felt uncomfortable with the likes of Walther, were the right place and the right time.

On his short walk to Villa Hildegard Walther understands. The integrity of some and the cowardice of others.

After a few days of the season's activities, including a session of mud baths at the Friedrichsbad in which, after too much hesitation, an exasperated Felix does indeed hurl Walther in one of the uninviting tubs, the best of news reaches Villa Hildegard: Fräulein Kahler is on the next train to Baden after a bruising campaign of Napoleonic proportions against her family's divisions.

Once reunited, they allow themselves to decline a few invitations here and there, their household back to the comforting Charlottenburg routine.

One day they plan a strolling expedition to the Rumanisch Orthodox Kapelle: a fairly long walk through the Kurpark which is not of much appeal to Charlotte. Walther is in the meantime diligently trying to catch up with the affairs of the estate.

Felix and Edda stroll along the Stourdzastrasse, an oak-lined path which leads to the Kapelle.

They cannot avoid it: at the crossing with another path, an older gentleman, his wife at his side holding his arm, walks right up to them by accident.

'Herr Kimmich!'

Edda observes Felix with the tail of her eye: his face is white, almost blue.

'Herr... Count.'

She fears Felix is about to faint: she can feel the trembling. She holds him up with an arm around his waist, the older couple silently wondering who she might be.

The Count's consort is a charming lady, elegantly dressed, if not on the cheaper side of couture. She is the one to volunteer some small talk.

'Delighted to see you, Herr Kimmich, the coincidence of both of us being in Baden for the season.'

Von Stolberg betrays no emotion and looks at Felix in the eyes. Cold, severe.

By good luck the pleasantries' exchange is brief and perfunctory. Von Stolberg wishing no more than Felix to linger any further.

She has led him slowly to a bench; his head drops in Edda's bosom, his eyes about to well up.

'No, Felix. Not here. People are looking.' He returns to the upright position, still pale and now staring aimlessly ahead. She squeezes his hand.

'I had to see my uncle again too.'

For a few days, and to the puzzlement of the household, he withdraws and remains uncharacteristically silent at every event.

But Edda's support is unflinching, and she also informs him that, while he remained absent-minded, the Von Stolbergs had revealed to her that they were about to leave

Baden soon. But she also warns him that the possibility of further encounters will always be there, he has to accept it.

Once he's sure that the Von Stolbergs have indeed departed, he adventures in the Kurpark by himself, in need of a solitary saunter.

He has skipped lunch as the continuous dining invitations are wreaking havoc with his delicate digestion; he wears the best of his morning suits, the cream coloured one with a tweed gilet, hat, gloves and stick. The early afternoon rays slash through the oaks lining the path.

'Herr Hagelstein!'

The voice has a youthful, almost insolent timbre. He turns and doffs his hat.

'Florian?'

He's standing a couple of metres away, hands in the pockets of a swanky suit, a soft cap and his endearing smirk.

'Fancy meeting you here, sir.'

'Indeed. What a pleasure. How in Baden?'

'The gentleman. You know, the one I told you in the note? You did get the note, did you?'

'Oh yes, of course. Well, you look in good form, young man.'

'And you, sir. Always the gentleman, you. Are you angry with me?'

'I never was, why should I be?'

'I bolted, didn't I?'

'I hope the gentleman is looking after you well.'

'Sort of. Anyway, you might not want to be seen with me here.'

'Is Baden awash with rumours and gossip about Florian's exploits?'

A boyish laugh.

'Not yet.'

'Then we better take a stroll before that happens.'

'I don't want to take up your time, sir.'

'My pleasure.'

They reach a small kiosk, Florian turns around.

'You wouldn't buy me an ice cream, would you?'

'Of course I would.'

They sit on a bench and due to the heat, the ice cream leaks on Florian's trousers, causing a short burst of improper language.

'The gentleman is staying at the Brenner-Park Hotel but I'm not. He's put me up at a dingy old pension. No outings, no meals together; almost every night after dinner I go to his suite and then back to my room. Thankfully. He had to buy me a nice suit otherwise the hotel staff might stop me in the lobby. Also a little cash. Well, sometimes.'

For some reason Von Stolberg's image crosses Felix's mind.

'He's not…I mean, he's not violent to you?'

'No, sometimes he just talks and then I leave.' He lowers his eyes. 'He's very old.'

'Oh, Florian.'

'Anyway, no more sad stories. Are you here alone?'

'No… with my wife.'

'No need to blush, you all have wives!'

He's hurt by that. He never considered himself as one of the 'all'.

They stroll back to Florian's pension. Once in front of the doorsteps they face each other.

'Well, here I am. Would love to invite you upstairs but the lady in charge is of the scary type: "No visitors!". That was the first thing she said when I arrived. Perhaps she had my sort all worked out.'

A little smile. Florian looks sideways a few times. The oak-lined path is almost deserted and the few solitary walkers seem to be immersed in contemplative thoughts. He leans over and kisses Felix on the cheek.

'You aren't an easy one to forget, sir.'

Felix puts his hand in the inside of his jacket.

'Let me...'

'No sir, please. Was great to see you again.' He forwards his hand, Felix takes it and shakes it gently. Shivers run through their bodies.

'Good bye, Florian.'

'Good bye, sir.'

He turns away and starts strolling back to Villa Hildegard. Love sometime flies by our lives and never enters them. We might know when it happens but rarely discover why.

On his way back to the villa he walks by a couple of governesses perched on a bench while their young charges play and run about. A little girl in a white and blue dress parades in front of him. She has picked a tiny bunch of violets and without saying a word she offers them to him. He kneels and takes them, thanking her before she runs back to the governesses who are clearly commenting on the exquisitely elegant and handsome young gentleman who has responded in so charming a way to the little girl's impromptu gift.

He turns, smiles and lifts his hat in greetings. The two young ladies nod. A new life perhaps. A new beginning.

* * *

He has reserved the best table for an afternoon tea at the Kaiserhof for Charlotte and Felix: 'It'll do you good,' Walther remarks to him in the study.

Winter is back, the first snow has fallen and the woods of Baden are already a fading memory. Some Christmas decorations have tentatively started to grace lamp posts and restaurants' entrances.

He's perusing the menu while a radiant Charlotte nods to the numerous fresh new acquaintances attained upon Baroness Von Mutthe's public display of their association.

'Herr and Frau Kimmich, we are honoured by your presence here at the Kaiserhof, how may I be of any help?'

His eyes leave the menu. There is a smiling young man standing in his dazzling uniform, his hands holding a tray behind his back.

'Florian?'

'Herr Kimmich, my pleasure.'

'You…you know my name?'

'It's on the guests list.'

'What a coincidence.'

'I'm still in training, but I love the position. My friend, I mean, the gentleman put in a good word for me.'

'Well, I'm being very rude. This is my wife: Frau Charlotte.'

'At your service, Frau Kimmich.'

After Florian has left with the order, he turns to Charlotte.

'Singular coincidence…is this Walther's work?'

She shrugs, tea is now laid out. When they are standing and ready to leave, Felix calls him at the table and places a few notes in his hand.

'Thank you young man, most excellent service.'

'My pleasure, Herr Kimmich. Always kind and generous, sir.'

Their eyes are fixed on each other, stirring a renewed thrill.

'I don't suppose I can tempt you for tea at Villa Augusta? I would be most delighted if you could attend.'

'I look forward to it, sir.'

'I'll leave the address at reception. By the way…' He turns to Charlotte, 'We'll be celebrating; my wife and I are expecting our first child.'

The typist

He cannot quite distinguish the column of smoke billowing from the tall chimney towering behind the barracks; it has snowed heavily overnight and a morning fog is concealing the courtyard too. He can barely discern the red bricks of the ammunition deposit on the opposite side. A knock at the door jolts him out of his thoughts.

'Come in.'

'Heil Hitler!'

'Heil Hitler! So, any luck?'

'I'm sorry, Herr Commandant, no results so far.'

'For crying out loud, how difficult is it to find one? Does any of you have any experience or qualifications rather than in…in…' He knows what he wants to say. 'What about you, Hocker, can you type?'

'I was a butcher, Herr Commandant.'

'Of course you were. Well, you'll have to find one. I have a backlog of documents which need to be typed and sent to Berlin. Why are they not sending me a typist? I keep requesting one!'

'Men are needed at the front, Herr Commandant.'

'We still have a front at least. Alright, you'll have to find one in the camp.'

Obersturmfürher Hocker abandons his rigid attention

position and leans forward, his head slightly turning in puzzlement to Obersturmbannführer Westphal.

'In the camp, sir?'

He waves his hand with impatience and extinguishes his cigarette in the ashtray on his desk.

'Yes, yes, in the camp. They must have a typist.'

'But sir, the documents might be confidential?'

He walks back to the window, the fog is starting to lift.

'Well, yes, some of them at least.'

'Isn't that dangerous, Herr Commandant? I mean, if...'

'I know very well what you mean. Easily solved. During the task you'll transfer the typist in isolation, no contacts with the others. When he has finished, then, well, you'll dispose of him, her, whoever he is.'

'At your orders, Herr Commandant! Heil Hitler!'

'Heil Hitler!'

He has held the position of Obersturmbannführer at the camp for the best part of three years. He has had reports of advances of Russian divisions but he has continued with his task. Those are still the orders.

He opens the bottle. Whisky at ten in the morning: he would have never done that back in Berlin, at his apartment on the Motzstrasse. He would have been at his desk at the bank anyway. But the party had promised anything that could be possibly promised to secure his organisational skills for a vital mission in the east. He was only twenty-five when that happened but too many men were already dead so they just went for anyone with a shred of brain cells. After all, how difficult can mass murder be? At that time he rightly concluded that refusal wouldn't have been the safest of options.

He walks into the adjacent room and lets himself crash on the camp bed with a thump, emptying the glass with a swift gulp. He wants to sleep again. There, in his Commandant's uniform. The Russians may do it: send him to sleep forever. He seldom spends any time in his villa at the edges of the camp. He has no family, there are no friends. And even if there were, there is no longer a glorious victory to discuss or gloat about. No one is sure whether they still have any relatives, loved ones or acquaintances to return to. The letters stopped coming long ago. Though still unsaid, everyone knows that the Red Army will end their lives here. In months, weeks or even days perhaps.

Obersturmführer Hocker knocks at the door. While walking in, he pushes a malnourished corpse in front of him in such a violent fashion that the young man tumbles on the floor, hitting his head on the frame of the desk. Hocker's boot is about to hit his ribs.

'Get up you…'

Westphal stops him with a raised hand.

'If this is the typist, I would rather have him alive?'

'Yes sir, Heil Hitler!'

The young man rises with a struggling effort and stands to attention, his face staring at the floor.

'Do you speak German?' The boy nods. 'Did you study typing?' Another nod.

'He put his hand up when I asked in the camp, sir. There were two or three of them.' Hocker shrugs, 'I suppose one is worth the other.'

'Good job, Hocker. Have you found a separate cell for him at night?'

'Yes, sir.'

'Can you wash him tomorrow morning? We are not in the camp here.'

'Will do, Herr Commandant.'

'Good, dismissed for now.'

'Heil Hitler!'

'Heil Hitler!'

The boy has remained motionless and hasn't raised his head. He's holding his cap in his hands. It's impossible for Westphal to fathom out his age, the malnutrition and the scarce hygiene befuddling his judgement.

'Sit at the desk.'

He sits down and places his hat on the side. Realising in terror that he has not been ordered yet to do so, he withdraws it with a sharp movement.

'Leave your cap there. Now type this, only a try to see how fast and good you are.'

He hands him not a document but a meaningless memo; the boy puts it on one side and starts reading it, then he places his fingers on the typewriter. They are bony and dirty but he types at speed and when Westphal snatches the paper from the roll, he can't find a single mistake, the margins are precise too.

'Good, we'll have to make you eat a bit more though while you do this.'

The boy stays silent. He then lifts his head, something which he's not supposed to do, to peer outside the window: a bright eastern sunny day, the rays hitting his face. He closes his eyes and warms his ravaged skin.

When he is thrown in by Hocker the following morning, he looks slightly different. He has been washed, scrubbed and fed something more substantial than the survival rations of the camp. His uniform is clean too. The yellow star almost gleams.

Westphal has left an inch-thick pile of papers on the side of the typewriter, some handwritten, some badly typed. The boy lifts his finger to be allowed to ask a question.

'Yes?'

'Am I allowed to ask you if I can't understand a word?'

He hears his voice for the first time. He still can't work out his age.

'Yes. If I'm not here, write it down and ask later.'

He sits at his desk in the middle of the big study, observing the boy's back, hunched over the machine, the keys clicking fast.

After about thirty minutes he checks the work and it's perfect. Then the boy stops. Still, his hands on the keys. Westphal thumps the glass of whisky on the desk.

'What's wrong?'

He hears no reply and the young man starts typing again. Westphal sees his hand wiping his eyes and walks up to him. He can see his frail bones trembling in fear, some tears on the desk.

He picks up the paper on the top of the pile. STRENG GEHEIM, NUR FÜR DIE REICHKANZLEI is stamped in red ink across the page. Under the warning, statistics, numbers, methods, results. He puts it back on the pile and leaves.

Once the boy had read that paper, his freshly acquired knowledge had turned into a death sentence. He now understands while he's held in isolation during his task. He will never be sent back to the camp.

But he can't stop either. He would be taken outside and promptly shot in the head by Hocker; although he has no idea of how many documents are left to type, they will prolong his life by perhaps a few days, or weeks. Or it will all end tomorrow.

After the third meal and the daily showers, the corpse is slowly starting to resemble a living human being again. Westphal is sending all the backlog of documents to Berlin and he has also started to dictate letters.

His shaved hair has started to regrow. Hocker has asked the Commandant if it should be shaved back again, but he has deemed it unnecessary as there are no head lice here.

Every day the pile of documents seems to grow and the boy has started to notice that some of them no longer appear to be of vital importance.

The only exchanges have happened when he had to ask about a few words so badly jotted as to be utterly incomprehensible; today he's asking about an unintelligible one and Westphal leans on the pile of papers to be closer to the script. His bony finger is still on the word and the Obersturmbannführer, not being sure which one he is pointing at, places his finger on the manuscript too. They touch, jolting the boy in fear; he withdraws the hand in sharp haste and keeps his head down, his eyes closed. Any wrong movement anticipates violence.

'I think it says "provisions", does it fit the context?' The boy checks and returns in position, nodding in agreement. 'Very well, "provisions" it is.'

It has been a week. The boy is astonished to be still alive and the pile of documents never seems to diminish in size. Some of them are now patently ludicrous and he has noticed that the Obersturmbannführer stows some of the typed papers away, with no intention of sending them anywhere.

It's almost time for Hocker to collect him with invariable violence, twisting his arms, hitting his back with the butt of his rifle. Westphal's voice cuts deep in the silence of the study.

'Come here.'

The young man stirs, grabs his cap and stands to attention in front of his desk.

'Head up.'

His skin has partly recovered and he's pale, his hair a light brown, his eyes either brown or black, Westphal cannot say. His features are more defined now and he reckons that he's probably twenty or perhaps younger.

'What's your name?'

There is a pause. His name is never asked. They have no names, only numbers.

'Adler.'

'Your first name.'

'Jacob. Jacob Adler.'

'Where are you from?'

'Berlin.'

'Scheunenviertel?' He nods but Hocker is at the door,

ready to drag him away.

The following morning he locks the door once Jacob has been ushered in by Hocker. The Obersturmführer never fails to take full advantage of the brief time in which he can unleash resentful violence on someone vastly more educated than himself.

Jacob is typing away, the documents now verging on the ridiculous. With the tail of his eye he sees Westphal's hand holding a small china plate, a portion of apfelstrudel and a fork on it. The plate is now at his side, yet he hears no order to eat it and he is at a loss to what to do. Despite the better rations, he's still permanently hungry and he hasn't eaten apfelstrudel since the night of the raid, when his parents' bodies were lying on the floor of the apartment in a pool of blood, the SS guards pulling him away by his hair.

He takes the strudel in his hands and starts to bite it, the smell and the flavour taking his mind back to that night. But he's still on the edge of starvation and he finishes it off in seconds, embarrassed by the indignity of famine.

Westphal returns and pulls the plate away, leaving a napkin on the side.

He receives something every morning though he's not quite sure whether the Commandant orders extra breakfast or goes without some of his; in the meantime he continues to type senseless documents.

The sun is bright this morning. So bright that he has to keep shielding his eyes with his hand to read the now clearly meaningless material the Obersturmbannführer piles up every day at the side of the typewriter.

Westphal approaches and lowers the blinds. Then closes them shut, the rays disappearing behind them. He is standing right behind Jacob who has stopped typing. He has no idea why; he felt he had to stop while Westphal was plunging the room in semidarkness.

He senses his presence, his uniform has a pungent scent of tobacco and whisky and he can't be more than two or three inches away.

Two fingers have unexpectedly landed on his neck and are slowly searching around his collar. They travel upwards and hold his earlobe for a fraction of a second before descending back onto his neck. One hand is now lying on the upper portion of his chest and when it travels downward, he feels one of his tiny nipples stroked by the rough fingers. He remains still, staring ahead. When the hand lands on the other nipple, he shuts his eyes, unable to define whether for pleasure, fear, or both.

The next day the blinds are already lowered. Westphal swiftly locks the door once butcher Hocker throws Jacob in with the usual kicking and shoving.

He sits at the desk without typing. The page on top of the pile at the side of the typewriter reads 'Officers Mess Dinner Menu'. The Commandant is desperately scraping a barrel but he's clearly near the bottom of it.

He's behind him. Jacob remains still while Westphal's fingers are caressing his now grown hair, the other hand pressing on his shoulder.

The Commandant hasn't asked. And he's in no need to:

he owns him, his mind, his body. He can have him and then murder him at his pleasure. He's supposed to be repelled by him. Yet he's presently stroking his hair.

He's asking himself whether Jacob's arousal is brought on by the thought of a maiden, rather than by an Obersturmbannführer's uniform reeking of whisky and tobacco. Yet we are at the end of life, possibly the world. Does consent matter when neither of them will be alive in a few weeks, maybe days?

He drags the chair backwards and lifts the boy up. Jacob is pinned against the wall and when their eyes meet Westphal knows that it was no maiden fluttering across his mind.

Jacob anticipates a violent kiss or maybe a bite: a persistent aura of ferocity and brutality permeates the camp, even among the officers and the lower ranks. Their exchanges are always sharp, angry, reproachful.

Instead he collides with inexplicable tenderness to which he abandons himself, as it might be the last he ever experiences.

When Westphal's lips detach, his breath is heavy, his eyes transfixed; he slowly kneels and Jacob feels his trousers being lowered. He's close and ready, yet veneration precedes possession.

But then he freezes and lifts himself up, Jacob's trousers still down, his manhood fully exposed. Westphal's face shows a puzzled darkness before he can speak.

'You're not?...'

'I am.'

He moves away while Jacob pulls his trousers up.

'But your...'

'I know. It's not.'

Westphal appears confused, his expression demanding an explanation.

'I am a Jew.'

'You can't be.'

'I am.' He turns his gaze to the typewriter, pensive. 'When I was seven the Scheunenviertel wasn't yet a ghetto and I lived there with my parents. Both died of tuberculosis and the Adlers decided to adopt me. They raised me in their faith but Father insisted that I was too old for the Brit Milah. The Rabbi was furious but he stood firm. I am a Jew.'

'But you aren't, you are an Aryan.'

'My race doesn't matter.'

He has raised his voice and he fears retribution. He suspects that the discovery might have softened his tormentor's hatred, though he's no longer sure if his tormentor is now his lover, his defender, his executioner.

'It could have saved you from the camp. Why didn't you tell the SS? You could have shown them and explained. You could have said anything: I don't know, that you were forced into the faith against your will. Why didn't you do it?'

'Even if I wanted to, I was being dragged away after they had massacred my family.' He pauses and turns his face away. 'In the living room. In front of me. They had protested. It was my silence that saved my life.'

Their eyes are fixed on each other but they have no way to know what their respective thoughts may be: fear, remorse, hatred, lust, foreboding. A discontinued jumble of feelings hits them. An overwhelming human cataclysm bouncing through a hall of shape-shifting mirrors.

Westphal turns and marches to the door.

'Hocker! Here, now!'

'Heil Hitler!'

'Yes, well, there's no more typing for today and I have some important issues to look into at once. Bring him back tomorrow at the same time.'

He sits at his desk and starts writing a note. Then he suddenly gets up and leaves. He follows the narrow path carved through the high snow across the courtyard which leads to the Reichspost shed. When he enters the young man at the desk raises his hand, clicks his heels and salutes.

'Yes, yes. I need to send a telegram to Berlin, the Reichsstandesamt. Urgent.'

Two days go by. There is no more conversation while he types and types ridiculous documents. On the third day, after he has eaten his pastry, he turns to Westphal and he finds him watching him. Impassive, immersed in his thoughts.

'Thank you for the pastry.' He grabs some papers from the pile, 'And these.'

Westphal gets up from his chair, opens the door and calls his aide.

'Hocker!'

'Heil Hitler!'

'Yes, yes. I have received some important documents from the Reichskanzlei. I need at least an hour to peruse the details. No calls and no one disturbing.'

'Heil Hitler!'

He closes and locks the door. Jacob has remained seated

but he has been following him with his eyes across the room. He walks to the adjacent room's entrance, opens the door and holds it for a few seconds before speaking.

'It's not an order.'

His head is resting on Westphal's hairy blond chest, his hand softly stroking the hidden nipples while he kisses his hair.

'You have to go.'

He puts his scrub on and quietly waits by the side of the bed until the Commandant is back in his uniform. He then follows him to the door but Westphal turns, his hand falls gently on Jacob's cheek and a soft kiss lands on his lips before shouting for Hocker.

Doctor Trzebinski is a lean man of forty-five, the only doctor for the camp's officers and guards. He has been summoned by Westphal at eleven and finds the request rather peculiar; nothing out of the ordinary has happened over the past few days. A few injuries, some drunken guards recovering, cuts and grazes.

He walks up the stairs of the Headquarters wearing his white scrub as he was unsure whether the Commandant had requested his presence because he was unwell. Hocker ushers him in and he now stands in front of Westphal.

'Heil Hitler!'

'Yes, yes, please Doctor Trzebinski, take a seat.'

He notices that the Obersturmbannführer appears to be in good health as he walks to the drinks cabinet and opens the glass doors.

'Perhaps a whisky?'

Trzebinski darts a cheeky look at the clock on the wall together with a mocking and reproachful frown at Westphal.

'Given the circumstances, the timing for a drink is immaterial, Herr Doctor, don't you think?' He pours two big glasses and lifts his arm. 'Heil Hitler!'

'Heil Hitler!' Trzebinski leans forward. 'The circumstances?'

'Doctor, I am of the opinion that you are an intelligent man.'

'Most grateful, Herr Commandant.'

'How far do you reckon the Red Army is from here?'

'I see. Maybe I'll have another glass.'

Westphal replenish their glasses.

'Doctor Trzebinski. I require a favour from you.'

Trzebinski is now listening carefully. These are times in which favours command high rewards.

'My typist, a young man of about twenty, has been hauled out of the camp to work for me.' Westphal takes a long sip. 'His name is Jacob Adler. But he's not a Jew.'

Trzebinski's attention is up a notch. He frowns.

'But the name?'

'That is not his real name. He was adopted.'

'How can you be sure? He might have told you a lie.'

He has left the desk and he's now at the window, fiddling with Jacob's papers.

'I've checked.'

'I see. Well, all you have to do... I mean, I can visit the boy and certify it. If that's what you are asking.'

'That could be done but it carries a risk. There is a chance that once we have your certification approved in Berlin, he'll be enrolled in the Wehrmacht and sent to the front

210

or, even worse, ordered to remain here as a guard. As an Aryan he'll be expected to serve the Führer. The Russians are on their way. When they get here, he'll find himself on the wrong side.'

'What did you have in mind?'

'To certify him as an Aryan and a homosexual.'

Trzebinski's eyes are on stalks.

'That is your plan?'

'I have a birth certificate here with his new name. I received it yesterday from the Reichsstandesamt in Berlin.'

He shows the certificate to the doctor who takes his spectacles out of his bag and peruses it.

'How did you obtain this?'

'A friend.'

The doctor looks up.

'Is it authentic?'

'The paper is but the name and date of birth are false. My friend can't run the risk of searching for the real one and the capital isn't in its best functioning mode to say the least. Doctor, we are not losing the war. We have lost it.'

'Herr Commandant, I'm not sure that...'

'Allow me to finish. You will certify the boy's homosexuality and we will issue him with a pink triangle. I will issue an order to deport him back to a camp in Germany as this camp is for Jews only. Not entirely true, I'm aware of that. Luckily, there aren't many officials left to question it and I am in charge after all. Only Berlin can reverse my orders and they are being bombed out of existence. I have found a camp which is about to be dismantled as the Allied Forces are too close. Unless some crazy officer goes on a rampage, he might have a chance.'

The doctor whistles.

'How do you rate this chance?'

'Minimal.'

'Herr Commandant, it's quite a risk you are asking me to take.'

He's back at his desk pouring more whisky in the empty glasses. He then opens the drawer and places an inch-thick wad of Reichsmarks on the writing leather mat. Out of a side drawer comes a 30-caliber Luger now lying by the wad of notes, pointed at Trzebinski. The doctor jolts in his chair.

'Herr Doctor, I have been given the information that you have left a wife and two young daughters in Munich when you joined us at the camp, is that correct?'

A worried nod. Westphal takes the wad of notes into his hands pretending to tidy it up.

'They'll need money. When the Red Army arrives, you'll no longer be in a position to help. This is half of the deal, the other half upon the boy's departure.' His hand is now on the Luger. 'Alternatively, we are in no need to wait for the Soviets.'

The doctor approaches the desk and grabs the wad of notes, swiftly storing them away in his bag.

'Send the boy to my surgery tomorrow afternoon. Three o'clock. Heil Hitler!'

'Heil Hitler!'

He's sitting at the desk and he has eaten his pastry. He's waiting for him to open the bedroom's door as he heard him locking the door. He hears his steps and the floor creaking;

they can have a few last days of meaningless bliss. He has typed all the top secret documents and although he somehow guesses that his liberators are not far from the camp, he's also aware that they might murder them all before defeat. Scorched earth.

Westphal grabs his shoulders, his fingers massaging his long thin neck, tickling his earlobe again.

'There is a brown envelope on my desk. You will deliver it to Doctor Trzebinski at three o'clock. Hocker will take you there; keep the envelope close to your chest.' He senses his shoulders shaking under his hands. 'Your birth certificate with your new Aryan name is inside the envelope. The certificate is authentic but the name and date of birth are false, you should be aware of that. Let the doctor open it, he knows what to do. He will visit you, take photographic evidence and issue a medical certificate confirming you are indeed an Aryan but also a homosexual. You will be issued with a new uniform marked with a pink triangle. The train leaves at seven. The doctor is already in possession of my order and you will be deported back to a camp which is about to be dismantled or so I have been informed, I can't be one hundred per cent sure.' A tear lands on one of Westphal's fingers. 'I believe the Americans to be close to the camp but again, I can't be sure. Once there, it will be up to you to seek safety. I must stress it to you: your chances are minimal. Here they are zero. I have no documents left.'

Jacob nods.

'Thank you.'

He takes his head into his hands and turns it gently toward the chimney. A thick column of black smoke has been belching from it all day long.

'I am the plague that befell you.'

His blood no longer warrants genocidal fury. Yet we rarely question the covenants of our survival. Perhaps because life stubbornly maintains its value even after being soiled by mankind's endless capacity for murderous depravity. Perhaps because we want to outlive the infernal insanity which so wants us dead. And maybe go and tell it on the mountain. Or, more prosaically, despair allows us no time for self-questioning. We just want to live.

'How does he prove I am a homosexual?'

He walks back to the spare room's door followed by Jacob's eyes.

'We have some time.'

'Hocker, Doctor Trzebinski and I are not to be disturbed.'

'Heil Hitler!'

He's at his desk, two glasses full of whisky on it.

'Safely departed, Herr Commandant.'

'There is nothing safe about his departure, you very well know that.'

'Yes. All the same, Prost!'

'Prost!'

He opens the drawer and a wad of notes more or less of the same size of the previous one appears on top of the desk. The doctor leans over and hurriedly hides the notes away in his bag.

'You could have kept him typing until the arrival of the Russians and he would have been liberated.'

'I was running out of work for him. I'm not certain of how

far the Red Army is either and it could be months if they meet strong resistance.'

'Well, he might have a chance. A shake for a change?'

His hand is met by a strong hold. Westphal has placed the Luger back on the desk, instantly noticed by Trzebinski.

'Are you finishing the bottle today, Herr Commandant?'

'Only half a glass left.'

He's about to leave but he turns around.

'As the camp's physician, I'm not in possession of a pistol, Herr Commandant.'

Westphal walks to a locked cabinet and takes out another Luger. He loads it with a magazine and hands it by the barrel to the doctor who swiftly puts it in his bag.

'You are a gentleman.'

He hears the shot when he's half way down the stairs. While officers, clerks and guards scamper to the Obersturmbannführer's office to check what has happened, he carries on walking until he's out in the open. It has started to snow again. He looks up to the Commandant's window before ambling head down to the Reichspost shed.

'Heil Hitler, Doctor Trzebinski!'

'Yes, well, I'd like to deposit this cash on my account. Then I would like you to wire the whole balance to my wife's account in Munich, you should have her details already as I did the same transfer yesterday.'

'It will be done, Doctor, Heil Hitler!'

'Yes, thank you, good bye.'

He strolls numbly to his small cottage at the side of the officers' quarters. Westphal allowed him to keep a German Shepherd who jumps up his legs as soon as he opens the door. He lights the fire and takes a bottle of whisky out of the drinks cabinet. Holding a full glass in his hand, he slumps in the armchair, staring at the flames.

The bottle is now empty and he has fallen asleep; it must be early evening. When he wakes up he pats the dog's head.

'Time, my friend.'

He gets up and slowly walks to the table where his bag has been lying unopened. With the Luger in his hand he strolls to the small patch of garden at the rear of the cottage. It has stopped snowing, the moon is shining. His war is over.

Zoologische Garten

The bell rings and the flood of students disgorges on the pavement. It has been a cold spring so far but this early day of May is exploding with warm sunlight and the young crowd reaches for it in eagerness.

He's looking for his mate. Max and Kaspar are of the same age but in different classes. He has to shout across the multitude of parents and children noisily calling each other. Once he has spotted him, he waves his hand high but Kaspar is distracted and fails to acknowledge the sign. Finally, he turns.

'Max!'

'Kaspar! I'll meet you on the other side!'

He nods in agreement and after a few pushes and shoves they are out of the chattering mob. They stroll towards the Tiergarten as on such a day it would be unthinkable to travel on the S-Bahn. They intend to walk all the way to the other end. They'll be home late but they have checked with each other: the homework load is light; perhaps the teachers want to encourage them to walk and enjoy the clear and warm spring day after all.

'Hey, Kaspar, how was your day?'

'Bored shitless. Latin and German. And again, and again.'

'More of a technical guy, aren't you?'

'Yes, I think I'll do engineering at university.'

'You might change your mind again, it's two years away.'

'What are you going to do then?'

'No idea. I like politics.'

'Not the right time to like politics, Max.'

'Why not? It's messy. Perfect time for a career.'

They are now at the ice-cream kiosk. Kaspar is fumbling for pfennigs in his pockets but his friend fishes a note out of his jacket.

'What flavour?'

'Vanilla. How come you always have money? I thought your dad lost his job.'

'He has.'

'Then?'

'Odd jobs, and he receives government support.'

'I thought they didn't have any money to pay for it.'

'They still do.'

No talking while slurping the ice cream. The temperature has risen, it melts fast and then it starts dripping along the cone. When they have gulped down the last chunk of the wafer cone, they throw their satchels on the grass and lie for a while in the sun. Away from teachers, parents, and the annoying world.

Max is a robust lad of sixteen, dark blond and blue eyes. Kaspar's frame is smaller, his features angular, his limbs rather thin. His dark brown hair is rarely cut so it flicks rebelliously around his sculpted face.

Their friendship is recent, brought about by a casual encounter outside the school gates. A fresh and inexplicable bond. Something they both seem to know about each other but cannot quite express in full.

They are late home. Kaspar and his parents live in a shabby two-bedroom apartment on the sixth floor of a late nineteenth century building in the Schöneberg district; a notice on the iron gate reports that the lift has broken down and the administration has no funds to repair it.

Good luck asking Dad, he thinks.

Once he steps on the landing of the third floor, one of the doors opens and a man of perhaps sixty or seventy appears, still wearing a black winter coat and a hat of the same colour. When he spots the boy on the landing, he doffs his hat, revealing a wispy batch of white and grey hair.

'Good evening, Herr Flugel.'

'Good evening, Kaspar, how are you today, young man?'

'Very well, thank you. The lift is broken again. Do you need any help to bring something back up to the apartment?'

'Thank you, that is very kind of you. I'm just going out to visit my sister, won't have any grocery with me. A few stairs will do me good.'

'Have a nice evening, Herr Flugel.'

'And you, Kaspar.'

Herr Flugel lives alone and Kaspar suspects that to have always been the case. He has heard his dad calling him 'one of them' though he wasn't quite sure what he meant by that. In any case he likes him; he is always kind and polite so he has never been much interested in finding out what his father had been implying.

'Mum, I'm home, sorry I'm late, walked through the park with Max and…'

His parents are at the table, two mugs of coffee in front

219

of them. His mother has been crying. He goes over and kisses her on the cheek, then turns to see his father's face but he is staring down at the mug while holding it tight with his hands.

'What's wrong? Has something happened?'

His mother strokes his cheek and takes his hand.

'Your father has lost his job at the factory.'

He sits down.

'I'm sorry, Dad.'

'Thank you, Son. Quite a few of us as a matter of fact.'

'Max's father has lost his job too and he seems to do the odd job here and there. I can do that.'

His mother is standing behind him now.

'No, you have to carry on going to school and university.'

'But what are we going to do without money?'

'I don't know, we'll think of something.'

Another sunny day and another walk through the park. Routine ice cream out of the way, another blissful break on the grass.

'My dad has lost his job.'

'Oh mate, sorry to hear that.'

Kaspar shrugs.

'I think we have about one or two months' rent saved up, then, who knows?'

'Nearly everyone is in the same situation.'

'Yes, bad, isn't it? Would like to find a job. Mother doesn't want me to, but what if we are evicted? You know your job and chores? Do they need another hand?'

Max is silent for a while before sitting up and staring

ahead, his arms around his knees.

'It's not exactly a job.'

He sits up too and shields his eyes from the sun with his hand.

'What do you mean? I thought you said…'

'Oh Kaspar, you're so naive. There are no jobs. There is no fucking work. Where have you been?'

He feels slightly offended; he's aware of his naivety but he resents being reminded of it.

'Sorry. I'm a bit stupid, I don't understand.'

Max gets up and lifts him up with a hand. They grab their satchels and start strolling towards Schöneberg. He would like to drop the subject but he never had anyone to confide in about it. He also knows that it might be Kaspar's family only chance of survival.

'After we go our ways I don't always go home.'

'You don't? Where do you go?'

'To the S-Bahn underpass at the Zoologische Garten.'

'To do what?'

He's driven crazy by Kaspar's innocence but he likes him and he's the only genuine friend he has. He stares at the grass.

'To meet men. Older men.'

He turns but there is no one at his side. Kaspar has stopped walking and stands a couple of metres behind him, his face white.

'You do what?'

All he can do is to open his arms in resignation.

'It's either that or hunger and eviction. We have no money.'

He's back at his side and they start walking again.

'But...how do you hide it from your parents?'

They keep walking in silence, then Kaspar sees him lifting his hand to wipe his eyes. He grabs his arm to stop him, his eyes wide in shock as he stammers.

'They... they know?'

They hug. Max needs it so much, he cannot let go. When they get to the end of the park, Kaspar turns to say goodbye.

'Are you going there now?'

'I can't do it tonight, not after telling you.' Max's head is swinging left and right in embarrassment. 'Are we still friends?'

'Same time tomorrow.'

'Thanks. Same time.'

A sleepless night; during the initial shock he felt a burst of hate for his friend but now he's calm, though worried about one recurring thought: it might be the only way to help his parents.

The weather has taken a turn for the worse again and it threatens rain. The S-Bahn journey is much shorter and they use the spare time to head for a cheap cafè off the Kurfürstendamm where they can still have an ice cream anyway.

They were silent on the train, Max's formerly secret activity obnoxiously squatting between them. The ice cream seems to have a strange power of relaxation on both.

'Did you actually tell your parents or they found out?'

'Neither. They aren't stupid, they know there are only two activities which pay at the moment and I can't do crime.'

'As far as I know that isn't legal either. What do they ask you to do?'

'Oh mate, you'll have to use your imagination for that, I can't tell you. Too embarrassing.'

'Yeah, not sure I want to hear it either.' A small laugh. 'But. Are they...I mean...do they treat you well?'

'Most do. Some are a bit weird but one gets used to it.'

'And the money?'

'Pretty good. It goes by age. We command the highest rate. Sorry, I meant "I".'

'It's alright. If you didn't have to do it, would you go with girls? I mean, do you like girls?'

He turns his head left and right, then down, then up. It slightly annoys Kaspar.

'No is the short answer.'

Kaspar lowers his gaze.

'Me neither. That's the longer answer.'

That provokes a good laugh and a long-awaited evaporation of any residual doubt. They now understand the connection that paired them up at the school gates and it comes as a relief. Kaspar toys nervously with the napkins' holder on the table.

'What would you think if I...if I give it a go?'

Max isn't taken aback. A few months earlier he found himself in the same situation and had gone through more or less the same conversation with another friend.

'If you can stomach it.'

'That I don't know until I try, would you help me out?'

'What do you need to know?'

'I don't need to know it, I need to do it first and I don't

want my first time to be with a stranger.'

Max leans across the table and whispers.

'You understand that your "first time" is worth a big wad of cash, don't you?'

'Maybe. But I'd like you to be my first.' Their knees are touching by chance now. 'If you don't find me unbearably unattractive, that is.'

'Don't be stupid, of course not. I'll make it as special as I can, mate.'

They are in a secluded booth. Their hands fidget on the table and travel towards one another until they meet and squeeze into a hold. Kaspar feels shivers down his spine, Max winks.

They hear the door opening and a small but loud mob of young men floods the premises. They untangle their hands fast and sit back; soon some of the lads are at their table. Kaspar has started noticing some of these boys outside the school gates, their perfectly ironed light brown uniforms ogled by admiring girls, the red bands around their arms standing out in a glare.

Kaspar is not a follower of politics as he's more of a maths and physics boy. He finds it difficult to understand why some people would fight so vehemently for their opinions. Science doesn't require an opinion and facts are what counts for him.

One of the boys drops a red pouch on their table.

'Any contribution for the party, lads?'

He looks at Max. He seems not to be overtly worried about the loutish and brawling character of the young crowd now harassing the other customers with leaflets and demands for donations. Kaspar replies without looking up.

'We're still at school, we don't have any money.'

The boy appears to appreciate his reasonable answer.

'Fair enough, here are some leaflets for you.'

Max takes the leaflets and a few coins appear in his hand.

'That's all I can spare.'

'Most grateful, anything will help the cause. Heil Hitler!'

They are gone. Kaspar feels rather uncomfortable.

'Why did you give them money?'

'They mean well, they are trying to save Germany and one day perhaps we won't need to do what we have to do at the moment.'

'I find them very aggressive. I don't like them.'

'You don't have to, it's just a new party, like the others.'

One of Max's regulars puts them up the following afternoon and despite a few awkward moments and clumsy false starts, it all goes surprisingly well. Max is sweet, gentle and patient, their youth excites them both in spite of the underlying feeling of being in a business transaction. Kaspar feels like he has been under some kind of training. It helps that although attracted to each other, it's quite obvious to both that they aren't in love with one another.

In any case protracted and tedious courtships are a girls' thing. Boys would rather dive straight into action, preferably without a single word uttered before it. Or after.

'Does it bother you that it wasn't with someone you have fallen in love with?'

'Can you fall in love with men? Have you?'

'No, but perhaps we will, too early to say.'

Kaspar is gathering his clothes. When he's back on the

bed he kisses Max on the lips.

'We might like girls later on, how do we know? But I enjoyed it. Thank you for being nice to me.'

'My pleasure. I must warn you, the guys down at the underpass aren't always this sweet, but I'll watch over you; there are a few to be definitely avoided, all the boys know who they are.'

Kaspar has stopped putting his clothes on.

'I'm still a bit nervous.'

'I have one of my regulars lined up for you; nice guy, owns a grocery shop so he still has a bit of money to throw about. It's five-hundred Marks for the privilege of having you in his bed for a couple of hours tomorrow afternoon.'

He drops his vest and turns, his eyes wide.

'Five-hundred Marks?'

'Told him you are my age and didn't mention this afternoon. So, make sure you play the super innocent. You know: the "I've never done it", "I'm a bit scared" thing, they love that rubbish.'

'That's two months of our rent!'

'Yes. About that. I wouldn't go running to your folks with that pile of cash in your hands. There aren't many ways in Berlin at the moment for a sixteen-year old to earn that kind of money. They'll become suspicious fast.'

'What should I say?'

'Hide it and feed them bit by bit. Just say you got a job with a shop. Actually, that guy can pretend you work for him if they want to enquire; he isn't married so he's quite chilled.'

Kaspar drops back dead-like on the bed, still almost

half-naked. Max is now stroking his hair.

'What time do we have to leave?'

'We don't.'

He has dropped his hand on Max's leg.

'I wouldn't mind doing it all over again.'

'Me too.'

The following day the S-Bahn carriage they are travelling in is stormed by another group of boys and men in the same brown uniform; Kaspar raises his eyes to the ceiling.

'They seem to be proliferating fast.'

When they are close to the Zoologische Garten stop he starts to shake and grabs Max's arm.

'I'm not sure I can do this.'

'Relax, always hard the first time.'

They walk down the stairs and turn right until they reach the underpass. He's keeping very close to Max. They fend off the crowd and head for a spot on the corner where a fair amount of young men seem to be gathered: some of them loitering, a few leaning against the wall, others frantically chatting with older gentlemen.

One the boys calls out to them. When they approach he seems to scrutinise Kaspar from head to toe and then whispers some comments into Max's ear. A few minutes later a gentleman of probably fifty stops in front of them and he introduces his trembling friend.

'No need to shake in fear, boy. I'm not about to kill you.'

The voice and deportment reassure him. He has a gentle, humble posture; he had been kept awake all night by the thought of a brutish and violent ogre. His nap in the classroom had been picked up by the teacher with a severe reprimand.

'I'll see you at the cafè in two hours. Make sure he pays first, though you can trust this one.' He sneaks a small pot of grey stuff in Kaspar's pocket. 'Make sure he uses it. It hurts like hell without it. And hide the notes in the safest place, other boys here are not to be trusted.'

He is in their usual booth with a mug of coffee on the table, the weather has gone cold again. He sees him coming through the door and looking around so he waves his hand to attract his attention. He's eager to know.

'Well?'

'Was fine.'

'Paid?'

'In my pants.'

They laugh at that. It helps.

'Did he treat you well?'

'Very. He even prepared a sandwich for me.'

'A sandwich? Mate, you are something else.'

Kaspar shrugs.

'I told him I was hungry. Sex makes me hungry.'

Max smiles, reassured. His friend can be surprisingly matter of fact.

'He's not a good-looking man but he was full of attentions. He kept telling me how beautiful he thought I was.'

'Sadly he isn't one of the richest, I doubt he'll be able to fork out the same sum for quite some time.'

'Does it have to be so high? I'm just doing it to help my folks, I don't really care about the money.'

'It'll go down, don't you worry. After a while you become, how can I put it, second-hand?'

'Charming.'

'There's nothing charming about this.'

'Need to go home now.'

He comes up with a good story. Deliveries for a grocery shop near the Savignyplatz, between three and six every other afternoon. He hands over what he thinks might reasonably be considered a decent cash-in-hand pay to his reproachful mother. He then hides the rest of the cash in his bedroom.

Max is very skilled in finding the right customers for him. The shopkeeper was right: Kaspar is a beautiful boy and for the time being he commands the highest fee. He's also warned by his more experienced friend to steer clear of some of the boys under the bridge; a few of them are young men with girlfriends who are in the profession because there is no other way to make money, but they are not to be messed with. Some customers have been badly burnt by these louts: blackmailed or viciously beaten up when their requests went a bit too far.

The pair of them though are now well known and thoroughly liked by the real gentlemen. They are clean, honest, discreet, compliant and never contemptuous of their age or desires. There is no shortage: American industrialists, former aristocrats, English writers, French diplomats and general staff dispatched to the city to ensure compliance with the very treaty causing the widespread moral and financial meltdown.

And they love Kaspar. He makes them laugh with his

naive wit and he seems to treat sex as a game. His services come without tension. A few gentlemen cautiously demand some incredibly eccentric forms of exhibitionism or decidedly weird performances, expecting the boy to demur. Instead, he invariably pretends to reflect on the proposal and just laughs with a hint of affection: 'Never thought about that one, sir. Well, why not?'

The man approaching has just alighted from a dark blue Mercedes. They are hanging out by the wall, chatting with other boys, smoking, laughing. Kaspar has become acquainted with some of the friendly ones and a surreal camaraderie has strangely ensued; and since he has no other friends at school except for Max, he's rather pleased with the development.

He's in a chauffeur uniform, the client obviously inside, waiting. Rich pickings, Max whispers in his friend's ear.

The driver doesn't quite ignore Kaspar but his partner in crime has the look of the more grown up so prospective customers sometimes talk to him first.

Max takes him aside.

'He wants us both.'

His eyes widen in shock.

'What?'

'You heard me.'

'At the same time?'

'What do you think?'

'I...I don't know.'

'If you aren't embarrassed, I'm not. We've been there anyway.'

'Yes, well, not quite the same.'

The chauffeur is waiting with an uncomfortable expression. Even in the early afternoon, this is not the most salutary area to be waiting, surrounded by prowling hustlers.

'He's waiting. Good money.'

He nods. He always feels safe in the company of his best friend anyway; they both lack prudishness and they haven't been together since his weird induction day, despite still feeling some sort of attraction to each other. In any case, having to perform every other afternoon has worn the novelty out for Kaspar. They follow the chauffeur who opens the rear door, swiftly ushering them in. They are now facing their buyer.

He introduces himself formally and in the highest possible German. He's slender and elegantly dressed; not KaDeWe garments, more Kurfürstendamm upmarket tailors.

He sports a pair of trimmed blond moustaches, deep blue eyes and a pale complexion. They can't figure out his age but they guess he must be in his early forties: money has clearly bought some groomed beauty.

There is no conversation in the car and the boys respect his wish; perhaps he's not keen on the chauffeur hearing any of it, though they guess he must be trusted if sent bartering for their services at the underpass.

The chauffeur drives the car along a round driveway and stops in front of a visibly opulent villa at the edges of the Tiergarten. Kaspar has spent the journey staring out of the window while daydreaming. At irregular intervals he looked up at the gentleman who smiled back at him in tender and loving fashion; when their eyes met Kaspar felt a little startled.

Once in the hallway he disappears briefly through one of the doors; when back, he drops an envelope in Max's hand.

'I trust you take care of the details?'

'I do. We're best friends.'

After being dropped by the chauffeur nearby the underpass they stroll to their regular cafè as they still have some time to burn. Once in their usual booth Max opens the envelope and more notes than they were both expecting fly out on the table.

'Generous gentleman. I think we gave him the afternoon of his life.'

Kaspar is not following in the wake of his laugh. Max splits the money and hands half to him. Then he grabs his hands, they still have the notes in it.

'My friend. Look at me. We don't fall for clients. It's dangerous.'

'What? I don't know what you're talking about.'

'Do you think I'm blind? Not that I mind, but I was doing all the work while you two were just kissing away. I could see you hardly minded that.'

'You are imagining things.'

'He's an attractive man. And clearly very rich. But you'll get burnt. They fall in love, treat you like a prince for a few weeks and then you never hear from them again. Happens all the time. We're still at school and you live at home. This was for an emergency, remember?'

He huffs at the scolding.

'You're talking rubbish. He just wanted to kiss me all the

time and I had to do it. I thought we were meant to please clients?'

'Maybe. Just be careful.'

He's tired. He's determined not to fall behind with his homework but now he's at the underpass three times a week and on those afternoons he has to complete them when he gets home, obviously exhausted.

Youth is energy though and there is no discernible change in his school grades. After a quick supper he's now in bed, toying with a visiting card in his hand; Max is right but he'll call him tomorrow anyway.

He wanted to send the chauffeur to pick him up but he's fine with the S-Bahn and he remembers the location of the villa. When the butler opens the door, he's admitted with a bow and led into the drawing room where Lars is sitting on the sofa, distractedly perusing the Morgenpost. He drops the paper and stands up, opening his arms wide for Kaspar to gently slide in them and let him kiss him.

They left the heavy drapes open as they both wanted to slowly gaze at their bodies in the afternoon light of a bright day of spring. The rushes through Kaspar's spine were fresh, raw, mysterious. His lips are singed by the incessant kissing. Lars' arm is now around him, his fingers caressing his chest, casually landing on his nipples.

'Thank you for calling me.'

'Thank you for having me here, sir.'

'Would you like to stay a bit longer? Perhaps the evening?'

'Can't do that, I live with my folks. And I'm still at school.'

'I thought as much. What pushed you into this?'

'Father lost his job and Mother doesn't have one. God, if they find out they'll kill me.'

He feels Lars' lips on his hair.

'A few hours in the afternoon will be good enough, I'll be generous.'

'You don't need to. I didn't come here for the money.'

They are silent for a little while. Their bodies are re-charging and they know they have enough time for another brief journey to paradise.

'Your name. You know, Stolberg. Is it just Stolberg?'

Lars fails to reply while his hand has stopped caressing his chest. Kaspar becomes worried as he hears him lighting another cigarette.

'Sorry, sir, none of my business.'

'It has a Von in front of it. Von Stolberg. Count Von Stolberg.'

Another long silence. He curses his big mouth.

'Sorry for asking that. As I said, none of my business.'

'It isn't exactly a secret, but I try not to divulge it. Before you ask, my grandfather was Count Von Stolberg.'

He interlocks his boyish fingers with Lars' more manly ones as an offer of apology. He has unearthed something hurtful and he just wants to push it back in.

'I gather you are familiar with the story.'

'Well, I wasn't even born but it's quite a famous one. I want to drop it, it's hurting you and that wasn't my intention.'

Lars has turned Kaspar around and he is hugging him tight as he prefers not to look at his face when he tells him. And he now feels the urge to tell him.

'It was my mother, his very daughter, who found us. I

was not yet fourteen. The screams, the scene. She was so distraught that she couldn't think about keeping it a secret. The servants were the first to know.' He wants him to stop. 'She was throwing pieces of furniture at him and shouting to get out while I was cowering in a corner, naked, arms over my head. I didn't even have to tell the Reichspolizei when they arrived; they examined me and found all the wounds from the beating and the whipping. He was a furious beast. The choice was to yield or be beaten to a pulp. He was cautious at the beginning but he became reckless with his lust. That day I even told him that Mother was at home but he was almost crazy with desire. When she found us he was inside me.'

He can feel his tears on his shoulder.

'Given his rank, the Oberinspektor didn't know what to do and the scandal had already broken. He offered him the only way out. For the sake of his name and his family he allowed him to return home to carry out the sentence himself. He accepted.'

'I'm so sorry, sir.'

'But worse was to come. You think family and society wouldn't remotely think of apportioning any blame to me, but that's exactly what they started doing. Why didn't he tell anyone? Why he kept hiding the wounds? Perhaps he was willing. You have no idea of the things which have been said about me. And to me. The best schools and colleges turned me down; they said I could be of bad influence on other pupils. I felt like I was contaminated with an infectious disease. That's why the title and the "Von" have gone. To no avail though, people still recognise me. As you did.'

Kaspar's lips are sealed with his. There is not much left of the afternoon.

He's now dressed and ready to go.

'I know you said you didn't want any money, but it would take you away from the underpass.'

'Thank you, sir, I was thinking of quitting anyway. I've saved a bit and I can pay my parents' rent for quite some time now.'

'Wise boy. Allow me to give you something. Please.'

He has taken the decision to quit the underpass. He'll tell Max about Lars Stolberg, knowing very well that he will be scolded for being so naive and that he'll be dropped like a stone after a few weeks. All the same, he has decided to take the risk.

Mothers do what mothers do, and one of the things all mothers do at any time in history is to tidy up their sons' bedrooms, mostly because their sons never do it.

The drawer is wide open and she's sitting on Kaspar chair, the thick wad of notes in her hands: more money that she has ever seen. More than she'll ever see. Suspicious about the prolonged silence, her husband comes in and sees it.

They sit at the table in silence, trying to figure out an explanation. Could be petty crime but there are thousands of Marks in the drawer, and they are most certainly not coming from a delivery job for a grocery shop.

He has come to say goodbye; not to Max, as he intends to remain friends with him at school, but to a few other boys who have been nice to him. He's of the loyal type and he'll miss them.

He's facing Max, who is leaning against the wall, and talking him through his newly taken decision. His friend shakes his head but there is a client looking at him behind Kaspar.

'Can I help you sir?'

Kaspar turns around and his heart dissolves. Blood rushes away from his face, now turned into cold stone.

The slap is violent and throws him on the floor. The boys run away fast and in less than a few seconds the place is deserted. It happens frequently: an infatuated older man, a father who discovers their unusual way to earn a living or, in this case, his father, now grabbing him by the collar of his jacket and slapping him with raging force on the head. Max hasn't fled but he has retreated in a corner. He knows what has happened.

'Home now, walk in front of me.'

Kaspar has tried to turn around and talk but he has shouted him down. As soon as the door opens, he kicks him inside. His mother runs to help him.

'Don't! I can't tell you how he has earned all that money. It's just too vile.'

He's shouting and beating him. With his hands, with his belt. Kaspar is neither screaming nor defending himself, he just cries.

He opens the door and grabs him by the scruff of the neck. In a second he's on the floor of the landing where he hits the bannister with his head.

'Never show your face here again! Never!'

He hears him walking fast through the apartment, his sobbing mother following him around. When his father reappears at the door, he finds himself covered by flying notes.

'We don't need your dirty money, you pervert.'

The door slams shut, leaving him sobbing on the floor. He gets up while collecting the banknotes and stuffing them in his pockets. He walks down a couple of floors and sits crying on the steps, not sure of what to do. He can't call Lars, it would be like asking to move in and that would freak him out. He walks down another floor and rings Herr Flugel's bell.

The old man is already in his night gown; Kaspar can hear the wireless blurting out some lively tunes from a local cabaret joint.

'Goodness, what has happened to you, young man?'

'I'm sorry, Herr Flugel, I need a place to stay, just for tonight. I'll slum it on the sofa, on the floor. Please.'

'But of course. Oh dear. Are you hurt?'

'No, I'm fine, thanks.'

Herr Flugel's apartment is small but quaint and well kept. A spacious living room with a kitchenette in the corner and a double bedroom.

He sits on the sofa with his head in his hands, still sobbing but slowly recovering. Herr Flugel goes back pottering in the kitchenette.

'I was preparing a soup for myself, there is enough for two.'

'Thank you, very kind. I'm not hungry.'

'No, I understand. Something terrible seems to have happened to you and food can't be on your mind right now. Well, I'll eat. You don't have to tell me what has happened and you can stay as long as you like. The sofa is rather comfortable and I have some nice bedding for you.'

'Thank you, very kind.'

He has finished his soup and shared some wine with Kaspar.

'And that's all really. I'm ruined. Probably I can't go back to school now. And I have nowhere to live.'

'Well, as I said, the place is small but I won't throw you out in the street, that would be cruel.'

'It hasn't stopped my dad.'

'Yes. He must be very distraught right now. It isn't a pleasant thing to find out, you must concur.'

He's putting the pan away in the kitchenette; when he turns Kaspar is there and throws himself in his arms, sobbing again. Herr Flugel can only pat him on the back promising that everything will be alright.

He has safely put him to bed. Exhausted by the events, he's now asleep and Herr Flugel turns the light off before quietly walking to his bedroom.

In the morning he prepares some pancakes which, together with the smell of coffee, wake Kaspar up.

'Good morning, young man, I trust you had a good rest.'

He's a bit lost waking up in a stranger's home, but he jumps out of bed and stretches. He's in one of Herr Flugel's pyjamas.

'Yes, thank you.'

'I hope you are hungry.'

'I am now, thank you.'

'Perhaps you should skip school today.'

'My satchel is in my bedroom anyway, not sure how I'm going to retrieve it.'

'Maybe I should go up and talk to your parents?'

'Dad has an opinion of you, and it ain't a good one.'

'I kind of figured that out. Nevertheless, you ought to know whether his decision is final or not.'

'I think it is. I disgust him.'

'That is parents' usual reaction, that's why mine never got to know.' Kaspar lifts his head from the plate. 'Do not worry yourself, I'm not about to sneak under your blanket while you are asleep.'

'I never thought you would.' He shrugs, 'Well, even if you did, what difference would it make? I've been used like a dirty rag anyway.'

'Don't talk like that, Kaspar. That nice gentleman you were telling me about last night seems to be genuinely interested in you.'

'I like him a lot. And he has a sad story too. But that's fantasy. When he tires of me, he'll drop me like a stone.'

'Not everyone drops people, Kaspar.'

Herr Flugel is dressed up to visit his sister but first he has an important call to make. He hasn't had anyone to care for in many years and there is a young man in need of help.

'Herr Flugel.'

Kaspar's father is in his underwear and vest, his unemployed days have ravaged his dignity, his pride, his will.

'Good morning, Herr Finkel. I'll come to the point quickly. I have put your son up in my living room as I understand you don't want him home for now, or ever, I'm not sure which. He needs his clothes and his satchel as he would like to continue to attend school. Would you mind allowing him to collect them?'

240

His wife has appeared behind her husband with an imploring look.

'How is he?'

Herr Finkel pushes her back.

'Just go back inside and don't interfere!'

Herr Flugel ignores the pig-headed rudeness. He's used to it: parents, employers, officials, his late partner's relatives. The list is always too long for comfort.

'Tell him to come around tomorrow morning, I'll be at the Arbeitsamt.'

'Thank you, most kind.'

When Kaspar appears at the door, his mother hugs him tight. She can't stop crying. He finds it difficult to look at her in the eyes as he's not exactly proud of what he has done, though he only did it to spare his family from eviction.

He collects all his stuff and when he's at the door he hands an envelope to her.

'Please take it. Hide it from Dad. You're going to need it.'

A bright day of spring again and a long walk through the Tiergarten. Ice cream break. Grass as your bed.

'Jesus, that freaked me out. Are you alright?'

'Sorry about my dad, but can you blame him? Finding me there. And you mistaking him for a client. That was gross.'

'How are you faring?'

'Herr Flugel is an angel. I sleep on the sofa and he feeds me. He saved me in a way.'

'And?'

'He's been very nice to me.'

'Won't last.'

'You keep saying that.'
'Because I know them.'
'You don't know this one.'
'I'm thinking of quitting the trade too.'
'Has your dad found a job?'
'No, but I have plans.'

He can now spend a few nights at Villa Stolberg and it feels like walking through the gates of heaven and back again. The love making is relentless and beyond ecstasy, the afternoon walks and the quiet evenings equally blissful. Sometimes he takes his homework back to the villa and Lars leaves him alone in his study for a couple of hours to complete them.

One day, somehow overwhelmed by the almost rural silence, he leaves his desk half-way through his history essay and walks in nimble steps to the drawing room, finding Lars sat at a small *écritoire,* distractedly perusing some documents. Reassured, he stammers a humble explanation between a tight lipped smile.

'I...I just wanted to check you were still here.'
'I have no plans to leave the house today.'
'Good.'

Lars takes him to his tailor on the Kurfürstendamm to have a couple of flannel suits fitted before reserving a table for dinner at the Adlon. Upon delivery of the first outfit Kaspar also braves Lars' barber for a rare haircut and mockingly stands to attention for inspection in the drawing room at the onset of an early summer dusk. Like a sergeant rounding a fresh recruit, Lars peruses him in jest, adjusting the knot of the tie, straightening the lapels of the jacket.

'Very dapper, young man. Here is the reservation for dinner at the Adlon. Read it carefully.'

Dear Herr Stolberg,

We are delighted to have reserved a table for you and your son for tonight. We look forward to welcoming you at the Adlon.

Regards

He looks up. Lars was expecting the frowning, disappointed face.

'Son?'

Lars lights a cigarette and walks to the French door, one hand in his pocket.

'There will be no candle on the table either. If there is one by mistake, they will remove it. I have been there.'

He sighs in wise resignation.

'We live in a malevolent world. And when it comes to our sort, the word I would use is "malignant". You are a kind and trusting soul, Kaspar, and you have yet to learn that most people aren't so.'

Kaspar stares at the floor. In his endearingly naive universe, he had spent the day dreaming of the two of them holding hands across the table, gaping intensely in each other's eyes.

Lars is making his heart beat fast tonight. His flaxen short hair and vulnerable pallor dazzle against his tailored dark navy suit. His glacial blue eyes and avuncular grin are slowly dissolving what little doubts Kaspar might still nurture.

'You are boarding at the Studiengenossen Internat in Münnerstadt and you are visiting your father who is treating you for dinner. Whether they believe that nonsense or not is immaterial; that is what they want to hear. I can see that it has never crossed your mind, but what we do is against the law. By at least four years. After that the legality will not make us any less detested. Before you ask, your consent is irrelevant. Trust me on this, if we are caught, they won't even ask you.'

He leaves the door and walks back to him. He lifts his chin up with a closed fist and softly kisses his forehead.

'Old Theodor was a beautiful boy of no means in the dying days of the last century. He put his irresistible beauty at the disposal of gentlemen who couldn't resist it. As you have. His arrest meant a permanent stain on his record. When he applied for the butler position, I spotted him gulping in resignation at yet another rejection when I turned the page of his application describing his conviction. You should have seen the shock on his face when he saw me crumpling it up and angrily throwing it in the waste bin. He has been in my service for nearly two decades now. It would be a waste of time to tell you the stories of all the other members of my staff. They are all very similar.'

'Theodor is always so nice to me.'

'Yes. But don't be fooled by this safe haven. Outside that gate the storm is permanent.'

Kaspar falls in his arms. He might be crying but he also

understands. Everything.

'I feels so safe with you at my side.'

* * *

The early summer heat has allowed them to enjoy a calm and pleasant dinner on the terrace of the villa. Theodor has attended to them with his usual avuncular affection, almost as if he feels that that more welcoming the villa is made for Kaspar the more likely he will become a permanent feature of it.

Lars has finished his wine and his hands are flat on the table, the sign of a momentous talk.

'Kaspar, I need to tell you something and I need you to listen carefully.'

He's never in any need to request respectful silences. Kaspar is an attentive listener.

'First, I'd like to ask you something: you have gone through some difficult times and you might have failed to notice what's happening around you, have you?'

'I have an idea.'

'Good. Kaspar, I'm leaving for Argentina in a week's time. All my assets have been transferred to Switzerland. It has taken some time, a conspicuous amount of bribes and efforts but the process is now almost complete. I have also invested in some silver mines, hopefully they will bring good returns. My staff will be joining me.'

Kaspar feels his heart sinking away.

'I can't predict what's coming to this country or, for that matter, to the whole of Europe, but I'm not prepared to take the risk. The omens are not good. If you have any doubts,

I'd suggest you pay a visit to your school friend.'

He struggles to comprehend and feels too dejected to speak at this very moment: Max was right, he's being dumped like many others before him perhaps.

Lars takes a sip of the wine.

'I would like you to come with me.'

He sees the boy's shock. He was expecting it.

'I have booked you on the SS Bremen in two weeks' time. It's a direct sail to Buenos Aires. Second class. You'll share your cabin with another gentleman. I thought First Class would be a bit overwhelming at your age. My notary can arrange your passport.' A card appears in Lars' hand. 'This is his number, all he needs is your details. He can be fully trusted. He knows how to get around the need for your parents' permission. He is himself decamping to Berne in a month's time. After that, you won't be able to change your mind.'

He stands behind him, holding his narrow shoulders in his hands while kissing his hair.

'You have time to think about it and I will understand if you decide against it. It's a big undertaking. You'll have total freedom: I'm not in the business of locking up boys of your age. All the same, it will be my honour to allow you to continue your education. It will be my mission. But you have to think about it carefully. It's a new life in a new world, a world you know nothing of.'

He's now leaning against the table, holding his hand.

'I cannot be sure of this, but if you stay you will find yourself among death, war and destruction.'

He rings the bell twice. Max has kind of disappeared lately. He has searched for him at the school gates and at the underpass. He has no idea what might have happened to him but he has decided to follow Lars' advice and pay him a visit.

His mother opens the door.

'Max, one of your friends is here to see you.'

He appears flustered when he finally arrives.

'What is it? Kaspar! Great to see you, come in!'

But he's frozen at the door and no longer sure that he wants to go in.

'Max?'

'Come in, I was just about to go out for the parade.'

'What parade? And why are you wearing that? What is that?'

'Don't be stupid. What do you mean "what is that?". You know perfectly well what it is. The parade is in an hour. Do you want to join us?'

'What? No. I don't want to. Why are you wearing that uniform? What have you got to do with these people?'

'These people are the future, my friend. No more underpass sewer, we are going to wash all that filth away.'

'Filth? We are that filth. We were there a few weeks ago. You took me there.'

'Yes, but now we are redeeming ourselves. We are redeeming Germany! You should join us.'

The heels click. The arm is up. Straight like a sword. The hand spearing the air. The eyes unblinking, beholden to a deceitful, dystopian destiny. They have taken him and made him their prisoner. Their lies are now his lies.

And he knows he has lost him. He stands still, aghast.

'Good bye, Max.'

'Hey, where are you going? Kaspar! Kaspar!'

But he's already on his way to the phone booth at the corner of the block, the card with Lars' notary's number in his hand.

Herr Flugel is frantically helping with the luggage. They are almost at the S-Bahn stop for the Lehrter Bahnhof. Kaspar is calming him down, they have time, he says.

They are on the platform now but they still have ten to fifteen minutes, the next service to Hamburg ready on the track, steam huffing from its underbelly.

'Well, young man, all I can say is: good luck.'

'You're not going to cry, are you?'

'Would love to but I'm just so happy for you.'

'I'm still scared. I don't know anything about Argentina and I don't speak a word of Spanish.'

'You'll learn fast. Young people do.'

'Don't forget the envelope for my mother. Lars has given me enough for their rent for a year. After that, well, I hope something comes up.'

'Don't worry. All in safe hands.'

'Thank you for helping me out, it has meant so much to me.'

'You've meant a lot to me, Kaspar, I hope great things will come to you.'

'Hope you'll be safe.'

He throws his arms wide.

'I'm an old man, what can they do to me?'

'Good bye, Herr Flugel.'

'Good bye, Kaspar.'

They hug tight, patting each other on the back. Neither of them knows who's in more danger: the young one sailing across the Atlantic to a new, mysterious continent, or this old and kind gentleman, staying put in what is about to become the most unkind place on earth.

* * *

The ashes of his cigarette flicker away like fireflies across the wake, the breeze of the Atlantic surprisingly warm, the crest of the waves silvery. He leans on the bannister, immersed in thoughts; the door behind him opens with a creak and closes back with a slam.

'Ah, here you are. I was wondering where you had ended up.'

'Needed fresh air.'

Lars takes a cigarette out of his holder and places it between his lips.

'You have a light?'

'You know what Doctor Fernandez said...'

'Well, yes. Still fancy one, sorry.'

Kaspar lights it up. Lars holds him by the upper arms.

'Let me look at you, that dinner jacket we bought makes you look so handsome.'

'Always the flatterer, you.'

'I think you had a considerable number of admirers in the dining room.'

'I never notice such things, you know me. Glad that it has never bothered you though.'

'And it still doesn't. It still amazes me that you have never taken advantage of the freedom I offered you. Twenty years of loyalty are rather extraordinary.'

'You know very well loyalty has never had anything to do with it.'

'I'm an old man now.'

'Two reasons why I never slept with anyone else: one silly, one serious.'

'Make me laugh.'

'Argentinian men do nothing for me. You know the serious one. In your car. Remember? I do.'

'I'll get ill, frail. I feel guilty.'

'We had this conversation over and over, Lars. Get it in your head: I'm not going anywhere. You'll have to kick me out of the house to get rid of me.'

He caresses his hair.

'I'm not sure how this is going to turn out. It was your idea and I respect it. I don't want you to become too upset though, we don't know what expects us there.'

'It has been six years, things must be better by now.'

Lars nods and turns around. They notice a lone gentleman walking past. He's not in dinner attire. They look at each other and frown, but Lars reassures him.

'Probably not. They are not so brazen. I wonder if they have put someone on the ship. They must have become suspicious of our decision to travel back to Germany after such a long time.'

After the first few years, German émigrés had started to flock to Buenos Aires. The incomers were mostly wealthy families who either didn't agree with National Socialism or had fallen foul of it for some reason or another. The outbreak of war abruptly stopped all the arrivals.

Lars and Kaspar were well established by then: fluent in Spanish and respected by the locals. A good income from the silver mines allowed them to reside in an opulent villa in Recoleta. Kaspar had graduated *cum laude* in civil engineering making Lars immensely proud.

The émigrés sought their friendship and advice but they remained cautious: reports filtering through from Germany were worsening daily and at one point his mother's letters ceased to land on the doorstep. They had to stop sending money to her as they were no longer sure of what had happened to his parents. Travelling back was no longer an option.

They became concerned about spies. Although they had done nothing wrong, they weren't too sure to how the Nazi party viewed citizens who had fled the motherland.

Lars was checking daily on Switzerland's situation. The bulk of his wealth was in Bern and his banker could not reassure him whether Germany would invade or not: 'If they do,' he cabled one day, 'we won't be able to push them back. I must warn you that, as a German exile, they might confiscate everything from you'.

He offered to try to secure some transfers to Argentina but despite their gilded exile in Buenos Aires, Lars had reservations about the financial stability of the country.

It hadn't been difficult to live in tranquil seclusion. Once he had set foot on the docks of Mar del Plata and had spotted Lars standing by his car in his white suit and hat,

Kaspar had instantly realised how much in love he was and that he had taken the right decision. The company of each other was enough for both and Kaspar was determined to spend his evenings studying hard to graduate.

Depression struck them hard over the war years as the reports of widespread carnage and destruction became more and more horrific as the days went by. They had no means to know what had happened to his parents or Max.

They tearfully hugged when Radio El Mundo announced Germany's surrender but thought wise to wait another six years before returning. The images of the devastation had left a lasting impression on them.

Then they started to notice some unwelcome developments. Though they scrupulously avoided socialising with fellow Germans in general, the few they were acquainted with reported on the new arrivals with an ominous warning to keep well away from them.

They followed their advice as the fresh incomers were being hunted by the newly established Mossad; suddenly having German surnames had become increasingly dangerous. Because of his silver mines and the never-ending stream of bribes required for the smooth running of them, Lars had solid connections with the Peronist administration, but the Mossad were efficient and ruthless. If unable to kidnap the war criminals back to Israel, they opted for elimination *in loco*. They had noticed that they were being followed though Lars had calmly reassured the worried young man: 'The Mossad are justifiably thirsty for justice and retribution but they are neither stupid nor reckless. They have probably checked that we fled Germany, not supported it. They know who we are and they aren't in the habit of wasting bullets. I suspect they don't want to harm us but they might be working out how to obtain information from us.'

They were never approached directly. Lars had considered informing them that they had never had any contact with the individuals they sought, but he had no idea how to approach the secret agents who were likely operating illegally in the country.

Kaspar lights another cigarette.

'Why are some of the ship's signs in German?'

'SS Liberté used to be German: SS Europa. War spoils, I guess. The French must have left out a few signs or they just couldn't be bothered.'

'Why were we invited to the Captain's table? I struggled with my French, my head felt like exploding.'

'I found it strange too. There aren't many other Germans on the ship, perhaps they fancied a change in the conversation.'

'I think Madame whatever-was-her-name was trying to pair me off with her daughter.'

'Can you blame her? The most handsome man on the ship?'

'At least my murder of French grammar put her off. How long will it take us?'

'We still have five days at sea before docking at Le Havre. The train to Paris will take no more than three hours and we'll spend the night there. Then it's a day and a night on the Wagons-Lits to Berlin. All reserved. Mind you, border crossing will be painfully slow. The train will be sealed through the DDR and then there will be checks by the Russians, the Americans, the British, heaven knows. We better enjoy the next five days, my dear boy.'

Kaspar kisses him on the cheek.

'I always feel safe with you at my side.'

They have spent twenty years without leaving Argentina and they are in a state of shock after the stringent controls at Le Havre docks. Lars tries some explaining: 'The whole of Europe might still be suspicious of us, Kaspar.'

He has been very quiet for the whole journey and Lars knows why. Although he can't be sure whether his parents are dead or alive, he nurtures no hopes: they have seen the images of the devastation caused by the Allied Forces' bombing. The chances of a survival are indeed negligible.

Lars knows that Kaspar wants to enquire about Max and although he judges that to be a bad idea, he has no intention of stopping him from going ahead. He would do anything for him, like he did when he asked him if he would take him back to Berlin. He's not planning to stay longer than necessary yet he's not so sure about Kaspar. Nostalgia for the city of his birth might sway him to remain.

Despite the luxury of their compartment and the excellent restaurant, they don't get much sleep on the Wagon-Lits service due to the frequent stopping and shunting. Kaspar takes the upper berth and spends the night peering through the curtains. He comes across a few buildings still in ruins and he feels unsettled. He has only seen the consequences of war in pictures or film reels: these are real, and a few metres from him. Some of the stations still have platforms and tracks surrounded by semi-demolished walls.

The train stops for hours before crossing into the DDR and one of the train guards enters the compartment to draw the curtains close with a stern order no to re-open them until well into West Berlin. The Russian checks are surprisingly fast but that's because they are directly entering the British sector. The corporal of the British Army politely asks them to alight and follow him. They are both fluent in English yet Lars warns Kaspar to let him do the talking.

They are ushered inside a tiny shed where they are invited to take a seat by what they believe to be a Captain or a Lieutenant, they have never been familiar with military ranks.

'Gentlemen, do you speak any English?'

They nod. The officer seems to be relieved by that, worrying Lars that he might anticipate a long conversation.

'Thank you for forwarding your travel plans in advance, it has made easier for us to check that everything is in order, but we still have a few questions.'

Kaspar's face is worried but Lars nods in agreement. This seems to please the officer.

'Mr. Stolberg, you left for Buenos Aires in 1931, shortly followed by Mr. Finkel. Why have you decided to return to Berlin now?'

'The situation prevented us from returning any earlier, you would agree on that, sir.'

'Yes, of course. May I ask you, what do you mean by "us"?'

'I trust you are a man of the world. Captain?'

'Yes, Captain.'

'Then you won't have any problem in guessing it?'

The officer scrutinises them both.

'I see.'

'Does that present a problem?'

'Not as far as we are concerned. Why did you leave?'

'We were not in agreement with the political developments. Events have proven us right, if I may point that out.'

'Yes, of course. No collusion with the regime then?'

'If there were, we wouldn't have left?'

'Indeed.' He peruses some papers on his desk, then speaks
without lifting his head. 'You are aware that several war
criminals are to this day still escaping to Argentina?'

'Sadly, yes.'

'Have you come into contact with any of them?'

'We have kept a salutary distance. You see, Captain,
neither of us are very political.'

'Certainly not, you didn't stay and fight.'

Lars feels insulted but wisely checks his outrage.

'Captain, even if we wanted to fight, there was hardly any
resistance in any shape or form. Sadly, almost the whole of
the country was behind the regime you have just defeated.
There was nothing to join. Would you have accepted
German nationals in the allied forces?'

'I see your point. It would be of great help to gather
further intelligence on the whereabouts of these escapees.
You have been living in Buenos Aires for twenty years and
must know the place well.'

'We do. Captain, if you have any doubt about us, let me
state very clearly that both my companion and I wish in
the strongest possible terms that these despicable individuals are secured to justice. If we could help, we would. We

haven't been threatened or been asked to hide them. We might be fellow Germans but we have kept a low profile. If anything, we are the ones in danger; if they come to us for assistance, I can assure you we won't offer any and we will report them. That might not please them a great deal, would you agree? These are people for whom violence is always an option.'

'I suppose. Are you planning to stay?'

He looks at Kaspar who is silent and looks intimidated by the interrogation.

'Unlikely.'

The officer hands him a card.

'This is our contact in Buenos Aires. Please feel free to call him if any information comes forward.'

'Will oblige, Captain.'

The officer orders his clerk to stamp their passports and bids a cold good bye.

When back in the compartment he notices the stressed and resentful expression on Kaspar's face and holds his hand in comfort. He sees him shaking.

'He treated us like a pair of criminals.' He blurts out in anger.

'Yes. Well. We've set a whole continent on fire so they are still a bit tetchy, but it'll go away one day. The train terminates at Zoologische Garten as the Lehrter Bahnhof is no more. We don't have to linger.'

'I'm fine with the memories. Without the underpass I wouldn't have met you.'

The Hotel Savoy is no luxury but it was miraculously left

standing and only needed a few repairs to start functioning again. It is also close to the Kurfürstendamm or what
is left of it. Lars notices Kaspar's discomfort at the number
of ruined buildings still dotting the landscape of the city.

'Six years is a short time after an apocalypse.' That is all
the comfort he can offer.

He discourages him to try to find out whether the building where he spent the first sixteen years of his life is still
standing. Most probably it's not and Schöneberg is in the
American sector. Travelling there will mean more checks
and more questions. They know that Herr Flugel died of
natural causes well before war broke out and they are glad
he had the fortune to avoid living through such catastrophe.

He wants to visit the Bunde Standesamt by himself and
Lars lets him. He understands it's something he wants to
do alone.

The building is still semi-derelict but a Teutonic order
has already been established in the offices and he's called
at the desk of the clerk rather quickly.

'Good morning. My name is Finkel, Kaspar Finkel. I
understand how difficult it must be right now and I don't
nurture any hope, however I'd like to find confirmation
whether my parents are dead or alive.'

'We were up and running three years ago. Why didn't
you come here earlier?'

'I've been abroad for a very long time. We didn't part in
good terms either.'

The expression isn't a friendly one. When the clerk, who
is probably in his early forties, moves to shuffle some papers
away, Kaspar discovers that his left arm is missing. His heart

sinks. He thinks of an excuse without realising it will make it worse.

'I left in 1931, well before the war.'

The clerk appears uninterested in the pleading explanation; his suit, with the sleeve folded in, is cheap and worn, his spectacles on the verge of falling apart. His cheeks reveal some severe gaps in his nutrition. It was a big mistake to wear his best suit this morning but Lars had promised to treat him to lunch as dinners are still not a grand affair in the still semi-occupied city.

'Their last address?'

He has written it down on a piece of paper and he leaves it on the desk. The clerk takes it and copies it on a file which he then inserts in a brown envelope. He writes Kaspar's name on it before lifting his head again.

'Your address in Berlin?'

'The Savoy Hotel, Fasanenstrasse, 9/10. I can't remember the post code...'

'I know the place.'

'Thank you. I have another request. I had a friend in Berlin and I wonder if you could look for him as well. I mean whether he is still...'

'I know what you mean.' Another paper and a brown cover appear on the desk. 'Name?'

'Westphal. Maximilian Westphal. Here is his last known address.' He leaves the address on the desk but the clerk hasn't raised his head.

'Is everything alright?'

The clerk now stares at him. The glare is icy.

'Do you know him? You seem to...'

'No, it's quite a common name.'

'If you do, I…'

'I said, it's quite a common name.' The voice is raised and angry. He does know him but he won't tell him, not here at least.

'How long will it take?'

'An enormous amount of records were destroyed, you'll need to be patient.'

He was prepared for this but he's still unsure what to do; back in Buenos Aires such hints would be every day's normal but this is Germany. On its knees, but still Germany. He decides to risk it and takes his wallet out of his jacket; the clerk follows his actions without a single move. His right hand lays a hundred dollar bill on the desk.

'I was wondering if there might be an extra fee for a faster service?' He lays another note of the same amount on top of the first one. 'And since you have two cases…'

The clerk covers the notes with the brown envelope.

'We will contact you at the hotel by post.'

'Most obliged, thank you.'

They have time to burn and not many places to visit. Villa Stolberg was razed to the ground though the land still belongs to Lars; he's not quite sure what to do with it but he will probably sell the plot to developers. Three days go by in hazy boredom.

He has left Lars in the suite and is walking through the hotel lobby on his way to buy some cigarettes.

'Herr Finkel!'

He turns around and recognises the clerk despite the

collar of his mac and his hat hiding half of his face. He holds a large brown envelope in his hand.

'Good morning, Herr...'

'My name is of no relevance, sir. I have the results of our search with me.'

'That's good news. Would you like to have a coffee by any chance?'

'No, thanks, very kind of you. I'm in a hurry.'

'I thought you were going to send them by post?'

'Yes. Well. I decided it might be best in person.'

Kaspar waits but the envelope is still in the clerk's hand, his gaze searching for some kind of confirmation. The question is sudden and brutal.

'You were one of us at the underpass, weren't you?' Kaspar freezes. Speechless. 'Don't worry, we never met.'

'You do know him.'

'He asked me to falsify a birth certificate back in 1945, that's all. Was he your lover?'

'No. Just a friend. My best friend.'

'I see. There were quite a few of us boys. Hard times. After you left, we went through a few raids. Not the Polizei, much nastier types. Some of those got a bit out of control.' His head flips gently on one side, pointing at his missing arm.

'I'm so sorry.'

'Never mind. If anything, it kept me out of the war. Here are our findings.' He hands over the envelope while staring at him. He is about to turn around but he stalls at Kaspar's question.

'And was he? Your lover, I mean.'

The clerk's expression is pained. Kaspar's suave

deportment inspires trust, but circumspection is still in order. Fallen regimes have no friends.

'Resentment makes us bitter, Herr Finkel. I don't recommend it.'

He's about to say good-bye but the clerk is already through the revolving door.

Lars is sitting in the armchair in their suite while Kaspar looks out of the window with the envelope in his hands.

'Would you prefer to read it alone?'

'No. I need you here.'

'I trust you haven't entertained any hope? I would hate to see you crushed by what's in that envelope.'

'I haven't.'

He opens it and reads it. A silence falls on the room, solemnly respected by Lars. He's not crying but remains glued to the window. In reflection. Dusk is upon them, a hint of a pastel spring sunset. He turns around, like suddenly out of a state of trance.

'Sorry, I'm keeping you on tenterhooks.'

'Not at all. Well?'

'The building was destroyed; they were unable to check who was inside, however no one under their names has ever re-registered at the Standesamt. They have been declared deceased.'

'I'm sorry, Kaspar.'

'I didn't nurture any hope, you don't have to worry.'

'Nevertheless, it's closure, I suppose. What about Max?'

Another long silence but Kaspar realises he's being cruel in withholding the information from Lars. He doesn't turn away from the window, a tentative knot in his voice.

'He became Obersturmbannführer of a camp in the east. He killed himself in his office six weeks before the liberation by the Red Army. He has been posthumously found guilty of genocide and declared a war criminal.'

Lars lowers his face in his hand.

'I'm so sorry, Kaspar.'

A week has gone by. They have laid a big wreath of flowers with his parents' names at the local Lutheran church. That was all they could do. Lars has convinced him to abandon the idea of having one made for Max: 'His name might be recognised. Remember him for who he was, not for what he had become.'

They are sitting at the hotel's cafè. The weather now allows a few tables outside.

'Kaspar, I've never told you what to do or not to do, but your life…our life, is in Buenos Aires.'

He is silent. As he has been over the past few days. Then a burst. Tears.

'How can anyone do anything like that? Max was a kind boy. He was my best friend. He couldn't hurt a fly. Why? Why?'

His fist lands on the table with a loud thump before sealing his lips in anger. He's shaking. The details of the charges will stay with him forever.

The waitress turns around but quickly returns to her chores; this kind of scene has been all too frequent over the past six years.

On the night of the discovery they had been unable to

get any sleep. Upon seeing him bent on the sink, vomiting in tearful spasms, Lars had picked up the witnesses' report from the bathroom floor. He had been unable to continue reading beyond the first few lines. With blood rapidly draining from his veins, he had perched himself on the edge of the bathtub, staring numbly at the floor. Incredulous. Speechless.

'I have no answer. Brain-washing, desperation. I don't know.'

Kaspar has seen enough.

'Take me home.'

'Wise.'

'Promise you'll never leave me.'

'I can't. I'm an old man, Kaspar.'

'I'll take care of you.'

Lars grabs his hands.

'Let's go home.'

Ruhe

The last brushstroke gives him an immense satisfaction. The last trace of the old colour gone; the dark, intense blue he has chosen now covering the whole of the hull.

He had woken up early this morning, it must have been five, too excited by the upcoming final touch. After a coffee and a pastry, he had collected the tin of paint and proceeded in earnest.

He's now on his third cappuccino, sitting cross-legged on the tarmac of the marina, in admiration of his own work. Patting himself on the back.

The sun is hot now and he'll have to take shelter soon. He only wears his swimming trunks on the boat, sometimes for too long; but hygiene quickly became secondary to the accomplishment of the task. Like all red-haired people his skin is too pink to endure the now blazing rays without burning to a crisp; it has happened to him so many times already.

He'll have a shower in the new cubicle just installed in the living quarters. It works perfectly. Changed into clean trunks and a white t-shirt, he starts tiding up paints and tools, some of which he intends to dispose of.

A new set of table and chairs bought at a sale of marine furniture is laid out on the veranda at the back. At the front there is enough space above the living quarters for a couple of mattresses for sunbathing, though, due to his complexion, not really his thing. Maybe a guest.

He'll sail along the Wannsee today. Anytime: that's the best aspect of it, not having a timetable to abide to.

Shaved and scrubbed of all the paint marks, he sits in the shade, researching the map of the network of lakes, rivers and canals dotting the great Berlin area. He hears the screeching brakes of a bike and lifts his head in the direction of the shore.

He has seen him every morning, briefly stopping on his bike and looking at his boat; or at him, perhaps admiring both, he's not quite sure. He has never engaged in conversation. That changes today.

'Good morning.'

'Good morning to you.'

'Looks like the job is finished.'

He turns in admiration of his own work.

'Yes, today.'

'You must be proud.'

'Very. I've noticed you stopping every day. You like boats?'

'I've never thought about it. Maybe. I certainly like yours. You've done an amazing job. But I'm being rude: I'm Roland.'

'Nice to meet you Roland. Heiko here. Would you like to share the fourth coffee of the morning with me? You've been following my work, time to step on it.'

'That's very kind of you, I feel like intruding.'

'Not at all. My boat and my boat only. All on my own, so company always sought.'

Heiko returns with two big mugs.

'Do you live around here?'

'Yes, I moved out of Berlin when I retired. A small flat just outside Potsdam, been fifteen years now.'

'And never thought about having a boat?'

'Well, yes and no. Too old now in any case.'

'You seem to be in good shape though.'

And he is. Roland has just turned seventy-four but he cycles twenty to thirty kilometres every morning in summer and goes swimming to the local public pool for a couple of hours every day in winter. He also eats healthily and that has helped him to maintain a slender figure. The full batch of wavy hair is silver but shaped in a modern cut. Hardly any line ruins his still handsome face.

'What made you buy one?'

'When I turned fifty I sold my business. I owned a bistro in the Tiergarten, you might have been there by chance. The Bismarck?'

'What made you name a bistro after such a person, I wonder?'

'I didn't. It was already called that when I bought it. I just added an Iron Cappuccino to the menu. Incidentally, the young lady who bought it kept the name. Strange. And a bit outdated now.'

They have finished the coffee. Roland is about to stand up.

'Well, thanks for the coffee and the talk. Most pleasant. I haven't noticed the name though.'

'The name?'

'Of the boat?'

'Oh, yes. I've yet to decide. It was called something banal

before but I want to choose something a bit more original. You can give me a suggestion if you'd like.'

'I'll have to think about it. Sailing today?'

'Yep, anytime.' Heiko clears up the mugs and then reappears from below the deck. 'If you fancy a ride, you are most welcome. No guests planned for quite some time.'

'Not possible today, but it's very kind of you.'

'What about tomorrow? Weather is supposed to hold.' Roland thinks for a moment. Heiko pats him on the arm. 'Come on, retirement can't be that busy.'

He laughs.

'It certainly isn't. Yes, tomorrow will be perfect.'

He arrives at around nine. They hadn't set up a time but they have all day ahead of them and Heiko was right: it's another splendid one, the sun already warm, the light blinding.

Heiko is in his swimming trunks and soon Roland disposes of his t-shirt, helping him with a few manoeuvres to set the boat off; then he starts emptying the big rucksack he has brought along.

'As a mark of gratitude for the invitation I thought I should take care of lunch. I didn't ask about your preferences though. Anything you don't eat? Vegetarian perhaps?'

'I eat everything, me.'

'That's a relief, where are we heading?'

'There's a quiet little bay where we can set anchor. I fancy a good splash.'

'Good plan.'

The quiet bay is blissful. No one around. They get rid of

the trunks and have a long athletic swim. Then, lunch time. Roland has brought along two bottles of Grüner Veltliner which have been kept chilled in the small fridge.

'All delicious, thanks Roland, much appreciated.'

'My pleasure, ride and swim have been heaven.' Heiko starts clearing the table. 'Are you actually retired? I mean, after selling the cafè? Are you going to do something else?'

'Not sure yet. I'm a bit young to stop. For the moment I'm happy to take a breather with the boat. I used some of the proceeds to buy and restore it. In winter I stay in the city. I rent a small apartment in Tempelhof.'

'Seems rather a good decision to me.'

He sails the boat to a shaded area which gives them the opportunity to go for an alcohol-induced nap on the two mattresses at the front.

They don't wake up before four. Heiko serves coffee and they slowly sail back to the marina. Roland is back on his bike.

'Thanks for the amazing day.'

'Pleasure, long summer ahead. No need to spend it alone. A boat is the best place to chat.'

'The day after tomorrow?'

'You got it.'

Roland's lunches become more and more delicious as the days go by and he feels confident enough with his new friend to confess that he hasn't prepared a meal for anyone over the past five years. This encounter has renewed his passion for cooking and his sailing mate's appreciation has made him dust off some buried recipe books.

'How come?'

'My partner passed away. He was ten years older than me so I was kind of prepared. He never had a strong constitution to stay fit so his health suffered.'

'Sorry to hear that.'

'Oh, it has been long enough. He was a good person.'

'How long were you together?'

'Thirty-odd years.'

'That is an achievement.' Heiko starts to clear up the plates and declines the offer to help. 'Do you have anyone now?'

'Time has well and truly passed for that, my friend.'

'You are still fit and healthy.'

'Even if it happened, the time left is bound to be short and with complications. Who wants to embark on that?'

'Don't you still feel the need for a bit of fun though?'

'Sometimes. When that happens I order a takeaway.'

Heiko bursts in a laugh, spitting the wine he was sipping.

'Sorry, that was funny.'

'Well, they aren't going to drop dead at my feet, aren't they?'

'Not judging, thought it was funny, that's all. I mean, the way you call it.'

'Lately I have a regular. Nice kid. Quiet and introvert. He grew up on the other side, so I suspect that all his life he's been told to keep his mouth shut. Still lives with his parents in one of those apartment blocks in the east. I don't do much in the bedroom anymore anyway: don't want to get a heart attack. Can you imagine the fright he would get? Sometimes he stays the night. It's nice to hold him, that's all.'

'I guessed you were the affectionate type. Is that enough for you? I mean, emotionally?'

'Well, it has to be. And there is no effort. At my age even love is an effort.' Heiko walks inside and returns with another bottle. 'I'll be an alcoholic at the end of summer.'

'Glad to hear your plans include these boat trips for the remainder of the season.'

'Only if you keep inviting me and don't feel you have to. I can become a bore, I know that. Old men do.'

'No chance mister. Great chats.'

The weather holds and the trips become a three day a week schedule. With almost the whole of the Wannsee explored, Heiko proposes a slow sail up to the city with an overnight stay on the boat. They sail up to Spandau then veer right towards the Spree. They set anchor for lunch before entering the river. Roland sees Heiko re-surfacing from down below with two chilled bottles of Riesling.

'I hope they don't do breathalysing for sailing.'

'You know, I'm not so sure.'

He fills both glasses anyway.

'I haven't asked much about you though. Not because I'm not interested, didn't want to pry.'

'You're such a proper gentleman, Roland. No problem. Fire away.'

'Do you have someone in your life?'

The pause somehow worries Roland.

'I'm married. Well, still married. Kind of.'

He puts his glass back on the table.

'If it's too complicated or painful really, you don't need to...'

'No, I think it's good to talk about it. And with you.' He takes a long sip. 'A boy of fifteen and a daughter of eighteen as well. They live with my wife.'

'Are you separated?'

'No.' He seems uncomfortable. 'Last year I came out to them.' He stands up and looks at the shore in sombre reflection. 'It didn't go well.'

He clears the plates and starts the engine.

'We better move on if we want to keep the berth I booked for the night.'

They sail up the Spree at a slow pace and finally dock. They take turns to have a good shave and a shower in the small bathroom and head for a biergarten Heiko knows about. The place is heaving with young people which pleases Roland no end.

'They are so alive and boisterous. It feels good to have them around.'

'Do you feel lonely?'

'At times. I'd be lying if I said I don't. You must have noticed that I haven't turned down a single one of your invites.'

They walk back in silence to the boat. Heiko rummages through the cupboard and comes back with two sleeping bags.

'Haven't got around to buy any bedding, sorry.'

'That's perfect.'

The four berths are located at each corner of the lower cabin, He lets Roland choose one of the three available and he's about to turn the light out.

'I do want to tell you but I need the right moment. It's

not a happy story.'

The morning is cloudy and when Roland wakes up, Heiko's berth is empty. He gets up and walks onto the deck in his underwear forgetting that this isn't the almost always deserted Wannsee marina; there are people walking up and down the river bank. He beats a hasty retreat and resurfaces in his trunks, t-shirts and a hoodie he had taken with him in case of a change of weather. Heiko has just arrived.

'There is a good Konditorei not far from here, thought for a change I'd provide the catering.'

The sail back is pleasantly melancholic, the sky grey, menacing a rain which fortunately never materialises.

The following week summer is back with temperatures in the thirties. The routine re-starts and after being invited to stay for supper, Roland goes shopping for groceries, on a mission to cook a sumptuous dinner on the single stove of the boat. He also stocks up with paper tablecloths, napkins and an electric candle, rightly thinking that a live one is a non-starter on a wooden boat.

'Roland, that was amazing. How did you manage with only one stove?'

'Well, had to pace things but I like a challenge.'

The dusk is darker, the Riesling flowing, the breeze warm. The only source of light is now the electric candle. Suddenly a bolt from Heiko.

'I was seeing a younger man. A nice thirty-something professional who wanted to progress into a more serious phase. You know, move in together, all that. After several rehearsals, I gathered my family in the kitchen and got it all out.'

Roland doesn't interrupt. He knows there is about to be a flood and it's no use trying to stem it.

'I've never been a girly type so they never had any suspicions. It hit them hard. Predictably, my wife cried and my daughter was shocked into silence. My son was fourteen at the time.'

He stands and walks inside to retrieve another bottle. He needs it.

'He jumped off his chair and started hitting me. I was trying to restrain him but there was a fury I could neither understand nor contain and I didn't want to harm him. He was like possessed by an uncontrollable anger. He called me everything under the sun, I didn't know what to do or say. Perhaps he had very homophobic schoolmates, I don't know. Then he ran away in the middle of the night. The police found him.'

He stands up and turns away from Roland.

'I put myself in their hands: if they wanted me to stay I would have left my partner and carried on as a family. For the children mostly. My wife asked me to leave so the only thing I could offer was financial support. But they weren't in forgiving mood.'

Roland is at a loss of what to say but he feels a break would benefit Heiko.

'How is your son now?'

'He followed us and attacked my partner. He had a knife with him.'

Roland raises a hand to cover his mouth.

'He's a small lad and we disarmed him quickly, but I understood then that his mental health had taken a battering. My partner was shocked and felt in danger. He left me. I just send the cheques now but I haven't spoken to any of them for over a year. I try. But they hang up on me.'

'Perhaps they were angry at losing you?'

'Perhaps.' Clearing up is done in silence. Roland is about to leave. 'Thank you for listening.'

* * *

The sun is still up and the breeze warm. These rides back are a further pleasure after the days on the boat. An early return today; they treated themselves to a robust lunch and he plans to be home for seven at the latest.

He's climbing uphill, only a short section in the woods before reaching the suburbs of Potsdam; good for sweating the wine off, the only aspect of the day trips Roland is worried about. He is fastidious with his fitness regime.

Another bike is behind him, tailing his wheel. Nowadays most people overtake him as he's no longer in a hurry for anything.

He makes a gesture to encourage the overtaking and the other cyclist is now at his side. Then he passes him. He wears a blue hoodie and he has seen that blue hoodie somewhere else though he cannot quite recall the exact time and location. All that wine.

The hooded cyclist slows down again and he's now back at his side. He has no time to wonder, the kick is sharp and violent. He tries to keep the handle bar steady but his bike veers off the kerb, sending him tumbling on the mossy ground until he luckily comes to halt before hitting a tree.

'What the hell...'

He stands up and checks himself for broken limbs, at his age this is already much more than they can take without snapping. He feels fine and he sets to search for his glasses; he finds them near the bike, wonky but wearable. Able to see clearly again, he lifts his head up and spots the cyclist standing at the kerb with his hands in his jeans' pockets, his bike flat on the pavement. Without removing his hood, he starts walking towards Roland with long and determined steps. Roland takes his wallet out of his shorts' back pocket and flags it up, waving it with his hands open wide.

'Please take it, there are a few Marks in it. No need for violence. Take the bike too if you want.'

While saying that he remains perplexed. There is hardly ever any crime in this area, it's much safer than the inner city. He has never thought this would happen to him. This is decidedly odd.

He can't tell how old the man is or if he's a man at all. He's young, of that he is sure, perhaps a boy. But he's unable to discern his face as the hood is closed tight.

He keeps walking in his direction. Perhaps not a thief but worse, a case of schizophrenia. He's really terrified now and his hands are pleading for calm.

The boy is standing in front of him now but all he seems to be doing is walking in a frenzy left to right, his hands still in his pockets, as if unsure of what to do next. Before Roland can utter another word, he walks beside him and starts kicking the trunk of a tree with angry force, scurrilous words interjecting savage grunts in an inexplicable furious outburst.

He puts the wallet away but he's still afraid. The boy might be indeed schizophrenic and when his anger against the tree is exhausted he might redirect it to him.

But after a few enraged kicks his bare fists are now hitting the rough cortex of the trunk. He jumps behind him and grabs his arms.

'Hey, hey, you're hurting yourself, you'll bleed. Stop that. What is wrong with you? What's the matter with you?'

The boy fights back a little but he can tell from the grip that his arms are thin and the body frame scrawny. His restraint is holding: his fists are still punching ahead yet they can't reach the tree as Roland notices a little bleeding already on one of them.

While holding him back he tries to reassure him.

'Can you calm down? You're going to get hurt. Just calm down for a second.'

He finally stops convulsing and grunting and when released from the grip, he walks forward and leans on the tree, still not a word.

Roland is exhausted, holding himself up with his hands on his knees, panting and fearing for his heart. This is no tussle for old men.

'Christ, what has got into you young man? You're not a thief, clearly. What is it that you want from me?'

He turns around and lowers the hood. The sun has set, yet it is still clear enough for Roland to see. The features and the red hair. The eyes.

'Oh Jesus. Listen young man, no matter what's going through your mind, listen to me: I am not your father's partner, boyfriend or lover. I am none of these things. I am his friend. Do you understand? We are just friends, and that's all.'

The boy's face is disfigured by a pained anger, either at Roland or himself, he's unable to tell.

'If you have a knife, please don't try to use it. I'm an old guy and I have no intention of harming you.' He looks at the boy's hands. 'You're bleeding.'

The boy shrugs and sets off for his bike. Roland is still in a state of shock but somehow relieved. He walks to his bike and starts checking it for damages. Thankfully the mossy terrain has lessened the blows and after having scrubbed away dirt and dry mud he regains the road.

The boy is still there, his hood up again, holding his bike at his side, about five to six metres ahead of him. He's unsure of what to do. He had noticed that blue hoodie on a bench near the boat's mooring. Quite a few evenings, he now recalls. He has been stalking him.

He decides to tentatively walk towards him and check his reaction. If he cycles away so be it. He's really in no need for this. When he reaches his side the boy neither moves nor looks at him. He's staring ahead, in the direction of the city.

'Are you ok?'

No reply. He sees a red streak dripping from one of his hands.

'Christ, I think I have some paper napkins in my rucksack, hold on.'

He takes them out. With one hand he holds his arm and with the other gently pats the wound which fortunately is merely a scratch. He stopped him in time.

'It isn't serious, just hold the napkin around your hand. We can walk back to Potsdam. Would you like to walk back?'

The boy turns around and sets off. 'Thanks for waiting,' he whispers to himself with raised eyes while fumbling with his rucksack and trying to hold the bike upright at the same time.

He's back at his side. The walk remains wordless for at least ten to fifteen minutes. The boy hasn't turned once.

'May I ask you your name?'

Still no turning.

'Oliver. But my mates and my girlfriend call me Ollie.'

'I'm Roland.'

They are in the city but he hasn't managed to extract any more vocabulary and he has lost any hope for a full and meaningful sentence. He's ready to say good-bye and nothing else. His age has steadily eroded his tolerance for most things and one of them is sulky teenagers.

'Ok, Oliver, not the best of circumstances but good luck anyway.'

He turns around for the first time.

'I'm hungry.'

'Are you now?'

'Yes, are you deaf? A burger?'

Roland rolls his head around, thinking aloud.

'Very well. Let's see. There must be a burger joint around here somewhere. If we walk a bit further into the centre we'll find one.'

He doesn't expect a reply and in any case Ollie has started walking again.

They find one. The stench of fried meat and potato churns

his stomach. Roland has ordered a small box of french fries while Ollie is now staring at a tall pile of meat, processed cheese and polyester bread buns. The beverage had to be the biggest, the tub of coke of such size that he can barely see him behind it.

The hood is down again. The resemblance with Heiko is even more evident under improved light, though, unlike his muscular father, his frame is scrawny, on the side of unhealthy.

'Isn't it a bit late? Shouldn't you be at home by now?'

A shrug.

'As if anyone gives a shit.'

'Your mother might.'

'Nah.'

Another bite. Roland picks up a fry, dips it in the mayonnaise box and munches half of it. He cringes. Ollie almost never raises his eyes from the plate.

'Are you telling my dad?'

'No, I won't do that.'

There is no further conversation. When they are outside he's preparing to say goodbye as he's now at the end of his tank of energy and he's running on fumes. He needs his bed.

'I get hungry after school.'

'Yes, that's normal.'

'Tomorrow at two then.'

He's about to reply but he's gone, cycling away, his hood up again.

When he shows up, Ollie is already sitting on a bench outside the burger bar with his hood up. He's staring at the pavement. His right knee jiggles rhythmically up and down. Roland has by now gathered that 'Hallo' and 'Goodbye' have gained neither meaning nor importance is his still short life. He looks up.

'You're late.'

Roland looks at his wristwatch and it shows two minutes past two.

'Well, it's only...' But he's already opening the door of the burger bar.

Ollie wants him to order exactly the same as the day before. When he returns to the table with the food, he notices the boy nervously adjusting the mustard, the ketchup bottles and the salt and pepper containers in a carefully aligned position in the middle; he could swear that they were in the very same position the day before.

He's also wearing the same clothes; clean, but exactly the same: jeans, trainers, a white t-shirt with no logo and the blue hoodie. Probably normal at that age though he finds the white t-shirt odd: teenagers usually prefer them to declare something on their behalf; normally something incredibly stupid but something all the same.

The flashbacks come thick and fast now. When he had noticed Ollie on a bench not too far from the boat's mooring, he was always perched on the right hand side with his bike exactly in the same position. The same position in which he found him outside today. He's now painstakingly adjusting the burger to the precise centre of the plate. He then moves the chips' carton box to his right; exactly like yesterday.

Roland tries to observe all of this unnoticed.

'How is your hand?'

He shows it to him. It has no bandage though a light crust is beginning to form on the skin. He thinks about asking why no one has medicated it but he resolves not to.

'School ok?'

'Shit.'

'Yes, it always is at your age.'

Another shrug. He struggles to see any point in these meetings as Ollie fails to put two words together at the best of times, but when they are outside he's met with another two-words order.

'Two again.'

'Ollie, tomorrow we are sailing out. With your dad.'

'After tomorrow then.'

'Yes, that's fine, but why don't you...'

But he's already cycling away. Does he ever wait for a reply, he wonders.

On the next encounter he becomes slightly conscious of being seen in the same burger bar with a visibly underage boy for the third time in a row. On the other hand Ollie's heterosexual brain hasn't processed the eventuality of their meetings being misunderstood by the burly Turkish owner. From time to time Roland works out an explanation in case a member of the Polizei turns up.

'Sorry about the kick.'

It has taken four days to receive one, but an apology is better than nothing, he thinks.

'No worries. No damage done.'

Together with the apology, his eyes now occasionally lift

from the table. A resounding progress which pushes Roland to try his luck.

'Ollie, you can't carry on trying to beat your dad's friends or lovers up. That is not what people do.'

'I'm not people. I'm shit.'

'That's not what I was trying to say. Why don't you try talking to him?'

'He hates me.'

'That isn't true, and you know it. Where did you get that shit from?'

He has noticed that swearwords make the young man more at ease.

'He left us.'

'He says you as a family kicked him out.'

'Mum did. I said nothing.'

Roland sighs.

'Why that doesn't surprise me. You could have said you wanted him to stay? He would have. He has told me so.'

The longest silence. Ollie's hands shape in two nervous fists, his eyes staring at the empty plate.

'How is he?'

'He's well. But sad. He misses you all. You must be missing him too.'

'Nah.'

'You are a crap liar, Ollie. Call him and ask him, you have his number, haven't you?'

A nod, yet not a promise.

He's worn out by these encounters and after working out the young man's obsessive compulsive disorders, he's now firmly convinced that Ollie is in dire need of professional help. He's an old queen, he thinks, one that has outlived his partner, his patience, his forbearance. Even occasional parenting stretches his tolerance.

But when Ollie requests his attendance for the following day at the end of every afternoon, he's afraid of what reaction a refusal would cause and he's not so keen on finding out, given the circumstances of their first encounter.

'Do you have trouble at school because of your father?' A nod. 'Bad shit? They bully you?'

'Kicks and punches. They call me names. Dad is a queer, so I'm the same.'

'That's total bollocks.' His attempts at swearing and slang are rather lame but they seem to have some effect. 'And you have a girlfriend anyway.'

'She's evil shit.'

There's no point in trying to figure out the logic of keeping a girlfriend who is 'evil shit'. That is if she is. Never mind whether she actually exists.

'Do you have anyone to talk to?'

The most preposterous of all his questions and one that is unsurprisingly met with a negative shaking of Ollie's head. If he had, he would hardly be sitting in a burger bar every given day talking in monosyllables to a man driving erratically along his very own sunset boulevard.

The next day, frustrated by the lack of progress, he resolves to go for broke.

'Ollie, what you have is shit. What has happened to you is shit, but it's by no means the worst shit. Not even close.'

He looks up, staring. Then frowning, confused, yet

curious.

'Perhaps you want to hear what happened to me when I was roughly your age, do you?'

He glues his lips into an eager nod. Trusting at last.

'And that is shit, you have been warned.'

* * *

They are lulling along the placid waters of the Wannsee.

'My young friend was over last night.'

'Has this boy got a name?'

'Jan.'

'You aren't blowing all your savings on him, are you?'

'Oh no, he's very reasonable.'

'Sounds like a nice lad.'

'He works for a delivery company, very down to earth. If I have to be frank, not the sharpest tool in the box, but the honest type.' They are close to the swimming bay. 'Not much fun in his life: shabby apartment, little money. He sounds lonelier than me sometimes.'

'You want to bring him along?'

'About that. He actually asked me. He's never been on a boat.'

'Can he swim?'

'Not sure.'

'Fine by me.'

Jan is indeed a quiet lad of twenty-five, Roland has never been quite sure about the age. Neither an oil painting nor a 'boy-next-door' type but fit and healthy all the same. His head rarely lifts from staring at the floor but when it happens, he's polite and thoughtful in the few words he utters. Once anchored at the swimming bay he is the first one to dispose of his trunks and dive with a thundering splash, patently having the time of his life. Roland was right, Heiko thinks, this boy doesn't get out much except for the few nights at the old man's apartment and maybe a few hook-ups with lads of his own age.

He has prepared another sumptuous picnic and, after some tentative sips, even Jan is apologetically enjoying the wine.

'More of a coke type, me. Sorry.'

As per every day's after-lunch routine, Heiko has sailed the boat to a shaded corner and dropped anchor for a deserved afternoon nap. Roland is out of it already on one of the mattresses at the bow. Jan walks along the side of the boat towards the stern where Heiko is still clearing plates and glasses.

'Fast asleep,' the boy says. And he raises a finger to his lips, recommending soft whispers.

'Yes, can hear the snoring.'

Jan raises his eyes in mocking jest.

'Tell me about it. Can I help with the washing-up?'

'No help needed. Just about to make a coffee, want some?'

'Yes, thank you.'

He's sitting cross-legged on one of the deck chairs when Heiko is back with the coffees.

'Thank you for inviting me. Stunning boat. Roland told me the restoration was all your work.'

'Yes. Rather proud of it. My pleasure by the way, it has been nice to have you around. Hope these two old queens haven't bored you to distraction.'

'No. Why?'

'I don't know, dull conversation about life. Ours is behind us, yours all ahead.'

'I'm not very intelligent so I'd rather listen than spout stupid stuff.'

'Who has told you that? I mean, that you are not very intelligent? That is a terrible thing to say. It's cruel.'

'DDR schools. They were only interested in the bright ones. To beat the West.'

'You must be glad that's over. Were you on the wall? Those nights, I mean?'

Jan stares at his cup.

'No. I didn't go.'

Heiko checks himself. He shouldn't assume.

'Don't get me wrong, it was a crap world. Even an idiot like me knows that. I'm glad it's gone.' He pauses, almost afraid of causing offence. 'But it was my world. Simple. Plain. Boring. Like me. They took it away and that was fine. But no one asked me if I wanted the change and I didn't know what to do. I was afraid of saying the wrong thing. My parents were Stasi informers; not agents, they weren't bright enough for that.'

Heiko detects that he's somehow pleased to be listened to. Maybe because no one ever takes any notice of him.

'A man at my school approached me to ask if I wanted to inform too. I refused and told them they could kill me if they wanted to as I wasn't that bothered. He seemed shocked but no one ever contacted me again as I mostly did as I was told. After the fall some people didn't treat us well. I understand why, but I was seventeen and stupid and never harmed anyone.'

'More coffee?'

'Thanks. I like coffee.'

All they can hear is the cicadas and, of course, Roland's snoring.

'He's still unemployed, my dad. He can't find a job to save his life. Maybe his file comes up every time he applies for one, I don't know. I like my delivery job though. I'm alone in the van and I'm not very good with crowds.'

'You seem to like coming over to Roland.'

'I don't do it as a profession. It just happened and he looks after me from time to time. Money is tight. But I don't take advantage and he asks for very little anyway. Sometimes nothing at all. You know, just to be there.'

He seems embarrassed by what he is about to say but he feels comfortable enough now.

'Sex is a bit too much for me, to tell the truth. When I sleep with guys of my age they go about it like bulldozers. It throws me. When I try to slow things down they make me feel like I'm lame.' He finishes the coffee with an embarrassed smile. 'Sorry, that was a bit personal.'

Heiko reassures him with a nod.

'It was amazing to be taken here today. I'm very grateful.' He stands up. 'I'll go and lie by him. He likes to hold me.'

They are ready to leave, Roland turns to Heiko.

'I've never seen him so happy. Thank you for letting him come.'

'My pleasure, smashing lad. Maybe you should tweak

some of your opinions about him a little bit.'

Jan has left the rucksack by his bike and has come back to the boat. Heiko offers his hand but he is now thanking him in his arms.

The summer plods along in the lazy heat, sporadically interrupted by invigorating thunderstorms. Jan joins them from time to time. He has unwittingly introduced an exhilarating spring of youth in their older lives and, unbeknown to them, he basks in the emotional safety of their company. The liberating relief of not having to be.

Now that he feels at ease, he has long afternoon chats with Heiko before returning to the bow and letting Roland hold him, Heiko now fully convinced that it was never really a chore.

Over the season they thumb through their lives' stories, some of them sad, others more uplifting. Roland's thirty years with his late partner were mostly uneventful; he has only good memories of that period and he nurtures them with affection.

One of the last dinners starts in the dark, evenings fall earlier now.

'One more week and then it's time for dry dock.'

'I would be lying if I said I'm not sad.'

'Same here. Thank you for this summer, Roland. It wouldn't have been the same.'

'We have told each other a lot of truths.' A tentative pause. 'But you've never asked about my early years.'

Heiko lowers his head, he's cutting a pear.

'No, I haven't.'

'You've seen it. On my arm.'

'That's why I haven't asked. Though I can guess.'

'Not the whole story though.'

The electric candle flickers upward, giving them ghostly faces. A ghostly past ready to spill over.

Almost midnight. Heiko has bathed in Roland's words. Each one of them.

'When I finally reached the camp in Germany, it had already been liberated by the US Army. The guards on the train surrendered immediately and I was freed on the spot. Roland is still the name he put on the false birth certificate. I never reverted back to the old one. There were other priorities, as you can imagine. You are the second person in the world to know. The first wasn't my partner.'

Four empty bottles of Riesling on the table and the breeze now on the chilly side. Both men have hoodies on. A long silence follows the end of the tale, Heiko's eyes glistening, his head shaking.

'The things we do.'

'Yes. It has been hard to keep faith in humanity. What I saw was beyond challenging. All the same, what choice do we have? The cruelty of men comes in waves, the lucky ones surf their way in between them.'

'What are your feelings about Westphal?'

'They have changed over the years. They were never defined in first place.'

'Do you think he sought redemption by saving you? Do you think he loved you?'

'I can't tell. And the time was brief and fraught. I think he knew hell was awaiting him, if there is such thing. I don't think he genuinely believed that one saved life would have made any difference. The chimneys were billowing all day long and you can't keep blaming orders indefinitely if it's you giving them.

I'm inclined to believe that he had been a kind human being before getting suckered into a never-ending tornado of evil depravity. I understand now that it happens to people. Easier than we'd like to believe.

Our brief time of love-making was so full of tenderness. It bewildered me. But I've never wanted to investigate his past and all I know of is his death. I guess he waited until I was on the train.'

'Too late to cycle home. I'll get the sleeping bags.'

The day before dry dock. Were they not mature gentlemen, there would be tears. Instead there is a firm promise to catch up from time to time over the long winter and a firm pledge to repeat the amazing summer the following year.

'I have some news.'

'Fire away.'

'My son called. Two days ago.'

'Any good?'

'A few grunts here and there but he wants to meet up. Not immediately. Sometime soon.'

'That is good news. It'll take time. Be patient.'

'He said he wants to go for a burger.'

'I'm afraid you'll have to endure that.'

'Some place in Potsdam. He goes there with his best mate apparently. After school.'

'He said that?'

He nods to confirm. Roland makes sure his tight-lipped smile remains unseen while he fakes a shrug.

'Well, you know, teenagers like that shit.'

Heiko frowns in mocking reproach.

'That's not you. Swearing?'

'Embarrassing attempt at sounding young.'

After a long hug he climbs on the ladder and unlocks his bike. Heiko shouts from the deck.

'Roland! We haven't come up with a name for the boat. We had the whole summer!'

'I have.'

'And?'

'*Ruhe.*'

He lifts his big strong hand to wave goodbye.

'*Ruhe.*'

Love, unseen

Full house.

He got drenched on his way to the Staatsoper; he forgot his umbrella and there are no balconies for shelter along the Unter den Linden. He had to dry himself in the holding hall and he was a bit late.

Kathryn, his fellow viola, is setting up her position and, as they share a desk, she's trying to attract his attention.

'Daniel? Daniel?' He turns around, the case still closed. He seems transfixed on the left-hand side of the front row. 'Daniel, the stand? Is it at the right angle? You are the page turner.'

'What? Yes, yes, of course, perfect.'

She's mothering him. When he successfully applied for the post, the conductor wisely paired him with suave and patient Kathryn, already four years in the post. He's the newest and the youngest of the fourteen violas, a real rookie. But at the audition the Maestro was impressed by his faultless technique.

'Daniel, he wants more brio in this movement, here, where Alfredo's brindisi is almost at the end, he said he will point it out...Daniel?'

'What? Yes, of course, Alfredo's brindisi...'

She gently lays her hand on his arm.

'When you are as new as you are, you ought to show a bit more concentration. He notices it. He notices everything, you must have worked that out by now. Your technique is spotless but you seem distracted sometimes.'

'Me? No, no, I'm ok. It's only Verdi, easy night.'

'Don't let him hear that. Are you expecting someone in the audience? You keep looking at the last seat in the corner.'

'No. Not at all. Let's tune.'

Kathryn has a reservoir of inexhaustible patience as she has a son of the same age, sadly with none of Daniel's talent.

'Let's tune.'

He hasn't come. There is a middle-aged man in the last seat of the front row near the side entrance, his wife at his side. He was determined to find the courage tonight, perhaps at the interval, but he hasn't come. He has seen him at the performances of Aida and Forza but tomorrow Lohengrin is on the programme and he might not be a fan of Wagner.

'What station do you walk to?'

'Stadtmitte.'

'I'll walk with you.'

She'll have to take a detour from Stadtmitte but she wants to speak to him and this is her only chance.

'I'm sorry for scolding you before; you know, mother hen.'

'No, not at all, Kathryn, I needed a little shove.'

'I know young men do sometimes. I have one at home who barely knows the difference between a viola and a clarinet.'

He smiles.

'Am I standing in for him?'

'You were waiting for someone in the stalls, were you?'

'Kind of.'

'Kind of?'

'It's really stupid. He seems to come only to Verdi's operas and tomorrow it's bloody Lohengrin.'

'Must be very attractive.'

'I don't really want to talk about it.'

The next morning is spent practicing, the old master works violas hard and he's a rookie after all. He still finds the time to go swimming at the local pool though, resigned to the fact that he won't show up tonight. Why does it have to be Lohengrin? Can they throw in a Macbeth? The old man wrote millions of operas and there's none on the programme for another week. He parts the water with angry force. Annoyance in the young comes in bursts.

Kathryn is going through a few movements and suggestions which the Maestro seems to relay only to her. Maybe he thinks that he's too young and new. He's following her with nervous attention as he won't come tonight anyway. But when her finger lands on the Elsa and Otrunde duet, his eyes spot him.

She lifts her head and, seeing the seat occupied, she turns to him with a questioning look but he quickly reverts back to the score.

'Ok, so, here where the quaver...'

At the first interval he leaps from his chair and leaves the pit in a hurry, Kathryn's eyes following him with a shake of her head. When he's near the seat he hesitates, but with the heart in his throat he claims the empty chair next to the young man.

'Hallo.'

Daniel is startled.

'Hallo. How do you know I've just sat here?'

'I can feel a human presence. How do you know I can't see you?'

'I've seen the stick.' He foolishly points to the long white stick next to the chair then withdraws his finger. 'And the rainbow sticker wrapped around it.'

'Yes. That was my idea. Mum wasn't impressed.'

'The lady who takes you in?' He nods. 'She doesn't stay?'

A little laugh.

'She hates opera.'

'I'm Daniel.'

'Can you place your hand in front of me please? He finds it and they shake with a soft but firm hold.

'Matthias.'

'Nice to meet you, Matthias.'

'Nice to meet you, Daniel, where are you seated?'

'Nowhere, I'm in the orchestra, one of the violas, the newest one. Rookie!'

'You play beautifully. I mean, the violas.'

'You can distinguish all the different instruments?'

'More than anyone else in here. May I ask you how old you are? I need to form an idea in my mind.'

'Twenty-six, and you?'

'Twenty-three. You must be very talented to have been selected at that age.'

'A bit of a prodigy, I was told.' The bell rings. 'Can I come back for a chat in the second interval?'

'Yes. That would be nice.'

He's back. Kathryn has observed him talking to a thin young man in dark trousers, blue jumper and white shirt, his complexion pale, the dark blond hair combed on one side with a hint of hair gel. She found it odd that he kept staring aimlessly ahead.

'Hallo again.'

'Hallo Daniel.'

'I thought you only came to Verdi's operas.'

'Have you been stalking me?'

'What? No. I just looked at the seat, you know, every night. Gosh, yes, that is stalking.'

A reassuring laugh.

'Don't worry, I won't tell my mother. This is always my seat, it's reserved for the disabled. I do like Verdi, the romanticism, the drama. And the tragedy. Tell me, how was Traviata? The production?'

'Violetta was wearing a huge white gown and a pearl necklace. She had fresh camellias in her hair and all the Parisian gentlemen were in white tie. Her salon had red velvet furniture and twenty chandeliers.'

'Really?'

'Well, no. She was in a Neapolitan slum, cooking spaghetti. And Alfredo was a Camorra gangster, you know directors these days.'

They laugh in unison.

'Sometimes it's better to imagine the stage.'

'Is that what you do?'

'More or less. I know the plot, I memorise the libretto and then I try to picture them in my mind. The costumes, the movements, the hugs and the cries. The music and the singing are inside me. Strangely it's easier in Italian than German; the passion in their operas is just unleashed and with no boundaries. Lohengrin is so long. How have they done the swan tonight?'

'A mechanical wing lowered from the ceiling.'

Matthias laughs.

'I imagined it to be a real one, carrying a handsome knight between his wings.'

'Some hope. And poor swan, Lohengrin is not on the light side tonight.' They laugh again. The bell rings. 'Have to go.'

'I like talking to you Daniel.'

'You wouldn't want to go for a coffee after the performance or is it too late? Do you have to get up early?'

'I doubt my mother will let me.'

'Let you?' He says that while frowning, still too early to be accustomed to the fact that Matthias cannot see his facial expressions.

'I'm not a normal twenty-three year old. I'll ask her though. Come back and I'll introduce you.' The bell rings again. 'Lohengrin won't be happy with thirteen violas.'

'Oh gosh, yes, better run.'

While the orchestra is standing to receive a deafening ovation, he sneaks out in haste with the case on his back. Kathryn notices that the conductor's gaze falls on them right at that moment.

He's at the seat, Matthias's mother has arrived and he has already told her about him. She is a stout lady, possibly in her early fifties, dressed simply and bereft of frills or make up, her face is more worn than it should be for her age.

'Mum, Daniel was asking if I could join him for a coffee.'

'It's a bit late.'

Her expression is not one of approval yet he detects a hesitant softness in the reply to her son.

'I can ask him to put me in a taxi afterwards, I have no lectures until ten tomorrow morning.'

'Alright. Did you say you were a member of the orchestra?'

He understands that she is reassured by his profession. She has to place her son's safety in the hands of a stranger but she agrees with reluctance and a motherly warning not to be too late.

When they are left alone it dawns on him that he has never led a blind person before and he's at a loss to what to do. He's standing there feeling a bit stupid with the viola case on his shoulders.

'Don't worry, all you have to do is grab my left arm, I'll have my stick in the right one. Just warn me of steps and of course, don't run me into a wall!'

They laugh in unison again and he finds it easier that he thought. Matthias is also used to it and he's quick to react to warnings about doors or steps.

The cafè is almost empty, it's rather late and Daniel hadn't realised how tired he is as he has played for five hours. His neck and back hurt.

The coffees are on the table, Matthias doesn't seem to need any help in finding his mug.

'It has stopped raining.'

Daniel looks through the windows.

'Is there anything you don't hear?'

'Very little. You must be tired.'

'I admit I am but it's nice to be here with you.'

'Thanks.'

There is a sudden silence during which he takes the chance to stare at Matthias' eyes. He finds them weird, glassy, the grey and blue colouring is almost like that of an alien. They still blink occasionally. Can they cry, he wonders.

'How do you find my eyes?'

'How did you know?'

'That's what people do when there is a silence.'

'Would you be offended if I say that they are beautiful?'

'No. But thanks. I don't know what they look like so I'll trust you.' Another laugh. 'I need to ask you something. You don't have to agree.'

'Ok.'

'It's important for me to form an image of you in my mind. I still don't know who I am talking to.'

'I understand.'

'Would you let me touch your face?'

'Yes. Of course.'

'You're not worried about people thinking we are weird?'

'The cafè is almost empty but no, I don't care.'

'Thank you, that is kind of you. What colour is your hair?'

'Dark brown.'

'Your eyes?'

'Same.'

He brings himself closer to the edge of the table and raises his right hand to Daniel's face. He stops for a fraction of a second, hesitant. Daniel gently grabs his wrist and leads it to his hair. He starts from there; then his small, slender fingers descend onto his eyes and like a silky, diaphanous veil glide over his eyelids, the nose and the ears. They are now tracing the contours of his jaw. Daniel's skin is smooth and the gentle contact is giving him goosebumps; despite his age, his facial hair is still a long way off, if it will ever appear. When his thumb lands on the lips it stops. He feels the lips moving and he presses it on them. Without a second thought Daniel kisses it. He withdraws his hand.

'You are a handsome man.'

'Blushing now.'

'I wouldn't…'

'I'm sorry, I didn't mean…'

'Don't be afraid to be clumsy. It's easy to forget.'

'Did I hear you have a lecture? Are you at university?'

'Yes, a special one. German literature, I'd like to be a teacher one day. It's getting a bit late now and I don't want to worry my mother. It's not easy for her. Can you find a taxi?'

'Sure, is Uber ok?'

'I prefer a taxi. Mum doesn't trust Uber. I can't see where they are taking me.'

'No worries.' He has found one, they walk outside to wait on the pavement. 'Will you be ok on your own?'

'Yes, if I ask they lead me to the door and then from there it's easy.'

'I'd like to see you again.'

'I'd like to meet you again.' He's not quite sure if that was meant as a joke, a reminder, both or neither, so he opts not to follow with any comment. 'Your phone?' Daniel hands him over his iPhone. He taps his number in without any difficulties. 'I can check your messages in audio. Type your number in mine.' The taxi is waiting. 'Stand in front of me please.'

He places the palm of his hand on Daniel's left cheek. When he has established the right location, he leans forward and a soft, quick kiss lands on the right one.

'Good night, Daniel.'

'Good night, Matthias.'

The week after the first encounter is always the hardest: when you are unsure whether the person you are slowly but unavoidably falling in love with has any intention of returning your affection.

After Lohengrin's matinee performance he's the one asking Kathryn out for a coffee; he doesn't possess a big circle of friends and not a best one to confide in as, despite being a prodigy, he still had to study and practise hard to get to where he is now.

'Tell me, Daniel, how do you manage to have your heart wandering somewhere and still play so perfectly?'

'What do you know about my heart?'

'I thought you invited me here to discuss just that? Or maybe I got it wrong, you lot don't like to talk much about your love affairs, my son is like a wall.'

His hands hug the mug.

'I find music is almost a detached part of me. I do wander out but maybe there's a part of the brain which just ploughs ahead, I don't know.'

'It's called a gift.'

'I'm lucky then. They would have kicked me out by now.'

'There's definitely something else on your mind, mother's

302

sixth sense here.' A brief pause. 'The boy you met at the interval last week?'

'Yes.'

'Did you go out with him after the performance?

'For a coffee. Here, as a matter of fact.'

'Nice lad?'

'Lovely one.'

'I know that the seat is reserved.'

He stares at the mug, she can almost hear the thoughts spinning around in his head: a Stravinskian rite of spring.

'He's blind.'

She pauses and takes a good sip of her coffee.

'And how do you feel about it? Are you going to meet up again?'

'Yes. Well. I don't know. He's coming to tomorrow's Rigoletto, he likes Verdi.'

'Must be the romantic type then.' But she realises that Daniel is in no mood for light jokes. 'You have doubts, haven't you?'

She was expecting the nods. They are pained and betray guilt. He's ashamed of those doubts and yet finds it impossible to chase them away.

'I don't know where we are heading, we have seen each other once.' His face makes a brusque turn. 'Damn, I have to stop using that word: see.'

Kathryn lays a hand on his forearm.

'There is no shame in having those doubts, how does he feel about his condition?'

'He seems chilled but how do I know it isn't just a front?'

'Do you want to see him again?'

'Very much. But, what if I can't cope with it? I don't want to hurt him down the line.'

'That is a risk you might have to run and he might understand that too.'

They are standing by the seat again, his mother's expression shows no displeasure but a constant worry, a recurring concern about the dangers Matthias might encounter; dangers people encounter every day but ones which might have more serious consequences for him.

Nonetheless she seems to be able to trust Daniel and she parts with the usual warnings. He has invited him for a coffee at his place and had started to call a taxi but Matthias explained that with him at his side it would be perfectly safe to use the U-Bahn.

The carriage is fairly empty on an early Sunday evening: a few members of the matinee's audience and a small crowd heading for restaurants and cafes.

'At least she didn't warn you not to be late.'

Matthias' reply takes some time, as if he's afraid of it.

'I told her that I might be back tomorrow.'

Daniel remains silent for a while, it's Matthias who has to speak again.

'I have offended you, sorry.'

'No, no, you haven't.'

'It wasn't in your plans, wasn't it? I'm not expecting it, I just thought it was a possibility which may arise. If I have misunderstood you, I apologise. As I can't read facial emotions I'm only able to guess your intentions. My encounters are not very frequent so I do make mistakes, sorry.'

The opposite seats are empty, daring Daniel to lean over to meet his lips. A cold shiver runs through both. He grabs Matthias' hand and holds it until they arrive at their stop.

He lives in Moabit. When it doesn't rain he usually cycles to the Oper, but it has been a wet and cold October and he was planning to invite Matthias over so cycling wouldn't have been an option.

He's renting a comfortable one-bedroom apartment with a decent-size balcony; the Staatsoper pays well but he's content with his small abode and he doesn't feel the need for anything bigger or more luxurious.

It has started raining again and they get a bit wet during the short walk from the stop, Matthias takes his shoes off once he has crossed the entrance door and asks Daniel for directions to the bathroom and the living room.

'Once I know where they are you won't need to show me again.'

Daniel is making coffee but on second thought he calls out from the kitchen.

'I wonder if you fancy a beer or a glass of wine instead of a coffee?'

'A beer would be great, thanks.'

They are side by side when he starts describing his apartment and the locations of furniture or items which he thinks could help Matthias to walk around without bumping into tables and chairs.

'Also there's a balcony right in front of you. Just be careful if you walk straight ahead.'

'I'll stop at the banister, don't worry, we have a balcony at home.'

Awkward silences break out between their conversation, then Daniel finds some courage.

'Sorry about before. You read me right though, I'd like you to stay.'

'Were you worried about being weird? That is normal.'

'Yes. I don't know. I'm kind of afraid of hurting you?'

'You mean in bed?'

'Yes.'

'I'm blind, not made of glass. Though admittedly my body is not on the muscular side. I do exercise though, I have a cycling and a running machine at home.'

Daniel feels a pang of pain: every activity has a special limitation; technology and ingenious inventiveness make some of them available to Matthias but invariably with some restriction attached. This thought keeps crossing his mind.

'I have to ask you to be delicate with me though. If you are into rough action, we have a problem.'

'Not into that, no.'

Daniel has grabbed his hand again.

'Knowing that I can't see your body will make you uncomfortable, you should know that. I've been there before.'

'They freaked out?'

'Some have. I don't have a long record: I'm twenty-three and blind. But if it helps, I have touched your face and when I touch your body I know I will like that too. I have been imagining you all week as a sexy man.'

Matthias laughs when saying that and it relaxes both of them as the conversation was on the verge of nerve-racking intensity. They kiss and pause, then kiss again. Daniel whispers in his ear.

'Bedroom time.'

He's about to ask if he wants the lights out and stops just in time; Matthias is happy with his clumsiness but that would have been spiteful, or at least that's what he thinks.

Their clothes have gone and they are still standing. And kissing. He has explored all of Daniel's body with his hands, slowly, softly, gently. He has aroused him no end and then Daniel feels Matthias' lips by his ear.

'I have been thinking about this moment all week.'

It's a grey morning, a proper October one. They are still asleep, entangled, the duvet at their waist as the heating in the apartment is of the tropical variety.

He stretches and, awake, contemplates Matthias' body: skinny but well formed, pale, sinuous. His eyelids are closed, and that was another stupid question he kept asking himself, fully aware of how stupid it was: of course he closes his eyes when asleep, what an ignorant thing to think.

The travelling aroma of the coffee machine brewing a frothy cappuccino awakes Matthias and he now stands naked at the kitchen door.

'Is this the kitchen? Are you in here?'

He gets closer and kisses him.

'You found the way.'

'I followed the smell.'

Daniel looks down.

'Shame we have to go back to the bedroom now.'

Matthias laughs. And for the first time there is joy in his laugh.

'Why not here? You'll have to guide me through before I

bang my head on something though.' And they laugh, then kiss, then laugh again. They are on the sofa, they fall and roll on the carpet. And a sudden, shimmering happiness runs through Daniel's home.

A few weeks have gone by. Kathryn has noticed Daniel's happiness and she knows the cause of it well before he confides in her.

'Are you a couple then?'

'Yes, he has asked me to be.'

'Asked? I thought you boys were more informal than that. Mind you, I'm used to my son, he just seems to order girls about.'

'He can be very formal but I think it comes with not being able to see me.'

'And your doubts?'

Hands are around the mug again.

'Still there. Can you be in love and still have doubts?'

'That's common, although yours are more, how can I put it, more specific. Is he in love with you?'

A happy nod.

'If your doubts win, you might hurt him badly, you know that, do you?'

A pained stare.

'There is no matinee this Sunday. When that happens I go to my parents for lunch.'

'Family duty.'

'I was wondering...'

'I know what you are wondering.'

'Yes. That was it.'

Matthias kisses him on the cheek. The duvet their little oyster.

'Are your parents ok with the gay thing?'

'Oh yes, I came out at fourteen. Dad is a doctor and Mum a nurse and they are uber-liberal. My little sister couldn't stop going around her school chattering about her cute gay brother.'

'So that's not your main problem.'

'I don't think there is a "main" problem.'

'Are you absolutely sure?'

Daniel gently turns away.

'No, how can I be?'

Matthias turns him over and hugs him tight.

'I'll come.'

Finally a clear day. When they leave the Zoologische Garten S-Bahn station they are hit by some warm rays as they walk through the underpass and stroll over to Savignyplatz where Daniel's parents have raised him and Sabine in a spacious apartment on the sixth floor.

After asking his boyfriend's opinion, he has informed his parents; Matthias was afraid that a sudden shock might have turned what was supposed to be a cheerful Sunday lunch into an embarrassingly fraught afternoon. The reaction was polite but rather mute and Daniel felt that.

The lunch is a great success and Matthias is in his best form. Both parents and sister ask a lot of questions and are genuinely pleased to hear of his progress with his studies. He also learns how proud they all are of Daniel's musical career and they can't help telling him that he had asked his musical director to briefly meet them before his first performance at the Staatsoper.

There are a few awkward moments, especially when his parents ask him about his mum and dad.

'My father left when I was very young and he travels around the world; he's quite a successful businessman. My mum has to look after me.' When he says that, Daniel notices a hint of distress in his mother's eyes, followed by an apprehensive gaze.

A long corridor separates the dining room from the kitchen and Daniel has volunteered to shuttle between the two to help his mother clear the plates.

'You stay with Dad and Sabine; just to warn you, they are a bit nosy.'

He's loading the dishwasher while his mother scrubs a dirty pan in the sink, her face staring at the wall tiles. He tries a spot of small talk, casually informing her of his intention to ask Matthias to move in with him. He then stops and puts a hand on her arm.

'Mum?...Mum?'

She's not turning and continues to scrape the pan but she can't help to lift a hand to wipe her eyes.

'Mum? Are you crying?'

'No. Yes. I mean, it's ok. I'm ok.'

'No, you're not. And I know why.'

He passes her a kitchen towel.

'He's a charming boy, Daniel, very sweet. I'm happy for you both.'

'But he's blind. Is that what you were going to say?'

'No, I wasn't. I'm just, you know, mother's worries.'

'Why should you be worried?'

'Please, Daniel, if you're happy...'

'I am happy, I love Matthias.'

He walks back and closes the door of the kitchen, just realising they could hear them.

'I don't have to look after him twenty-four hours a day, you know? He can be quite independent. As a matter of fact...But why do I have to justify myself?'

She gently strokes his cheek.

'You don't have to, you know that. You two look great together.'

'You know it's important for me that you and Dad like him, that's why I brought him here.'

'We do, we really do.'

'I know it's not going to be easy, I'm not stupid.'

But his mother has no more words, only worries.

It grows stronger and the sleepovers more frequent. Matthias enjoys Daniel's morning practice though he wonders how the neighbours don't get annoyed as he repeats a few passages countless times. Apparently he has struck a deal with them on the hours he is allowed to play.

Daniel was over the moon when he discovered that Matthias could swim and he had the right to reserve a lane at the public sport centre on specific hours.

'If you come along, you can swim in front of me and warn me of the edge so I can turn. Won't need a tapper then.'

'A tapper?'

'He's a volunteer who taps your head to warn you of the edge.'

The morning at the centre is fun and their newly devised system works perfectly. Matthias follows him about half a metre behind and when they are close to the edge Daniel shouts 'turn!' and he gyrates with faultless technique. When they are resting by the edge of the pool Matthias casually lays a hand on Daniel's bottom.

'I knew you were wearing speedos, you must look so sexy.'

'Well, I thought, since you are wearing them too.'

Matthias gets closer and kisses him.

'How did you know there's no one in the pool?'

'I didn't.'

They shop for clothes together and Daniel loves his boyfriend's total reliance on him for style, sizes and colour though he feels a hint of guilt for treating him like a fashion dummy. This is duly noted by Matthias after the tenth jumper is laid on his chest and commented upon how good he looks in it.

Coffee break in KaDeWe is a restful moment, though to Daniel's surprise Matthias really enjoys shopping. Perhaps its frivolity takes him away from a constantly serious life, one with a single issue which never goes away.

'How do you know about colours?'

'I don't, you only do if you become blind.'

'But you commented on them.'

He perceives a pause of discomfort.

'You can train yourself a bit on their characteristics. For instance, I know blue is a dark and more tranquil colour and the colour of the sky. Or red is quite strong and flashy. But I have no idea what they look like. I can't distinguish between light and dark.' They attack the lattes and the chocolate cakes. 'You said you wanted to ask me something.'

'Yes.'

'Must be important.'

Daniel takes his hand.

'Would you move in with me?' He doesn't react though Daniel feels a squeeze. 'If you want to. The reason I'm asking is because I love you.'

'I do. And I do love you too.'

'We can get a bigger place.'

'I want to, I don't know if my mother will let me.'

Daniel is not taken aback, he knows the hold she has on him and he is admittedly becoming tired of it.

'Does your mother have to let you?'

'Not in theory, but…'

'But?'

'Don't take this the wrong way but if it doesn't work out, my only option is to go back to her. She hasn't been nice to you, that I know, but she's afraid for me. Given the circumstances I would ask you not to blame her too much.'

'I don't blame her for anything.'

'You will when she says no.'

Her refusal ushers in a difficult period. Although they have continued with their three days a week routine, Daniel has woken up a few times in the middle of the night to an empty bed. Invariably he finds Matthias on the sofa, curled up in the foetal position, a few tears on his cheeks. He consoles him and overstates how unimportant it is if they cannot move in together. Matthias knows that to be a lie.

Unbeknown to Daniel, he goes on the attack almost every

evening. The match invariably descends into a blackmailing contest. He points out how well he's doing at university instead of being a layabout. She threatens not to take him back if and when they break up. When no one is listening there is not much point in talking.

His mobile rings while he's on his way home from rehearsal. There is no performance tonight and it's not a 'Matthias' night. He has planned for a quiet evening with a film and a glass of wine. He has been given Matthias' mother's phone number and her name appears on the screen. He hesitates as she has never called him since their first meeting at the Staatsoper.

'Hallo.'

'Hallo Daniel, it's Matthias' mother here.'

'Yes, I know, good evening.'

'Good evening Daniel, I'd like to speak to you if you don't mind.'

He does, but he can't be rude and, besides, it might be an opportunity to advance his case. Their case.

'Yes, sure.'

'Are you free now?'

'Yes, I was just going home, if you want you can…'

'No, thanks, I will meet you at Cafè Einstein, the one on the corner around your block.'

A quick look at his watch and the next U-Bahn station.

'Ok, I should be there in about fifteen minutes.'

'Thank you.'

When he arrives, he spots her sitting in a corner, a finished cup of coffee on the table. She's wearing a cheap mac, her hair is grey and untidy; one thing he never had the time to notice is how so unkempt she always looks. They greet each other politely but the frost has never thawed and is not about to melt anytime soon.

'I'll get to the point quickly, Daniel.'

'Please.'

'You probably think I'm being very hard in not allowing my son to come and live with you.' He nods. 'I just want you to know that it has nothing to do with the gay thing. I have accepted Matthias. With great difficulty, but I have.'

'What is it then?'

She pauses. She looks worn out, exhausted.

'There are quite a few details which my son might not have relayed to you.' He's unable to hide a worried look, though he wants to. 'You're underestimating the strength you'll need to be living with him.'

'I don't, I think I'm perfectly capable of looking after Matthias.'

'Let me ask you something Daniel, do you cycle?'

'Yes, of course I do, so?'

'That's something you won't be able to do together.'

'Well, yes, but there is so much else. We went swimming together.'

'Do you like to go to the cinema? The theatre? Or watch television?'

'But we do, and he comes to the Oper to listen to me playing.'

'No, you don't. While you're looking at all those things, he's only listening to them.'

'But we don't have a problem with it.'

'You don't but he does. He just can't tell you. It might be a bed of roses now, it can quickly become one of spines. You have no idea of the challenge.'

'You're lying to keep your son away from me. You're being cruel.'

'I'm not keeping him away from you. I haven't forbidden him to see you. I just don't want to go through the motions of him coming back home again.'

He jolts.

'Again? What do you mean by that? I've asked him, he had a few short affairs but he never had a boyfriend, he has never left home.'

'That is not true.'

'I don't believe you, Matthias doesn't lie to me, you'll do and say anything to keep us apart.'

She opens her purse, takes a paper out and puts it on the table.

'What is it?'

'His ex-boyfriend. He's a thirty-something professor at Matthias' university, though he wasn't teaching him when they met.'

He takes the paper and reads it.

'What do you want me to do with this?'

'You can do anything you want with it. For instance, you could talk to him.'

'I don't want to.'

'But you will. Good bye Daniel.'

No sleep. He turns, gets up, walks to the kitchen, drinks some water and back to the sitting room, the paper on the coffee table. Perhaps he should talk to Matthias first and ask for an explanation. But that might cause an almighty row, and perhaps a huge argument with his mother.

'Herr Dieffenbach?'

'Speaking.'

'You don't know me, my name is Daniel and…'

'Hang on, are you selling something?'

'What? No, no. I need to speak to you. I mean, I would like to speak to you.'

'Are you one of my students? I might have a few Daniels, I need a surname.'

'No, I'm not. It's about Matthias.'

He expected the pause.

'What about him? Has something happened to him?'

'No, nothing, he's well.'

'And who are you?'

'I'm his boyfriend.'

Another short silence.

'Has he given you my number?'

'His mother.'

'I see. Look, I'm not sure it's a good idea. Why do you need to speak to me?'

'Please, Herr Dieffenbach. Please.'

He perceives a hint of distress in the young man's voice.

'Ok, let me see, I'm free this afternoon for an hour. Two o'clock?'

'That's fine.'

'Do you know the Bismarck Bistro? At the edge of the Tiergarten? It's not far from the faculty so I can meet you there for an hour.'

'See you there.'

When he arrives he realises that he has never seen him before but he receives a message telling him where he's sat so he joins him in earnest. Ella shouts at Karl who's furiously tapping away on the phone.

'Karl! Customers! Put away that phone!'

He rushes over and he's now standing ready. They order and an embarrassed silence falls until the coffees are on the table.

Udo Dieffenbach is a fairly handsome man of just over thirty, wearing rather clichéd professorial attire: tweed jacket, crumpled shirt, round spectacles. Daniel has come in jeans, trainers, a Gap hoodie and a waterproof jacket. When he doffs his woolly hat, his hair explodes in all directions.

The coffees break the ice. It has started to snow again though the bistro's temperature is positively equatorial.

'How's young Matthias?'

'He's well, thank you.'

'His studies?'

'Going well.'

'I'm glad to hear it. So, young man, you obviously wanted to ask me something and it must be about Matthias.'

'Yes, sir.'

'I'm a professor but no need to call me that, thanks.'

'Did Matthias come to live with you?'

'He did. For six months.'

'Why did it end? Who ended it? What went wrong?'

Dieffenbach takes a sip.

'That is a hell of a lot of personal questions. Why should

I tell you?'

Daniel hadn't thought about it. Dieffenbach isn't under any obligation to give him any information.

'I've asked Matthias to move in with me.'

'And my experience or opinion is relevant because...?'

'His mother won't let him.'

'Yes, I expected that. Daniel, what has Matthias' mother told you?'

'That he moved in with you and then he went back to live with her, and that I won't be able to look after him.'

'Look after him? He's blind, not paraplegic.'

'Well, that's what she thinks.'

Dieffenbach has noticed his nervousness.

'Why would my opinion make any difference? Do you love each other?'

'Yes.'

'Then ignore Matthias' mother, we did.'

'He's scared of having to go back again.'

'That's understandable. What do you do for a living?'

'I am a viola at the Staatsoper.'

'You must be really talented, such a young age. Tell me, does your profession require a lot of your time and energy? It might sound an ignorant question but I'm not much of a musician so I don't really know. Do you have to practise and rehearse every day?'

'Most days. But we spend three nights together every week; we went shopping and swimming together, we had quite a few days all for ourselves and there haven't been any issues.' The flood is too intense to fool Dieffenbach.

'Not at all?'

319

He lowers his head. He has always found lying difficult.

'Well, some. One is that he didn't tell me about you.'

'Not everyone tells their new boyfriends the full history of their previous lovers.'

'He said he had never lived with anyone though. He lied.'

'I see. Perhaps you shouldn't focus too much on details. Matthias is a good kid and the world turned upside down when he lost his sight.'

Dieffenbach sees his expression and immediately knows. His hand reaches his eyes for a brief cover.

'He hasn't told you that either.'

'How many lies has he told me?'

'I think I've said enough. I'm not sure I should be here giving out this information. You two should have a long conversation.'

'No, please. I want to know.'

Dieffenbach thinks for a moment. He's asking him to interfere in something very private. But he sees his distress.

'Very well, what has he told you about his father?'

'He left and he's a businessman who travels around the world.'

Dieffenbach's head turns away in a long and pensive stare at the silvery landscape, as if he's counting the snowflakes. Daniel exhales.

'Even that isn't true, is it?'

'His father is in Plötzensee. For battery or grievous bodily harm, I'm not really sure and I wasn't interested enough to find out. He's a very violent man with a history of manic depression and I reckon mild schizophrenia too. He used to beat his wife.' He's still doubtful about the wisdom of revealing what he knows. 'And Matthias.'

Daniel is motionless.

'When he was ten or thereabouts, he threw him against a chest of drawers or a table, I don't know. The hit damaged the optic nerve and that was it, his sight never returned. I thought you knew as he knows about colours which he wouldn't if he had been blind from birth.'

'He lied about that too.'

'Daniel, there might be a reason why he has kept all this hidden from you, I wouldn't read too much into it if I were you.'

'Why did he reveal all this to you and not to me? Did you leave him?'

'Yes.'

'Why?'

'Matthias' mother is not a nice person but that doesn't mean she isn't right. After a few months it became increasingly difficult. He's not as comfortable with his disability as he might pretend and we had some very trying days which then became weeks. You should know this: he has inherited some of his father's characteristics and when things started to go wrong, I was unable to deal with the depression.' Dieffenbach is uncomfortable but he has come to like Daniel over this brief encounter. 'It's very sad but when that happens, he uses his condition to get at you: it's heartbreaking and you can't defend yourself without passing for cruel and insensitive. I couldn't cope with it.'

He calls Karl and asks to pay for the coffees. Daniel is stunned and he has to shake him to get his attention.

'I have to go back to the faculty. I think this was all that you wanted to know?' He nods. 'You clearly love him but you have to be prepared. It's not an easy life. Good bye Daniel.'

The screen is overloaded with messages. He hasn't contacted him for two days and they are showing signs of distress. He finally replies and Matthias is over now. On the sofa. In silence.

'What I don't understand is why you had to lie to me about all that.'

But there is no reply. If he could offer a look it would be one of resignation and he's also exhausted by the pain of having to listen to Daniel's long and reproachful rant.

'You could tell me.' He shouts.

'I don't have an answer. I'm not a perfect human being. I make mistakes like everyone else. All I know is that I love you.'

'Yes, I love you too but I haven't lied to you about anything, have I?'

'The sound of that is not how you say to someone that you love them. Perhaps you didn't have anything to lie about?'

'Don't use your affliction to hit back at me!' He immediately realises the enormity of what he has just said and stops. Matthias can't see that he has a hand on his mouth, in horror. He wishes he could take it back but it cannot be unsaid. He remembers what Dieffenbach said to him. A tear is on Matthias' cheek.

'No. I didn't mean it that way, I'm sorry, I really didn't.'

He's hugging him but with no response: the blow was low and likely irreversible.

'I think I'd better go home.'

'No, please, don't.'

'Don't make it worse. We need a break to reflect and you need some space, I can tell.'

'Please stay.'

Matthias has called a taxi with his special app.

'Take care for now, Daniel.'

Dinner time. His mother has called him twice. He sits in silence, barely touching the food.

'Are you going to do this every time?'

'I don't know what you mean.'

'You do, I'm asking: are you?'

'You need protection. You must have forgotten how bad it was when you came back from the professor's house. You almost dropped out of university. I have to think about you. They have no idea how difficult it is. I don't want you to get hurt again.'

'I take that as a yes.'

'Well, I haven't forbidden you to have your affairs, but living with someone has already proved a terrible idea, do you want to go through that again?'

He leaves his dinner unfinished.

'I have some revision to do.'

In his bedroom, he activates the voice command on his desktop computer and prints out what he has dictated:

Daniel,
we lie because we don't want to hurt the ones we love.
M

He folds it and puts it in an envelope; after sealing it, he drops it in his rucksack and walks to his mother's room. It's nearly midnight and he can easily hear the light snoring across the door. He returns to his bedroom and calls a taxi. When he's downstairs he feels the snowflakes on his face. It must be one the coldest days of the year as he feels a layer of ice under his shoes when he stands on the pavement waiting for the cab.

'This address first, please.'

When they are in front of Daniel's apartment's block, he asks the driver to accompany him to the letter boxes and show him number eighteen. He drops the envelope in it and returns to the car.

The new address is fictitious, just close to the Marschallbrucke though far enough to avoid raising suspicions with the driver.

He follows the voice of his smartphone map until he hits the wall of the bridge. He now knows where he stands and he only has to hope that no one is around, that no one will notice him. It's late and the city is deserted, the temperature well below freezing.

He finds the stairs and when he reaches the riverbank he kneels to touch the water. He knows that at this temperature there will be stationary or slow-floating ice packs.

He sits for a moment with his legs crossed but he can't afford to wait too long as someone might come. He's alert for footsteps.

He stands up and starts to undress. He folds his clothes onto the rucksack.

When all is off, he dives and hits a thick sheet of ice. He takes a dip under it and waits. It won't take long.

She's perching on the edge of the armchair. Lately she has been summoned a few times in his dressing room and invariably to talk about one thing and one thing only. He's in his chair at his desk, his fingers holding his chin.

'What's your opinion, Kathryn?'

She touches her forehead with the tip of her fingers; she has ran out of excuses and he knows it.

'The technique is still faultless, I'm sure you can hear it too.'

'The heart?'

She lowers her gaze.

'I agree, not in it, but…'

He raises his hand to stop her.

'I know what happened. We don't need to go through that again. You are paired with him and you have a career too. Do you think he's still interested in this?'

'I'm not sure he's interested in anything anymore, to tell the truth. I'm genuinely worried for him.'

'Yes, so am I. I'm responsible for the whole of the orchestra, Kathryn, there is only so far I can go. He had six months off and admittedly he practiced during those, I could tell. But will he ever be over it?'

'Maestro, I don't know.'

'I'm concerned about tonight. Have you spoken to him?'

'I have. He has asked the theatre to leave the seat empty. And it was during Lohengrin they met. He seemed serene though.'

He will probably be asking Daniel for a chat after the performance. What he will say, he's not quite sure yet; he likes him and he has tried everything, but it has been challenging. He talks very little these days and he barely acknowledges the other members of the orchestra. As soon as rehearsals or performances are over, he sneaks out in a hurry without saying goodbye to anyone. Everyone understands but it's not good for morale. Kathryn has tried to breach the wall but with no success, and she is uncertain of how much support he's receiving from family or friends.

One year today. It's the ninth of January and, like the previous year, the city is under a layer of snow half a metre deep, the temperature a teeth-rattling minus ten degrees.

It was still snowing hard when Daniel arrived at the Staatsoper and Kathryn had tried to ascertain if he was in a fit state to play.

'I think he wants me to play,' he had whispered. The hint of denial in the present tense hadn't reassured her.

His eyes are circled by a thin red line, the weight still hasn't come back and his gaze is haunted, vacant, spent.

While they are setting up their desk, the conductor and Kathryn exchange worried looks. Daniel has turned his head around a few times in the direction of the empty seat. They exchange a few suggestions and he nods in silent approval. She's not convinced that he's here at all but she remembers how detached he can become when he plays, how his heart can wander while his mind processes the score.

And his faultless technique takes him through the long prelude. Clean, perfect, not a tempo or a note wrong.

A rarefied silence cuts through the brief pause before the curtain is raised. His head bows and his arms droop, the viola and the bow in his hands almost touching the floor, one of his cheeks wet. Kathryn feels a rush of panic as the Maestro's baton is almost up again. But he stops when his eye catches Daniel. The conductor swiftly turns a questioning look to Kathryn who has her hand on his arm, trying to shake him, his viola and bow still dangling and now touching the floor. The other members of the orchestra are turning and whispering while a suffused murmur runs through the audience. The first rule is always to carry on playing but he might be seriously ill, he might need help.

The curtain is up, the singers and choir motionless as the music has yet to start. She feels Daniel moving and turns to the Maestro nodding to go ahead. He lifts the baton; covered by the sound, Daniel drops the viola and the bow on the floor. The thump resonates across the auditorium but the orchestra carries on. He gets up and starts walking clumsily across the pit's floor, stepping on his fellow musicians' shoes, bumping into stands. The conductor has his eyes on him and Kathryn has no choice but to abandon her post and follow him in the most discreet way she can.

But he's running to the exit. He's there already, the snowflakes landing on his wet face, the sadness mysteriously dissolved.

He turns left and starts running at full speed; he can hear Kathryn shouting his name, desperate, holding her face in her hands. She can't run after him, she's in a long dress and shivering, it's probably minus fifteen. She doesn't have her phone with her so she takes the decision to go back inside and call the Polizei. She is a mother. She knows.

He's at full throttle along the Unter den Linden, towards the Brandenburg Gate. The city is deserted; something, someone is giving him the energy.

When he reaches the square before the gate he turns

right, still at full speed, towards the Marschallbrucke, the snow up to his ankles, the flakes brushing his cheeks. There are no passers-by and he starts with the white tie, then the jacket, the shirt, the shoes, the trousers, the watch, the boxer shorts, the socks. He's still running and he feels warm, elated, peaceful. He has stopped fighting it.

When he reaches the bridge he runs down the stairs to the river bank, where they found his clothes piled up on his rucksack. He stops, panting. In the morning he had left a single white tulip by the spot and it's miraculously still there.

He takes it, throws it in the water and approaches the bank. The ice packs are static or moving at a slow pace, he can't tell. The snowflakes are starting to stick to his naked blue body when he sees a large enough opening. He's a good diver and he hits the target with determined precision.

Mein lieber Schwan! -
Ach, diese letzte, traurige Fahrt,
Wie gern hätt' ich sie dir erspart!

We are born to fight fury, for righteous rage is what propels us to offend. Yet we leave earthly grief in happiness when atonement idles away from our path. No swan. And no knight.

Yet a wing of white is all around him, a fog perhaps, a haze: warm, soft, cloud-like. He feels his hand leading him away. And the grey and blue of his eyes.

The eyes of the king

I was born in a remote hamlet a few miles from Wroclaw. In the mud. A lot of it.

The last of seven children. Several others had died before my appearance but that was nothing out of the ordinary in my time. When one died of malnutrition, unspecified infections or a combination of the two, my mother was most of the times already with child again. Often birth led straight to burial.

The son of peasants, and among the poorest ones. We never saw the nobleman who owned the estate; all we knew was that he owned us too.

It would be natural to describe my childhood as unhappy and deprived, and while it was certainly the latter, I was usually described by everyone as a cheerful lad.

We had nothing else to measure our deprivation against. All of us were born in it and meekly accepted it. Hard toil to provide hard meals. Hard meals to sustain hard toil. A not very merry go round which rarely stood the challenge of longevity. None of us lived long enough to experience middle age.

Playing and fooling around lasted only for the first few years and then it was fields: from dark mornings to dark nights. We only really inhabited our huts on Sundays: a bath to prepare for church, our single good suits and dresses, a lunch which involved some vague form of meat, tea and bedtime. And back in the mud.

In the run up to the day when our backs would be ready to be bent and broken chasing potatoes, we were sent to the local parish school. A crumbling shed containing a few woodworm-infested desks and chairs.

I have fond memories of those five years. Unlike other schools, where a fiendish headmaster invariably meted out more back-breaking whipping than education, we were blessed with a kind young lady who had stressed from year one the importance of learning both Polish and German.

This hadn't entirely pleased my parents who regarded themselves as Silesian-Polish and bitterly resented Prussian rule despite having known no other: Silesia had been annexed by King Frederick in 1740 and forty-one years had gone by.

The strange and guttural idiom tickled my interest though and I applied myself with vigour. I remember Fräulein Kaminsky stroking my curly blond hair while commenting with glee on how strenuously I applied myself to the 'more useful' of the two languages.

Make no mistake, we did receive a few hits of her ruler on our open palms when we went over to the slacking side.

When on the cusp of surviving my tenth year, my father went to talk to Fräulein Kaminsky, determined to withstand any objection: 'We need Kazimierz in the fields.'

I could tell she was heartbroken. My two languages fully mastered in reading and writing, she probably thought I could make it to teaching or something equally honourable but potatoes were beckoning. And they did. For a good five years.

I was a healthy lad and the fields failed to break me. Fire did.

I had just turned fifteen when the hut went up in flames. With my folks in it. Actually, with the whole of my family in it. The pastor held my shoulders while my glassy blue eyes contemplated a dusk bonfire of my family.

No peasant could afford a ceremony in those days. The burial was simple and fast and there wasn't much left to bury anyway. Another family of destitute peasants were at the ready to move onto the land, rebuild the wooden hut and call it home.

The pastor and Fräulein Kaminsky pleaded with them to add a young orphan to their already vast collection of loitering brats, but they were met with polite yet stern refusal. Too many mouths, not enough gruel.

The pastor absently enquired of my whereabouts during the raging inferno.

'I was with Bartek, Father. In the fields.'

'Doing what?'

'Playing.'

Fräulein Kaminsky collected donations for me but she was hopelessly poor herself. When she handed the small bag of coins to me she was at a loss as to what to say.

'What are you going to do? No one wants you. They have too many children already.'

'I'll walk.'

'Where to?'

'The capital.'

She had always been pro-Prussian and I could detect some excitement in her eyes. She added some extra coins which I tried to refuse, well aware of her dire financial straits.

'I'm glad your German has improved so well. It'll come to be of great help.'

I went to say goodbye to my best and only friend Bartek and while strolling along a remote corner of the fields I received my first kiss. He insisted on a full one. Noting my reaction of abandonment instead of one of rejection, he took my hand and led me to an even more remote spot. He was determined to send me away without my virginity.

I set off on an early morning of a sunny day of May. This was a journey best undertaken at the onset of spring and to be categorically avoided in the winter season, when frost and snowstorms brought the whole region to a standstill.

Marek, the village boot-maker, hadn't given me any money, offering instead a sturdy pair of low boots. I had also stowed in my satchel all the clean long socks I possessed. The pastor had written down directions, villages and cities. The nobleman had issued a sort of document outlining my situation and my good character. I thanked him profusely, not expecting any money with it. And none was given.

I had no idea of how long it would have taken me and it was of no importance to me. As long as I could feed myself, I was determined to enjoy my freedom.

I mostly slept under trees as I wasn't sure my coins were enough to buy me lodgings. I also wanted to arrive in Berlin with some pfennigs in my pocket and I only had the grand total of two Thalers at my disposal.

When the first early summer thunderstorm struck though, I reached the door of an inn a few miles from Zielona Gora with water flooding out of my boots like a river bursting its levies.

The innkeeper, a stout Prussian lady, addressed me in German, I guess ready to slam the door in my face had I replied in Polish. I would be told in later days that my German had a soft, melodic accent; perhaps the sound of it melted her heart.

I asked her for permission to sleep in the stables as I could not afford a room. I remember her turning to her husband with her hands on her hips.

'That's some respect from the lad. Most of these scoundrels would sneak in there without asking!'

My innocence and good manners earned me a sack to cover my dignity while my clothes were hung out to dry, a bowl of potato soup and bread which I devoured in a flash, and a share of the beds allocated to the serving boys.

Possessing no night shirt and in need of none due to the searing heat, it didn't take long for the lad next to me to enrol me in a mutual release of energy, the other boys either giggling, sleeping or joining in. He seemed to the ladies inclined yet with no ladies available to be inclined to. I suppose my long, blond curls made for a decent alternative. His lips sealed mine in a successful attempt to avoid waking the whole inn up, yet it was never meant to be a kiss.

In the morning I received a decent fare for breakfast. On a full stomach I walked to the laundry room to check on my clothes and boots. The inn-keeper was behind me, her hands on my shoulders. Everyone always seemed to want to place their hands on my shoulders. I wasn't very tall, I thought, perhaps that's why.

'What is your name, boy?'

'Kazimierz, madam.'

'How old are you, Kazimierz? Your German is very good, your accent is musical.'

'Thank you. I am almost sixteen years of age.'

'And not a bone of insolence, I could tell that from the start. I think you need to grow another foot, young man. Have you been feeding yourself enough?'

'What I can afford.'

'You need some pork and potatoes at your age.'

'I think my clothes are almost dry, madam.'

'Are you in a hurry? Where are you heading?'

'The capital.'

'That's still some journey, and you come from?'

'An estate not far from Wroclaw.'

'I see. Well, up to you. But there is work here for lads who know how to behave. And food and lodgings. We've just lost our stable boy, the ungrateful rascal ran away. How good are you with horses? Travellers like their charges scrubbed and polished before they leave.'

'I learn fast.'

'Yes, I thought you would.'

After a week, my small purse was starting to bulge with pfennigs. Some of the horses were old and scruffy and some beautiful, but I scrubbed, polished and fed them all with care and affection. I also led them in front of the inn saddled, visibly happy and ready to trot away, the guests remarking to the inn-keeper what a fine stable lad she had acquired, more coins landing in my hand.

There was also the nightly fun with the boy next to my allocated space. Games mostly. He never really became my friend; perhaps he became suspicious of my lack of protesting when, with still no ladies in sight, he unilaterally decided that I was the one to lose his innocence with. Asking permission wasn't in his character; he just held me down and sealed my mouth with his dirty hand. The other boys heard the heavy breathing followed by a muted final gasp and didn't take kindly to the violation of a defenceless newcomer. In the morning an older boy offered to beat him up on my behalf but I pleaded with him to leave him alone. He was rather shocked when I shrugged and remarked that it wasn't a big deal. In any case, the marking of his territory was swiftly followed by a complete loss of interest. Conquest does that to people.

After two weeks of motherly affection, my heart was beating fast when I found the courage to tell the innkeeper that I was ready to be back on my way to Berlin. She was mending socks when I told her.

'You are a free man. I'm sad to see you leave. If you fail to find what you look for in the capital, you are welcome back anytime. Your home.'

'You have been very kind. I won't forget.'

König, the German Pointer who had first befriended me and then become inseparable, burst in, perhaps sensing that I was about to abandon him.

'I think you need a companion for your journey, Kazimierz.'

'I couldn't possibly...'

'I don't think you'll be able to leave him behind.'

As I ventured into Prussia proper, the time spent at check-points increased in length as the nobleman's name on my safe-conduct became less and less known. Fräulein Kaminski had been right: my knowledge of the language and my suave accent dispelled many suspicions.

I had enough Thalers for lodgings now but when the nights were warm and dry, I still preferred a good sleep under a tree, König now snuggling up with me and licking my face clean in the morning.

I still have no idea how long it took to reach the gates of the city: weeks? Months? The sense of time dispersed itself along the journey and there was no need to recover it; I had a life in front of me.

I found cheap lodgings at an inn not far from the Hackescher Markt. Although exhausted, the excitement of being in the capital brought me out in earnest with König merrily trotting in tow.

Another avuncular innkeeper had suggested to leave most of my money in the safe and just carry a few pfennigs to treat myself to an apple or even a cake at the Markt.

I glued my nose to the window of a Konditorei.

There were no price tags on the pastries so, once inside, I had no choice but to pester the burly shopkeeper with questions until I could find a pastry suited to my meagre budget. I was ready to be thrown out without much ado but, having noticed my red cheeks and other customers waiting, he exhaled in exasperation.

'Boy, how much do you have in your pocket?'

I extracted the coins and started counting them.

'Twenty pfennings, sir.'

'That will do. Choose one.'

'May I have the chocolate eclair, sir?'

'Here it is.'

I had never tasted one. I was in ecstasy after the first bite. With a stomach at the height of happiness and hands in my pockets, I started a merry stroll along the Unter den Linden.

It had rained all night and large puddles of mud dotted the wide boulevards of the city. Spellbound by the beauty of the buildings and the garments of the noblemen and grand dames ambling in the morning sun, I entered a state of daydreaming, failing to notice a gold and white carriage driving at considerable speed only a foot or two away.

When the wheels plunged in rapid succession into a large puddle, König and I suddenly turned into statues of mud. As I kept walking in a blind state while he was spinning himself clean to the invectives of the passers-by, I knocked my forehead against a lamp post, provoking loud laughter by the same people drenched by my companion.

I was holding my nose in pain while trying to clean my face from the mud when I heard the noise of a stick banging against the frame of the carriage. I then saw a gloved hand emerging from the window, its fingers summoning me. A middle-aged gentleman in a blue and gold livery appeared through the opening.

'You. Boy. Come here!'

I approached while still peeling mud away from my face, König at my side. I bowed.

'Your Excellency.'

He frowned in puzzlement.

'What happened to you?'

'I was blinded by the mud and hit the lamp post, Your Excellency.'

'You only need to address me as such once, boy. After that "Sir" will do.'

'My apology, sir.'

'I believe we are responsible for your predicament, aren't we?'

'Not at all, sir, I was daydreaming, me.'

'Daydreaming? How peculiar. Your accent, where are you from?'

'Wroclaw, sir.'

'A Silesian boy with such a mellow accent. Interesting. Have you just arrived?'

'Yes, sir.'

The gentleman leaned out of the window.

'Are you hurt?'

'Nothing serious, sir, just a scratch. One of the many.'

'You are in a state, though.'

'I was born in the mud, sir. You are under no duty to trouble yourself for me.'

He disappeared for a moment. When I saw him again, he was holding a small purse.

'Catch!'

I caught it with one hand. It was fairly heavy.

'Sir, that is too generous, I've been of no service to you.'

'Hide it. Berlin is not a Silesian village.'

'At your orders, sir.'

'Your dog?'

I stood in proud attention.

'My loyal friend, sir. His name is König.'

He burst into a laugh and I heard other people laughing inside the carriage.

'König?'

'That is what he was called when he befriended me. I've tried to change it but he only responds to that. Do you think it offensive to His Majesty? I would never be knowingly disrespectful, sir.'

He struggled to halt the now mild laughter while he turned to the other occupants.

'I don't know. He might like it, who knows? He loves dogs. What are you called?'

'Kazimierz, sir. At your service.'

'And your business in Berlin?'

'Putting food on the table for myself and König, sir. For the time being, at least.'

'What have you learned in your still short existence, Kazimierz?'

'German and Polish. Worked in the fields and looked after horses, sir.'

He retreated inside once again and I heard some whispering among the occupants of the carriage.

'Do you have you any knowledge of the palace of Sans Souci?'

'That is where His Majesty resides, sir.'

'Indeed. Present yourself at the servants' quarters tomorrow morning. Any time after nine. They will know your name. You have access to a bath at your lodgings?'

'I believe so, sir.'

'Good, you might scare them with all that mud!'

I bowed at his mild laughter. There was neither malice nor scorn in it.

I had to pay a little extra for the evening bath but enjoyed the bliss every time the innkeeper's daughter emptied another bucket of hot water over my head. She insisted in wanting to wash my long blond curls while commenting on their beauty. I struggled to show my lack of interest in the most polite of ways as I had no intention of offending her. In the end I managed to convey the message by shielding my private parts with my hands upon her impertinent offer to wash those too.

I found a passage to Potsdam on a hansom. There had been nearly three Thalers in the black purse.

Somehow I was prepared to be shown the door. Whoever the nobleman was, he seemed to be of the highest rank and had very likely forgotten about me as soon as his carriage had sped away.

To my relief, someone who appeared to be a footman, let me in and took me to a small and shabby study where the royal housekeeper, a man of probably fifty, greeted me in a cold but polite way.

'Kazimierz, His Excellency the Chamberlain, Grand Duke Von Schlieben, has passed your name on to me for employment in the royal household.'

'He has, sir?'

'Yes, I believe he met you yesterday?'

'Yes. Well. I didn't know he was His Excellency, sir, he didn't tell me.'

'He is under no obligation to tell you who he is.'

'No. Of course not, sir. My apology.'

'Very well. It will be the royal stables for you. Food and lodgings, the clerk will let you know the pay.'

'Very grateful, sir.'

'I was told to inform you that you can keep your dog. Even with that insolent name of his.'

'I can try to change it, sir. I do not intend to cause offence.'

'Apparently His Majesty laughed out loud when he heard about it.'

'His Majesty? They talked about me and my dog?'

'They found it hilarious.'

The servants' quarters were spartan but, to a certain extent, so were the courtiers' and even the king's apartments. Sans Souci had been built in the most tasteful and restrained style and His Majesty took a dim view of French and Austrian wasteful grandeur when it came to court pomp. The stables though were full of thoroughbred horses to which I dedicated my day with earnest care.

Except for a few Feldmarschalls and noblemen though, I rarely saw any riders; the housekeeper told me that I could take them out for exercise but was disappointed when I revealed that I couldn't ride.

Von Schlieben never rode and neither did the king. 'Too old', one of the footmen informed me.

After a few weeks, my care and dedication had apparently been reported to higher echelons and one day I startled at hearing Von Schlieben's voice while scrubbing one of my charges. I stopped and bowed.

'Your Excellency.'

'Kazimierz, I've had good reports about your efforts.'

'At your service, sir.'

'And your demeanour in the servants' quarter. The keeper describes a discreet and reserved boy. Of no trouble.'

'Too kind, sir.'

He held his chin between his fingers, pensive.

'He also informed me that you can't ride.'

'It is a pursuit for gentlemen and noblemen, sir.'

'His Majesty is of different opinion.'

König appeared barking and running through the Chamberlain's legs. I called him and held him.

'I'm so very sorry, sir. He gets on well with the horses though.'

'They must know he's a king!'

He left with his customary affectionate laugh and the following morning I received a visit from a young soldier carrying a pair of riding boots and a whip.

'His Majesty's horses require exercise. Boots on.' That was all he said.

I made good progress and the young soldier must have reported my diligent enthusiasm back to Von Schlieben. After a week, more suitable trousers, gloves and a jacket appeared folded on my bed.

A month had gone by. On a sunny September afternoon I had taken a short break and was rolling barefoot with König on the lawn at the side of the stables. After a few tumbles, him trying to bite my arms and legs, me laughing silly all on my own, I landed flat on the grass. My eyes met with a row of tall black boots with shining rectangular buckles.

I stood on my hands and looked up. I had seen the portraits in inns and houses and there was one hung in the servants' dining hall. I grabbed König by the neck in fear that he would jump on him and bowed while still on my knees, trembling like a leaf in the wind.

'Your Majesty.'

'Up, boy.'

I stood up the best I could while holding König. He handed his stick to the gentleman to his right and stooped down with some effort.

'You can let him go.'

König ran to his hands and started licking them with utter pleasure, his tail wild. He lifted his head towards Von Schlieben.

'Now, gentlemen, see how fellow monarchs love each other!' I was relieved to hear the general laughter. He stood up. 'Boy, you are under no duty to keep your head bowed forever. You are allowed to look at your king.'

He seemed frail but still martial and imposing. His watery eyes were transfixed on me from above, yet with no discerning trace of any arrogance.

'We have been informed of the happiness of our horses. And that you are now able of exercising them too.'

I didn't know what to reply so I briefly looked at Von Schlieben who nodded in reassurance. I bowed further. He turned to his Chamberlain.

'You were right. Not a bone of insolence.' He turned back to face me. 'Kazimierz, that is your name, correct?'

'Yes, your Majesty.'

'Kazimierz, you and your loyal companion must meet my Italian hounds.'

He turned with no further words; he had dropped the *pluralis majestatis* after only one sentence. I stood without knowing what to do next until one of the gentlemen turned around and made a gesture to follow them.

The four hounds were kept in sumptuous quarters adjacent to the palace and when they were freed to roam they barked and circled König. I was terrified that a fight might ensue but they started to play, the barking louder and louder. He kneeled to stroke them.

'Kazimierz! Come here!'

'Your Majesty.'

'This is Phillis. And these rather energetic ladies are called Hasenfuss and Alcmens. Biche is named after another one I had but she left us during one of my campaigns.'

To his evident satisfaction they started licking my face, their tails wagging furiously. I stroked them a bit and they seemed to go wild with pleasure. While kneeling I found myself very close to him but somehow my fear had subsided. I didn't find him menacing anymore.

He pensively spoke to himself .

'They know kindness.'

Then he grabbed my arm with his wrinkled hand.

'I might need your help to stand up, Kazimierz.'

'Your Majesty.'

I offered my arm and he leaned on it with a gentle grasp. When up, he stretched himself with some effort and patted my shoulder.

'We'll take them for a walk tomorrow morning. You only

have to address me with that Majesty nonsense the first time of the day, then just "Sir". It is dreadfully tedious.'

'Your servant, sir.'

To my surprise, once the dogs were free to roam and were circling our legs in excitement, he dismissed the courtiers and made a sign to start walking. I shuddered at the thought of being alone with him.

'Where is König?'

'I thought I shouldn't bring him along, sir.'

'He is a good fellow, do bring him along next time. These ladies are at risk of becoming a bit supercilious with their Italian breed and all.'

We walked in silence as I was not supposed to initiate any conversation, only to reply to questions.

'Tell me: do they still detest me in the land of Silesia?'

'Not everyone, sir. My parents did, Fräulein Kaminski doesn't.'

'Fräulein Kaminski?'

'My teacher, we went to the village school for five years, sir.'

'You can read and write? In German, I mean.'

'Yes, sir.'

He became pensive. The longer we walked the more at ease I started to feel.

'They did? Are your parents deceased?'

'Yes sir, in a fire. The whole family.'

'My condolences.'

'Sir.'

'Well, your place of birth belonged to Austria before I took

345

it. It was never meant to belong to Poland. Marie Thérèse and I dismembered that land anyway. That is a fact. Her pompous, insufferable ambassador kept whining to me that his empress wept for any acre of land taken from the Poles. She wept but she took. Dreadful lady, never trust women, Kazimierz.'

I understood very little of politics, though I had gained a fairly balanced view by listening patiently to my parents' anti-Prussian rants and Fräulein Kaminski's pro-German teaching.

He stopped walking and looked at me in what seemed to be an expression of benign puzzlement, perhaps trying to figure out whether I was understanding any of his words.

'Well. No more of that.'

His frailty was verbal too, the enthusiasm for long conversations vanished. He had already said everything that he had wanted to say. His life had made history. A sentence would be followed by a long silence before any words were uttered again.

At the end of our third morning walk I returned to the servants' quarters to find my bed stripped and my satchel and small trunk packed on the side. I shuddered in fear while trying to recall when and where I had offended him. I was trying to figure out what I had said but I was aware that you cannot apologise to monarchs. When you lose their favour, it is the end.

I was sitting on the edge of the bed with my head in my hands when my riding instructor appeared in his soldier's uniform and grabbed one handle of my trunk.

'What is the matter, Kazimierz? Grab that handle, you have new quarters. At the palace.'

I was assigned a tiny room with a much more comfortable bed, a wash cabinet with a big jug and a small desk. I was also given a clean and embroidered livery.

The following morning, while preparing myself for the walk with the dogs, Von Schlieben came into my room.

'You do not thank the king. Remember that. His orders are not favours.'

He was happy to see König with me when he arrived with his courtiers. He dismissed them all at once when the hounds were out of their quarters.

'Have you read any books?'

'I have never been able to afford them, sir.'

'Of course. Silly question.'

The four ladies were now my friends. Every morning they greeted me with affectionate barking and jumps on my legs, the tail of my eye spotting his approval and satisfaction. At the end of the walk he summoned me in the library. Coffee was being served.

'Young Kazimierz will have a cup too,' he informed a stunned footman.

He sat behind his desk in the narrow alcove between the bookshelves. I stood in the middle of the room with my hands behind my back, overwhelmed by the resplendent decor, the oak-panelled walls, the gold reliefs, the soft rug. For a moment I thought I was about to faint.

'Sit.'

My eyes widened in disbelief.

'Sir?'

'I'm giving you permission to sit. You have nothing to fear. I'm the king.'

The butler approached me with a cup and a saucer which rattled in my hands until I managed to have a sip and safely position them on my legs.

'I read in French. German is barely useful to talk to horses if they can bear the sound of it and my hounds are Italian. A few years ago we availed ourselves of the services of a Kapellmeister from Venice or thereabouts who flatly refused to learn it. He pompously declared that merely hearing 'Guten Morgen' ruined his breakfast. We had a good laugh behind his back at his well-paid arrogance. His French was atrocious anyway. They know about music though. That said, I might be leaving this world by the time you master the language.'

He turned with a sweep of his hand towards the shelves.

'We have some literature in German, mainly translations from the classics. That will do. Your accent reminds me of my flute playing. Soothing, pleasing.'

As he stood up I rose at such speed that it was a miracle the cup and saucer hadn't catapulted away.

'Sit! You are not required to stand up.'

I felt his hands on my shoulders. The shoulders again.

'Among other things, my sight is failing me. I haven't read for a long time. After an early supper, you will come to my apartments and read to me. You will be my eyes. The eyes of the king.'

I rose before dawn to walk to the stables in my leather apron and dirty boots. I found a young lad preparing the horses for a wash and a scrub. He said he was the new stable boy and addressed me with "Sir", making me rather uncomfortable. The housekeeper explained my new orders: 'You are to exercise them but not to attend to them anymore. Do that before walking the king's dogs. Do not be late for that.'

I was mildly disappointed as I had enjoyed looking after them and I knew all their names and peculiar little habits. On the walk with the dogs I did well to remember Von Schlieben's words: 'You do not thank the king'. Or, worse, question his orders.

When tired, he now freely leaned on my arm and, when returning back to the dogs' quarters in such fashion, I spotted the waiting courtiers and officers whispering to each other.

After an earlier than usual supper, I presented myself at his apartments, the valets promptly opening the double doors wide for my entrance.

His bedroom was comparatively small but elegant. His single bed positioned across in an alcove with white drapes at the side. Some of the walls were white too, with silver reliefs. The mantelpiece sat under a vast mirror, a fire raging in it.

He was sitting in his armchair and already in his night gown, his feet in velvet slippers, perched on a silk footstool. I bowed and stood in silence. There was an upright and visibly less comfortable chair about a foot or two from his. Autumn had arrived and the heavy drapes were tightly drawn, the only source of light a few candles on oversized candelabras.

'I'd like to revisit Homer. There is a decent translation

on the table.'

I picked it up and waited for his order to sit.

'Sit down. Kazimierz, you are in no need to ask my permission when you are here to read for me.'

Every night I read until his eyes closed. Then I would call his valet to wake him up and take him to his bed.

We were making good progress. On the fourth night, while he interrupted my reading to order me to take a sip of water, he commented in a distracted yet tender way: 'I could listen to your accent for hours.'

In less than a week we were more than half way. I struggled to follow the poetry. It was just too difficult for me and I think he detected my embarrassment.

'Come closer.'

I moved the chair and he gently took my small and soft hand in his. He was now squeezing it, seeking comfort.

'Agamemnon was a terrible man and an even more terrible father. Not a good king either. He only thought himself as such. He lured his daughter Iphigenia to Aulis to sacrifice her to cruel gods. You understand how cruel men can be, Kazimierz?'

'I have a vague idea, sir.'

'When I was your age I formed an attachment with a handsome boy barely a year older than myself. Peter Karl had no education but he was intelligent and sensitive. We became inseparable. We loved each other. The king did not take kindly to such liaison and he dispatched him to a regiment on the Dutch frontier, not before inflicting a savage beating on us both. I never saw him again.'

His fingers were now interlocking with mine and squeezing harder.

'Soon after my eighteenth birthday I made another friend, Hans Hermann. A handsome and kind fellow. We fell in love and tried to flee the court but were arrested and brought back to Berlin. My father had him executed. I was forced to watch when they cut his head off with a sword.'

He paused and looked away.

'I fainted.'

He detected my trembling.

'No fear, my boy. No such thing will happen to you. I think that is enough for tonight, no need to call my valet, I will make it to bed by myself. Good night, Kazimierz.'

He held my hand for a few minutes every night. We young invariably fail to notice the ravages of old age but I did. Some of his teeth were missing and the skin seem to always suffer from a yellow tinge, regardless of the time and light of the day. He suffered from gout and personal hygiene was famously never his priority. Yet I found myself looking forward to the walks with his dogs and the reading hours. One evening I didn't wait for him and took his hand in mine, his eyes more watery than usual.

'There will be no reading tomorrow, we are having a small concert in the music room. You will accompany me.'

I couldn't sleep that night. I was happy to be his charge but I had no ambition of becoming a courtier. I knew my place and I sensed that the king's favourite invariably made countless enemies. I pleaded with Von Schlieben to send me the plainest of liveries and he complied. The valet passed a message to me.

'His Excellency would like to reassure you that you have no reason to worry.'

A frosty hush welcomed us in the music room when he marched in holding on his stick with me trailing in his wake. When we took our seats he whispered in my year.

'No fear, Kazimierz, they bark louder than my hounds but they don't bite.'

We were now sailing through Plato's Republic. I gave up at the beginning in trying to make any sense of it all; I put my efforts into concentrating on the best pronunciation I could muster and it pleased him no end.

'I must apologise, Kazimierz, this must make no sense at all to you. I need to find something simpler for you to enjoy too.'

'Sir.'

'Take me to my bed. I'm tired tonight. I will look for something else in my library tomorrow.'

I led him to the alcove and once he was sat on the edge he waved at me, signalling not to call the valet. I stood a few feet away, intensively thinking about what I was about to say, weighing its offensiveness against its demonstration of unbridled devotion.

'Perhaps His Majesty's wish is for me to remain at his side?'

The effrontery of the assumption was a risk I hadn't calculated but one that somehow I had been prepared to take.

He looked up.

'Come here, Kazimierz.'

I stood in front of him, my legs between his. As I was

still not very tall, his face was merely a foot or even less below my chin.

He started undoing the laces of my shirt. When my blue, hairless, bony chest became exposed, he kissed it all the way down from my nipples, landing the last peck on my belly button. Then he detached himself but remained positioned a few inches from it, noticing the goose bumps.

'Such celestial beauty would let the king leave this world the happiest of men.'

He lifted his head up, his watery eyes fixed on my tiny blue gems.

'Yet an act of such cruelty would soil the company I so treasure. The scent of your youth is all your king needs. It is all your king wishes.'

He took my hands in his, his thumbs caressing them. I kneeled down and let my head fall in his lap. I felt his hands searching through my long curls, stroking my neck.

'Your offer is beyond generous. My acceptance would be gruesome. Good night, Kazimierz, the king wishes you a safe sleep.'

The next day he took his Chamberlain aside.

'Von Schlieben, it would be ungentlemanly to take advantage of young Kazimierz's unquestioning devotion. The boy is spending too much of his time in the company of gentlemen of age. That is not healthy and loneliness will make him unhappy.'

He was staring at the gardens now strewn with amber leaves, his hands behind his back.

'A suitable companion must be found at once. Perhaps a

young officer of honour and integrity.'

'Your wish, sir.'

'As you rightly pointed out, not a bone of insolence can be found in his body. Sensitivity and kindness must be prerequisites. He is in no way suited to the scheming or cruelties of the kind we see at court.'

'Understood, sir.'

The Chamberlain was about to depart.

'Von Schlieben.'

'Sir.'

'I'm in debt to you. For your find.'

A bow.

'Your Majesty.'

Von Schlieben was undisputed master at court. He made sure that, for my benefit, I was never to become a full member of it. He had subtle ways of extending his sway. A pompous and over-powdered Margrave once foolishly revealed his lust for the unsettling beauty of His Majesty's favourite: the Silesian angel, he had dared call me. A thoroughly unfazed Chamberlain had taken him aside.

'Margrave, you are a gentleman of too many words. One of them could easily lead to the gallows.'

The Margrave, aware of his perilous faux pas, had bowed before attempting to move away.

'Not so fast. Loose talkers are always in debt to their listeners, Margrave. You are a frightful gossip: you'll have no trouble in dispersing a casual warning of the ultimate consequences of such reckless desires among courtiers suffering with similar lust for Silesian angels. You and your fellow peers of the Reich surely appreciate the danger of crossing His Majesty.'

There was also laughter between us and I had become happy with my routine. He had managed to rescue some low-brow novels which made him smile, though visibly relieved at seeing me finally understanding some albeit ludicrous plots. We had started to discuss the ridiculous characters and my silly questions had him burst into affectionate laughter. I noticed that when he saw me smile, his eyes sparkled with contentedness.

I had also become close to my riding instructor: newly-promoted Lieutenant Schulze. He was barely two and half years my senior. The speed at which the letter of promotion had landed on his bed had raised a few eyebrows. The very same eyebrows had lowered in silent haste when word spread that the seal on the envelope had been of the red and gold variety. Upon learning that the initials V.S. were apparently scribbled at the bottom of the letter, everyone bowed and congratulated the flabbergasted young man for his 'well-known' military skills.

At the end of a long ride Schulze approached me in the stables and kissed me without giving it too much thought. I attempted a little resistance but he was handsome and charming and my limbs surrendered when he took me in his arms; it had been a long time since my games with Bartek and the boy at the Silesian inn.

The warmth of the hay allowed us a few moments of blissful peace before putting our clothes back on. He noticed my sombre expression and the tension in my face.

'I haven't offended you, I hope.'

'No. But I belong to the king. He has no wish for me to share the royal bedchamber. All the same, I am his property.'

'You say that with gladness.'

'My affection is sincere.'

A tender smile appeared on his mouth while shaking his head.

'These are his orders. The best ones I have ever received.'

He saw my shocked frown and caressed my cheek.

'Monarchs don't wish unhappiness on their favourites. This one certainly doesn't wish it on you and he's worried about you being lonely. Von Schlieben has demanded our friendship to be explored and nurtured. I look forward to it. Only if you do too.'

Schulze had what the king had requested. He never involved himself in court's intrigues and, despite having chosen a military career, he was kind and sensitive.

The king was pleased and after a few weeks he was invited to join us walking the dogs; his martial deportment, respectful silence and polite, intelligent replies further reassuring him that the right companion had been chosen.

I turned down an offer of better lodgings. I liked my small room and I had grown fond of the few pieces of furniture. Von Schlieben was flabbergasted when the only complaint I would forward was that I didn't possess a portrait of my sovereign. This was duly presented to me on the day of my seventeenth birthday and it graced the wall by my bed for the following four years. When a Chamberlain inured to ever-demanding, pestering courtiers reported my modest request to the king, he smiled with a touch of pride.

Schulze and I grew closer under his watchful and encouraging eyes but he was now grappling with the devastations of a premature old age. At the onset of my fifth year at court, our reading evenings became shorter and shorter, his eyes closing after only a few pages.

One sweltering summer night, while rushing through the last book of Marcus Aurelius' Meditations, I felt his hand becoming colder. I looked up and saw his eyes closed, his head turned in my direction. My hope is that my heavenly beauty soothed his journey to an eternity bereft of sorrow. A garden of peace.

I put the book down on the table and kneeled in front of his armchair. Then I took his hands in mine and held them against my face, before letting my head drop in his lap.

My king.

* * *

I recall all of this from the future he secured for us. As usual, the loyal Von Schlieben had taken care of all the details. When he informed me of the mansion and the land left to me in the king's instructions, he pointed out that the absence of a title was His Majesty's specific wish: 'Aristocracy is something I hope young Kazimierz will never meddle with,' he had solemnly declared to his Chamberlain.

The windswept steppes of Brandenburg at the eastern end of the city are now our home. His generosity has bestowed on us a sizeable villa, farmers, servants and the four Italian hounds. His nephew, now on the throne, has never suspended or even questioned the substantial royal allowance.

A gently sloping path on the left-hand side of the entrance gates leads to a small but rather scenic lake. We plan to build a chapel not far from the shore.

We are, of course, childless but not without future lineage. Consumption regularly ravages our farmers' families and the Kimmichs passed away only a few days apart, leaving newly-born Alexander an orphan. I have made him my ward and his name will hopefully secure descendants. My Silesian one will die with me.

The best part of fifteen years have gone by and Alexander has grown into a healthy and charming young man. We were relieved at learning that he is to the ladies inclined as the future of the estate will be in his hands.

The fertile land has produced good harvests and, by virtue of Schulze's skilful administration, I am now one of the wealthiest landowners of Brandenburg though we continue to conduct our existence in the most frugal of ways. I'd like to think His Majesty would be proud of such endeavour.

My private secretary and I wish for a serene and secluded life, yet history might be upon us: a young French general is presently putting the continent to the sword.

Von Schlieben continued to offer his services as Chamberlain to the new monarch, Frederick William II. He is old and frail now and his beloved wife passed away shortly after our king did.

He has numerous children and grandchildren yet he regularly pays us visits for lunch, tea or supper, occasionally spending the night here. We don't talk much though and soon after the first few evenings, I offered to read for him, knowing that he was too much of a gentleman to put forward such a request himself. He soon interrupted me by raising his hand: 'His Majesty once revealed to me that he used to spend the whole day relishing the time you would walk through the door with a book in your hand. Now I know why.'

Tiergarten

'Children! Children! Come down! Jurgen is waiting.'
They rumble down the staircase in their finest attire and in youthful morning energy, followed by auntie Edda, the youngest holding her hand.

'Come on now, you're going to get a good telling off by Jurgen.'

They flood out on the steps and hug their driver. He grabs the youngest, who simply adores being lifted by his enormous arms, and deposits him in his carriage as he would never ride in the other one, come what may. The eldest runs up to Charlotte and kisses her on the cheek.

'Mother, may I ride up with Jurgen?'

She caresses his cheek and nods.

'Of course, my dear. But let's move on, shall we?'

Walther sits in the second carriage, looking after the rest of the lively young things. Edda, Wenzel and Jonas are on the doorstep waving at the carriages finally setting off.

It's a splendid morning at the onset of spring. Still frosty but clear, crisp, blinding.

Jurgen loves driving the horses on the road to the Kimmichs' family home: a long, narrow trail which slices through the deserted and windswept Brandenburg steppes, sparsely dotted by reddish barns and a few farmers working the fields.

The Berliner breeze gradually turns into a gale lashing their faces; he hands the bridles to the boy for a few minutes with a stern warning not to tell his mother about it.

The gates of the estate's grounds are open; the carriages trundle past the grand main entrance and veer left, down the path which leads to the lake.

They come to a dusty stop in front of the chapel. A creaky gate leads to a path through a small garden, the dark blue waters of the lake in full view behind the low spire.

They dust themselves off. The whistling of the wind and the singing of the birds are suddenly interrupted by the children's chattering. Charlotte, Walther and Jurgen try to restore some order.

They eventually succeed in soldiering the boys along the garden ground and line them up respectfully; when one of the middle ones keeps picking his nose, Charlotte lowers his hand down and softly strokes his hair.

Walther takes a handkerchief out of his pocket and does his best to sweep the dust off the white marble stone. Charlotte kneels and places a small bouquet of white tulips inside the pewter flowers' holder.

FELIX ALEXANDER KIMMICH

1863 - 1897

Beloved son

Faithful husband

Loyal companion

There had been sneers in some quarters when the text of the inscription had been reported back to the city. Society never suffers from shortage of people with a hopelessly limited view of human nature and its meanders of acceptance and denial, its unyielding capacity for understanding, forgiveness and, ultimately, its destructive fear of not being loved.

Only the years are engraved: on the very same day of his fatal fall down Villa Augusta's steep staircase, a grisly murder had been discovered by the outer edges of the Tiergarten. A man in his thirties had been found stabbed to death. He had no clothes on, his wallet had been stolen and a lad of Polish origins had been arrested and charged. The victim was apparently an unidentified young sailor without fixed abode; or at least that was what the Reichspolizei's report said he was. Case closed. Somewhere in Berlin an Oberinspektor and a Reichgericht Mediziner had stumbled onto a small fortune.

Perhaps there is no such thing as succumbing to a broken heart. Nonetheless, Herr Kimmich now lies next to his son, as requested in capital letters on the first page of his will. Frau Augusta rests peacefully at his right side.

He was found slumped at his desk a few months after Felix's passing, his hands clutching the boxing trophy. After his son's burial, no one, save for his loyal butler, ever saw him again. Meagre meals were served in his study but they regularly returned untouched.

In his heroic and futile attempt to save his son, he had provided him with a loyal companion, a respectable wife and a pretorian guard of loyal servants. All to no avail: Felix's relentless, pounding quest hauled from the darkest and most irresistible of our yearnings. Unhappy ones.

Too afraid of their father, once Frau Augusta's husband had also passed away, Stephan and Renate had moved to avenge themselves of all the love and affection bestowed on their brother. She was briefed on the most lurid and degrading details with evil callousness and extraordinary precision. They had scant regard to the possibility that her frail heart might not withstand the horror of hearing the kind of depraved abyss her son had descended into.

She had been unable to find the strength to inform them that Felix had settled all of Stephan's debts out of his own income and that he had set aside a substantial dowry for Renate to ensure that she could marry in the best of the Junkers families. All she could do in the end was to ban them from the family home for the rest of their lives.

The following morning she had strolled to the chapel in her mourning dress. Like every morning since the death of her son, she had sat motionless on the bench installed by the servants at the foot of the graves.

When they had lifted her veil in the early hours of the afternoon, a serene smile was gracing her anguished face, happy to be reunited with her beautiful boy.

Charlotte and Walther grab the eldest boys' shoulders: their signal for silence, respect and a short prayer before returning in sombre order to the carriages.

He stays behind with the eldest, side by side, quietly staring at the grave.

Walther is now a slender lad of almost fourteen: healthy, good-natured, gregarious and well-liked by everyone; he has taken up boxing in his first year at military school.

He turns his head and meets his uncle's gaze; his wavy chestnut hair is wispy, furiously swept along his forehead by the fierce gale, his skin levigated alabaster, the eyes sharp, the emeralds twinkling. He also sports a light trace of soft brown hair above his upper lip. Under it, that smile.

Walther gently brushes his thumb along the fine, almost transparent fluff, tickling the boy's nose.

'Are you going to grow those, young man?'

'I most certainly am, uncle Walther!'

He turns and walks back to the carriages. Elegant. Deer-like.

A few years have gone by but debris of jagged grief still rattles in Walther's fibres. When the wind sweeps his face, he feels his hand, his soft moustaches, his searching lips.

He breaks into a silent laugh as he remembers his friend's tasteless quip upon the birth of the fourth boy: 'I'm convinced that at least one of those brats will be found at Franz's one day!' Felix had his very own way with shameless behaviour.

After the first born had ushered in an almost unhinged elation among their parents, Felix and Charlotte had proceeded to fill the nursery rooms. Over the following years Villa Augusta had turned into a busy, happy crossroad of nannies, governesses and screaming infants.

He had doted on them, assiduously visiting the nurseries, apprehensive for their health. Walther was duly instructed to set up trust funds for their education.

He had also reported to him that, mercifully, a single mission to his wife's quarters seemed to be enough to produce results. He now remembers Felix's earthy laugh at his reply: 'I was the first to witness the evidence of your fertility.'

Edda had finally moved in and become the auntie from nowhere. There is always one in every family: ladies rejected by an unforgiving world.

On one life-changing evening, nailed for the umpteenth time to a chair in the drawing room and forced to entertain another pompous, oafish suitor, she had suddenly stood up and had calmly proceeded to pour the entire content of a sizeable jug of cream on his head. Then, without collecting a single item of clothing, she had walked all the way to Villa Augusta and was never to be seen again at her family home. Felix had been the one to open the door and had instantly realised what had happened.

'Welcome home, Edda.' That is all he said.

While working his way up at the Kaiserhof, Florian had become a regular guest, often sharing the night with Felix. And Walther. Or both. For the first two or three weeks, the transgressive nature of their liaison had made them reach for dizzying heights of pleasure; on the fourth one, Wenzel had found the three young men sitting cross-legged on the rug, playing a game of cards in their night gowns, Felix winning every hand.

But Florian was Florian and one day he once again vanished in the morning mist. In his typical generosity, Felix had merely remarked to Walther that he was now worried that the young man might not find someone to look after him.

When they come to pay their respects they always find a full-blown red rose in the pewter vase. They know who comes to visit yet they wonder how he undertakes the long and arduous journey. Perhaps the kindness of a gentleman friend. And a sumptuous carriage. Perhaps.

On the day of the funeral, Walther had noticed a small wreath pinned on the side of the hearse. It was a tribute from the working men's boxing club, likely initiated by Jurgen. He felt moved that they had remembered him. Felix had entered these men's hardened hearts with his boyish charm, his gregarious demeanour, his endearing dedication and schoolboy-like respect for his instructor. He had quickly become the club's mascot: 'Little Felix'. Upon his appearance in the filthy canteen, those unshaven, vest-clad wife-beaters, rascals and sailors would slap his shoulders (nearly toppling him over) and ruffle his hair, proceeding in earnest to get him dangerously drunk. Manly love in the abysses of reprobation.

He shakes his head with a tight-lipped smile: *Felix*.

At the burial, a black carriage had stopped some fifty yards away from the ceremony, its occupant not alighting. Only Charlotte had turned; a lady in mourning attire had lifted her veil and offered a single brief nod through the lowered window, a hint of grief in her watery eyes. She had then instructed her driver to quietly trot away.

Baroness Von Mutthe's visits to Villa Augusta never resumed. Maybe she chose not to intrude in the immense grief suddenly befallen on this adorable yet most peculiar of households. Or the solution had once more miserably failed and people were talking again. Charlotte would never know.

Felix's downfall had never been far away. When Franz's was raided and closed down for good, he had reverted to stalking the Charlottenburg Baths and a few hair-raising districts where adventure, mischief and relief could be found in equal yet perilous quantities. Then the outer edges of the Tiergarten had become the new game in town for disreputable activities. These were frequently interrupted by a murderous gang of young Slavic lads of no Hellenistic persuasion who used their angelic beauty to lure unsuspecting old men. Or not so old.

Walther, still handsome and athletic, had forced himself out of his self-imposed sensual decline and had knocked a few times at his friend's door to find yet again an empty room, his hat and coat gone. A very late Felix would often find him asleep in his bedroom's armchair, in his pyjamas, waiting for his brother-in-arms.

Jurgen had spent night after night by the woods. Waiting, worried sick, unable to do anything to save his master. And that fateful night he had himself been moved away by the night watch who were far too insistent in wanting to know the whereabouts of his squire. When he had been allowed to return, he had scoured the woods until early morning to no avail.

He sweeps the grave again with his handkerchief, the boys are hungry and are calling their uncle back.

He closes his eyes and the knot returns. He still misses

him terribly; on some nights he finds it unbearable. He stares longingly at the lake behind the chapel: the welcoming haven for the long summer swims of their youth. Where they lazed by its shore for hours, their clothes scattered on the grass. Where at the onset of the first green shoots of adolescent, mysterious desires, Felix had taken the first of the many risks of his life. He had laid his burning lips on his sleeping friend's mouth, taking the chance to collide either with angry blows or requited affection.

Walther will never know that when the steel blade had clicked and flickered in the moonlight, Felix had not tried to flee, calmly waiting for a demonically beautiful angel of death to dispatch him to his freedom. And theirs: he had long decided on his sinful unworthiness of the ones who loved him with the most unyielding of devotions.

He had always been well aware of the lurking dangers of his ways and had left behind a cast-iron will, entrusting everything to Walther. His extended family will now be taken care of down to the last grandchild.

It is his duty to stay strong. Felix's four sons must one day know what a special person their father was, flaws and all. Their future has been entrusted to him in times of uncertainty and deep foreboding: winds of war are now lashing the steppes of Brandenburg.

Fräulein Kahler's formidable resilience had rescued the family's name from scandal and shame. Upon returning to Villa Augusta at the onset of dawn, Jurgen had dispatched Maria to wake her up without disturbing Charlotte.

While on the phone to the Reichspolizei's Headquarters,

he had noticed her face gradually losing her characteristic rosy complexion, her hand holding the padded armrest of the chair with feral strength, a fireball of grief blasting in her chest. After replacing the handset she had been ready to faint, yet she knew what to do and that she was the only one who could do it.

'Jurgen. Master Felix has been murdered in the Tiergarten.'

She had grabbed his big hands with extraordinary force.

'There is no time for tears. We must save his name and that of his family. There are four children upstairs.'

The driver, frozen in shock, had barely been able to nod.

'We need Wenzel and Jonas but tell no one else. Get your carriage ready. Call another two coaches. Find a cart which can transport a body and tell the driver to wait at the back entrance of the Reichspolizei Headquarters. Tell all these people that we'll pay them good money. Go in haste.'

She had then summoned the governess and ordered her to wake the boys up, dress them, pack some of their clothes as quickly as possible and wait upstairs, ready to leave. She had no time to offer an explanation.

As she had anticipated, Charlotte and Walther were beyond distraught when she reported the news. She had hugged them both but time was precious.

'We must save the family's name. There is no time for grieving.'

She had to shake Walther to gain his attention.

'The Oberinspektor knows Felix's father. Call him right now and ask him to divulge no information until we arrive. Tell him that we'll be slightly delayed by an urgent stop at the family's bank. He'll understand the hint. We'll need further funds for the Reichgericht Mediziner. Do you have access to them?'

'Unlimited.'

'Charlotte, the boys and the governess are ready to leave. Two carriages will be here shortly. We'll go upstairs and be ready. You will travel to the family home. It falls on you to inform your sons and his parents. I think it's for the best though it's a lot to ask of you. I cannot come with you, Walther needs me. I must go with him to the Reichspolizei. Try to evade any questioning until we call you at the Kimmichs. If we succeed, Felix had a fall down the stairs: here at the villa.'

She had taken Charlotte's face in her hands and kissed her.

'If we do not, we are ruined. The boys will be ruined. I trust I need not to reveal the circumstances of the murder. It's important that you prepare yourself for this eventuality.'

Fräulein Kahler knew all too well the corrupted ways of the world they inhabited; the two leather briefcases Walther had carried with him to the Reichspolizei Headquarters had been more than adequate to satisfy the lurid venality of the two top officials.

After Doctor Falckenberg had certified the fall and left in dignified sadness, Edda had walked out of the room, leaving Walther by the side of the bed, knelt in lacerating grief.

Alone in her room, the heroic strength which had held her up until that moment had suddenly evaporated and she had collapsed in the armchair by the window, the tears and the sobbing uncontrollable yet liberating.

After all, she had always understood Felix better than

anyone else: 'Friendship is everything for boys. But they are incapable of giving up their freedom'.

He slowly turns around and sees a perturbed Jurgen watching him. Over the past few years he has witnessed his master's youth peeling away, despoiled by punishing sorrow. No longer a boy.

At times he feels a compulsion to visit the grave alone and the ever loyal driver never questions the long journey. He solemnly waits by the carriage while Walther sits on the bench for a short time. When he hears him cry, he ties the horses to the railings and quietly leaves.

The gusts are fierce, Jurgen's waxed cape flaps violently with a clanking noise and the horses stir with a loud whine. Time to leave. He has tried, and he tries today.

Then he is chased by a murmur in the whistling hush.

We are inseparable.

Author's note

Paragraph 175 of the German Criminal Code was adopted in 1871, shortly after unification. Rather astonishingly, it wasn't repealed until 1994.

It appears that over the years it was applied more or less vigorously and to the letter depending on the regime of the day.

Curiously, convictions went down in number during the early years of the National Socialists' rise to power. Later, of course, they became no longer necessary as deportations to camps hardly required legislative backing.

Over the last decade of the nineteenth century there were some timid attempts at forming a movement demanding the de-criminalisation of homosexuality - the modern concept of 'gay rights' being non-existent at that time - and the head of the Social Democratic Party, August Bebel, tried unsuccessfully to have Paragraph 175 abolished.

As for the attitudes of society in general, the picture seems to be more nuanced.

Convictions ran at an average of five to six hundred a year, though, unlike late Victorian Britain, it appears that the police acted almost exclusively on information passed on by citizens or spies and were mainly interested in corruption of minors, at that time anyone under twenty-one years of age. Entrapment in public facilities seemed to be largely unheard of and was likely considered a waste of police time.

For all its illegality, homoeroticism, unintended or otherwise, was in any case at the very centre of Prussian militarism and widespread among Ernst Röhm's SA before their demise on the night of the long knives. Röhm, himself a homosexual, held some curious and, in my opinion, largely contrived and self-serving views on the 'homosocial' nature of National Socialism.

Under Kaiser Wilhelm II, a great deal of emphasis was placed on loyalty, male companionship, camaraderie and manly bonding. These are not to be confused with our modern concept of gay relationships.

These strong and lasting unions might have been more of the Hellenistic variety, warrior-like. Felix and Walther's relationship never seems to leave adolescence behind and the sexual side is treated more like a side game.

And the sexual side of many of these unions might have been indeed incidental, not always present, and at times only partially carried out for the purpose of much-needed release of pounding testosterone. While loyalty and friendship were proudly flaunted, discretion remained imperative in cases of more intimate understandings. For such special friendships to be in any way tolerated, they had to firmly remain a gentlemen's affair.

A case in point was, of course, Wilhelm II himself. Arguments and speculations have yet to be settled on whether he was in the end a severely repressed homosexual or merely an eccentric and slightly deranged human being. A likely option is that the repression might have precipitated the derangement. Besides the lurid innuendos about his passion for bracelets and all kind of trinkets, it is indeed true that he had confessed in more than one occasion of only feeling happy when in the company of Potsdam's 'Liebenberg Circle', where 'One feels free with the beautiful nature around you and soldiers as much as you like, for I love my dear Regiment very much, those such kind nice young men in it.'

Well. I just leave it there.

Against this backdrop, 'solutions' similar to the one concocted by Herr Kimmich the elder to protect his beloved son were not uncommon, though mostly found among upper middle class families in the French Republic or the German Reich. Aristocracy placed formidable obstacles to such schemes, given that marriages, though still arranged, served the sole purpose of lineage's conservation or families' alliances.

Wealth seemed to be the primary common denominator as certain conditions needed to be met for such plans to work: vast residences where husbands and wives could lead separate lives and the financial means to allow them to travel and build parallel, alternative lives.

It was of immense help that conventions allowed - even required - married couples to retire for the night to separate boudoirs, with husbands visiting their consorts exclusively for procreation purposes.

The Charlottenburg Baths were not yet in existence in 1890. They are fictional but so are the events described.

We cannot be sure whether the S-Bahn underpass at the Zoologische Garten stop was such a market of forbidden pleasures in 1931 or, for that matter, at any other time. It's a place like any other. All the same, as any fellow gay man would happily confirm to you, when such a place doesn't exist, we'll make one up. There is, after all, 'an inevitability to it'.

No one in their right mind would name a hipster bistro after the Iron Chancellor, that much is clear. I confess to the absurdity of the creation but then again, more often than not it serves coffee and cakes to people living through absurd personal stories.

If you find disposing of swimming trunks before diving for a good swim counter-intuitive, you have clearly never cycled along the shores of the Wannsee.

Frederick the Great died alone in his armchair in the month of August 1786, no Silesian angel reading classics at his side. He is a largely forgotten yet still controversial figure despite his achievements on the battlefield. Mischievously co-opted by Goebbels for his propaganda wars, his social reforms and cultural enlightenment are, in my opinion, overlooked. History seems to prefer dwelling on his brutish character.

There is no doubt that he was a misogynous homosexual.

By his own admission, not only did he find women physically repulsive, but he actively avoided their presence. Sans Souci was an all-male court, though, in all fairness, more homosocial than fully homosexual. A few of the dignitaries and officers were married and had no interest in physical relationships with their fellow courtiers. All the same, they seemed to enjoy the martial atmosphere. That said, although he banned his wife from Potsdam for the rest of her life, his sister Wilhelmina remained his best friend and confidante until her death.

When I learned of it, I found the callous cruelty of his father, Frederick William I, deeply shocking. I still find such behaviour disturbing. Think for a moment how you would behave for the rest of your life after witnessing such wanton ferocity.

It is all an invention. Of course it is. And yet all of it could have easily happened.

Either in fear or as jealous custodians, we dissemble and hide our inexplicable universe from the disapproving gaze of *faux moralité*. The gods might be mocking us, but they are the ones seeking pleasure in our passionate embrace: tender and savage. Rarely fettered.

Some of us will always strive for the dreary greyness of routine normality, yet they forget what holds us back from achieving such unremarkable Holy Grail: we are no ordinary people.

Berlin is not for everyone and not everyone is for Berlin.

Its unique, relentlessly brooding melancholy can easily

overwhelm you; the casual bleakness is never more than a Strasse away. It has the intensity of history breathing down your neck. Day after day. Corner after corner. The experience is every bit surreal, yet its vibrancy and mysterious darkness makes you perpetually shudder with renewed curiosity. A city of questions seemingly incapable of providing an answer.

And in the end, we are only as strong as the world we inhabit allows us to be. After all, tradition and hypocrisy remain locked in a poisonous yet unbreakable union: the blood they spill and the lives they destroy are merely wedding gifts which keep on giving.

More often than not, our kind, kings and paupers alike, lands in this world riding a luckless rainbow comet. Sometimes we survive to tell the tale of an unwelcome tribe.

Acknowledgements

Special thanks go to my partner David for sharing with me his vast knowledge of Prussian history and society on a daily basis.

I would like to thank my publisher James Essinger of The Conrad Press for believing in what is perhaps a rather eccentric book.

And I would like to thank my friend Raymond Yiu. A talented and well-known conductor and composer, he shared with me his knowledge of the workings of a classical orchestra which helped me immensely with the character of Daniel in 'Love, unseen'.

I would also like to thank the owners of Caffè La Storta in Milan, Federico and his mum, for allowing me to sit al fresco for hours on end, while revising and re-editing the book countless times over a scorching Italian summer. I enthusiastically recommend his cappuccino, *caffè freddo* and *torte salate*.